# YOU
# ARE
# HERE

The Other North - Book One

ALISON GOLOSKY

One Printers Way
Altona, MB R0G 0B0
Canada

www.friesenpress.com

**Copyright © 2021 by Alison Golosky**
First Edition — 2021

ISBN
978-1-03-912652-7 (Hardcover)
978-1-03-912651-0 (Paperback)
978-1-03-912653-4 (eBook)

*1. FICTION, SCIENCE FICTION*

Distributed to the trade by The Ingram Book Company

For Jackie.

This being human is a guesthouse
Every morning a new arrival

A joy, a depression, a meanness,
some momentary awareness comes
as an unexpected visitor

Welcome and entertain them all
even if they're a crowd of sorrows
who violently sweep your house
empty of its furniture,
still, treat each guest honourably—
he may be cleaning you out
for some new delight

Be grateful for whoever comes,
because each has been sent
as a guide from beyond

Rumi

# PART I

# CHAPTER ONE

*Marcy, 13*

"I don't think I like your friend with the fake cough," says Marcy, eyeing Grace, the cougher, suspiciously.

"She can't help it," says Bernadette. "She has asthma."

Marcy watches with disgust as Grace, one of her least favourite people in the entire school, swipes one hand across her nose, making zero effort to cover her mouth as another cough explodes out of her. "Yeah," Grace agrees, clearing her throat. "I got asthma. *And* a cold."

"Well maybe," Marcy suggests, her eyes narrowed in what she hopes to be a menacing way, "you shouldn't be smoking."

She takes one last drag from her own cigarette, then crushes it out against the brick exterior of her junior high school. She feels totally annoyed. Bernadette is her best friend, no question, but why she hangs out with losers like Grace is a total mystery. Bernadette is just way too nice, which Marcy has told her, like, a million times, but every time she does, Bernadette says, "well *you* seem to like me." Marcy can't argue with that.

Right now, however, she has bigger things to think about; namely, The Dancetasticks. The Dancetasticks is an all-girl (and one boy) dance troupe at her school, and they are going to perform at the end-of-year assembly in just two weeks. Marcy danced with them at the Christmas concert last year, but this time she and

1

Bernadette will be performing a duet. This is totally exciting but also totally nerve-wracking. Their routine will be set to Madonna's 'Papa Don't Preach,' Marcy's favourite song of all-time—she doesn't care how old it is—and at the end, they are going to light real sparklers on fire!

"Come on," says Marcy, turning her body slightly so that she is facing only her best friend and giving Grace the literal cold shoulder, "we gotta get going."

Bernadette looks sheepish. "Yeah...okay. But, um, Grace is coming with us, okay?"

"What?!" Marcy stares in disbelief. "But we're supposed to practice! We gotta get that routine down, Bernadette!"

"I know. We still can. Grace won't get in the way. She's just gonna watch."

Marcy opens her eyes as wide as they can possibly go, signalling silently but not subtly that this really isn't cool. Behind her, the dreaded Grace whoops out another loud cough.

"You need to go to the doctor!" Marcy snaps.

"I thought you wanted the chance to try out the routine in front of someone," says Bernadette. "Grace can be, like, the make-believe audience."

This last word has an involuntary effect: Marcy doesn't *want* to hang out with Grace, that's for sure, but one thing she doesn't mind is an audience. And if Grace is just sitting there watching, then they're not really hanging out anyway.

"Okay, fine," Marcy relents. "But let's *go*, then. We're gonna miss the bus."

"Um...," Bernadette pauses, "well, we don't have to take the bus. Grace's mom is gonna pick her up, so she can take us to my place and we can practice there."

Marcy turns back around. "Why is your *mom* coming to get you?"

Grace seems unfazed. "I'm not allowed to ride the bus," she says simply.

*Oh my God,* thinks Marcy. *This kid really is a loser.* Being seen with a loser is bad enough, but being seen with a loser *and* the loser's mom while being driven around like a baby is out of the question. She can't afford this—not in Junior High. She groans loudly.

"Urgh! Just forget it!"

Turning away from the other girls, Marcy heads toward the transit stop.

"Oh, come on, Marcy!" Bernadette calls after her.

"Whatever!" Marcy snaps, breaking into a run.

How can this be happening? Did Bernadette and Grace make all these plans without her? It sure sounds like it. Since when do best friends make plans with other people and not tell each other until the last possible second?

Furious, Marcy stomps onto the bus wishing she could sit in the back where the grade niners are, opting instead for an empty seat half-way down. She tosses her books onto the seat next to her, letting everyone else know she's not interested in sharing. On the ride home her anger festers. Now she and Bernadette aren't going to have enough time to practice before the recital. They're going to totally suck in front of the entire school, and it'll be all Grace's fault!

When she gets home, she uses the key around her neck to let herself in. Her mom is still at work and she doesn't care where her older sister or younger brother are. She helps herself to a can of pop before stomping downstairs to her bedroom. The tiny space is a complete mess, as usual, but to Marcy it fits perfectly with her mood. She flops onto her bed, grabs her Discman from the night-stand, and puts the headphones over her ears. She presses play and listens to 'Papa Don't Preach' over and over. In her mind, she sees herself and Bernadette in their sequined leotards—leaping, spinning, and break-dancing across the stage. In real life, neither of them knows how to breakdance, though God knows Marcy has tried. But in her fantasy world they are total experts. She pictures the adoring audience on their feet cheering in admiration.

An hour later, inspiration over-taking her earlier annoyance, she decides she had better call Bernadette after all.

"What's going on?"

"Nothing," says Bernadette. "Grace's mom smelled smoke on us, so she got really mad and wouldn't let her come over. She *really* freaked out."

"Oh." Marcy looks at her cuticles. "Well, do you wanna practice tonight? Like, after dinner? Because we missed today's practice!"

"That wasn't *my* fault," says Bernadette.

"Well, it wasn't exactly mine," says Marcy, keeping her voice even. Silence on the other end of the line.

"Look," she says. "Do you even want to practice or not?"

She hears Bernadette sigh. "Yeah. I do."

"Good. Then I'll see you tonight."

\*\*\*

*Chet, 17*

The voice coming through the crackly drive-thru speaker sounds like it belongs to a total bitch.

"No cheese on the burger!" the voice barks. "And I want extra mayo! The last time I came here, I asked for extra and I didn't get *any*!"

*I'm not surprised you're not getting any,* Chet thinks. He would love to tell customers like her that if they want five-star service they shouldn't eat at a dump like this.

"Is that everything for you today?" he asks in his friendliest of tones. When she says yes, he tells her to please proceed to the next window.

He reaches in to the pass, grabs a burger and a large fries, and shoves them into the bottom of a to-go bag. Then he grabs a large handful of ketchup and mayo packets, tosses them in, and expertly folds the top of the bag shut. Filling a large cup with coffee, he grabs a lid and surreptitiously glances around the corner into the main kitchen. Confident that no one is looking, he generously licks the underside of the lid, making sure to get a serious amount of spit on it before securing it to the top of the cup.

With a most-pleasant expression, he opens the drive-thru window and greets the 30-something bitch behind the wheel. His appearance immediately disarms her. He is used to this response from women—especially the older ones, like her. He knows they think he's hot.

Chet hands her the bag and smiles. "I made sure you got the extra mayo," he tells her, doing everything short of actually winking.

"Oh!" she says, suddenly self-conscious. "Thanks!"

He hands her the coffee with an overly-concerned warning. "Be careful—it's really hot."

"Oh, I... I didn't order a large."

"I know," he smiles, "it's on the house."

"Oh!" she says again, touching her Jennifer-Aniston-haircut. "Thank you!"

"Have a good day."

"You too!" She rolls up her window.

"Enjoy your coffee," he mutters, chuckling to himself.

At 8:00 p.m., the restaurant's grimy little manager pokes his head out of his grimy little office.

"Eight o'clock!" he hollers. "Chet—you're outta here!"

Already untying the back of his apron, Chet hollers back, "Yup!"

No one needs to tell him what time it is. Grabbing the stupid-ass hat off his head, he dreams of the day when he will no longer have to work in this shit-hole. Just three more months before he starts university and then he can kiss this dump goodbye.

On his way out he sneaks up behind Devon, a fellow teenaged co-worker, who is placing limp tomato slices onto rows of even-more-limp burger patties. Stealthily, Chet reaches around and punches the back of Devon's hand, completely submerging it into the tomato container.

"Dickhead!" Devon exclaims.

He throws a tomato slice at Chet, who ducks and laughs.

"Smell ya later, douche!"

Exiting out the back of the restaurant, Chet makes his way through the parking lot and over to his car, a brand-new Ford

Escort. It's an early graduation gift from his parents, although it's far from his first choice for a vehicle. He had wanted something a little more slick, like a Mustang or a Trans Am—something with a bit more power under the hood. But still, a new car is a new car.

He gets in behind the wheel and almost immediately smells the grease from the restaurant on his clothes, his hair, his skin. He knows that even after he showers tonight, the smell will still be in his nostrils, permeating every frickin' internal organ he's got. He rolls the windows all the way down in an attempt to escape from it.

Firing up the car, he skids out of the parking lot, making his way over to the library on 106th Street. It's only eight o'clock—it's practically summer, but already the streets are virtually empty. Edmonton is such a dead city. He wishes he could have applied to one of the universities in B.C., with their beaches and skiing, but his parents were too cheap.

He parks his car in the near-empty library lot and heads inside. His best buddy Raja is crouched around a large table inside, along with a bunch of other kids from their school.

"Whaddup," Chet says, nonchalantly addressing the group. "You guys ready to motor, or what?"

Chet told his parents that he would be studying at the library after work, but that's not going to happen. Instead, he and a bunch of other Grade 12 students are going to celebrate their last full day of classes by drinking behind the bleachers at school. It seems a fitting farewell.

"Did you get the booze?" he asks.

"Yup." Raja opens his jacket to reveal a six-pack of beer.

"Where's the rest of it?" Chet asks.

"This *is* the rest of it."

"What happened to the money I gave you?"

"This *is* the money you gave me!"

Chet rolls his eyes. In three weeks, he will turn eighteen and be able to buy his own booze. He can't wait.

Together, the group of high schoolers leaves the library and heads back out to the parking lot. As Chet nears his car, he twirls his keys on his index finger, tosses them high into the air, then bends down low to catch them just before they hit the ground.

"Nice one," says Raja.

"O-kay." Chet turns around to face the rest of the group, now walking backwards. "Who's riding with me?"

"I am," Raja calls.

"I know *you* are, knucklehead. Who else? I got room for a couple more."

"We'll ride with you," says Lindsay as she and her friend Jessica make their way over.

"Aren't you riding with Terry?" he asks. Terry and Lindsay have been going out all year.

"Nah, we wanna ride with you guys."

Raja looks over at Chet and raises one eyebrow.

"Yeah, okay," says Chet. What does he care? His own girlfriend, Kelley, is staying home tonight—she won't be around to give him shit for it.

"Shotgun!" Raja calls, rushing past the girls and jumping into the front seat.

As Lindsay and Jessica get into the back, he reaches around and places the six-pack on the seat between them.

"For safe-keeping," he winks.

Chet slides into the driver's seat, puts the key in the ignition, and guns it out of the parking lot, taking off so fast that all four heads inside the car swing back in unison.

"God, I'm so glad I'm not riding with Terry!" says Lindsay. "He drives like an old woman!"

"You mean," says Chet, his voice deadpan, "he doesn't do... this?"

Suddenly, he swerves the car hard to the left.

"Whoa!" Raja hollers, as all four bodies veer forcefully to the right side of the car. The girls shriek in surprise.

"Or, this?" Chet asks again, this time swerving violently to the right.

"How about this?!"

He zig-zags his way down the street while Raja hollers and laughs and the girls scream with delight until suddenly, from out of nowhere, Chet sees the unmistakeable flash of red and blue lights. Immediately, he slows down to a cringing halt.

"Sssssssshit!" Raja exclaims.

"Shut up!" Chet snaps. "Don't say anything!"

In the rear-view mirror he watches the police officer approach his car. Taking a deep breath, he calmly rolls down his window, a look of innocence on his face.

"Licence and registration."

"Yes, Sir."

Chet reaches into the glove box, retrieves the items, then politely hands them over.

"Have you been drinking tonight?"

"No, Sir." No one says 'sir' or 'ma'am' in this part of the world. Chet has picked this up from American movies and TV and uses it when he needs to.

"You kids been partying?"

"No, Sir. I just got off work and I'm driving my friends home from the library."

The cop looks briefly inside the car's interior. In the rear-view mirror Chet sees the six-pack of beer still sitting between the girls, neither of whom make any attempt to cover it. That's good—they must instinctively know that any move toward it would draw attention.

After only a quick glance inside, the officer hands Chet back his documents.

"Make sure you and your friends get home safe," he says.

"Yes, Sir."

Chet sits with both hands gripping the wheel, not moving until he sees the cop get back into his own car. With a deep breath, he rolls up his window, puts on the indicator light, and slowly begins to drive away.

"Yes, Sir!" Raja mimics in a high-pitched voice. "Aye, aye, Captain!"

"Whatever," Chet mutters, unbothered. "If you'd been doing the talking, we'd all be in jail right now."

"How did we not just get a ticket?" asks Lindsay, clearly baffled.

"It's this guy," Raja explains, gesturing to Chet. "He's got horse-shoes up his ass."

"But you were driving *so* crazy," she says. "And it seemed like he looked right at the booze!"

"Horseshoes, I tell ya," says Raja. "You wouldn't believe the shit this guy gets away with."

Chet shrugs. "What're ya gonna do, man."

\*\*\*

*Dannicka, 27*

Dannicka's life feels like an absolute mess. For starters, the name-change isn't going well - most of her friends and all of her family continue to call her 'Maureen,' despite the legal name change she made six months ago. It wasn't cheap, either—she paid $185 of her non-existent savings to have it done. She then had to face her dad who, in a rare show of emotion, told her just how unhappy he was.

"Your mother gave you that name," he'd said, angry with her for the first time in her adult life. "It's not good enough for you, now?"

"It's not that," she'd argued, although she wasn't able to articu-late why she had done it—why she had needed to. She hated how bratty she had sounded, hated that she'd opened an old wound between them in having to discuss her mother. It was the only real fight she and her dad have ever had, and now, months later, it con-tinues to linger between them. She hates this even more.

Her new boyfriend, Todd, has only ever known her as Dannicka. Sometimes she wonders if that's the only reason she stays with him. Lately, Todd has taken to calling her Danni—not her ideal nick-name, but at least it's a world away from Maureen, and that's how she wants it.

"Beavis and Butthead is starting!" Todd hollers from the living room.

"I'll be there in a minute!" she calls back.

She stands in her bedroom where she's been pretending to look for an allegedly-missing pair of pants, contemplating her next move. Within seconds of Todd's announcement, she hears him laugh at his favourite show. Swiftly, she makes a move toward the phone on her nightstand.

*If I'm going to do this,* she thinks, *it'll have to be now. Right now.*

Quietly, she picks up the receiver and dials the number for her boss. She waits impatiently for his out-going message to kick in and when it finally does, she whispers into the phone.

"Hi, it's Dannicka—I'm not going to be in tomorrow... I think I have a bladder infection?? I'm gonna go to my doctor. I should be back in on Monday. Sorry... um, thanks."

She quickly hangs up the phone and curses herself. Bladder infection? Really? Why didn't she think of something even more embarrassing, like, say gonorrhea? She prays that her boss won't listen to the message on speaker phone, then resigns herself to the fact that he likely will. Speaker phone is his new favourite invention. Oh well, there's nothing she can do about it now.

Plodding back down the hall and into the living room, she tries to give off an air of normalcy as she sits beside Todd on the couch.

"I found the pants," she says, keeping up with her alibi.

"That's good," he says, clearly unconcerned. "C'mere!"

He holds one arm out for her to snuggle under, which she does.

Already, she feels incredibly guilty.

\*\*\*

## Ryan, 29

"Don't pack it in so tight! You'll never be able to light it!"

"I know what I'm doing," says Ryan tersely. "This isn't amateur hour."

Cory, one of the only two people in the world that Ryan still hangs out with, giggles. "I'm with you, man. Pack it in there! Smoke 'em if you got 'em, right?"

Rob, the only other person that Ryan still hangs out with, shrugs. "Don't blame me if you can't fire it up."

"Give me the lighter."

Ryan presses his lips over the mouthpiece of the bong and holds the flame to the expertly packed bowl. He takes a long pull off the homemade contraption, filling his lungs with a most-welcome plume of smoke.

"See?!" Cory claps his hands. "Success!"

\*\*\*

*Julian, 40*

Julian is sitting through what he considers to be pure and abject torture. Trudy, his wife, has dragged him to many bad live-theatre productions over the years, but this one really takes the cake. It's only been ten minutes since the ratty seen-better-days curtains have parted and yet it feels like he has been here for an hour.

*Just give it a minute,* he tells himself, something his dad use to say when the show they watched on TV seemed boring. But he has given it a minute. He's given it ten minutes. Ten minutes of torture. It's all just a bunch of audience-hungry, artsy-fartsy attention-seekers wearing costumes that have nothing to do with either each other, or the sparse yet confusing set. Dialogue seems to consist of only non-sequiturs so far and Julian has yet to determine just how anyone thought this was worthy of charging admission. It couldn't possibly get any worse.

It gets worse. The actors—of which there are ten, so far—start to sing.

"You didn't tell me it was a musical!" he whispers, but Trudy only holds a finger to her lips.

As though the visual and audio assault is not enough, Julian's olfactory sense is experiencing its own type of torture: the woman seated next to him is wearing so much perfume that he is actually beginning to taste it. What is the matter with people? Don't their noses work? He shifts in his seat, crossing his right arm under his chest to prop up his left elbow. He balls his left hand into a fist and buries his nose into it, trying desperately to counter the overwhelming bouquet.

The worst part about this entire situation, though, is that he's missing the golf game for this. Yes, Trudy has programmed the VCR to tape the tournament, but Julian knows that one of the kids will have taped over it before he'll be able to watch it.

A new character appears on stage now, as if this will make any difference. For reasons unclear, at least to Julian, the actor is clad in seventeenth century dress which clashes with the supposed twentieth century garbage man with whom he is sharing the scene. A monologue is delivered—one so agonizingly dull that Julian actually contemplates crying.

Is this the longest play ever written? He begins to count the buttons on the actor's coat. Seven. Eight? Eight. No, seven. It's decided: this *is* the longest play ever written.

Several scenes later, the seventeenth century man appears to be flying a plane, and has been joined by a stewardess who is dressed like a flapper.

"Excuse me, Captain, but there's a passenger who wants to see you."

"Send him in," says the seventeenth century man.

When an actor in a beaver costume joins the other two in the cockpit, Julian begins to laugh but is quickly silenced by a sharp jab to his side. Apparently, this isn't supposed to be funny.

"May I please be excused?" asks the beaver.

*What the hell is going on?!* Julian wishes desperately that he could be excused.

Finally—thankfully—Intermission comes, although it only serves as a reminder that this tire-fire of a show is only half over. In the lobby, Julian gazes wistfully at the other theatre-goers flocking around the bar. He hasn't had a drink in eight years and, for the first time in ages, he sincerely wishes he could.

"Well, Tawnee's really out-done herself this time," says Trudy. Tawnee is Trudy's second cousin, and the playwright of this atrocity.

"She sure has," Julian agrees.

At the bar, he orders a glass of white wine for his wife and settles on ginger ale for himself, which he sips patiently. With even more patience, he nods and mm-hm's while Trudy delves into her cousin's foray into playwriting.

"Ladies and gentlemen," a disembodied voice soon announces. "Please take your seats for the beginning of Act Two."

"More like Round Two," Julian mutters.

"What?"

"Nothing. Let's just get'er done."

Trudy frowns, but Julian thwarts her off at the pass, forcing a smile and placing one hand on the small of her back. Regretfully, he leads her back into the theatre.

Nothing about the play improves. Half-way through the second act, the beaver returns and sings a sad song about how complicated his life has become. In his paw (is it called a paw on a beaver? Do beavers have paws?) he holds a hand gun. Julian pictures himself storming the stage, wrestling the gun away from the beaver, and shooting himself in the head. No, wait—he'll shoot the beaver first, then himself. He stifles a laugh.

Beside him, Perfume Lady dabs at her eyes with a tissue. She must have sprayed herself down with more perfume during the intermission—another waft of it floats over and once again, he futilely shoves his nose into one fist.

When the play is finally over, Julian wonders if this is how prisoners feel upon their release. It has been a complete and total waste of a night.

"I found the beaver absolutely heartbreaking," says Trudy, getting into their car.

He can't help it. He bursts out laughing.

"God, you're so immature!" she exclaims. "Do you have to make a joke out of everything?!"

"Oh, give me a break!" he shoots back, his patience finally gone. "It's a beaver! With a gun! It's so stupid!"

"The beaver is a metaphor," she says, her voice rising, "for our declining environment! Or didn't you get that?"

"I got it," he mutters.

"Just because it isn't some stupid action movie doesn't mean it's not worth paying attention!"

Not wanting to escalate things any further, Julian says nothing. They spend the rest of the ride in silence. When they get home, he wants nothing more than to check out the sports highlights on TV, but thinks better of it. He doesn't want to annoy Trudy any further, and he hates fighting. He brushes his teeth then strips down to his underwear before getting into bed. When Trudy walks into the room, he pulls back the covers on her side.

"Come on," he says. "I'll give you a back rub."

Silently, she lets him.

"I'm allowed to not like something," he says, "but I shouldn't have laughed. I'm sorry."

She doesn't respond.

"Okay?" he asks gently.

"Okay," she says.

She turns out the light and in a few short minutes he can tell she's fallen asleep. He doesn't know how she does it.

\*\*\*

*Carole, 42*

Carole has had a late dinner with friends and gets home just before midnight. Mr. Biscuits greets her at the door, his stump of a tail wagging in double-time.

"Hi, sweet pea," she says, scooping him up in her arms. "Sorry I'm so late. Come on, let's go outside."

She carries the tiny dog out to the backyard and sets him down on the grass, then looks up at the stars. It's early June here in Edmonton. Despite the late hour, the sun hasn't set completely— Carole can still see a faint light along the horizon—and, in a few short hours, it will work its way back up into the sky.

Mr. Biscuits sniffs the grass intently, searching for just the right spot. The mere sight of him makes her happy, although the first time she laid eyes on him was a startling experience. Mr. Biscuits was, and still is, one of the strangest-looking dogs she's ever seen— the front and back halves of his body look as though they belong to two completely different animals. He doesn't necessarily even resemble a dog.

Her little charge used to belong to Holly, one of Carole's best friends. Eight years ago now, Holly got sick and asked Carole to look after him. It's hard to believe that was nearly a decade ago. Carole still misses her dearly.

Mr. Biscuits, now finished his business, waddles over to Carole and looks up at her lovingly. In all of her forty-two years, she has never seen a sweeter face.

It's late—she should go to bed now, but she doesn't feel like it. She feels like painting and tonight seems like a perfect time for one of what she calls 'No Thinks'. 'No Thinks' are a style of painting that she came up with in response to her work as a graphic artist. After having to be creative on a deadline and within specific parameters, she found her own artistry becoming stagnant. As an exercise, she began to paint while allowing herself to think about anything *except* the painting. Now she uses this technique to clear her mind and ground herself. She finds it incredibly calming.

Mr. Biscuits follows her in to what is supposed to be the master suite, but has become her studio. What does she need a master suite for, anyway? She has the whole house to herself.

He curls up contentedly in his little bed while Carole puts on one of her smocks. A record player sits in one corner and she takes a moment to flip through her old record collection. No one puts out vinyl records anymore, which she thinks is a shame. Those CD's they make now do a grave injustice to the album artwork, shrinking it down to a ridiculously small size that leaves her thinking, why bother? Any lyrics now printed on the inner booklets require a magnifying glass to read. While she's a fan of new technology in general, this is one area that has been a disappointment for Carole.

Halfway through her stack of vinyls, she comes across the Fleetwood Mac 'Rumours' album. It has been awhile since she heard it. Carefully removing the record from its sleeve, she places it on the turntable.

After prepping a large canvas, she begins to mix her colours. Shades of white, pale yellow, pale blues and greens being to emerge on the palette. She starts to paint, not at all mindful of what, and almost instantly begins to think about Corinne.

Corinne is her identical twin, although the term seems less and less accurate the older they get. They had been so close while growing up that they may as well have been conjoined. Now, they regularly go for months at a time without seeing each other, despite living in the same city. To add to this, Carole can't honestly remember the last time the sisters spent any time together alone.

In 1965, when they were twelve years old, they had made a pact; they weren't going to have normal, boring, regular lives. They weren't going to tie themselves down to husbands, cooking and cleaning all day, or anything else that resembled proper domestic life. Carole and Corinne were going to have adventures—when *they* finished high school they were going to move to Europe and become artists. They would hang out with the Beatles and, maybe, one day meet the Queen.

By the time they graduated, the Beatles had broken up. Instead of moving to Europe and becoming artists, they went to the University of Alberta and majored in Art. Carole had wanted to study somewhere exciting like Italy or France, but Corinne found the idea too daunting. As a compromise, Corinne suggested they spend one of their summer breaks in Europe.

"We could go between third and fourth year," she'd said. "That'll give us time to save enough money so we could actually see everything, not just be limited to a few places. We could go to Italy, and France, and Austria..."

Carole agreed. She spent their first two summer breaks working, and she did save up a fair bit of money. When the time came to make actual plans, however, Corinne backed out. And although Carole was upset, she wasn't surprised—for their entire third year of university, Corinne had been glued to the side of an Engineering student named Barry.

"I just don't have time to traipse around Europe like a gypsy," Corinne said. "Barry's parents are flying us to Ontario to meet them!"

She'd said this as though Carole was somehow supposed to be as excited about this as she was.

"You can't meet his parents *and* go to Europe?" Carole asked. "You could fly out from Ontario after the visit."

"We're going for an entire *month*," Corinne said, adding, "this is really serious. I'm *really* in love."

Carole somehow doubted this. She'd seen her sister all gaga over guys before, and this wasn't it—Corinne's feelings for Barry struck her more like a business decision. His family was rich, something he didn't seem to have a problem announcing, and Corinne seemed hypnotized by this. Is this really who her sister was?

"You're really in love, all right," Carole had said. "But not with him."

"What do you mean by that?" Corinne demanded.

"You know what I mean—you're in love with his money."

Corinne never really forgave her for saying this. Looking back, Carole knows that comment was the beginning of the end between them. Maybe she was just the tiniest bit jealous that her twin was attaching herself to someone else, but even so, she still stands by that comment. She was right about Corinne's priorities, and she didn't respect her for it.

Side A of the record comes to an end and Carole gets up to flip it over. She hums along with Fleetwood Mac as they sing about never breaking the chain. She sits back down in front of the easel and resumes painting.

It's not Corinne breaking their pact that Carole finds upsetting—promises made by twelve-year old girls are not always the most practical—it's that Corinne seems to have forgotten the sentiment behind their pact. In the twenty-one years since they finished their undergraduate degrees, Carole and Corinne have led two very different lives. Carole has travelled and lived in many parts of the world, working in whatever capacity she can in order to experience as much of life as possible. She has meditated with Buddhist Monks in Thailand, taught English in Korea, served as an Au Père in France, and smoked hash with a guru in India. She had psychic surgery in the Philippines (a scam, she soon discovered, although the experience was more than worth it), and was romanced, then robbed, by the same man in Greece (also worth it). Never tied down, never in one place too long, she spent years as a virtual nomad.

When her dad became ill five years ago, Carole gave up her travels and moved back to Edmonton, assisting with his care until he died. She now spends much of her free time with her widowed mother—her old lifestyle a distant memory.

Corinne, on the other hand, never left Edmonton. She married the wealthy Barry, had two children, and has spent most of her time focused on her career in real estate. She has shown little to no interest in Carole's 'galivanting,' (even going so far as to call it irresponsible) and prefers to discuss more important issues like her much-lauded landscaper and her suspicion that her maids are stealing from her. Corinne worries that her children, now sixteen and fourteen, will one day be kidnapped. She finds it only fair that Carole manages the lion's share of their mother's needs since Carole 'doesn't have much going on'. Carole wonders how long it has been since Corinne was actually happy.

Carole puts down her paint brush and slowly begins to come back to the present. It has been a few hours since the record ended, and daylight now peeks in through the blinds. Squinting in the light, she realizes that she has painted straight through the night. It has been ages since she last pulled an all-nighter. She will definitely have to go to bed now—hopefully, she can catch a few hours of sleep before starting work. Thankfully, she'll be working from home today.

Getting to her feet, she steps away from the easel and performs a short series of stretches to work out the kinks now in her neck and back. She opens the blinds to let the morning sun in before returning to the easel to survey her night's work. When she does, a small gasp escapes her. Despite her varied palette it looks as though she has painted the entire canvas white.

# CHAPTER TWO

Dannicka's alarm goes off at 7:15 a.m., just as it does every weekday morning. Unlike every other weekday morning, though, she is already wide awake.

Todd, who has slept over, mumbles something incoherent.

"Sshhh," she whispers, not wanting him to wake up. "Go back to sleep. I'll see you after work."

Quietly she gets ready, putting more effort into her appearance than usual. She puts on the outfit she set out last night (something else she never usually does) and then tip-toes into her bathroom to put the finishing touches on her hair and carefully-applied makeup. At the front door, she slips into a pair of heels and a light dress coat, grabs her purse, and carefully picks up her keys so they don't rattle. Stealthily, she slips out into the main hall of her apartment., lockng the door behind her. Once outside, she dashes across the street and over to the bus stop.

The Edmonton House Hotel is only two blocks from her office, which is risky. She will need to take a detour to get there. If she runs into anyone from work, she has decided she will tell them that she's on her way to the doctor. This won't explain why she's so dressed up with her hair and makeup expertly done, but she hasn't thought of everything. She has never done anything like this before.

She arrives at the hotel and quickly glances behind her before going inside. Coast clear, she walks through the lobby to the elevators. When the doors slide open, she enters, takes a deep breath, and presses '6'.

One year ago, Dannicka (who was still going by Maureen at the time) and her boyfriend, Eric, broke up. They had been dating for three years and living together for two of those years. She had hinted at getting married and, while he hadn't come out and officially asked her, he hadn't said the idea was off-limits either—it seemed inevitable that they would, eventually. Eric had applied to a pre-med program in Quebec and Dannicka was sure they would get married before he got a residency placement. She didn't mind waiting.

When Eric's application was approved, Dannicka immediately began picturing her new life. Moving to Quebec would be daunting, no doubt. She would miss her dad and her friends, but she was going to be the wife of a doctor. She wouldn't have to work if she didn't want to, they would have a nice house and cars, they could have two, maybe three, or even four kids. She wanted a big family; she had been lonely growing up. Her mom died when she was twelve, and she had no brothers or sisters. Although her step-mom was nice enough, they'd never been close. Now, for the first time since her mother's death, something really good was happening to her.

She should have seen it coming. The closer they got to leaving, the quieter and more distant Eric became. *He's nervous,* she'd tell herself. *He's got a lot to think about.* Meanwhile, she continued to make plans and pack up their apartment. She drafted a resignation letter to her boss and was about to give their landlord one month's notice when Eric finally stopped her.

"I need to do this alone," he'd said.

"You want to go there first?" she'd asked, confused. "Like, to get settled and stuff? I can go earlier if you need to..."

She did not want to make such a long trip by herself and couldn't figure out why he would want to either. He wasn't making sense.

He went on to explain that he wasn't going to have the time and energy it would take to 'maintain a relationship' while in school—he had talked to enough students in the program to have realistic expectations.

She could not believe what she was hearing. There was no way she could handle living that far away from him for eight months of the year while he'd be in school.

"But I'll get a job there, I'll make friends," she had pleaded. "I'll have my own things going on!"

"What's the point of uprooting your whole life for that?" he'd asked.

Uprooting her life? Eric *was* her life.

"I thought the point was to *be* together!" she had exclaimed. He may not have asked her to marry him, but at many points in their three years together he'd said he wanted to be with her always. He'd *said* those words. What else could he have meant?

She started to cry. "Are you breaking up with me?"

He wouldn't look at her.

"Are you breaking up with me?!" she demanded.

"It wouldn't be fair to you to move..." he began.

"Oh, you can't even say it!" she'd wailed. "*This* isn't fair!"

The break-up sent her flying into a panic. Being dumped by Eric made her feel like she was twelve years old again—abandoned by the death of her mother. In the days that followed, he moved back into his parents' house and she, alone in their one-bedroom apartment, crumbled. She called him at all hours of the day and night, alternately pleading, threatening, and sobbing uncontrollably. Her behaviour was repellant, even to herself. Before Eric left, she humiliated herself even further by all-out begging. He seemed impervious to her feelings, and to the fact that he was single-handedly causing her to meltdown.

Had he ever really loved her? Or even liked her? She wondered how a person could suddenly turn so cold and calculated. Even after he left, she held out the hope that once they were apart, he'd realize what he was missing and come back. He didn't.

Six months later, with no contact from him, she resigned herself to the fact that it was never going to happen. She legally changed her name to Dannicka, although she wasn't sure where she had heard the name before. She began dating Todd—almost as an after-thought—and went through the motions of daily life like an automaton. She heard nothing from Eric until yesterday when, out-of-the-blue, he called her at work.

"I've been in town for a course. Sorry I didn't call earlier, but I've been swamped. Anyways, I don't start again until noon tomorrow. Do you want to meet for breakfast?"

She'd heard herself say "sure" before even giving herself a moment to think.

She could have told Todd—it was just breakfast, no big deal—but she didn't. Instead, she lied to her boss, took the day off work, and wondered if Eric wanted to get back together. The thought sent a thrill up her spine.

The elevator chimes and the doors slide open at the sixth floor. Dannicka takes a deep breath and smooths a hand over her hair. She steps out into the hall, heart thudding, and walks toward Eric's room.

"Hi," she says when he answers the door. She smiles—she can't help herself.

He orders some breakfast and they eat together in his room. They laugh like old friends, catch up on each other's lives, and tell each other they look good.

"So, it's 'Dannicka' now, right?" he asks, looking slightly amused.

She straightens up in her chair and tries to appear more self-assured than she feels. "That's right!"

"So, no more 'Mo-Mo'?"

The sound of her former nickname, the one only he ever used, takes her aback.

She doesn't mean for anything more to happen. She tries to convince herself that she hadn't even considered the possibility; but it's just so easy, so familiar. Afterwards, they spoon under the covers like they used to and, for the first time in a year, Dannicka feels like she's home.

"I've missed you" she says.

Her statement hangs in the air. And hangs there. And hangs there. With each moment that passes, reality creeps in.

Eventually, Eric replies. "It's 11:30," he says. "I gotta get going."

"Sure," she says, hoping to sound casual. She climbs out of the king-size bed as if on auto-pilot and begins to get dressed. In the mirror she sees that her makeup is smudged and her hair is a mess.

"Do you want to get together for dinner?" he asks. "I should be done around six."

"I can't," she tells him. "We're having dinner with Todd's parents." She laughs woodenly, adding, "kinda makes you wonder what I got up to when *we* were together."

He stops doing up his pants mid-zip.

"Don't say that," he says, looking directly at her.

"It was just a joke."

Her reply is said by way of apology, but secretly, she is glad that it got to him. She never cheated on him while they were together—never even considered it—but now he can wonder if she did. She knows his ego won't be able to take the hit.

In the lobby, he kisses her on the cheek and tells her to 'take care.' She has never felt so awful. What was she thinking?! Todd is a nice guy; he doesn't deserve this. *She* doesn't deserve this.

In this moment, alone in the hotel lobby, Dannicka feels like she might explode.

\*\*\*

Every morning, Ryan wakes up in considerable pain. This morning is no exception.

He lies on his right side, curled up in the fetal position, mentally preparing himself for his first movement of the day. He takes a deep breath, squeezes his still-shut eyes so that they are closed even tighter, and braces himself. Then, slowly, he begins to straighten his left leg. This movement releases some of the pain and stiffness in his back, but creates a series of new pains that shoot up his leg and into his side. He winces, groans, and when the leg is finally straight, releases the breath he has been holding.

Allowing himself a moment to recover, he lies perfectly still and anticipates his next course of action. When he is ready, he takes another deep breath and repeats the same process with his right leg.

With both legs straightened, he uses his left arm to roll himself slowly onto his back where, breathing hard, he rests for a few more moments with his eyes still squeezed shut. The next order of business is to sit up, but before he can attempt this, he'll need to open his eyes. And that, amid everything else, is the most dreaded part of his day.

When Ryan opens his eyes for the first time each morning, there's a good chance he will see stars. He has calculated the odds of this happening—it's about one in five. Stars signal that he is about to have a migraine, in which case the entire day will be a total write-off. If the stars appear, he'll have about ten, maybe fifteen, minutes to take his migraine medication if there is any chance of it working. Even then, it rarely does.

*Okay,* he tells himself. *Here goes nothing.*

Just then, he feels a small pressure over his right eyelid. This is no cause for worry, though—he knows what this is, and it's not a headache. It's a paw.

Slowly, he opens his eyes (no stars, thank God), and finds himself nose-to-nose with his cat.

"Hey, buddy," he croaks.

"Mawr," Roland replies.

Ryan takes another deep breath and begins the slow process of sitting up. By the time he has done it, he is sweating from exertion. It's hard to believe that there was ever a time when he could wake up and just get out of bed. That seems like science fiction to him now.

"Mawr," Roland reminds him.

"I know, I know," he says. "You're starving to death."

He pulls the comforter away from his body and slowly swings one leg over the side of the bed. He lets out another groan—that one hurt. Grunting, he does the same with the left. Now, finally, it's time to stand up.

Ryan's bones creak and snap as he pads slowly to the bathroom, then just as slowly into the kitchen. Grimacing, he bends down to open one of the lower cupboards, Roland helpfully noses his way inside as though reminding him that the cat food is housed there.

"I know," he says, scooping the stinky nuggets into Roland's bowl.

Slowly, he straightens back upright and glances at the clock. 11:30. He looks at the calendar tacked to the wall above the cat dishes. It's June 2nd, and on today's square he has written 'Physio—1:30'.

Ryan is conflicted about his physiotherapy—on one hand it can seem like torture, but on the other his physiotherapist is super cute. It's the closest he gets to any female action these days and it's about all he can handle.

Glancing into the living room, he sees a total disaster. Rob and Cory were over until three in the morning, smoking pot and playing video games. If Ryan's mom knew much pot he smoked now she would probably faint. He doesn't care—it's the only thing that takes the edge off. Besides, he tries not to smoke during the day, which should count for something. His 'real' painkillers, for which he has a long-standing prescription, wreak havoc on his stomach. He would rather smoke pot any day of the week; and he does.

Back in the bathroom, Ryan steps into the shower and makes the water as hot as he can handle. It turns his skin pink but soothes his aching muscles. Slumping down in the tub, he allows the spray to fall down his neck and back. Slowly, the ever-present tension begins to release, not completely—never anything *close* to completely—but enough that he starts to feel like something resembling human.

The phone rings while he towels himself off; he makes no attempt to answer. Soon, he hears his own recorded voice.

"You know what to do."

"Ryan, it's Mom. Are you there? Pick up the phone, please. [Pause.] You shouldn't be sleeping this late, it's not good for you. Ryan?"

Her voice is so grating. He begins loudly humming nothing in particular in an attempt to drown it out.

"You probably need groceries, so I'll go shopping for you today. The last time I was over, I went through your cupboards and you were out of everything..."

He thinks about the last time his mom came over, which was just a few days ago. When did she have time to go through his cupboards? She showed up unannounced, which she knows he hates, and then lied about having been in the neighbourhood. He had been tempted to lie to her in return and say he was just on his way out, but he knew that would only trigger a barrage of questions: Where was he going? For how long? Was he remembering not to over-do it? Did he need a ride? Did he want her to come with him? Instead, he just told her he was about to take a nap.

"Oh, that's okay," she had said. "I'll only stay five minutes."

Five minutes turned into forty-five during which he was subjected to another chapter of Who's-Bothering-His-Mother-Now. He'd left the room once to go to the bathroom. He couldn't have been gone for more than two minutes, but clearly it was long enough for his mother to snoop through his kitchen. He swears under his breath. He hates it when she goes through his shit.

Her voice on his answering machine drones on while Ryan makes as much noise as he can to drown it out. God, when will she shut up? She's right about needing groceries, but he sure as hell doesn't need *her* buying them. She always treated him like a baby, but she has become downright unbearable since the accident.

Back when he was still living in the hospital, he over-heard the resident shrink tell his parents that, to have any semblance of an independent life, he was supposed to do as much for himself as possible once he got out. He knew the instructions were falling on deaf ears—he is pretty sure his mother's exact words were 'what the hell do *they* know?' If she had her way, she would be over at Ryan's apartment on a daily basis doing everything short of wiping his ass. Or, better yet, she would move him back home to live with her and his dad.

Ryan doesn't blame Amy for dumping him. It wasn't the accident after-math she had found too overwhelming—it was his mom. He knows that.

Finally, the answering machine clicks off. Ryan, who had started singing out loud, stops. He wraps the towel around his waist and walks back into the kitchen. Opening a cupboard, he sees that he is out of coffee and slams the door shut with a loud bang. Fuck! He can't get groceries *and* go to physio today; it'll be too much. He can't not get coffee either—if he doesn't have one in the next couple of hours, he'll get a massive headache for sure. He'll have to stop for one on the way to the appointment and that is going to be a huge pain in the ass.

Here's where he tells himself it's time to quit drinking coffee altogether—that would solve the problem.

"Fuck that," he says aloud. He's had to give up enough shit in his life already.

*** 

"Marcy, stay after class, please."

"But I didn't do anything!" she protests, in a knee-jerk reaction.

As the rest of the kids in the classroom make a hasty exit, Marcy plods upstream toward her homeroom teacher's desk.

"I didn't do anything," she repeats, quickly running through the last hour in her mind, trying to figure out what Mrs. J might have seen her get up to.

"I take it your mother didn't see you before you left for school today," Mrs. J says dryly.

"Huh? I dunno."

"Do you have any idea how much makeup you've got on?"

"Well, I'm the one who put it on," Marcy replies cheekily. "So... yeah." Is this why she's in trouble?

Mrs. J sighs. "Anyway, the reason I wanted to talk to you is because of the song you chose for the recital. It's not appropriate."

"Why not?" Marcy loves 'Papa Don't Preach'. She wishes her own parents would stop being so preachy.

"Because it's a song about teenage pregnancy, Marcy, which you know."

Marcy hadn't, in fact, known this.

"And it's not an appropriate subject matter for junior high school. Pick another song."

"But that's the song that works with our choreography! I don't have another song!"

Her teacher, also the school dance coach, is unmoved. "Well, you'll need to find one or I guess there will be no duet. Unless you want to dance in complete silence."

"But I can't!" Marcy wails. That's the only song that–"

"This isn't up for debate," Mrs. J interrupts. "Find another song, or don't perform. It's up to you."

Marcy feels a sudden burst of fury and helplessness. This can't be happening! She can't even argue, can't even let her real feelings be known or she could lose everything! How could Mrs. J do this to her?!

All she can do is nod. If she opens her mouth, something rude might come out.

"And I need your new selection by Monday, okay?"

Marcy nods again before turning away. Once out of the classroom, she stomps down the hallway forcing herself not to break into a run. She bursts through the front doors of the school and scans the area for Bernadette, already planning out how she'll break the news of this dramatic turn of events. She sees her best friend sitting on the grass eating her lunch. She's not gonna want to eat when she hears what Marcy has to tell her.

In just a few steps, Marcy sees that Bernadette is not alone. Grace is sitting right beside her, coughing as usual, and laughing. Without breaking stride, Marcy walks right past them.

"Marcy!" Bernadette calls.

Marcy ignores her.

"Hey, Marcy!" Louder this time.

Furious, Marcy stops in her tracks. "I'm going home!" she yells, the thought of leaving is suddenly the only logical choice.

"Are you sick?"

"What do you care!?" She turns on her heel and makes a run for the transit stop, purposely getting on the wrong bus. She doesn't care where she goes, as long as it's away from this stupid school!

She flashes her bus pass to the driver and stomps down the aisle to the very back of the nearly-empty bus. She slumps into the last seat, blinking back the tears which threaten to fall. She is not going to let herself cry over Mrs. J, that's for sure. Not that old bag.

***

Dannicka stands in the hotel lobby and watches Eric leave. Being seen by her co-workers would be bad, but being seen leaving a hotel with her ex in the middle of the work day would be disastrous. She waits a moment, then walks out the front doors and stands blinking in the sunshine. She needs to get out of the downtown core—it's lunch time and the chance of being seen by someone she knows is pretty high. She can't go back to her apartment in the southside, though. Not yet. Todd has the day off and could still be there. She's definitely not ready to face him right now.

Turning left, she begins heading west down 100th Avenue, steering clear of Jasper Ave—the main drag. She thinks about what just happened and starts to cry. How could she have been so stupid? After all the soul-searching she has done in the last year, after everything she has been through, after starting over from scratch, she has destroyed any progress she made since the break-up with one moment of weakness.

But it wasn't really one moment, was it? She could have hung up on Eric yesterday—told him where to go. She could have told Todd about her plan to meet with him, or even invited Todd to come along. She could have stopped Eric when he began to kiss her. She could have kept her clothes on.

She cries her way through the streets of downtown, past the neighbourhood of Oliver, and into the west end neighbourhood of Glenora. A small block called The High Street separates the two neighbourhoods and when Dannicka gets there, she stops walking and looks around. There are some boutique stores, and a Grabbajabba coffee shop. She decides that the coffee shop will be as good a place as any to hide out. She wipes her face, adjusts her sunglasses, and goes inside.

The shop is practically empty. She orders a large coffee and a muffin, although she doesn't think she can eat. She chooses a small table beside one of the large windows at the back. As soon as she sits down, she has the disheartening realization that she is going to miss a full day's pay. Why hadn't she thought of this before? Did she really think Eric was going to carry her off into the sunset? She already lives paycheque to paycheque. How is she going to pay her bills at the end of the month? She feels like crying again but chokes it down with a gulp of coffee instead.

***

Marcy has been crossing her legs for the last several blocks. She really has to pee but there's nowhere to go. She can't just knock on someone's door and ask to use their john—what if the person who answers is a kidnapper or a pervert? She can't even go in the bushes because it's broad daylight and anyone could see her. Oh God, she has to go so bad! She has to get off this bus before she pees her pants!

Just when she thinks she might cry she recognizes the upcoming corner. There are stores up there—thank God! She jumps up and yanks the cord signal, then races up the aisle. When the bus comes to a stop, she bursts out the door and runs to the closest coffee shop. Once inside, she asks the man behind the counter for the bathroom key.

"Bathrooms are for customers only" he tells her. "You planning on buying anything?"

Her face crumples. She can't pee her pants in public, she'll just die.

"Uh," she begins, wondering if she has any money on her.

"Forget it," she says. She'll just have to try one of the other places.

As she turns to leave, another man behind the counter—an older one—stops what he's doing and hands her the key.

"Here you go," he says, smiling.

"Oh, *thank* you!"

"Sorry," says the Grabbajabba employee. "I thought we weren't supposed to give the bathroom key to non-customers."

"Ah, she's just a kid," says Julian. "And it looked like she really had to go. I don't think she'll be a problem."

The kid in question, aside from a face full of makeup, looks about the same age as Julian's own daughters.

"It's pretty dead in here," he tells the employee. "Why don't you go on your break? I'll hold down the fort."

"Okay." Removing his Gabbajabba apron, the younger employee heads out the back door of the coffee shop.

Julian could use a break, too. He left his house in Calgary for the three-hour drive to Edmonton at six o'clock this morning, after getting home late from that stupid play last night. As a district manager for Grabbajabba, he is required to make the trip once a month. He likes having the time to himself in the car; his house is always so noisy with the kids doing God-knows-what and it's the only quiet Julian ever seems to get. This morning's drive was even more enjoyable than usual, thanks to the cassette-tape he found at the back of the glovebox. On it was the album he'd recorded with his old 80s band, 'New Clear Winter'. Julian had been the drummer and still thinks they could've gone somewhere if their lead singer hadn't quit.

> *Burning ashes from a cigarette*
> *There's just one thing that I still regret*
> *It's stepping onto that private jet*
> *And leaving you behind...*

In his car, Julian sang along, impressed that he still remembered every word.

> *The limo's long and it drives all night*
> *Party on 'til the morning light*

> *But something still just don't feel right*
> *It's leaving you behind...*

Okay, maybe not the best lyrics, but still, he thinks his band rocked. Cranking up the stereo, he belted out the chorus. *"Leaving you behind, Babe. Whoa, leaving you behind, mama..."*

Now, standing in the quiet Grabbajabba, he imagines switching the mellow Sarah McLachlan tape for the New Clear Winter one and laughs.

A few moments later, the bathroom door opens and the girl with all the makeup comes out. She looks like she's been through the ringer.

"Can I get a hot chocolate?" she sniffs.

Julian nods. "Coming right up."

*\*\*\**

After a whopping two and a half hours of sleep Carole should be exhausted, but she isn't. She hasn't painted through the night like that in years and it's left her feeling energized. She's been working from home all morning, glancing occasionally at last night's painting, and is even ahead of her work schedule.

At noon, she lifts her head from her desk and stretches her back, deciding she may as well take a break.

"Come on, love," she says to a sleeping Mr. Biscuits. "Time for a walk."

She puts her shoes on at the front door, attaches the dog's leash, and grabs her bag. Together they walk out into the sunshine and head down the street.

*\*\*\**

"I feel sorry for monkeys," says Raja.

Chet flicks on his indicator switch, changes his mind and turns it off, then changes his mind again and turns sharply to the left. The car behind him honks its horn. "What're you talking about?"

"Monkeys are kinda like humans that didn't quite make it," Raja explains. "We're, like, riding around in cars and stuff, and they're still swinging from trees like morons."

Chet hears Lindsay and Jessica laughing from the back seat. He was supposed to take his girlfriend Kelley to West Edmonton Mall today, but at the last minute, she'd said she was "too busy." He knows that she's just pissed at him for driving Lindsay and Jessica to the bleachers last night. He tried to tell her that nothing had happened but she didn't want to hear it.

"*We're* the morons," says Chet. "We're the ones sitting in school all day for years on end. Then we gotta get jobs so we can afford to live! Monkeys just wake up and do whatever the hell they want to do, every day."

"This is true..." Raja trails off thoughtfully. "Still, I feel like there had to have been some kind of fork-in-the-road thing. Like, some of the monkeys were fine with the way things were going, but then some *other* monkeys were, like, 'we don't want to pick our noses in front of each other; we don't want to keep flinging our shit around the woods...' and *those* were the monkeys that became us humans."

The girls in the back seat laugh again.

"Ladies and gentlemen!" Chet booms, in a loud, over-the-top announcer's voice. "This has been 'Evolution with Raja'—Canada's answer to Stephen Hawking!"

"I'm right," says Raja. "It makes total sense. It was all, like, free will and stuff. The humans just decided they wanted something more. Like, bigger houses and whatever."

"Tell me again how you got in to university for next year?"

"I'm telling you—if you get into the study of evolution, you'll find out I'm right."

"You are *really* scraping the bottom of the barrel with that one," says Chet.

"I'm not the bottom of the barrel!"

"I never said *you* were the bottom of the barrel—I said you were *scraping* the bottom of the barrel. You're, like, an inch from the bottom of the barrel."

"What if the barrel is only an inch deep?"

"Then it's not a barrel—it's a dish."

"Hey!" says Lindsay. She leans forward between the two boys, pointing at the group of shops and cafes now on their left. "Can we stop?"

Without answering, Chet jerks the wheel to the left, cutting off an on-coming truck that is forced to screech to a halt.

"Fuck's sakes!" Raja exclaims. "Give us some notice!"

Chet squeals past the angry truck driver and peels into the High Street parking lot.

"Ladies?" he says gallantly, as if he's just brought their horse-drawn carriage to a gentle stop.

"Hang on," says Lindsay, reaching for her purse.

"It's okay," says Chet, feeling generous. "What do you guys want? I'll get it."

"Really?" Lindsay smiles.

He doesn't ask himself why he's just offered to pick up the tab for a car-load of friends, one of whom (Raja) usually has more money than he does. He doesn't ask himself, because he wouldn't want to admit that he's trying to impress the girls—namely, Lindsay. And if his girlfriend didn't like him driving Lindsay and Jessica to the bleachers last night, she'd definitely be mad at him for buying them drinks today.

"Okay, I got it," he says, taking their orders. "Be back in a second."

*** 

Carole is amused by the number of coffee shops that have sprung up around town. A few years ago, there were only a handful of them in Edmonton, but now people can't seem to function without one on every corner. Though she finds this funny, it doesn't stop her from being a regular customer. They remind her of sanitized, homogenized versions of the cafes she loved going to in Europe. She just wishes Canadians weren't so uptight when it comes to dogs. Luckily, Mr. Biscuits is small and quiet; when Carole puts him in her over-sized shoulder bag, no one even knows he's there.

\*\*\*

There is a coffee shop half a block from the physiotherapy clinic which would not be a big deal for most people; for Ryan, however, it's a huge deal. It means that many more steps, each one more difficult to make. It means adding an additional half-hour to his outing—not just because he walks so slowly, but because he can't trust himself to walk while carrying a hot beverage. He uses a cane, which is embarrassing enough, and when he buys groceries, he has to carry them in a backpack. He can't do that with a coffee.

When he walks into the shop, he's glad to see that it's not busy. There are only two people ahead of him in line, but it quickly becomes apparent that he could be waiting a while. The kid at the counter has apparently ordered a ton of drinks with special instructions so elaborate that it has to be a joke. Ryan balances uncomfortably on his cane, shifting his weight from one side to the other. Standing too long is sometimes worse than walking—it messes with his balance and makes his legs stiffen up. He silently prays that the guy making the drinks will hurry up and get his shit together.

The other person ahead of Ryan is a woman he's seen here before, and with any luck her drink order won't be quite as ridiculous——unless she gets something for whatever that is inside her bag. He sees the large, over-the-shoulder bag twitch periodically and wonders exactly what is in there. Probably a small dog, or a ferret, maybe even a rabbit? He imagines trying to smuggle his cat in—as if that would work!

He shifts his weight again. God, what is taking so long? He checks his watch—it's nearly one o'clock. That leaves only a half-hour to drink his coffee (if he ever frickin' gets it) and get himself to the clinic.

He glances around the shop at the only other customers, each sitting alone at separate tables. One is a pre-teen girl wearing a pile of makeup and drinking the largest hot chocolate he's ever seen. The other is a really cute girl, about his age, staring out the window like she's a million miles away. He looks back at the kid up front and the flustered dude trying to make all the drinks.

*Hurry the fuck up*, he silently commands.

\*\*\*

When the earthquake hits—at precisely 1:00 p.m.—Ryan is the only one who isn't surprised. Since the accident, he's been prone to dizzy spells and often feels like objects are moving around him. So, when that familiar swaying sensation begins, he grips the countertop and hopes he doesn't look too stupid. It's not until a large decorative teapot falls from its shelf and smashes to the ground that he realizes this isn't a dizzy spell.

What starts as a gentle rocking now feels like a giant jackhammer has descended upon the entire shop floor. One of the girls screams, Ryan doesn't know which, and the kid at the front, who had just been given a cardboard tray of drinks, drops them.

After several seconds, the shaking stops and everything suddenly goes quiet. Next comes a deep thrumming so low that Ryan feels it rather than hears it. At the same time, something in the back right corner of the shop catches his eye. He looks over to see the air pulling downwards, somehow, as though a giant invisible straw has been inserted through the ceiling. Still gripping the countertop, Ryan watches in fascination as this distortion of air sweeps from one side of the shop to the other, reminiscent of a massive vertical photocopier. It moves at a moderate pace, bending and distorting everything in its path but moving nothing, as though it was never there.

After that, all is still.

"Is everyone okay?" Julian shouts, breaking the mesmerized silence. What the hell was that? "Is everyone okay?!" he shouts again, louder this time. He moves quickly out from behind the counter, making a beeline for the young girl.

"What's your name, honey?"

Marcy begins to cry. She is sitting at her small table, both arms desperately gripping the sides, her hot chocolate splattered on the floor.

"It's...Marcy."

"Are you hurt, Marcy?"

"I...I don't think so."

Julian places a hand on her shoulder and glances around the shop. He sees a young woman curled up in a ball under a table and rushes over to her.

"Are you hurt?"

Dannicka lifts her head. "No—I'm okay." She had screamed earlier and now feels embarrassed.

Carole has been through an earthquake before, once when she was in Australia, and that felt similar to this; but earthquakes aren't supposed to happen in this part of the world. And what the hell was that thing at the end? Whatever it was, it caused Mr. Biscuits to howl like a miniature wolf. Instinctively, Carole had crouched down, covering her bag with her body. She barely noticed the contents of the boy's drinks spraying her as they splattered to the floor, just inches from her head. Now, getting back to her feet, she is relieved to see that the coffee shop's owner is taking charge. Mr. Biscuits seems none the worse for wear, so she turns her attention to the teenaged boy in front of her; he is drenched and seems very confused.

"Did you get burned?" she asks.

"No," he says slowly, not understanding her question at first. After a second, he gets it. "The drinks were all cold," he tells her.

"Oh, good." She turns to the man behind her, who is clutching a cane. "Are you alright?"

"I'm fine," he says. "What about you?"

She realizes then that her hair is wet and brushes a strand from her face. "I'm okay."

"Can everyone please stay put?" Julian hollers. "I'm going to call 9-1-1 and just make sure that everything is okay."

He goes to the back room to use the phone, realizing that his hands are shaking.

Chet, soaking wet and not at all understanding what's just happened, puts down the now-empty tray and begins heading for the door.

"Whoa, just a second," says Ryan, holding out an arm.

"My friends are outside in the car," Chet tells him. "I just wanna check on them."

"Oh, okay." Ryan sees that the kid might be in shock. "Just don't leave yet, okay?"

"I won't," says Chet, woodenly.

Deciding to keep an eye on him, Ryan watches as the kid walks out the door and over to one of the cars in the lot.

"9-1-1, do you require police, fire or an ambulance?"

"I'm not sure," says Julian. "I'm calling because of the earthquake."

"What earthquake?"

He does his best to describe the incident. "It just happened a few minutes ago."

"There've been no reports of an earthquake," says the operator.

"Well, whatever it was!" he snaps, losing patience. "I'm at the Grabbajabba on 102nd Avenue and 125th Street. I'm the manager here and something *like* an earthquake has just happened! I've got customers in here and I don't know if any of them are hurt!"

"Stay on the line," the operator instructs. "I'm dispatching help."

\*\*\*

"What the fuck happened to you?!" Raja asks, laughing. "Did you get in a fight in there?"

Chet looks at his friends, sitting in the car. They all seem totally fine. He feels stunned. Looking down, he realizes that his shirt is dripping with the sugary contents of four complicated coffee drinks. Raja gets out of the car, looking a little confused himself.

"Seriously, dude—what happened?"

"Are you okay?" Lindsay asks as she also gets out of the car.

Chet hears sirens. Within seconds, a police car and fire truck pull into the parking lot.

"Stay here," he tells his friends. Before anyone can respond, he turns and heads back into the shop.

\*\*\*

It's nearly two o'clock. Each of the people inside the Grabbajabba—Carole, Julian, Ryan, Dannicka, Chet and Marcy—have all been checked over by the paramedics and questioned by the police. No one appears to have suffered any injuries from the incident, only a momentary shock followed by the unsettling feeling that no one else seems to have an answer as to what just happened.

"None of the other stores here have experienced anything like you described," says an officer. "There *is* some construction going on a block over... that could have something to do with it."

The elder four stare at the officer, dumbfounded.

"That would have to be some pretty impressive construction," Carole says, deadpan.

"In the meantime," the officer continues, "please feel free to contact us if you have any further questions or remember any other details."

Julian isn't satisfied by this and he knows the others feel the same. He scans the faces of the five people who have experienced this strange event with him, and when he looks at Carole, he does a double-take.

"Do I know you?" he asks. "I mean, from before today."

"I don't know," she says. "I come here quite a bit..." She clutches her large bag gingerly, sensing that Mr. Biscuits is becoming restless. "You've probably seen me in here before."

The front door swings open and Marcy's dad, who had been contacted earlier at his work, bursts in. She already knows the first thing he'll say and she's ready for it.

"Why aren't you in school?"

On cue, she bursts into tears. "I didn't feel good!" she cries. "I accidentally got on the wrong bus and then I had to go to the bathroom and I stopped here..."

"What the hell happened?"

Julian steps forward, calmly introduces himself, and offers a brief summation. He's grateful for the police presence, not sure if the girl's dad might escalate things. God knows, if he found one of his own kids in this situation, he wouldn't be too calm either.

"Anyway," says the office in charge, "we'll be investigating." He turns to Julian. "You're gonna need to shut down for the rest of the day."

"Of course. Wait—" he adds, before any of the customers leave. "I'll give you my business cards. I want you to call me if you have any concerns, or if there are any problems as a result of...today."

Carole takes a business card from Julian's outstretched hand.

"Thanks," she says, tossing it into her bag with what she hopes comes off as a normal gesture, but doesn't. She should have just put it in her pocket. Instead, she opens the top of the large bag just a sliver, not wanting anyone to catch glimpse of what's inside, while trying not to startle Mr. Biscuits by tossing the card onto his face.

"Thanks," she says again, smiling guiltily at Julian who, if he's realized that there's an animal in her bag, doesn't let on. Turning around, she heads out the door.

"I'll take one of those," says Marcy's dad in a slightly intimidating tone.

"Absolutely." Julian smiles, wondering if this guy is thinking about suing Grabbajabba. "Call me anytime," he adds in his best customer service voice.

"Thank you," says Dannicka, also taking a card from Julian. She puts it in her wallet. As she walks out of the shop, she realizes that it's the first time in the last 24 hours she hasn't thought about Eric. *It only took an earthquake,* she thinks, angry with herself.

Ryan takes the card with a brief, "No worries, man," as it's handed to him. He's missed his appointment. Should he go to the clinic anyway? See if they can take him? He still hasn't had his coffee.

This is the first time an adult—or anyone, for that matter—has given Chet a business card.

"Thanks," he says. He still feels out of it and weird, like he's not really in his body or something. As he heads for the door, Julian calls out after him.

"Wait! Let me make you more drinks! You didn't even—"

"No thanks," he says. He doesn't want them anymore. He just wants to go home.

# CHAPTER THREE

"Hey, Marcy!"

Marcy turns around and looks down the main corridor of her school, searching for the owner of the voice. In the sea of bobbing faces she spots Bernadette waving and pushing her way through the crowd. For once, Grace is not glued to her side.

"Hey! Wait up!"

From this distance, Marcy notices that her friend is starting to look more like a grown-up—all willowy arms and legs—and it feels strange. They've been friends for more than half their lives and now, for the first time since they met (all the way back in Grade One), Bernadette is the taller of the two. Next to her, Marcy feels like a stunted work horse.

"Where's your flunky?" Marcy asks, unable to stop herself from sounding snotty.

Bernadette adjusts her backpack. "Don't be mean. Grace didn't feel good today, so she went home."

"Yeah, right," Marcy mutters.

"Did you find us a new song for the routine?"

Marcy had all weekend to find a new song. Well, not exactly all weekend—because of that weird construction problem at that coffee shop on Friday, she got caught skipping school, although it seemed like her dad believed her about not feeling good. She spent the weekend at his place and had all day Saturday and Sunday to find a new song, but nothing presented itself. She wracked her brains and her dad's boring old record collection, but couldn't come up with anything close to what she wanted. On Sunday night she'd even asked her dad to play the radio while he drove her back to her mom's place, and still, nothing. This morning, with no time left, she broke her sister's 'stay out of my room' rule, randomly grabbing one of her CD's while she was in the shower, and shoving it into her backpack.

"Yeah, I found one," Marcy lies.

"What's it called?"

"I forget. Come on, we're gonna be late."

Marcy and Bernadette head to the girls' gym where The Dancetasticks rehearse every week. They change into their dance clothes and find their spots on the gym floor, arriving just in time to begin the familiar warm-up. Marcy could perform the warm-up in her sleep, she knows it that well. In fact, she has easily memorized all of their routines.

"Okay, everybody!" Mrs. J addresses the group. "Get into your positions for the opening routine! And I want to see some smiles!" She presses 'play' on the tape player and shouts, "a 5, 6, 7, 8!"

Marcy knows this routine especially well, and begins to dance with her usual confidence. A few bars into the song, however, she seems to make a mistake. She's not sure how—she knows this routine inside and out—but she's ended up alone on stage-right, while the rest of the troupe have side-stepped their way in the opposite direction. She rushes to catch up, making one more apparent mistake, and then, unbelievably, another.

"Pay attention, Marcy!" Mrs. J yells above the music.

She is totally confused. She knows this choreography—she does! Not only does she practice nearly every day, but she thinks about it when she's lying in bed at night. She's gone over and over it, and now, it's almost completely different. When did it change? She was at last week's practice... did they get together without her on the weekend?

"*Left,* Marcy!"

Marcy tries desperately to keep up with the other girls (and Cody, the one and only boy), sometimes bumping right into them. It's *so* incredibly embarrassing. This is definitely new choreography, and she would just love to know when it changed.

By the time the song is over, Marcy, evidently standing in the wrong place judging by the puzzled looks from the others, is more than confused. She's pissed off.

"Come *on,* you guys!" Mrs. J reprimands. "This is nowhere *near* where it's supposed to be! The recital is in *two weeks*! Marcy, are you even awake?!"

"Yes," she snaps back, irritated. A couple of the girls behind her giggle, and she feels her cheeks turn red.

"Let's run it again!" Mrs. J hollers. "A 5, 6, 7, 8!"

They run the routine twice more and by the time they are done, Marcy has picked up the new steps. She's still angry, though, and someone is definitely going to hear about it.

"Let's see if the closing routine is any better," Mrs. J shouts, adding, "It'd better be!"

With trepidation, Marcy takes her place for this routine, glancing around at the others to see if anything about this choreography has also changed. Bernadette catches her eye and gives her an encouraging nod, which is somehow even more irritating. Turning away, Marcy tries to concentrate.

As the song begins, she cautiously moves through the routine, her usual confidence now gone. Only when the song is over does she finally relax, knowing that at least *this* choreography has stayed the same.

The rest of their practice runs in a similar pattern: Marcy is cautious as they start rehearsing each number, then relieved to find it familiar. So—it's only the opening number that has changed.

"Marcy!" Mrs. J calls. "Stay after practice, please!"

This time, she is glad to stay after class. She would love to get to the bottom of this; if they've been having extra rehearsals without telling her, then that's really unfair.

"I'll wait outside," says Bernadette, heading off to the changeroom.

Marcy, panting from the workout, walks over to where her teacher is standing.

"What was going on out there, today? You seemed lost at the beginning."

"I didn't know the choreography changed," Marcy replies tersely. "No one told me."

"Marcy, that choreography changed two weeks ago. And last week, you had it down, so that's no excuse. You need to stay focused."

"Uh-uh!" Marcy insists. "I swear to God, I've never seen that choreography before!"

"Can you watch your tone, please?"

"Okay, sorry! But you guys must've had an extra practice or something because –"

"I don't want to hear any excuses. You need to keep your focus and not be daydreaming—that's what happens when you think you know something so well that you don't have to pay attention. That's when mistakes get made."

Marcy bites her lip as tears of frustration spring to her eyes. She knows she never saw that choreography before today—she *knows* it! They *had* to have had another rehearsal, or something, without telling her! Maybe Mrs. J forgot to tell her and thinks she did? Maybe she's having some kind of mid-life crisis—Marcy has heard about that happening to adults. If she didn't have the recital to worry about, she'd accuse Mrs. J of going through one of those crises right now.

"Now, do you have your new song picked out yet?"

"Yes," Marcy lies.

She had looked at her sister's CD during lunch, but didn't recognize any of the songs. If only there been some way to listen to it. She reaches into her backpack and hands the CD to Mrs. J. She'll have to wing it, but it'll be better than not getting to do the duet at all.

"Alanis," says Mrs. J. "I've never heard of her. Which song is it?"

"Um, I forget the name of it. Can I look at the back again?"

She scrolls down the list of song titles, choosing one at random.

"Um, 'Iconic'."

She hands the CD back.

"Oh, you mean, 'Ironic'."

"Yeah," says Marcy. She doesn't know what the word 'ironic' means and looks at the teacher to gauge her reaction.

"Okay, well, let's have a listen."

The song starts out slow and, to Marcy's ears, boring. There's no way she and Bernadette can dance to this—they're no ballerinas, that's for sure.

"This is really different for you," says Mrs. J. "I'm impressed."

Marcy decides to tell Mrs. J she's made a mistake, that this isn't the song she meant to choose, but as she opens her mouth to speak, the song changes. The drums kick in loudly and Alanis begins singing in a way that Marcy's never heard before. It's almost like she's yelling; like she's not even trying to sound pretty. It's so... powerful. If Marcy could sing, this is exactly how she would want to sound.

"This is the song I want," she says, definitively.

Mrs. J says yes..

***

SATURDAY, JUNE 10

Dannicka is keeping two big secrets. The first is that she slept with Eric. That was a huge mistake and something that Todd never needs to know about. The second is what happened at the Grabbajabba. She wishes she could tell Todd how strange it was and how out-of-sorts she's been feeling ever since, but there's no way to explain why she was there. She hasn't told her friends either, knowing that they'd care less about the coffee shop and more about her getting together with Eric. She just can't deal with the inevitable 'Evils of Eric' lecture right now, so she keeps her two big secrets to herself.

To make up for the missed day of pay, she has arranged to come in today and sort through the filing cabinets. This has needed to be done for a long time, but is something she can't fit in during a regular work day. Thankfully, her boss agreed to it. That's one problem solved.

Alone in the empty office, she begins by removing all the files from the first cabinet and placing them in stacks on the floor. Sitting cross-legged on the floor, she goes through each document one by one. She recognizes her own handwriting on many of the documents, having worked here for three years now. It was supposed to be a temporary job—six months tops—while she figured out what she really wanted to do with her life. Three years later, she still doesn't know what that is.

About an hour into this work, something catches her eye at the top of a questionnaire: 'Company of Origin,' after which is written, 'Belgium.'

It's funny that she hadn't caught that typo before—it's obviously supposed to say 'Country.' In the next stack of papers however, on completely different documents, Dannicka comes across the same typo. It is the same in the next stack, and the next one after that. 'The Company of Canada has issued an announcement regarding immigration practices related to...' How could she have missed this error over and over? How could everyone else in the office have missed it?

Nervously, she thumbs through document after document. Maybe this entire group of files have been grouped together *because* of the typo. Maybe someone else caught it and put them all together. She sees a post-it note on one of the papers, her own familiar handwriting staring back at her. *Client has only lived in the company for 5 months.* Dannicka feels a chill at the back of her neck. Something is very wrong.

Her first instinct is to leave the office. She needs air—she can't seem to catch a breath. Looking down at the absolute mess she has created, she knows she can't just leave an entire filing cabinet's worth of papers all over the floor. What should she do? Helplessly, she glances around the open area of the office as though looking for someone, or something, to answer her question.

*Don't freak out*, she thinks to herself. *There has to be some explanation.*

She takes a few deep breaths, drinks from her water bottle, and gets back to work. By 4:30 p.m., she is done. As she leaves, she grabs a few papers from the "shred" pile and shoves them into her bag. She can figure this out when she gets home.

Outside, the fresh air comes as a relief. She begins walking towards the nearest transit stop, then changes her mind. The last thing she wants to do right now is sit on the bus. Instead she chooses to make the forty-five-minute walk home and uses the time to think. She supposes she could have missed the typo. Doesn't the brain fill in things that it expects to see? She's always so busy when she's at work and today was the only time the office was quiet. Or, maybe in a certain context 'company' is substituted for 'country.' Maybe it's some legal term she's not familiar with.

She walks through the river valley and on to the High Level bridge, one of her favourite places to walk in the city. She loves seeing the river, one hundred and fifty feet below, the rush of air as cars race past her on the industrial-looking bridge which resembles a giant cage. The walkways on both sides of the bridge are busy today, the weather being unusually warm for this time of year. She takes her jacket off as she walks, tying the arms around her waist and allowing herself to enjoy what is probably the nicest day they've had since last summer.

By the time she gets home she has convinced herself that she was over-reacting. She doesn't look at the papers in her bag—she doesn't need to. It's either a typo or a legal term. She'll ask her boss on Monday and it will all be straightened out.

Still, she can't quite erase the feeling of doubt. She, herself, wrote that word on the post-it note—it's pretty hard to explain that. She doesn't own a dictionary or an atlas, but she does have a music collection. Finding one of her mixed tapes, she puts it in the tape deck and rewinds to the beginning of Side 2. In a moment, John Lennon's 'Imagine' begins to play. She listens to the familiar song, almost embarrassed by what she's doing. What is she trying to prove? Does she honestly think anything about the song will suddenly be different?

As the second verse begins, however, her confidence falters.

*Here it comes,* she thinks, and there it is: "Imagine there's no companies."

She stops the tape, rewinds it, and plays it again. "Imagine there's no companies."

She shakes her head. It must only sound like 'companies' because she's expecting to hear it. She remembers the 1980s band she used to listen to called 'Big Country.' She still has their album. Flipping through her stack of records, she finds it near the back. Her heart beats loudly as she lifts it out of the pile. On the front of the album cover, in large block letters, it says: 'Big Company.'

Shaking, she turns the record over and looks at the list of songs. One of her favourites titled 'In a Big Country' now reads 'In a Big Company.' Beside this is written 'Property of Maureen' in her own teen-age scrawl.

She thinks about phoning someone— Todd, her dad, or her friends—then decides against it. What would she say? She thinks about her mom. Ever since her mother's death, Dannicka has maintained what she knows to be an unrealistic fantasy about her—she has always believed that no matter what was going wrong in her life, her mom would understand and have the power to make it better. Right now, even this thought cannot comfort her.

For the rest of the night, Dannicka does not sleep.

***

Ryan dreams that he is sitting in his bed, propped up as if someone has lifted him from under the armpits and set him here like a ragdoll. It's a strange sensation. He feels as though he's floating, while simultaneously feeling grounded to the weight of the bed beneath him.

Roland, his cat, jumps up from the floor and sits at the foot of the bed facing him. The room is very dark but Ryan can see Roland easily thanks to a small spotlight focused only on the cat.

"Roland's on stage," Ryan murmurs, smiling drowsily.

Roland blinks purposefully as though preparing to say something, which Ryan finds very funny; then, fantastically, Roland does.

"Hello, Ryan."

"Whaaat?" Ryan chuckles, amused.

"We say 'hello'."

"You can talk, man? So awesome."

Somehow this all makes sense, and Ryan finds himself wondering why he's never talked to his cat before.

"Hey, Roland," he says, still sounding more than half asleep. "Wus going on with you? Hey?"

The cat blinks again, in that same deliberate way. "You may call us that."

He notices that Roland has an accent and tries to place it. English?

"Hey—are you from England?"

Ryan wakes up.

\*\*\*

## SUNDAY, JUNE 11

"Trudy!" Julian hollers. "I'm gonna run to the mall and get a present for my Dad! I'll see ya later!"

At the sound of his voice, Trudy barrels down the stairs and over to the front door where Julian is standing.

"Please take the girls with you," she says. "They're driving me up the wall."

Julian takes one look at his wife and sees that she's exhausted.

"You bet. Girls!" he hollers. "Get over here!"

An eleven-year-old Pandora and an eight-year-old Lexie emerge from two different areas of the house. As is often the case, he is struck by the miracle and the mystery that are his daughters. How did he produce two human beings? And such (in his opinion, anyway) incredible ones? Having grown up with only brothers, being the odd man out in a house full of estrogen is even more of a mystery.

"What?" asks his eldest, already put out by whatever will be asked of her, before knowing what it is.

"We're going to the mall," he says. "Get your shoes on."

"Do I have to go?"

"Yes. You two are driving your mother crazy."

"No, we're not," says Lexie. "I'm pretty sure."

He kisses the top of her head.

"You drive everyone crazy," he tells her. "C'mon, let's get a move on."

Julian and his daughters walk out to the driveway and get in to their minivan. This was an excursion he'd wanted to make solo. Yes, he had planned on going to the mall to get a Father's Day present, but he also wanted to make a detour out past the city limits. Now he won't be able to do that without his daughters questioning him.

Julian has driven back and forth from Calgary to Edmonton hundreds of times—he knows every stretch of the highway. But when he drove back to Calgary the day after the earthquake, or whatever that was, he noticed that something was missing. Something rather significant. Something that's incredibly difficult to believe could suddenly be gone: the foothills on the outskirts of Calgary.

Julian was more shaken up about what had happened at work than he felt comfortable admitting. He was obviously mistaken about not seeing the mountains and must have misjudged where he was on the highway. Or maybe he'd just been preoccupied and didn't register seeing them. Maybe his eyes are starting to go. There are a million possible reasons why he might have missed them.

The only real problem, however, is that he's been unable to get the thought out of his mind. He knows that a missing mountain range is ridiculous, but it's been eight days since that trip and the thought continues to nag at him. If he could just drive to the outskirts of town and see for himself, it would put his mind at ease.

He pulls into the mall parking lot and finds a space.

"Everyone stick together," he says.

They walk into the mall and head straight to one of the record stores. Julian reads the headings on the store shelves, looking for the 'Country and Western' section, finding 'Cowboy and Western' instead. He chuckles to himself when he sees that one. Calgary is so cowboy-crazy. The store must have changed their signage in preparation for the upcoming Stampede.

In this new 'Cowboy and Western' section, he finds what he's looking for; the newest Shania Twain album. Not his taste, although he doesn't mind checking her out in her music videos, but he knows his dad will love it.

"Can we go to The Gap?" Pandora asks, already bored.

"I'm not authorized to do any other shopping," Julian tells her. Before she can protest, he adds, "I *am* allowed to buy you guys some ice-cream, though."

After a stop at Baskin-Robbins, he and the girls get back into the minivan and he suddenly has an idea: "Why don't we go for a drive?" he says. "We can give your mom some more time to herself."

"Can we go to the zoo?" asks Lexie.

"The zoo is for babies," says Pandora.

"The zoo is for all ages," says Julian, "but that's not a drive. I'm driving, so I get to pick."

"But we can't drive!" Lexie exclaims. "So, it's not fair!"

"You get to pick the music, though," he tells her. "So, that's pretty good."

"Can we listen to The Spice Girls, then?"

Julian groans loudly, "Oh, God, no! Not The Spice Girls! Please! Anything but that!"

Lexie giggles. "You said I get to pick!"

He sighs. "You're right—I did say that. A deal's a deal. And then Pandy gets to pick the next one. Oh—and *no* singing."

His youngest laughs. His elder, eleven-going-on-eighteen, rolls her eyes.

Julian drives away from the mall and on to Deerfoot trail, heading North. In the back seat, both girls sing along with The Spice Girls. Julian half-wonders about the appropriateness of the lyrics, but his mind has shifted now to the task at hand. The closer they get to his destination, the more nervous he feels.

*This is stupid*, he tells himself. What's to be nervous about? They'll drive by, see the foothills that are supposed to be there, that have always been there, and then they'll go home.

But that's not what happens. Instead, he drives past the spot that's been plaguing him for more than a week and sees, or rather doesn't see, the same thing he noticed eight days ago: the foothills are gone.

They should be on his left now, sticking out over that row of buildings across the highway, but instead, there's only sky. There is nothing wrong with his eyesight and, as if to emphasize this, Julian clearly sees three birds soaring leisurely off in the distance. He glances into the rear-view mirror to see how the girls react, to see if they have noticed anything out of the ordinary. They look bored. He thinks of the phrase 'love can move mountains' and stifles a manic laugh.

"Can we go home now?" Pandora asks. "We've been gone forever."

"Sure," he says. He takes the next exit back onto the highway, heading South. Still, no foothills. His hands, gripping the steering wheel, begin to shake.

*I must be losing my shit!* he thinks. What the hell is going on? Has there been some kind of rock-blasting taking place? Even if there was, why would there be? And how could they have wiped out an entire range overnight?

*Calm down,* he tells himself. *Just focus on driving and get the girls home.*

***

## MONDAY, JUNE 12

The Grad Committee at Chet's high school has chosen 'The 1970s' as this year's grad theme. Plans have been made to transform the gym into one large disco, and a theme song has been chosen: "We May Never Pass This Way Again", by a band Chet has never heard of.

Months earlier, he was selected to be the Class Historian. He accepted the honour happily, having no idea how difficult speech-writing would be. Now, with the ceremony just four days away, he is feeling more nervous than ever.

Chet has never been an anxious person, but since the incident at Grabbajabba ten days ago, he has definitely been on edge. Twice, he's woken up in the middle of the night in a total panic; heart racing and feeling like he couldn't breathe. He hasn't mentioned this to the friends that were there that day (none of whom seem bothered, or anxious, or different in any way) and he also hasn't mentioned it to his parents. When he told them about the weird-as-shit experience, his dad asked if he and his friends had taken any drugs.

The buzzer screams through the hallways of the school, and Chet jumps. Embarrassed, he checks to see if anyone noticed before slamming his locker shut. It's exam time. He's already written his finals for Bio, Math and Chem, and today is Social Studies. He hasn't bothered to study for this exam, but he's not worried; he's been kicking ass in this class all semester.

Walking into the gym, he sees the long rows of desks that have been set up. He chooses a seat near the back, noticing that his girl-friend, Kelley, is already seated up ahead in another row. Not far from her sits Lindsay, who sees him and smiles. He smiles back, thankful that Kelley isn't looking. She's still pissed at him for going to the mall with Lindsay and Jessica last week—or at least, for trying to go. After the Grabbajabba stop, he felt really weird and disoriented and had to get Raja to drive his car home.

Chet's ballcap suddenly flips off his head. Startled, and trying not to show it, he spins around.

"Nervous, much?" asks Raja. "You need to lay off the caffeine." He slides into the empty seat beside Chet.

"Oh, ha, ha."

"Let's get this *over* with," Raja announces, adding, "I can't wait to be *done* with this shit."

Before Chet can agree, one of the school's Social Studies teachers walks to the front of the desks, clapping his hands.

"Okay, everybody!" he hollers. "Settle down!"

Once settled, he continues. "Do not open your exams until I instruct you to do so! You will have ninety minutes to write the exam. If you finish early, you may hand it in to me, after which point you will exit the gym. QUI-ET-LY. Are there any questions?"

Raja shoots a hand up into the air. "Do you have the time?"

"Any *real* questions?" the instructor snaps. "No? Okay."

He checks his watch. "You may begin."

Feeling on edge, Chet works his way through the first two questions. When he gets to the third, he does a double-take. 'Canada is a Company which...' Company? He scans the rest of the exam, finding the word pop up a few more times. He stifles a laugh. It appears that the geniuses who made up this thing have substituted the word 'company' for 'country' throughout the entire test. What a bunch of morons! Suddenly, his anxiety takes a back seat. Now calm, he makes his way through the rest of the exam.

After an hour and fifteen minutes, he is done. Collecting his things, he quietly gets to his feet, delivering a subtle kick to one of Raja's runners. His friend keeps his head down, still buried in the exam, but one middle finger salutes Chet as he brushes by.

At the front of the room, he hands in his paper.

"How's your speech coming along?" the teacher whispers.

"It's done," Chet whispers back, lying. *When it actually is done,* he thinks to himself, *it's going to suck.*

He leaves the gym and makes his way over to the cafeteria. Moments later, he is joined by Raja, who throws his backpack on the floor and slumps into a chair.

"Thank God, *that's* over."

"Did you check out that major typo?" Chet laughs.

"What typo?"

"You know, the one where they kept saying 'company', like, 'Canada is a company where..."

"Huh?"

"God, you're stunned! Open your frickin' eyes next time!"

Raja gives him a blank look. Chet is about to say something further on the subject when he sees Kelley walk past the cafeteria entrance without coming in. The excitement he usually feels when he sees her has lately been accompanied by unmistakeable dread. It's like she's always mad at him and, half the time, he doesn't even know why. Did she see him wave at Lindsay back in the gym? Did she see him just now and pretend not to?

"I gotta go," he says, groaning. He wishes he didn't have to, but if he doesn't go after her now he'll end up in more shit than he's probably in already.

\*\*\*

Since giving up her worldly travels a few years ago, Carole has stayed put in Edmonton. Now, for the first time in five years, she feels like she is travelling again. And this could be the most thrilling trip of all.

Carole believes that what happened at the Grabbajabba was supernatural. What other explanation could there be? That wasn't like any other earthquake she's aware of, and it sure as hell wasn't caused by any construction, either. Since that day, she's been feeling a disconnect between herself and her surroundings, as though she somehow doesn't fit in anymore; like a puzzle piece that has gotten wet and has swelled beyond its intended borders. This feeling is everywhere she goes; in her house, at her work, and in every other place she frequents. Things around her appear normal; the people she encounters look and act the same, and yet, something is very different. She finds herself looking for some indication, other than her intuition, to tell her she's right. So far, none has come.

Although the feeling is unsettling, it's also exciting. She has returned to the Grabbajabba four times over the last ten days— each time, she has felt anxious and hopeful when she arrives, but leaves with a sense of disappointment. Is she actually expecting an extraordinary out-of-this-world experience each time she steps over the threshold? Somehow, yes.

Tonight, she would love nothing more than to go back there again tonight —to bring a book and stay until closing—but a deadline is looming on a work project. Instead, she picks up Mr. Biscuits and carries him into her studio.

The Fleetwood Mac album is still on the turntable, and she turns it on again. She begins to assemble her work materials, turning her thoughts now to the assignment in front of her. The last 'No Think' painting, the one she did the night before the earthquake-that-wasn't-an-earthquake, still sits on the easel and she glances at it briefly. Her mind is focused on the current assignment and it takes her a moment to register that something about the painting is different. After a double-take, she sets down her pad and pencil and walks over to take a closer look. The painting, made using a few pale shades of yellow, green and blue, still looks entirely white. But now, in the upper left-hand corner, there are three small perfect circles painted in a bright, can't-miss-it cobalt blue. She knows for a fact that she did not paint them.

For ten days Carole has been searching for any evidence that something extraordinary has happened, only to find that it was right here in her own studio, all along; in bright cobalt blue on white. A shiver runs up her spine. She stares intently at the circles and a nervous smile slowly spreads across her mouth.

"Mr. Biscuits," she says, "I don't think we're in Edmonton anymore."

# CHAPTER FOUR

Once again, Ryan dreams he is sitting in his bed, propped up as though he has been placed there by invisible hands. Roland sits at the foot of the bed facing him with the same small spotlight (coming from where?) focused on his little body.

"Hello, Ryan."

Ryan smiles slowly, dreamily.

"Talking Roland," he murmurs. "Talking cat!"

"Ryan, we need you to listen."

That isn't an English accent at all. It's...Australian. New Zealand?

"Ryan, we need you to focus."

He nods. "Focus." This must be serious.

"There has been an error."

Roland's foreboding tone tells Ryan that this matter is indeed serious. Something is dreadfully wrong. He doesn't know what that something might be, but he trusts his cat. He trusts the soothing voice coming through his cat.

"Ryan, we need you to gather the others. Do you understand?"

"Yes."

Instinctively, he knows exactly who Roland is referring to. What he doesn't understand is why he needs to collect them. As though reading his mind, Roland continues.

"The others are starting to find discrepancies. You need to gather them so this error can be corrected."

"Gather?"

"Ryan, we need you to––"
Ryan wakes up.

***

Ryan takes a deep breath and opens his eyes slowly. No stars. Incredible! He hasn't had a migraine since...he thinks for a minute— today is the 13th, which makes two weeks since his last migraine. It's the longest he has gone without one in years. He doesn't know what he should attribute this to and he's wary of becoming hopeful— every night he goes to bed dreading the possibility of waking up to a migraine, but for the last two weeks, he has been waking up with 'Get Out of Jail Free' passes. He's not complaining, although it *is* disconcerting; the longer he goes without a migraine, the more sure he is that the next day will be The Big One.

He sits up in his bed with half the effort it usually takes. This, too, seems to have become part of the new normal. Is it possible that years of torturous physiotherapy is finally having some real effect? He shouldn't think about it—he might jinx himself. And anyway, it's probably just a fluke and before long, he'll be back in the depths of his familiar agony.

He throws the comforter off his legs and nearly shits his pants— Roland, who he didn't know was under there, sits staring at him with his piercing green eyes.

"You nearly gave me a heart attack, buddy!" he says, clutching his chest and laughing. "What're you doing under there?"

Suddenly, the memory of last night's dream comes flooding back. He eyes the cat cautiously, half-expecting him to speak. Instead, Roland begins to groom himself and Ryan feels an sense of embarrassed relief.

They were weird dreams though, no doubt about it. The first one was sort of funny, although thinking about it now, Ryan doesn't feel like laughing. This last one, from just a couple of hours ago, felt very different. It felt...ominous—and real despite its fantastical nature. Now that he's remembered it, he can't shake off the feeling it's given him.

He wanders into the kitchen and feeds an appreciative Roland, then heads into the bathroom. He turns the water on and steps into the shower. What happened at the Grabbajabba was not normal. The dreams are probably just his subconscious trying to make sense of things. He had plenty of nightmares in the wake of the accident; in them, he re-lived the trauma (what he remembers of it, anyway) over and over. Then again, these more recent dreams are not a re-enactment of what happened at the coffee shop; more like a continuation.

*This is so stupid*, he tells himself. Dreams are just the brain's way of compartmentalizing day-to-day life. They're like putting your thoughts into a mental filing cabinet—they're not real. It would be like saying hallucinations are real.

He turns off the water, grabs a towel from the rack and begins to dry off.

"I clearly don't have enough going on in my own boring life," he says out loud, "that I have to entertain myself with this shit. Honest to God."

He plods back into the bedroom, gets dressed, then heads into the living room where he plunks himself down in front of the TV. He turns on his Sony PlayStation, a gift he bought himself with the settlement money, but he can't concentrate enough to actually play. He feels restless, like he wants to move. This in itself is unusual. For the first time since the accident, Ryan actually feels like going for a walk. Without a second thought, he gets to his feet, grabs his keys and his cane from the entryway, and heads out the door.

It's nice out. Wishing he had brought sunglasses, he squints in the sunshine while he decides where to go. It's strange to be outside with no specific task or destination. Without any reason, he begins walking south up his street.

He tries to think of something other than those two bizarre dreams but he can't get them out of his mind. He should have brought his Walkman. He tries to hum softly to himself, tries to take in his surroundings, but he can't seem to block out Roland's solemn words—there has been an 'error' and Ryan needs to 'gather the others' because they are starting to find discrepancies. Huh? He knows, somehow, that 'the others' refers to the five people who were with him at Grabbajabba that day, but what the hell is the error? And the discrepancies that the others are finding?

*It's not a code to be deciphered*, he tells himself. *It's just a couple of whacked-out dreams*. But that voice coming from his cat—it was so clear, so...calming. And so believable.

He stops walking, suddenly aware that he is standing directly across the street from the Grabbajabba. He hadn't been paying attention to where he was going. Did he subconsciously bring himself here? Or did something else?

A shiver runs up his spine, bristling the hairs on the back of his neck. He *was* brought here. There has been an error and he now understands this to be true. He stands, transfixed, staring at the coffee shop, comprehension suddenly dawning on him like an actual lightbulb turning on in his brain.

There has been an error; and that error felt a lot like an earthquake.

***

## FRIDAY, JUNE 16

"I am so proud of you!" Chet's mother says. "I don't know where the time has gone."

Her eyes begin to well with tears.

"Okay, let's keep it together," says Chet's dad. "We haven't even left the house yet."

"I just want one more picture. Why don't the two of you stand beside the car?"

"Mom, I'm gonna be late," Chet complains, but he smiles briefly beside his dad for the photo.

"Do you have your speech?" she asks.

"Right here." He flashes the folded piece of paper in his hand. Getting into his car, he tosses the paper onto the passenger seat beside the corsage he's bought for Kelley.

"Okay, I'll see you guys there" he calls, reversing out of the driveway.

As he drives the familiar route to his girlfriend's house, he begins to feel more and more anxious with each passing block. The inside of his mouth feels like it'ss lined with sawdust and his stomach gurgles with acid. What is the matter with him? He hasn't given a shit about grad all year, and now he wonders if he will be able to get through the ceremony without a panic attack.

When he arrives at Kelley's place, he is unable to park in his usual spot in the driveway because a limo is already there. He parks on the street instead and gets out of his car, then goes back to grab the corsage.

As he walks toward the house, the front door bursts open and two girls from his grad class, both in dramatic off-the-shoulder gowns, run out giggling. Chet is surprised—he didn't know Kelley invited other people over. It sounds like there is a party going on inside.

"He's here!" shouts one of the girls.

Kelley yells from inside the house, "Stay where you are!"

Chet stands at the bottom of the front steps, wishing to God he was anywhere but here. A moment later, his girlfriend appears in the doorway. She is decked out in a dark red, off-the-shoulder dress with a skirt so long that it trails two feet behind her.

"Ta-da!" she announces, twirling before him.

Chet whistles in appreciation because he knows he's supposed to. Secretly, she reminds him of a giant tube of cinnamon toothpaste, its contents partially squirted out onto the ground.

"*And* my nails," she says, holding out a perfectly manicured hand for his inspection.

"Very nice," he tells her.

Since the beginning of the school year, Kelley has been teaching him to appreciate such things—manicures, hair styles, romantic gestures. Chet hadn't really minded, assuming it's all par for the course with girls, but for the last few weeks it's grated on his nerves. The more anxious he becomes, the less patience he has for her trivialities.

He endures having several photos taken while pinning on the corsage (white roses, as per her request), then poses for several more pictures while standing beside her.

"Smile!" her mom instructs. "It's not a funeral!"

He almost wishes it were—at least then he wouldn't have to plaster a fake smile over his ever-darkening mood. Standing behind his girlfriend now, he wraps his arms around her waist and slouches down so that their heads aren't too far apart. The perfume she's wearing makes him want to gag. She seems like she's in heaven, completely in her element, unaware of how uncomfortable and short-tempered he's feeling. He considers putting an end to this bogus photoshoot, wondering how best to present the idea, when Kelley's mom makes the call.

"Okay!" she hollers, clapping her hands. "Everyone into the limo!"

"Where'd that come from?" Chet asks. A boy he recognizes from his English class runs past them and dives head-first into the back seat.

Kelley looks at him with mild disbelief. "My parents rented it—I've told you about it a hundred times!"

She looks at her two girlfriends.

"We couldn't exactly show up to grad in *your* car!"

She and the girls laugh. Chet laughs along with them, but he feels stung. She sure didn't mind being chauffeured all around town in his car. She didn't seem to mind making out in the back seat of it, either.

"Right," he says, thinking to himself that her big-ass dress wouldn't fit in his car anyway.

"My dress wouldn't even fit in your car anyway!" she says, laughing again.

When the limo arrives at the school, it draws attention. Some of the kids and parents look at it in surprise, no one has ever done this before, while others deliberately look away, not wanting to give them any further attention. As he climbs out of the stupidly-long car, Chet feels a rush of embarrassment.

"That was so awesome!" exclaims the boy from Chet's English class, climbing out after him. He raises his hand for a high-five but Chet ignores him and walks purposefully toward the school.

"Wait up!" Kelley hisses, and he stops.

"I thought you were right behind me," he lies.

"We're supposed to walk in together," she scolds, linking an arm through his. Lifting the train of her gown, she proceeds forward and the word 'promenade' pops into his head. His girlfriend is suddenly treating the dusty parking lot of their shitty high school like a Hollywood red carpet.

Entering the cafeteria, they get into the line to receive their caps and gowns. Chet catches sight of Lindsay almost immediately; she's wearing a long simple dress that clings to her curves. He hadn't noticed until now that she has a great body. She sees him too, and offers a small wave. He smiles back, but only after checking to make sure Kelley isn't looking.

"Okay, grads!" the vice-principal hollers. "Everyone line-up the way we rehearsed! Two by two, alphabetical order!"

"I wish we could walk together," Kelley complains. "They've got me walking with this loser I don't even know. Meet me back here right after, okay?"

"Okay."

He finds his place in line next to a nerdy-looking girl whose name escapes him. He smiles politely but she looks down.

Near the end of the long, winding line, he spots Raja, who kindly gives him the finger. After returning the favour, Chet makes a sudden, pants-shitting realization: he doesn't have his speech. He pictures it, sitting on the seat of his car which is still parked back at Kelley's house.

"Fuck!" he stage-whispers. The girl beside him jumps.

"Sorry," he says.

"Hi, Chet." He turns toward the sound of the voice and sees Lindsay heading for the front of the line. When she sees the look on his face, she stops.

"Are you okay? You look sick. I mean, you look fine, but you're really pale."

"I just realized that I forgot my speech," he says.

"Oh, shit!" She looks at him with sympathy. "Do you remember any of it?"

"Some of it, I guess. I dunno."

"That sucks." She places her hand reassuringly on his forearm. "Just say whatever. This whole thing is bullshit anyway." She smiles before rushing off to her place in line. In her wake, she leaves behind a sense of something close to calm, which a moment ago would have seemed impossible. As the grad march begins, he can still feel the touch of her hand on his arm as though she's left an imprint.

"Ladies and gentlemen!" a voice booms through the loudspeaker. "Please rise for your graduating class of 1995!"

Chet hears the opening notes of the grad theme song, 'We May Never Pass This Way Again.' He's never heard the song before today, but by the time the grads have all marched through the gymnasium, he's heard it four times and that's more than enough.

Sitting through the boring ceremonies, his anxiety begins to creep back up to the surface. How the hell is he going to make it through his forgotten speech? His collar feels way too tight, he can't seem to get a decent breath. He needs to get out of here.

"Ladies and gentlemen, next up we have your Class Historian!"

*Fuck me*, he thinks.

The crowd applauds heartily as Chet makes his way up to the stage, hands shaking, his heart pounding loudly over the noise.

He stands behind the podium and clears his throat into the microphone. The sound is shockingly loud. Ahead of him, a sea of mortar boards undulates across the first half of the audience, inflicting a moment of unsteady motion sickness.

*Oh, God*, he prays. *Please don't let me puke up here.* He suddenly envisions his entire high school career, where he somehow sailed by in both popularity and academics, capped off with an on-stage hurl-fest in front of the entire school.

"Good afternoon parents and teachers, friends and family, fellow grads," he begins unsteadily. "Thank you for electing me as your Class Historian—we all knew I had no shot at being the Valedictorian—like I could ever have the highest marks in the whole school!"

Laughter. He clears his throat again.

"As your Class Historian, it is my job to recount the things that have happened in the last three years—the good, the bad, and the ugly!"

More laughter. Usually, this reaction would be a good thing—but without an actual written speech in front of him, he can't appreciate it.

From that point on, Chet's speech becomes conversational, as he no longer remembers the exact wording of what he'd written. He talks about a few funny incidents, including "Students Dress Up Your Teacher Day," and tells the crowd how funny the vice-principal looked, dressed up in Drag. This draws big laughter from the audience. After that, Chet draws a blank. He cannot for the life of him remember what comes next, or anything else he'd written.

*You were there, doofus!* he thinks. *Talk about something! Anything!*

A hush falls over the entire crowd and time stands still. He wants to die.

"Come on, Chester!" Raja yells from somewhere out in the crowd. A smattering of laughter follows.

Chet looks down at the podium, willing his written speech into existence but it doesn't happen. After another excruciating moment of silence, he lifts his head.

"In closing," he says, his speech nowhere near closing, "I'd like to wish all of you the best of luck in your futures, whatever they may be. And like the song says, 'We May Never Pass This Way Again.' Thank God, eh? Now, let's party!"

He doesn't hang around to bask in the moment. Instead, he walks off stage as fast as he can without actually running, feeling totally and completely humiliated. He doesn't deserve the hearty applause that follows, and that makes him feel even worse. He did a complete shit-job and they still liked it.

*I really could have puked up there,* he thinks, *and they probably would have clapped for that, too.*

As he heads toward his seat, he catches Lindsay's eye. She raises on eyebrow and makes a '50/50' hand gesture. Then she breaks into a grin and applauds along with the rest of the crowd. Once again, she has done the impossible—at this most dismal moment in his life, she has managed to make him feel better. He makes a decision—tonight, he is going to ask her to dance and he doesn't give a shit about Kelley's thoughts on the matter.

***

## SATURDAY, JUNE 17

Julian has been watching the news for the last half-hour but, if questioned, would not be able to recall a single thing he's seen. He has been tuned out, thinking about Uncle Ribbons for the first time in years.

Uncle Ribbons is his mom's younger brother. His real name is Uncle Ritchie, but after Julian over-heard his grandma say that his brain must be cut to ribbons, the nickname stuck. Naturally, he and his brothers kept the nickname to themselves; their mom would have killed them if she'd known.

Uncle Ribbons was the black sheep of the family; eccentric, erratic, maybe even a bit scary sometimes. To be fair, he could also be a lot of fun, too, although any happy memories of him were long ago overshadowed by what happened after.

On that particular day, Julian's uncle showed up to their house, completely naked. He had left his own house without a stitch of clothing––not even shoes––and driven across town. He said he wanted to stop by for 'coffee and freedom.' Julian had been home sick from school that day and saw the whole show. His mother had freaked out, throwing her husband's bathrobe over her brother, and sent Julian to his room. He could hear her on the phone crying and telling someone that her brother was 'very sick.' Within minutes, a police car and an ambulance showed up, and from his bedroom window, Julian watched his crazy uncle being carried away into the back of the ambulance. After that, they never saw him again.

*Maybe it's hereditary*, Julian thinks now. Maybe this is how it starts; you see something that no one else does, like an entire range of hills on the outskirts of the city you've lived in for your entire life, and one day it vanishes into thin air. Only *you* remember it ever being there and still, you'd bet your life on it. After that, what? A slow descent into madness until you find yourself driving around naked in search of coffee and freedom?

He can't tell his wife—he just can't. Her first reaction would be accusatory, assuming he'd fallen off the wagon and had gone back to drinking and talking nonsense. That would be bad enough, but when he could prove his sobriety, the truth would be even worse. He has to keep this to himself, at least for now. Oh, sweet Jesus, how long does he have?

"Dinner's ready!" Trudy hollers. Julian shuts off the TV and walks over to the table, sitting in his usual place. His daughters are soon to follow.

"The chicken's a bit over-done," Trudy says by way of apology. "I got distracted by Tawnee's phone call."

Julian's obvious concerns about his life have not quashed his annoyance with Trudy's cousin. He's still mad at his wife for making him sit through that piece-of-shit play.

"Don't you want to know how she's doing?" Trudy asks, putting a jug of water on the table.

"Why?" Julian asks absent-mindedly. He helps himself to a baked potato.

"Because her play opens next week," she replies, annoyed.

"It's opening next week? Shouldn't it be closing?"

"Seriously? I know she's not your favourite person, but you could show some support! God, you always have to be so sarcastic!"

Julian hadn't meant to be sarcastic at all. He sat through that stupid beaver play over two weeks ago; he *knows* he didn't invent that.

"Sorry," he says, swallowing hard. He thinks for a moment, wondering how best to navigate this. "So, where's the play opening?"

"I told you, it's at the Cobalt Theatre. You know, if one of *your* family members made it to Off-Broadway, I bet you wouldn't forget the details."

Julian practically chokes. Broadway? This has to be a joke. When he looks at Trudy, though, he can see she isn't joking at all.

"Anyway," she continues, "you still have to get your holiday time sorted out. I want to book our flights as soon as possible; see if we can get a seat sale. Tawnee said she'll book the hotel. God, I can't believe I'm finally going to New York!"

Julian says nothing. He reaches for his water glass and takes a long drink, wishing it were something much stronger than water.

"How come we can't go?" Lexie asks.

"New York is super expensive," says Trudy. "And the play is for adults."

She looks at Julian. "So, can you sort out your holidays on Monday?"

"Sure," he says woodenly. What else can he say?

Right now, he knows he can no longer pretend that everything is fine, at least, not to himself. If his brain is playing tricks on him, letting him believe that he's the only one who has noticed a major disappearance, that's one thing. Tawnee's shit-show opening in New York is another.

He must be going insane.

\*\*\*


## WEDNESDAY, JUNE 21

Marcy sits at the make-shift dressing table set up in one of the classrooms at her school.

"Trust me," she tells the other girls. "You're gonna have to wear *way* more make up than usual." She takes a black eyeliner pencil and uses it to exaggerate her eyebrows. "I know it looks weird right now, but when you get on stage it'll look just right. If you don't wear enough you'll look like a ghost."

She turns to Cody, the only boy in the dance troupe.

"You too," she tells him. "You gotta wear *some* makeup. Seriously."

Cody's cheeks turn pink. "No way," he says.

"Okay!" Mrs. J hollers, addressing her troupe of dancers. "Girls! I mean, people! Sorry, Cody." She claps her hands three times. "We're on in five minutes!"

Bernadette sidles over the Marcy and squeezes her arm. "I'm so nervous!" she half-whispers, half-squeals.

Marcy can't help but admire how stunning her friend looks. Bernadette always looks pretty, it's true, but tonight, with her shimmery eye shadow and sparkling leotard, Marcy can hardly take her eyes off of her.

"Now, listen up!" Mrs. J continues. "I want you guys to get out there and do exactly what you did this afternoon—but this time with more sparkle, right? Remember what we talked about, with stage presence? And energy?"

When the Dancetasticks performed one of their routines for the entire school earlier that day, Marcy had half-worried that the choreography would once again mysteriously change. It hadn't, and tonight she feels confident.

"Alright, let's go!"

Mrs. J leads her group of young dancers out of the classroom and into the area behind the school's stage. While they wait together in the wings, full of anxious energy, their teacher walks out on stage to address the audience.

"Thank you all for coming tonight," she begins. "The Dancetasticks have been working very hard since you last saw them at the Christmas concert, and tonight they are very pleased to be performing for you once again. We also have a special treat in store for you, in that a few of our chosen girls—I mean, people, will be performing solos and duets. I think you will all notice how much improved the entire troupe is. So, without further ado, ladies and gentlemen, The Dancetasticks!"

The audience applauds as each dancer solemnly takes their place on stage. Marcy stands with her back to the audience and, when the music starts, she spins around. She strikes a defiant pose as if challenging the entire crowd, loving the way her sequins flash under the stage lights.

She knows she isn't the best dancer in the group. There are at least two, or possibly three girls who are better than her, but tonight she doesn't care; tonight she feels like a star. When the opening number is over, she basks in the applause. Two more routines follow before it's time for Marcy and Bernadette's duet. She can hardly wait.

Once again, they wait in the wings while Mrs. J introduces them, Marcy jumps up and down in exhilarated preparation, vigorously shaking her arms and legs. This is it. This is the moment she's been waiting for, for months!

"I don't feel very good," Bernadette whispers.

"You're just nervous," Marcy whispers back.

"No, I mean, I *really* don't feel good."

Marcy looks at her, incredulous. "What do you mean?"

"I mean, I gotta go!"

"Oh, come *on*, Bernadette!"

Out on the stage, Mrs. J announces their names. Marcy takes two steps forward, then turns back to look at her friend who, unbelievably, is running away. Stunned, Marcy catches the eye of her teacher and shakes her head vigorously.

Mrs. J hurries over. "What's wrong?"

"She took off!" Marcy sputters. "She's sick or something!"

"We'll have to go on to the next number, then."

Marcy gives her teacher a stricken look. She cannot believe this is happening! All that hard work for nothing!

"You could do it on your own," Mrs. J suggests. "You know how to improvise."

Marcy feels paralyzed by the thought.

"I need an answer, or we're going to have to move on—it's up to you."

Oh, God—what should she do?

"Well, I..." Marcy looks out at the empty stage, the bright lights seeming to call her name. She can do this, can't she?

"Yeah," she nods. "Okay."

Without further discussion, Mrs. J walks back to the microphone.

"Change of plans, ladies and gentlemen—our duet has just become a solo."

As Marcy walks nervously out onto the stage, she sees Bernadette's mom jump out of her seat and make a hasty exit. Her own parents are both here, sitting on opposite sides of the gym, naturally, and although Marcy knows exactly where they are, she avoids looking at either.

The Alanis Morrissette song she had randomly chosen begins to play. For two weeks, she and Bernadette have worked on this routine, and after listening to the song over and over, Marcy has learned to love it.

She adapts the choreography that was meant for two dancers as best she can. Never before in her entire life has she ever felt so vulnerable. She tries to fill in Bernadette's steps with other moves she has learned but they don't seem to fit properly. Eventually, she gives up on the choreography altogether and opts for basic dancefloor moves instead—nothing the average person couldn't do in a heartbeat, wishing with each passing bar that this stupid song would just end. Why did she ever agree to this?

As it finally comes to a close, Marcy dances slowly over to a small table, which has been placed on stage for the routine. On it sits a lit candle and two unlit sparklers. She picks the sparklers up and dips them into the flame. Only one ignites; the other simply refuses. She gives up trying and slowly walks to the front of the stage, facing the audience. In each hand, she holds a sparkler; one sputtering with fire, the other completely dead. She stands awkwardly in one spot, where Bernadette is supposed to be dancing around her. Having exhausted her arsenal of choreography, there's nothing left for her to do but stand and listen to the rest of the song. Alanis sings with a tenderness that Marcy had begun to find beautiful. But right now, she isn't paying attention to that—all she can do is stare helplessly out at the crowd.

As the song finally ends, the audience bursts into cheers of support. Marcy doesn't even notice. She runs off stage, completely humiliated.

Backstage, she does not want to talk to or see anyone. She pushes past the others and slumps into a dark corner, covering her face with her hands. There's absolutely no *way* she can go back out there for the last number—she can't face that audience again! She just can't!

While the rest of the routines are performed, Marcy thinks of all the times Mrs. J has told them that 'the show must go on'. She knows in her heart that it's true. She'll have to go back on stage, like it or lump it. She now knows first hand what it means to be left in the lurch and she can't do that to the rest of the troupe.

When the final routine is announced, she bravely gets to her feet, wiping underneath her eyes for any smudged eyeliner. She lines up in the wings, avoiding looking at anyone in particular, her face set in a defiant, leave-me-alone expression.

She is so determined to appear strong that she doesn't realize at first who is standing right in front of her, also preparing to go on; it's Bernadette. She is talking animatedly with one of the other dancers and, unbelievably, giggling.

*She doesn't look sick at all*, Marcy thinks, furious. *Unless it was the shortest flu on record, like, five minutes long.*

*I can't believe you just ran out on me,* Marcy thinks. *You left me out there to die!* What kind of person does that to a friend? And not just any friend, but a best friend?

Someone who isn't a friend at all, she realizes.

In that moment, Marcy vows that she will never speak to Bernadette again, never forgive her. Not as long as she's on this planet.

\*\*\*

## SATURDAY, JUNE 24

Carole is walking through a large field with one arm linked companionably through her mother's.

"I'm sure glad it didn't rain today," her mother says. "The last game I went to, the field was just a mucky mess."

"I remember," says Carole. "I had to hose off my runners afterwards."

"Oh, there's your sister." Her mother returns Corinne's frantic wave, but Carole does not.

It used to be difficult to tell the twin sisters apart, but these days, it's rather easy. For example, Carole is wearing a simple sundress with a wide-brimmed hat, her hair pulled back into a low ponytail. Corinne, on the other hand, looks like she's just stepped off the runway wearing what are probably designer clothes, and perfectly coiffed hair. She is adorned in her usual array of gold and diamond jewellery despite standing next to a dusty ball diamond in the middle of a teenage softball tournament.

*God forbid she should be mistaken for someone who isn't rich,* Carole thinks.

"They're just about to start the fourth inning," Corinne says as they approach. This statement is disguised as information, but Carole reads her sister's disappointment loud and clear.

"We got here as soon as we could," says Carole, defensively. "I told you I had to work today." *And if it was so important,* she adds inwardly, *why didn't you pick up Mom?*

While getting situated on the bleachers, Corinne fills them in on the details of the game.

"Our girls are in trouble tonight," she tells them. "The pitcher on the other team is a bit of a problem."

Corinne's husband Barry chimes in "She's got a pistol for an arm," he says sounding undeniably impressed.

"She's aggressive," Corinne snaps. "I don't know what her problem is, if she's on steroids, or what."

"I doubt that steroids are a problem in the junior-high circuit," Carole says dryly.

"You have *no* idea what these kids get into today," her sister says.

What Carole wants to say now is 'of course I don't—I'm not a parent, blah, blah' but because their mom is here, she keeps her mouth shut.

Carole tries to settle in on the uncomfortable bench seating, wishing she could bring a book to these games. She loves her niece but watching a bunch of kids play softball is like watching paint dry.

Making an effort, she looks out at the diamond and sees the two teams of thirteen and fourteen-year-old girls, huddled into their separate groups for what surely must be life or death strategizing. After a moment, both groups break apart with a loud cheer. The players scatter to take their positions for the start of the inning.

Striding confidently to the pitcher's mound is a young girl with a face full of makeup. This on its own is amusing considering the setting, but becomes less interesting when Carole realizes that it is the girl from the coffee shop. Carole has never been the most maternal person, but when she sees Marcy she is overcome with an intense desire to hug her, which takes her by surprise.

Marcy stands atop the pitcher's mound, both arms at her sides, and stares intently at the batter before her. Without warning, she springs into action and delivers a pitch equal to that of a college-level player.

"Strike one!" yells the umpire.

"See what I mean?" Corinne complains. "She shouldn't be allowed to play in this league!"

"She's something, alright," their mother agrees. "Wow!"

Carole can't take her eyes off Marcy, and it's not because of her impressive athletic ability; in fact, she barely notices that. What catches her attention is that the girl seems somehow...brighter than everyone else. It's as though the entire world is grey and Marcy is the only thing in colour.

"Strike two!"

The longer she looks at her, the more vibrant Marcy becomes—it's as if her entire being is alight. Carole has never seen anything like it.

"Strike three!"

The dejected batter walks away and the next victim steps up to the plate. Unfortunately, it is Emily, Carole's niece.

"Come on, Emily!" shouts Barry, cupping his hands around his mouth.

"You can do it, girl!" Corinne hollers.

Carole hasn't even given Emily a single look, still mesmerized by Marcy. Maybe it's the way the sun is hitting her...Carole knows this doesn't make sense, but how else can she explain the now-brilliantly glowing girl? Has anyone else noticed?

Marcy effortlessly strikes Emily out, then systematically does the same with the next batter. The short inning now over, Marcy breaks her concentration and glances over to the crowd. When she does, her smile instantly fades.

\*\*\*

*That's weird,* Marcy thinks. Something is shining in the stands. Curious, she holds one hand over her eyes to shield the sun, trying to figure out where it could be coming from. It wasn't there before, or she would have noticed it for sure. Squinting, the object comes into focus. It's not a thing—it's a person; a lady. A glowing lady.

Marcy shifts her head a few times, changing her perspective, but the lady still looks like she's shining. In fact, the more Marcy looks at her, the brighter she becomes.

Marcy follows the rest of her team off the field and into the dugout area. The lady in the bleachers continues to glow. Marcy, forgetting about the ballgame entirely, stares at the lady while trying not to look like she is. No one else seems to see it, though Marcy isn't the least concerned about anyone else right now. By the time she goes up to bat, she is so distracted that the opposing team's pitcher strikes her out in three pitches. Barely noticing, Marcy walks back to the dugout like she's in a trance.

At the start of the fifth inning, one of Marcy's teammates takes over at the pitcher's mound, much to the delight and relief of the opposing team. Marcy sits out the rest of the game and Carole, noticing a sudden change in her behaviour, grows concerned. Ignoring the game entirely, she keeps an eye on the glowing Marcy sitting on the grass with her knees tucked up to her chest.

When the game is finally over, Carole tells her family that she'll be right back. She walks in a straight line toward Marcy, who now appears to be hiding behind her dad.

"Hi," says Carole. "Remember me?"

Marcy's dad is momentarily puzzled before recognizing Carole. "Oh," he says, "that coffee shop, right?"

"Yes," Carole replies. "I came here to see my niece play—she's on the other team. I was quite surprised to see you here, Marcy."

Surprised doesn't quite cover it. Up close, the incredible glow is even more so.

Marcy says nothing. She stares at Carole with what looks like a mix of disbelief and fear.

*It's not just me, then,* Carole thinks. *I must look to her like I'm all lit up, too.*

The very thought is beyond exciting. If she'd had any doubts about something supernatural going on, they are now completely gone.

"You're quite the pitcher," Carole continues, hoping to set the girl at ease. "I really enjoyed watching you play."

Marcy, still silent, continues to stare at this weird glowing lady, freaked out and interested all at once. What's wrong with her? Is she, like, radioactive, or something? Why can't her dad see it? Or anyone else, for that matter?

Unaware of what she's doing, Marcy takes a cautious step behind her dad.

Carole returns the gaze, smiling gently, willing the girl to read her mind. *It's okay,* she tries to convey. *I see it, too.*

"Yeah, well, I guess she's not feeling too good today," says Marcy's dad, giving his daughter a concerned look. "It's not normal for her to quit in the middle of a game."

"I've been feeling a little strange, myself," Carole replies, hoping that Marcy will pick up on her meaning. "But, I'm sure it's nothing to worry about."

She smiles again, but Marcy, looking down at the grass, will not acknowledge her.

"I hope you feel better soon," Carole adds. She finds herself wishing there was some other reason to stay in her company, but she can tell how anxious Marcy is to leave.

"Well, it was nice seeing you both..." Carole trails off. "Take care!"

She doesn't want to go. Practically forcing herself, she turns around and walks away.

I've been so selfish, she thinks. She has been so enamoured with the idea of something fantastical happening to her that she never stopped to think what that might mean for the others. What she considers an exciting adventure could be terrifying for someone else, especially someone Marcy's age.

What should she do?

***

## SUNDAY, JUNE 25

Todd is regaling Dannicka with the latest in the saga of the World Wrestling Federation. She's mostly tuning him out, not only because she has no interest but also because she has spent the last two weeks feeling paranoid and preoccupied. Apparently, the word 'country' no longer exists and no one else on the planet seems to have noticed. She's gone to three different libraries, seeking out a wide range of atlases, history books, maps and the like, and all she's seen is 'company, company, company.' The continents are still around—all seven of them, so that's something, she supposes.

Did she have a stroke, or some other brain problem recently? Something that has disrupted her memory? Was it caused by that bizarre event at the Grabbajabba? She recalls the wave-like ripple at the end... that could have disrupted something.

"And the crowd's just going crazy," Todd says, "you know, like, booing and—"

"Todd," she says, pointing to the empty space ahead, which he hasn't noticed.

"Oh."

He pulls up beside the drive-through speaker and leans out the window.

"Yeah, I'll have a large coke, two double cheeseburgers, and two large fries."

He turns to Dannicka. "You want anything?"

"Just fries."

"Make that three large fries," he adds. The voice from the speaker tells them to proceed to the next window.

"So, anyway," Todd continues. "The Rock, you know who he is, right? Well, he chases the other guy into the stands, and they end up wrestling right in the middle of the crowd! Like, smashing into other people..."

He looks at Dannicka, raises one eyebrow, and recites The Rock's catchphrase: "Can you *smell* what The Rock is cooking?"

She bursts out laughing, despite herself. Todd does have a knack for impressions.

He pulls up to the drive-thru window and an employee pushes aside the glass panel. As Todd rifles through his wallet, Dannicka suddenly sucks in her breath—the employee at the window is the kid that was at that Grabbajabba that day—the one with the huge drink order.

This on its own would be interesting, but what really stuns her is that he appears to be glowing. She has never done acid or any other hallucinogenic drug, but she thinks this must be what it's like. Before he has a chance to see her, she turns away and looks out her window, heart thudding in her chest. Something is wrong with her, alright—something is definitely screwed up inside her brain, but added to this is the worry that he'll recognize her and she'll have no way to explain to Todd how they know each other.

Unable to help herself, she turns her head ever so slightly toward him, only to find *he* is literally staring at her, mouth hanging open. Todd, who is trying to hand over his money, has to prompt him.

"Oh. Sorry," the kid says. As though in a trance, he takes the money, then hangs back out the window, completely aglow.

"Hear ya go," he says woodenly, handing the food to Todd with his large, illuminated hand. Dannicka catches his eye then, and shakes her head no.

*Don't say anything,* she pleads inwardly, praying he gets the message. *Don't say anything.*

"Have a good day!" he says, almost robotically.

He closes the drive-thru window and she quietly exhales.

"Man, that kid was *out* of it!" Todd laughs. "Smoke another one, dude!"

***

Chet thinks he's picked a shitty time for an acid flashback. He did acid once, last winter, which seems far enough in the past, but what else could that have been? That chick in the last care was glowing like a neon sign!

He looks around the restaurant's kitchen, the row of tills, then back out the window. Everything else looks normal, so far. Shit, is he about to really flip out? Maybe he should ask to leave early.

***

"Wait—can you pull over and park?" Dannicka tries to keep her voice casual, but her heart is beating in double-time.

"But you just went before we left," Todd says.

"Well, I have to go again. I can't help it. I'll be right back—just wait here."

She hops out of the car and back over to the restaurant, dashing toward the counter.

"What can I get for you today?" asks a young girl behind one of the tills.

"I just went through the drive-thru," Dannicka says, "and I'd like to talk to the guy who served us at the window."

"Is there a problem?" asks an older man, who has over-heard. He must be a manager.

"Oh, no, not at all," Dannicka stammers. "He was really great. The service was great. I just want to thank him. In person. Can I talk to him?"

"Devon!" the manager hollers. "Cover for Chet. Chet! Someone to see you!"

Chet removes the headset and hands it to Devon, who laughs and says, "She's a bit old for you, but she's pretty hot!"

He comes out from behind the take-out alcove, stopping in his tracks at the still-glowing chick from the car he had just served. She looks even brighter now than she did in the car. She takes off her sunglasses and only then does he recognize her. Standing still with the counter between them, he waits for her to speak. Maybe tiny butterflies will fly out of her mouth.

"I don't have long," she says, her voice lowered. "Ever since that day, things have been weird. What about you?"

He stares at her, not sure if this is really happening.

"Hello? It's Chet, right?"

He nods.

"I'm Dannicka—we were both at the same Grabbajabba..."

He nods again.

"Have you noticed anything weird, or even crazy, lately?"

*This is pretty crazy*, he thinks.

"Yup," is all he can manage.

"This is gonna sound nuts," she says, "but to me, right now, you look like you're glowing."

She's taking a chance by saying this, but she doesn't care—she has nothing to lose.

Chet feels his knees begin to buckle. This is no acid flashback. This is actually happening.

"You, too," he finally says.

"Me, too? Do you mean I'm glowing, too?"

"Yup."

"Okay. I'm giving you my phone number. Can you please call me later?" She thinks for a moment. Todd will be out with his friends tonight. "Like, tonight? After seven?"

"Uh... okay."

She reaches into her purse for the pen she keeps in there, and scribbles her number on the back of an old receipt.

"Call me!" she says before leaving. "Please!"

Stunned, Chet walks back to his alcove. What the hell just happened?

"Score!" Devon exclaims, passing the headset back to him. "You got her number and everything! Sweet! Don't worry, I won't tell Kelley."

Chet barely hears him. Right now, Kelley is the furthest thing from his mind.

\*\*\*


## TUESDAY, JUNE 27

Once again, Ryan dreams that he is propped up in his bed in what is becoming a familiar position. This time, however, he is prepared.

With a great deal of effort, he pushes back the covers and attempts to get out of the bed. His body feels incredibly heavy, as though he is moving through quick-drying concrete. Roland, sitting in his usual position at the foot of the bed, spotlight in place, watches politely as Ryan struggles to stand.

"Hel—..." Roland begins.

"You need to tell me what's going on," Ryan snaps, cutting him off.

"—lo, Ryan."

"Yes. Hello. You need to tell me what the hell is going on here. Who *are* you?"

Roland blinks. "Ryan, you need to collect the other five..."

"For what?!" he asks, exasperated. "This isn't even happening! This is just a stupid dream!"

"There has been an error..."

"What error? You mean the earthquake?"

"It is complex."

"Try me."

Roland blinks once, twice, then sits silently for a moment. Ryan continues to stare at the cat, refusing to back down. "I'm not doing anything until you..."

"The six of you did not make the shift," Roland finally says.

"The shift? What are you talking about?"

"You were sent into a...facsimile."

"A what?"

Ryan doesn't understand. He sees the light around Roland start to fade, he sees the foot of the bed beginning to fade. He feels like he's about to walk up, and the thought causes panic.

"I will NOT wake up!" he says out loud, commanding himself to stay here, wherever here is. He doesn't want to end this dream, or meeting, or whatever the hell this is. He has too many questions.

"Why do *I* have to get everyone together?" he asks desperately. "Why can't you talk to Julian? He's the manager!"

"We cannot reach Julian."

"But you can reach me? Why?"

Roland blinks, pauses, then says, "Your accident...dislodged you. You could not shift and you pulled the others..."

"I WILL NOT WAKE UP!" Ryan shouts, feeling himself beginning to fade.

Ryan wakes up.

# CHAPTER FIVE

For the past four years, Ryan has felt stuck while life around him has continued to move on. People he knows met new people and formed new relationships; they have had new experiences, traveled to different places; they obtained new Degrees and got new careers; they got engaged and, in a few cases, have even had children. Whenever this has happened, Ryan pretends to be happy for their accomplishments. And he is—for the most part. It's just that each new milestone reached by someone else seems to highlight the stagnancy of his own life. Most days, his only accomplishment is getting out of bed. He has pictured himself as an old man, still in pain, still living in the same shitty apartment, playing video games day in-day out, counting down the hours until the day is over.

But lately, something has been happening to him. He's not just 'feeling better', his body is actually beginning to heal. Rapidly. It's not exactly where he used to be, but it's getting pretty damn close. Each day he feels stronger than the last and now, for the first time in years, he has allowed himself the luxury of imagining a different future.

In the first few years following his accident, Ryan used to pray for, even *beg* for, the phenomenon of 'spontaneous healing'. But he had finally accepted that it was never going to happen. Now, it's as though his prayers have finally been answered. What else could it be? He has cancelled his last four physiotherapy appointments—why bother? He has seen enough medical personnel for eight lifetimes. He just wishes he could enjoy this new-found health without feeling guilty; but as he lays in bed, drenched in a pool of sweat from last night's dream, he knows he cannot continue to ignore what's really going on.

What happened to him and the others may have been an 'error,' but it's also the reason Ryan has been getting better. He knows this is true. Why would anyone want to correct that? And even if he did want to, what could he possibly do? Call everyone who was at the coffee shop that day and say, "Hey guys! My cat thinks it's super important that we all get together! And you know how I know this? Because he's been telling me in my dreams!"

Aside from the manager, Julian, and the younger girl, Marcy, Ryan doesn't even know the names of the others.

*You have Julian's business card*, he thinks. *You could start by calling him.*

He rubs his face with the palms of both hands.

"Fuck!" he says out loud.

With minimal effort he gets out of bed, and plods into the kitchen. He fills Roland's bowl with food, but Roland is hiding under the kitchen table and does not appear interested in eating.

Maybe he should just call Julian and feel him out, no big deal. He could make up some fake reason for calling, and if Julian seems normal and fine (and why wouldn't he) then Ryan can set his mind at ease, and no one could say he didn't try.

"Okay," he says aloud. "I'll call."

And he will.

Soon.

Probably.

\*\*\*

"There are many states of being. There are many levels of consciousness. There are higher frequencies on which we all may resonate, guiding us toward total enlightenment..." These are some of the teachings bestowed upon Carole nearly two decades ago, during her time in India.

This must be what the gurus were talking about––this heightened state she has been experiencing. She wants to immerse herself in this new realm where artwork appears changed as if by magic, and where people glow like fireflies. She wants to savour each new discovery, for surely there will be others. She wants to be fully present for what just might be the spiritual journey of a lifetime. She wants all these things, but right now this is not possible—not while she feels responsible for Marcy's well-being.

For three days, Carole has been turning her house upside down in search of Julian's business card. She knows she put it in her bag on that fateful day, but it's not there now—she has taken everything out of it twice. Yesterday she went to the Grabbajabba, but the employee there refused to give her Julian's number. The best she could do was give Carole the regional office's 1-800 number, but when Carole called, she was told all *they* could do was pass a message on to Julian. She's left four so far.

Ever since the ballgame last Saturday, Carole has not stopped worrying about Marcy. She did come up with a few ideas as to how she might be able to help, but none of them seemed very plausible She has decided that the best option is to call Julian––Marcy seemed receptive to him that day, and it would appear more legitimate if he were to call and check up on her, wouldn't it? Now all she needs is his damn phone number.

After another morning spent working from her home office, she takes a break for lunch. Deciding to throw in a load of laundry, she begins collecting a few items from her bedroom floor and tossing them into the basket. Bending down, she takes the blanket out of Mr. Biscuits' bed and shakes it out before adding it to the pile. Something falls out and, when she sees what it is, she laughs with delight.

"Mr. Biscuits!" she exclaims.

Assuming he is being summoned, the little dog appears in the doorway.

"Have you been hiding this on me?" She holds up Julian's business card in mock accusation, then leans down and kisses the dog on the top of his tiny snout.

***

Julian sits at his desk and stares out the window, oblivious to how long he has been in this position. The cursor on his computer screen blinks incessantly, as does the message light on his phone. Both go ignored. On his desk is a pile of sales reports and statistical analysis charts which he has not even bothered to glance at. He feels paralyzed by the world, or his perception of the world. He has to tell someone, but who? His wife? His doctor? He doesn't know which would be worse. If he tells his doctor it would at least be confidential, but any appointment would have to be kept secret from Trudy. If she found out he had gone to the doctor on his own, she would flip out. She would probably jump to the worst-case scenario and assume he was dying.

The second he has this thought, a rush of blood drains from his face. He hadn't even considered that as a possibility. What if he *is* dying? What if he has some kind of horrible disease, or a brain tumour?

He can't go on like this, anxiously second-guessing his sanity from one moment to the next, wondering how long it will take before his own nephews come up with their version of a derogatory nickname, like Uncle Ribbons. He thinks for a moment—what would his be? Uncle...Loonian? That might almost be funny if it wasn't so accurate. He feels a sudden pang of guilt for how he treated his own crazy uncle.

His thoughts are interrupted by the phone on his desk as its high-pitched electronic ring jars him out of his daze. He reaches for the receiver.

"Julian speaking."

"Hi," says a female voice. "It's Dannicka."

He draws a blank.

"From the Grabbajabba in Edmonton."

He sits up, instantly intrigued. "Oh, hi. How are you?"

"Feeling weird, actually," she replies. "I'm sorry but I can't talk for long, I'm at work and I'm not really supposed to be using the phone right now."

"Oh, okay."

"I'll just get to it. Things have been really...weird, ever since we were all there that day, and a few days ago, I ran into Chet. You know, the high school kid that was there, too?"

"Uh-huh."

"Well, we had a long talk and he's a bit of a mess, and we talked about some...things we've both been noticing, and, I don't even know what you could do about it or why I'm even calling..."

Julian feels a wave of relief wash over him. Apparently, he isn't the only one losing his mind.

"I think I might know what you mean," he says carefully.

"You do?" He hears the relief in her voice.

"Yes. I've been...well, let's just say I think I get it. Listen, I'm actually going to be back in Edmonton this Friday," he says. "Do you and Chet want to meet me at the shop or something? Maybe you'd have more time to explain what's happening, or..."

He trails off, aware that he has just asked a younger woman he doesn't know to secretly meet him, realizing how it might sound.

At the other end of the line, Dannicka feels a combination of relief and fear, each emotion competing for the prime spot.

"Could we just meet in the parking lot?" she says. "I would like to meet, and I think Chet would too, but I don't think I can go back in there."

He understands completely. He's been wondering the same thing himself.

"I work until 5," she says. "Is 5:30 okay?"

"That'll be fine." He can't believe he's having this conversation.

"Oh, and don't be surprised if Chet and I appear to be glowing, okay?"

"What?"

"I gotta go." The line suddenly goes dead.

Julian continues holding the receiver to his ear for several seconds before hanging up. Did that call actually happen? Or did he imagine it? He can't trust anything anymore. He supposes there is only one way to know for sure, and that's if Dannicka and Chet show up next Friday. Then again, he could *think* they're there and just be hallucinating...He'll drive himself crazy with that reasoning, if he's not already. Opening up his day timer, he writes 'Dannicka—5:30' on Friday's page.

Before he can think about this any further, the phone rings again.

"Julian speaking."

"Oh, hi Julian! My name is Carole, I was at the Grabbajabba with you in Edmonton a few weeks ago."

He freezes. How can this be happening? Two calls from two of the people who were there, one right after the other?

"Yes," he says cautiously. "I remember. How are you?"

"I'm well. How are you?"

"Fine." Julian notices that, unlike Dannicka, Carole sounds at ease.

"I was wondering if we could talk for a few minutes. Is this a bad time?"

He looks at the pile of work on his desk.

"Not at all."

"Good. Listen, I'm not sure how else to say this, but ever since that incident a few weeks ago, I've been noticing a few things that are... out of the ordinary. Some pretty major things."

Still cautious, he says nothing.

"Are you still there?"

"Yes. Sorry."

"Well, I saw Marcy the other day, you know who I'm talking about?"

"I do."

"Okay, bear with me." She pauses. "I saw her playing softball and she looked to me like she was glowing."

Silence.

"Please don't hang up." Carole begins speaking quickly. "I know how crazy it sounds and I wouldn't bother you except that when I went over to talk to her she looked at me like I was an alien. She looked terrified. I probably looked to her like I was glowing too."

More silence.

"I can take care of myself; you know? But she's just a kid. If something happened to us that day and *we* don't even understand it, how can she be expected to deal with it?"

She pauses. "Are you still there?"

He clears his throat. "Yes. It's just...right before you called me, I got a call from Dannicka. She was the other woman there that day."

"Oh."

"She said she ran into the high school kid who was also there, the one ordering all the drinks. We made plans to meet up this Friday when I'm back in town because she said they've also been experiencing...some strange stuff. And she said to me..." he pauses. "Don't be surprised if we look like we're glowing."

Now it's Carole's turn to be silent. After a moment, she speaks. "This is really happening, isn't it."

"I don't know," he says thickly. "I think so."

"When exactly are the three of you planning on getting together?" she asks. "I'd like to join you, if that's okay."

It's more than okay, thinks Julian. The cautious relief he had felt when Dannicka called is beginning to blossom into actual relief.

"Of course," he says, giving her the details.

"You know," she says, thoughtfully, "I've been back there quite a few times, just wondering if anything else will happen...and wishing something would. It was really incredible, wasn't it?"

This statement gets to Julian almost more than anything he's heard today. She isn't afraid. She has been actively seeking out something more. Suddenly, he feels almost ashamed of himself.

When the call ends, he sees that it is one o'clock. For the first time in weeks, he feels like he can actually get some work done, now that he knows he isn't alone.

At 5:00 p.m., Julian shuts down his computer and clears off his desk. For weeks he has been dreading the return trip to Edmonton, but now he is actually looking forward to it. Maybe now he'll get some answers, or at the very least, a support group.

There was one other guy there that day, younger than Julian who walked with a cane. What did he say his name was? Jason? Ryan? He wonders if he might hear from him, too.

After closing the office door behind him, he wishes his receptionist a good night. Just as he turns to leave, the phone in his office rings.

"I'll take it," says the receptionist, reaching for the receiver on her desk.

"That's okay," he tells her. "I've got it." He rushes back to answer.

"Julian speaking."

Silence.

"Hello? It's Julian."

"Uh, hi. Um, I don't know if you remember me, but my name is Ryan..."

Julian cuts him off.

"Yes, I remember you. And you might not believe this, or maybe you will, but I had a feeling you were going to call."

***

"For the tenth time, Marcy. Get. To. Bed."

Marcy has been lingering in the kitchen, in the living room, in the bathroom and in the TV room, all in an attempt to stay up as long as possible. She's never been afraid to sleep alone, and she's not afraid now, either. Not exactly. It's just that every time she closes her eyes, all she can see is the glowing lady. She's not afraid of the glowing lady; not really, she just doesn't want to think about her.

"Okay, okay—I'm going! But I have a question for you."

"What is it?"

There's no way she'll ask her mother this particular question in front of her sister, who will make fun of her for sure.

"It's private," Marcy says. Her mother sighs.

She plods into her bedroom followed by her mother. "What's your question?"

Marcy climbs into bed. "Is there such a thing as glowing people?"

"What?"

"Like, people who look like they're glowing. Like, there's a really big lightbulb inside of them."

"Oh, my God," her mother groans. "You really will think of anything to stay up late."

She kisses her daughter on the top of her head. "Now go to sleep. I mean it."

Marcy always feigns indifference when her parents show her affection, though secretly she doesn't mind. But tonight, for some reason, she is not comforted by her mother's gesture. Not at all.

Marcy's mom turns out the light and closes the door as she exits the room. Marcy keeps her eyes wide open, waiting for them to adjust to the dark.

What's there to be scared of? Nothing. She's just being a total baby for some reason. It's not as if the glowing lady is hiding in her closet or anything...that's totally impossible.

*But so are glowing people,* she thinks. *And I definitely saw one of those.*

Marcy squeezes her eyes shut and ducks under the blankets.

*Think about something else,* she tells herself. *Anything. Think about Bernadette.*

\*\*\*

## FRIDAY, JUNE 30

Chet waits until his parents have both left for the day before calling his manager. Sitting on his bed, he lifts the receiver from his nightstand and dials the number.

"I can't come in today," he says. "I'm sick."

His manager from the restaurant groans. "You high school kids," he complains. "Totally unreliable."

*I'm not in high school anymore,* Chet wants to say. *I graduated.*

"Let me guess; is the 26-ounce flu?"

"No, I'm really sick."

And he is. His heart is pounding like a jackhammer in what is, unfortunately, a now-familiar sensation. He's suddenly very cold, and the palms of his hands are sweating profusely.

"I thought you wanted more shifts this summer," the manager says.

"I did." Chet insists. He's having trouble breathing. And now, to his absolute horror, he feels like he's going to cry.

"Well, that's pretty funny, because you've called in sick three times in the last two weeks..."

"I gotta go!" Chet exclaims, slamming down the phone.

He feels like he's about to faint, or throw up, or both. Still sitting on his bed, he bends over and shoves his head between his knees. He keeps trying to take deep breaths but his lungs feel constricted.

What the hell is going on with him? He's turning into a total loser! It's like he's afraid of the entire world, lately. He's supposed to meet Dannicka later today but he doesn't see how he can––not like this. He wouldn't even be able to drive in this state.

After a few minutes, the faint feeling begins to subside. He takes another slow breath, then cautiously raises his head. In one continuous motion he lifts the comforter and crawls underneath, curling up into the fetal position. Pulling the blankets up and over his head, he buries himself completely.

*\*\*\**

Today must be the longest day in Dannicka's employment history. No matter how much work she gives herself, the morning drags on and on as though every clock in the office has slowed down. All she can think about is her meeting at the Grabbajabba later today.

During her lunch break, she calls Todd and tells him she'll be going out for drinks after work. It's just another lie to add to the list of lies she has been telling him all month.

"That's good," he tells her. "Some of the guys are going to Whyte Ave tonight…"

She tunes out the details of his plans, aware only that she won't have to see him later.

Just before five o'clock, she tidies up her desk and gathers her things, trying not to look too eager to leave. Behind her she hears the familiar sound of her boss' door opening, and soon he is walking past her desk.

"Any big plans for the long weekend?"

She smiles weakly. "Nothing major." *I'm just going to meet up with a few people I thought I went through an earthquake with to find out if we're losing our minds.*

"What about you?"

"We're heading to Jasper," he says. "I wanted to go camping but the wife's insisting on a hotel."

"Sounds nice." *Let me out of here!* She thinks. *Stop talking!*

He smiles. "Well, have a good one."

"You, too." She's never understood that saying. Have a good *what*?

The moment he's gone, she grabs her shoulder bag and heads to the elevator. On the way down she wonders, not for the first time today, whether or not Chet will actually show up. Judging by their conversations, she thinks he is going through some real anxiety. And who can blame him? She herself has barely slept a wink in the last three weeks, alternating between there-has-to-be-a-logical-explanation and total denial. Finding Chet last weekend has provided the only real sense of calm—and now the thought of reconnecting with Julian, too, fills her with hope.

She stands on the street outside her office building and waits impatiently as the minutes tick by. If Chet doesn't get here by 5:20 p.m., she'll just have to start walking. She stares intently at the rows of cars driving past, feeling her disappointment grow.

*Come on, Chet,* she prays. *Please.*

Just when she has given up hope, she spots a car down the block that matches the description Chet gave her. She can't help but feel a twinge of jealousy when she sees that the car he is driving is brand-new. At twenty-seven years old, she still can't afford *any* kind of car, let alone a new one.

*Must be nice to have Mommy and Daddy helping out,* she thinks acidly, in a knee-jerk reaction; but the feeling fades the instant the car comes close enough for her to see its glowing driver. He looks... unbelievable. Dannicka lifts her arm high in the air and waives.

***

Any fears or anxieties that Chet has had dissipate the moment he sees the radiantly-glowing Dannicka. How could he have even entertained the idea of not meeting her today? Just being in this proximity to her makes him feel, for the first time in nearly a month, almost normal. She is somehow familiar to him, as though they have known each other their entire lives.

He slows down and pulls over to the side of the street. Dannicka steps forward, bending down so that she can look at him through the rolled-down window, all lit up like a trippy sci-fi movie.

"Hi," she giggles. She opens the door and gets in. "I guess we're still glowing."

He grins involuntarily. "Maybe even more."

***

Julian stands at the window inside the 125<sup>th</sup> Street Grabbajabba. It's 5:35 p.m. and none of the others have arrived. He tells himself it's still early. It's Friday rush hour, after all; they could be stuck in traffic. Five minutes is nothing. He continues to watch the parking lot, refusing to give up hope despite the voice in his head telling him that he really is crazy.

*See,* he thinks, *you probably invented this whole thing—the phone calls, the plans...*

He silences his thoughts and checks his watch once more. 5:38 p.m.

Maybe they've changed their minds – even he had trouble stepping across the threshold this morning, worried that being back inside so-called Ground Zero might result in some other unsettling phenomena. He thought about Carole and how she had been back to the shop multiple times; he thought about the two other employees who were already inside working. Finally, feeling ridiculous, he slowly walked into the shop. And so far, nothing catastrophic has happened.

At 5:42 p.m., he walks outside and into the parking lot, stopping when he reaches the sidewalk.

*Come on*, he thinks. *Someone. Any one of you...*

Turning to face the other direction, something immediately catches his eye—there, on 104th Ave, about two blocks from where he is standing, a woman is walking toward him. It's not just any woman, though. It's a brilliantly glowing woman.

Julian is grateful that he'd had some warning, because without it he probably would have fainted. Even expecting to see it has not prepared him for this sight. It's unbelievable.

The woman is too far away to make out any features, but he knows without a doubt that it's Carole. The closer she gets, the more he stares at her and the more intensely she glows. It's as though she is lit up from within. Every inch of her skin, every strand of her hair, each facial feature (which Julian can now distinguish) is an exaggerated burst of colour, framed by a brilliant white light. Everything around her seems two-dimensional by comparison.

Carole approaches the equally-dazzling Julian and laughs at the expression on his face.

"Was I exaggerating?"

"No," he replies, unable to stop looking at her.

"I'm sorry I'm late. Am I the last one here?"

"You're the only one here." He feels almost mesmerized, unable to speak; or even think. This is the single most remarkable thing he has ever seen in his entire life, and that includes the birth of his two children. Why aren't the passing cars slamming on their brakes?

Why isn't there a group of curious people surrounding her right now? How is no one else seeing this?

"It's happening to you, too," she says as though reading his mind. "Julian, you look *incredible*."

Dumbfounded, he stares down at his hands, searching for any evidence that he is also glowing, but sees none.

"We can't see it in ourselves," she says. "I don't know why."

A new Ford Escort drives into the parking lot. Inside sit two glowing people and Carole laughs out loud when she sees them.

"I guess that's them!"

Chet isn't laughing. He pulls into an empty parking space and turns off the car, staring at the unbelievable sight before him. Together, their light is even more intense than Dannicka's.

He doesn't know what to do with this. It's just so fucking weird.

Dannicka sees his white-knuckled grip on the steering wheel. "I know," she says gently, understanding exactly how he feels without him having to speak. "It's a lot."

They open their doors at the same time and get out of the car. Dannicka suddenly feels like crying, though she's not sure why. She walks directly over to Carole and embraces her as though she is a long-lost friend, then does the same with Julian. Taking a step back, she looks at all three, seeing how their light greatly increases when they're together.

"Oh!" she exclaims. "It gets brighter when—"

"Yes," says Carole, finishing the thought. Carole has stopped laughing, but she cannot take the smile off her face. She can't remember the last time she felt this happy.

For Julian there is a mixture of relief and near-euphoria. He's spent the last month thinking he was losing his mind. Now he knows this is real—whatever 'this' is—and although he barely knows these people, they seem as much his family now as his own wife and children.

"Two of us are missing," says Dannicka, who didn't even know Carole would be here. As intense as this is, it still feels incomplete.

"I didn't call Marcy," says Julian, "but Ryan said he'd be here."
He looks at Dannicka and Chet. "I know you two don't want to come
inside. Would you feel comfortable sitting on the patio? We can get
to it through that gate over there."

Dannika and Chet exchange a glance.

"Yeah, ok," says Chet.

They all make their way over to the outdoor patio located beside
the coffee shop. They choose a table as far from the shop's entrance
as possible, grateful to be the only people there. This location,
tucked away from the main road, is rarely busy, and on a Friday
evening it's usually dead. They are all grateful for the privacy.

"Can I get anything for you guys?" says Julian. "My treat."

He takes their drink orders, then hesitates briefly in the doorway.
Will anything happen now that the others have joined him? He
takes a breath and steps gingerly inside. Nothing out of the ordinary, besides the already extraordinary, happens.

***

Ryan stands across the street, tucked behind an office building
where he has been hiding for the last fifteen minutes. Inside the
Grabbajabba, he saw what he thought was a giant light, until that
light walked outside and was joined by another giant light. Two
more lights drove up in a car and, when they all stood together, the
lights merged to become one. Julian had warned Ryan that something like this might happen, but Ryan hadn't really believed it.
Even now, watching it happen right in front of him, he can't quite
accept it.

*Look at them,* he thinks. *They're so happy.* Maybe their lives
have improved as much as his, maybe even more.

Why would we want to change that, he wonders, not realizing
that he has already referred to himself as part of the group.

The more Ryan looks at them, the more drawn to them he feels;
compelled, actually. He has to force himself to keep his post, praying
that his own light (which he knows he probably has—he won't
bother kidding himself that it's not there) will be mostly covered

by the building he is hiding behind. Luckily, the group appears too enamoured with each other to bother with their surroundings.

After a few moments, he sees them leave the parking lot and settle at a table on the patio area at the side of the shop. He can't see them once they sit down, except for the faint glow of residual light peeking through the surrounding trees

He should leave right now.

\*\*\*

Julian returns to the table with a tray of drinks.

"For me," Dannicka says, "it was that the word 'country' had disappeared. It's 'company' instead. Have you guys noticed that? When I saw the word written in my own handwriting, I knew something was wrong."

Chet makes a face. "Oh, man—they kept using 'company' all over my Social Studies exam. I just thought it was a typo."

"I never even noticed," says Julian, sitting down at the table. "But I guess I had enough to worry about when the foothills outside of Calgary literally disappeared."

"Wow," says Carole, clearly impressed. "That's pretty significant."

"Even that didn't completely convince me," he says. He tells them about Tawnee's play and how it couldn't possibly be Broadway, or even off-Broadway, material.

"You should see this thing," he says. "First of all, it's a musical. I mean, kill me now, right?"

"I like musicals," says Carole.

"Yea, but you probably like the good ones. This one features a giant singing beaver that keeps threatening to shoot himself."

Chet laughs.

"Exactly—that's what *I* thought, too. But it's supposed to be this dramatic tear-jerker. Anyways, when I found out it's going to be an off-Broadway hit, I knew something was drastically wrong."

He turns to Carole. "What about you? What did you notice?"

She tells them about her painting and the three perfect circles that mysteriously appeared overnight, then about running into Marcy. After that, the table falls silent.

"What's happening to us?" asks Dannicka. "Did that eruption, or soundwave or whatever it was, interfere with our brains? Are we all hallucinating?"

"Well, that's definitely a possibility," Julian replies, wondering why he hadn't thought of it himself. It would be a lot easier to accept than dying of some horrible brain disease, or turning into Uncle Ribbons.

"But why are we the only people, or things, that are glowing?" Chet asks. "What if we're, like, radioactive?"

"I think," Carole begins cautiously. She wonders if she should say what she's about to at the risk of scaring Chet. Technically he is an adult, though he said his eighteenth birthday was only ten days ago. She takes a breath and continues. "The real question is, *where* are we? When I saw Marcy last week, it seemed like she was the only thing, other than me, that was actually real. And now, seeing the three of you, I feel the exact same way."

This thought sends a chill up the back of Chet's neck, and seeing the others nod in agreement makes hm believe it to be true. Warily, he looks around at the tree-lined street, at the houses tucked in behind, at the other cars on the lot. If none of this is real then what is it?

"I wish Ryan and Marcy were here," says Dannicka, who hadn't been expecting to see them; but the group feels incomplete—uncomfortably so.

"Ryan's not ready," says Carole. She thinks for a minute. "I don't know why I just said that. And, as for Marcy, well, she's really afraid and we need to do something about it."

There is a murmur of consent around the table.

Ten days earlier, when Chet turned eighteen, his father had said, "Welcome to the Adult World." In his wildest dreams, he never imagined it would be like this.

\*\*\*

Ryan feels drawn to the other four like a magnet, but has forced himself to keep his distance. Now, with an even greater effort, he turns and walks away.

When he gets home, Roland appears agitated, following Ryan around the apartment and circling his ankles in a repetitive figure-eight. Ignoring him, Ryan slumps down in front of the TV and turns on his Sony PlayStation. After it boots up, he immediately turns it off. He picks up the phone and calls Cory, one of the few friends he still sees.

"Hey man, you feel like hangin' out tonight?"

"I can't," Cory says. "Marshall's having a party."

"Maybe I'll go, too."

"Yeah, right!" Cory laughs. Ryan hasn't been to a party in three years.

"Seriously. I'll go too."

"No shit?!"

"No shit."

"Wow. Okay—I'll come pick you up."

\*\*\*

Navigating his way through the maze of bodies at the crowded house-party, Ryan is met with looks of disbelief and cheers.

"No frickin' way!" screams a girl he used to party with.

"What died in the bush?!" exclaims Marshall, the host of the party and Ryan's old dorm-mate. He claps Ryan heartily on the back.

"Not much, man."

Cory thrusts a beer into Ryan's hand and he downs the whole thing in one go.

"Ry-an! Ry-an!" chants the crowd. Someone hands him another.

\*\*\*

At ten o'clock, a server walks out onto the patio where Julian and the others are still sitting.

"Did you guys want anything else?" she asks. "We're about to start cleaning up."

Julian checks his watch. "Is it that time already!?" It's always light so late at this time of year. More so in Edmonton than in Calgary, he notices.

Over the last four hours, he and the others have discussed a number of possibilities to explain what is happening to them, and have come up with one potential plan to reach Marcy. So far, the only thing Julian knows for sure is that he is going to get himself a hotel for the night. Trudy is going to be angry—he should have been back in Calgary at least an hour ago—but right now, he doesn't care.

"That'll be fine, thanks," he tells the server. He looks at the others, knowing none of them want to leave.

"I don't wanna go back out there," says Dannicka. "I agree with Carole—I don't think any of it is real."

The thought of leaving this group, of going back to her place and to life-as-usual fills her with worry, and she knows she isn't the only one.

"We'll see each other tomorrow," says Julian in an attempt to reassure them. "Nothing really *bad* has happened." Apart from the obvious. "I mean, we're not in any danger. We'll see each other in a few hours, actually."

"You guys can call me anytime," Carole jumps in. "I mean it. Even if it's the middle of the night."

They get to their feet and take turns hugging one another as though they might never see each other again. As they walk back to the parking lot, they prepare to go their separate ways.

"Do you want a ride?" Julian asks Carole. "It's getting dark."

"I suppose I could," she says, not wanting Mr. Biscuits to wait for her much longer. She hadn't meant to be gone so long. "Thank you."

"My car's just over here."

As the four pair off into groups of two, there is an almost-physical sensation of breaking apart. A look is shared amongst them, but no one says anything about it.

"Goodnight, you two!" Carole calls. "I'll see you in the morning!"

"Goodnight!" Dannicka and Chet reply. Dannicka gets into Chet's car feeling grateful that she'll have a few more minutes before separating from him, too. The drive back to her apartment is spent in comfortable silence. There's nothing more to say right now, not after the intense meeting they've just had.

As they cross the High Level bridge, she stares out her window, unable to get the thought out of her mind that nothing she sees is real. Thank God she won't have to face Todd tonight; whoever or whatever he is.

Outside her apartment building, Chet pulls a U-turn, taking more care behind the wheel than usual.

"Thanks for the ride," she says, wishing she didn't have to leave. "I'll see you tomorrow."

"For sure."

He watches her incredible light––made even more brilliant by the surrounding darkness––as she walks up to the door of the lobby and lets herself in. Not wanting to leave either, he sits in his car and waits until her light is swallowed up by the building.

*** 

Ryan is sprawled out at one end of a ratty old couch, barely able to keep his eyes open. It's been ages since he's been this drunk. The other end of the couch is occupied by an also-drunk couple, who sporadically and lazily make out, though Ryan takes little notice. A face hovers into his view, and he has to squint his eyes to focus. It's a semi-familiar face, a female face, but he can't quite figure out who it belongs to.

"I haven't seen you since that night," she slurs, her eye makeup running down her cheeks. "*You* know...*that* night...when..."

But she doesn't get to the end of her sentence. Marshall appears, as if from nowhere, one hand clamped firmly on her shoulder.

"We're not gonna talk about that," he says. "No one needs to talk about that night."

"But I waz jus' gonna say..."

"Come on." Marshall lifts her to her feet. "Ryan doesn't need that. Let's dance."

He leans over and cranks up the stereo. One of the speakers sits perched beside Ryan's head but he makes no effort to move away from the blasting music. He knows this song and slurs along to half-remembered lyrics about love, and peace, and harmony, which could only exist in the next world.

"Ohh..." he croons until it suddenly hits him like a tonne of bricks—the earthquake, the weird dreams with his cat, the glowing people, everything. It all becomes clear.

"I'M ALREADY IN THE NEXT WORLD!" he shouts at the drunk couple who, between bouts of catatonia, are still making out. Unable to hear him over the blaring music, they stop kissing.

"HUH?" shouts the girl.

"HE SAYS," her companion yells, "HE'S ALREADY *IN* THE NEXT WORLD!"

The girl-half of the couple stares blearily at Ryan for a moment, trying to comprehend.

"FUCKIN'-A!" she yells. She starts to laugh.

Ryan starts laughing, too. He laughs so hard that he falls off the couch and onto the filthy carpet.

# CHAPTER SIX

"Hello, Ryan."

Ryan is sitting up in his bed, in the now all-too-familiar position. This time, however, he isn't at all worked up about it. He isn't worried, and in fact, he doesn't really care what their problem is. He has absolutely no desire to engage these...well, whatever the hell they are.

"Ryan," Roland begins, spotlight in place.

"Why doncha jus' fugoff," Ryan slurs. Even in his dream he is drunk.

Roland blinks in that weird, re-setting thing he does before going on. "Ryan, it's important that you listen."

"I don't *have* to listen to you," Ryan says belligerently. "I don' even know who the fuck you are. An' I don't like whatcher doing to my cat. I rilly don' think he'd be on my case for—".

"Ryan, you *need* to collect the other five."

Roland's voice remains calm and steady despite Ryan's insolence, which is even more of a piss-off. Ryan can't handle those piercing green eyes. It's like they're boring through his very soul. He tries to shut his own eyes but can't. Even in his drunken stupor he can tell that their hold on him has gotten stronger.

"Ryan—"

"They already got together," he snaps, "so why doncha talk to *them!*"

"Ryan," Roland calmly repeats. "The six of you need to all be together in the same place at the same time in order for us to shift you back."

Ryan tries to slam his fist onto the bed but is unable to move his arm.

"I don't WANT to shift back!" he shouts, feeling his desperation rise. "Do whatever the hell you want with the others, I don't give a shit! I'm staying here!"

"Ryan." The word is now a command. "This 'here' is only a facsimile. It is not permanent and it *will not last*."

He doesn't need to listen to this. He needs to wake up now—Roland's voice is hurting his head.

"If you choose to do nothing," Roland continues, the voice now seeming to drill right into his skull, "there will be nothing to 'live' in. And *you* will be responsible for the deaths of the other five."

Deaths? The word is like a laser, splitting his brain in two. Why did they have to say that?

"But I..."

Roland lets him go.

\*\*\*

When Ryan gets out of bed in the morning, he sees that Roland has been sick on the carpet. Ryan feels like he might do the same. It's been years since he's had a hangover and yet the feeling is entirely familiar. *Like riding a bike*, he thinks wryly.

He remembers when he used to think that hangovers were the worst thing in the world. Now the hangover, as shitty as it is, feels like a parade down Main Street compared to what he's had to contend with on an average day.

In the kitchen he finds a can of Coke, best hang-over cure in the world, and cracks it open. He takes two large swigs, then belches loudly before going back to deal with the cat puke. One shower and the rest of the Coke later, he feels almost normal again.

Back in the bedroom, he gets dressed, then sees that Roland has been sick twice more in the last few minutes. A sinking feeling drops down to the pit of his stomach. Getting down on his hands and knees, he checks under the bed to where Roland hides whenever he's ill or embarrassed.

"You okay, buddy?" Small green eyes peer back at him from deep under the bed. "Maybe we should take you to the vet?"

A trip to the vet isn't going to help though—he knows this. He shifts into a sitting position on the floor and groans.

"Fine!" he says out loud to whomever, or whatever, is listening. "I'll fucking go!"

***

The server at Grabbajabba looks surprised.

"Oh!" she says. "I didn't know you were working today."

"I'm not," Julian tells her. "I just stopped by to see if I left my sunglasses here last night."

"You mean these?" She holds out a pair that have been sitting behind the counter.

"That's them," he smiles. "Thanks."

"So, I guess you're heading home, now?"

"That's right," he lies. He's not going home, at least, not yet. He's going to Carole's.

"See you next month," he says, not at all sure that this is true.

He walks out to his car, unlocks the door, and is just about to open it when he sees a ball of light out of the corner of his eye. He stops and looks over at the glowing figure with an immense feeling of relief as it approaches.

"Hi," says Ryan. He doesn't know what else to say. There's no point in, 'it's Julian, right?' or 'I'm Ryan, we spoke on the phone...' It is so beyond that, now.

He looks at Julian, feeling that same magnetic draw he had felt yesterday, only it's much stronger at this close proximity. And what appeared to be a giant ball of light from yesterday's vantage point is now, he realizes, so much more than that. Everything about the person standing before him is alight: his face, his hands, his head, his arms. Even clothing does not contain the light that seems to burst from every seam, collar, and hem. Ryan has never seen anything like this in his entire life. He couldn't walk away now, even if he wanted to.

"How did you know I'd be here?" Julian asks, surprised.

"I didn't. I just thought...well, I couldn't be here last night..." Excuses feels so lame now. "I thought I'd start here and then..." he trails off, realizing that he had no plan. He'd just assumed he would find one of them, and he has.

"Don't worry about it," says Julian. "You're here now. And I was just on my way to Carole's to meet with Chet and Dannicka. Do you think you could come, too?"

Before he has time to think, Ryan hears himself say yes, as though there was never any doubt. Once inside the car, Julian rolls down all of the windows. He already thinks of Ryan as family in the same way he does the others, but the smell is a bit much. It's as if Ryan has been swimming in a pool of whiskey. Julian does not miss that part of his drinking days.

"Sorry," Ryan mutters, as though reading his mind. "I went a bit overboard last night."

"Been there myself."

Julian changes the topic to more pressing matters, spending the remainder of the drive filling Ryan in on the previous night's discussion. Ryan listens silently. The more he hears about the other five, the more responsible he feels. It's his fault that this is happening and he is going to have to come clean.

"This is it," Julian says, pulling up in front of a 1960s ranch-style house. He stops behind Chet's already-parked car and turns off the engine. For a moment, both men simply sit and stare at the intense light radiating from the house's large living room window.

Julian lets out a short laugh. "She'd never need to tell us what her house number is—we're all shining like beacons!" He turns to Ryan. "Shall we?"

The front door opens before they reach the porch. Ryan sees Carole, Dannicka, and Chet standing expectantly before him, looking at him like a long-lost brother. The sight nearly bowls him over.

"We know," says Carole, her voice solemn. She holds out her arms to embrace him and, although he's never been an affectionate person, he returns the embrace like it's the most natural thing in the world. Then he does the same with Dannicka. Suddenly, he feels more connected to these people than he has ever felt to anyone.

"Come in," says Carole. "We were just sitting around the table."

They make their way through the large living room and over to the dining room, where they all take a seat. Without prompting, Ryan begins to speak, telling them about the accident he had four years ago which he has never shared with anyone before. He tells them about the constant and excruciating pain he has lived with every day since, he tells them about the chronic migraines, his sense of hopelessness and how he sometimes thinks about killing himself. They listen with sympathy and without judgement.

"And so, I hope you'll be able to forgive me," he says contritely. When he sees the puzzled looks on their faces, he takes a deep breath before continuing. Never one for more than a few words, he feels comfortable sharing with these people, knowing they will understand.

"I've had a series of dreams," he says.

He describes each one with great detail, and when he's done, he is met with understandable silence.

"I know," he says. "I should've gotten in touch sooner. I was just...feeling so much better than I had before the accident, and I knew it had something to with this, and...I'm sorry. I—"

Carole places a hand over his. "Don't be. It's a lot to take in."

A facsimile world. It's the most unbelievable thing she has ever heard, and yet, it explains everything. They've just spent the last month living somewhere that isn't the real world. The real world 'shifts' periodically—Ryan wasn't told how often, but he said that this shift is sort of like a computer screen refreshing itself; it's just something that's always happened. He said his understanding is limited, and therefore so is his explanation.

*They sent us into a facsimile world when we didn't make 'the shift'*, she thinks. *And they intended to send us right back without our even knowing*. Has this happened before? Does this happen to people all the time?

She looks back at him, only now realizing that this bombshell news has eclipsed the terrible description of his accident. What happened to him is almost unthinkable. A wave of sympathy washes over her.

"I knew it," says Dannicka, in a small voice. "I just *knew* this place wasn't real."

"So," Chet begins slowly. "Does that mean *everything* is fake? Even my parents?" He thinks about his grad ceremony. Does this mean he never gave that God-awful speech to the entire school? He thinks about Lindsay—he had kissed her that night, and not just a peck on the cheek, either; they had really gone for it, and that definitely felt real. If that wasn't Lindsay, who was it?

"Are we just imagining everything?" he asks. "Are we all hallucinating?"

"I don't know," Ryan answers. "We're all real, but I don't know what the rest of it is."

Julian thinks about his wife and daughters and a wave of nausea creeps over him. What *are* they? He immediately sweeps the thought away. He can worry about that later. As upsetting as it is, there is a more pressing issue at hand.

"What did your cat, or *they*, mean when they said this 'facsimile' won't last long? Exactly how much time do we have?"

"I don't know," Ryan says again, feeling helpless and even more guilty. Why didn't he at least try? How could he have been so cavalier about the fates of these people?

Carole, sensing his angst, jumps in.

"I think the important thing to focus on is that there *is* a way back, and that's all. Now, they said that as long as the six of us are together at the same time, then we can...shift back. Is that right?"

"Yes," Ryan says.

"So, let's keep our plan to see Marcy tonight," she says. She turns to Ryan. "Marcy's in a softball tournament and her team will be playing against my niece's team at seven o'clock tonight. Julian and I were going to go, but now I think we all should. It might be our only chance to be together."

"But if she got that upset just from seeing you," Dannicka asks, "what'll she do when she sees all of us?"

"Maybe she doesn't have to actually see us," Julian suggests. "Maybe there's some way that we could get close enough to her without her even knowing we're there. I mean, we weren't exactly holding hands the first time it happened."

"But, look how bright we are," says Dannicka. "Even if we're hiding in the middle of a crowd a mile away, she's going to see us!"

"Okay," says Carole, taking a moment to think. "There are a couple of buildings in the field where they're playing—two schools and, I think, maybe a community centre and some kind of shed."

"Yeah," says Chet. "That's right. I went to the Junior High there, and there are two buildings right by the ball diamond."

"Okay—we could stay behind whichever one is the closest to her. She might still see some light around the building, but I don't think she'd necessarily think it's coming from us...the light is so much brighter with all of us together that she might just think it's the building that's glowing."

Julian lets out a long, low sigh.

"I can't believe I'm having this conversation," he mutters. He still hasn't entirely dismissed the possibility that this whole situation is only happening in his head; but either way, he's invested now.

"I don't really see any other way around it," he says. "Do you guys?"

"But, if we get close enough to do the shift-thing," asks Chet, "won't we pull in everyone else around us?"

The table goes quiet.

"None of them are real," Dannicka says, patiently.

"But what if we pull them in anyway? Then we'll have real people with fake ones..."

Julian cuts him off. "I think we'll just have to take that chance."

Mr. Biscuits, who had been sleeping in the bedroom, chooses this moment to make an entrance. Chet notices him first and grimaces, involuntarily. Yikes! What kind of dog *is* this?

"Your dog is glowing," he tells Carole.

"He is?"

Everyone stops to look at the small animal.

"Yes, he is," says Dannicka.

"That's funny," Carole replies, "I don't see it."

"Why would your dog be glowing?" Julian asks, slightly unnerved by Mr. Biscuits' bizarre appearance, glowing or not. *Is it sick?* He wants to ask, then thinks better of it. That's exactly the type of crack he would make that would elicit a glare from his wife.

"He was with me that day," Carole explains, sheepishly.

"He was? I didn't see him." Julian definitely would have remembered that.

"She carries him in her bag," says Ryan.

Carole looks at him in surprise. "Was it that obvious?"

He simply smiles in return.

"Well," says Julian. "We'd better take him with us. I don't want to risk anything."

***

"I'm *not* going," Marcy tells her mother defiantly. She sits on her bed, arms crossed.

"You can't let your entire team down just because you don't feel like it."

"It's not that," Marcy insists. "There's more to it."

Her mother sighs. "Look—I know you and Bernadette are having some problems, but you're going to have to face her sometime. Being part of a team means putting aside your personal feelings for the sake of others."

Her mom obviously thinks that Bernadette is the reason she wants to skip the ball game, but that's not the half of it. Sometimes parents can be so clueless. Marcy overheard her mom talking to one of her aunts the other day and she knew they were talking about her. Her mom said, "hormones, hormones," and burst out laughing. Marcy thought that was incredibly rude, not to mention totally wrong.

Maybe she doesn't want to face Bernadette, but she's more worried about seeing that glowing lady again. At the same time, though, she kind of *does* want to see her. She doesn't know what she wants. If only she could talk to Bernadette about it—she's the only person Marcy can trust not to laugh at her. But keeping the promise she made to herself, she hasn't spoken to her ex-friend since the recital.

Her mom sits on the bed. "Listen—you keep telling us that you're not a little kid anymore. So, if you want us to believe that, you're going to have act a little more grown up. Grown-ups have responsibilities."

"To play softball?"

"To keep their commitments," her mother snaps.

Marcy pouts and thinks for a minute. What if the glowing lady is there? What if she isn't? She probably won't be. It probably never even happened.

"Fine," she says. "I'll go."

\*\*\*

Dannicka sits in the front seat of Chet's car, aware of Ryan's presence behind her in the back seat. He's a very...interesting person. Although she has never thought in these terms before, she would have to say that he has a very strong energy. Like the rest of the group, he is a complete stranger, and yet entirely familiar.

Chet, driving decently for the first time since his driving exam, keeps his eyes on Julian's car, following at a polite distance.

"So, when we get to the 'real' world," he says, "do you guys think that it'll be exactly like this one, like the same time and the same things are happening but just with real people? Or do you think we'll zap back to the Grabbajabba and it'll be the same time as when we left?"

"I don't know for sure, obviously," says Dannicka, "but the feeling I get, is that time there has continued to move on. I don't think the world has stopped just because we're not in it." She thinks for a moment. "As far as everyone there is concerned, we're probably considered missing. They probably think we've all disappeared." She pauses again before adding, "I guess we have."

Ryan remains quiet in the back seat. Absentmindedly he checks his pockets to see if he still has the small container of pills that he never leaves home without. He hasn't taken anything at all, except pot, for more than a week, but he still carries them with him just in case. And God knows what'll happen to him when he shifts back.

Dannicka, as if reading his mind, turns around to face him.

"Maybe going back doesn't have to mean that you'll have the same problems...I mean, you feel better, right? Maybe what happened to us, like, just having gone through that, had some kind of... healing effect—so, it's not this place, necessarily..."

She trails off, feeling suddenly inadequate. How does she know anything about what's going on, or what he's feeling?

Ryan meets her eye, knowing she's only trying to help. "Could be."

He attempts a smile but finds his jaw is too tense to cooperate.

\*\*\*

At Carole's instruction, Julian turns off the main road and into the southside neighbourhood of Lendrum. Aside from giving directions, Carole and Julian have been quiet during this drive, both too preoccupied with what is about to transpire, and with what already has. After driving a few more blocks, a large park comes into view.

"You can park anywhere here," she says.

Julian slows down and pulls over. In his rear-view mirror he sees that Chet has done the same. All five get out of the cars and stand together on the sidewalk. Mr. Biscuits, having sat on Carole's lap during the trip, seems content to settle back into the comfort and security of her shoulder bag.

"The ball diamond is straight ahead of us at the other end of the park," Carole tells the others. "Do you see that little building over there? The green one? It's just to the left of the diamond."

"Yeah, that's the one I was picturing," says Chet.

"If we get behind it," Carole continues, "we should be close enough to Marcy without being seen. We should wait until after the game starts so we'll know exactly where she is, and then we can go around the edge of the park and sneak in that way."

"It looks *really* small," says Julian. "We're gonna light that thing up like a Christmas tree—there's no way we'll go undetected. What about that other building? The one further up the hill?"

"I know it's bigger, but I don't think it's close enough."

"How about we start there," says Dannicka, "and then, if we need to, we can move closer, like get behind the little green one. And if she sees our light, then it hopefully won't matter—we can 'shift', or whatever, and deal with the consequences later."

"I'm good with that," says Julian. "You guys?"

Chet is surprised to be asked. "Yup."

Carole says yes, and Ryan gives a quick nod.

"Okay, then." Carole checks her watch. "I'll go over there now, just to get a good look and make sure that it'll be close enough. It's only 6:15 —Marcy won't be here yet."

Dannicka looks at the crowds of people already gathering throughout the park, all engaged in various Canada Day festivities. "What if she came early?"

"She hasn't," Carole says with certainty. She looks to Dannicka. "Do you think she's here?"

Dannicka thinks for a moment. "No. You're right, she's not."

"I'll be back in a minute."

"I'll go with you," Julian offers.

Together they begin walking through the park, keeping their eyes peeled in search of Marcy's glowing being.

"I keep expecting people to stop and stare at us, or start scream-ing, or *something*," says Julian. Seeing the lit-up Carole against throngs of dull-by-comparison people, and knowing he, too, is a-light, makes the glow even more outstanding.

"I know," says Carole. "I still can't quite believe this is actually happening. And I don't mean to make light or anything—in fact, I mean quite the opposite—but, isn't this an incredible gift?"

Julian raises an eyebrow. "That's one word for it."

"I wish we had some time to just... take it in before we have to go back, you know?"

*She must not have much to go back to*, he thinks initially, then realizes her point. It *is* quite incredible, when you think about it.

When they reach the centre of the park, they stop walking and survey the area. Spotting the buildings in question, Carole takes a moment to consider.

"I think that one should be close enough," she says, referring to the bigger of the two small community buildings.

"It might be," Julian agrees.

"And, if not, we can always move in behind that little green shed. Hopefully it won't take too long to see if—"

"Carole?"

Carole and Julian turn around and find themselves face to face with Carole's twin sister Corinne. Julian's mouth drops open.

"I didn't know you'd be here tonight," Corinne says, giving Julian a quick once-over. "Why didn't you say anything?"

Julian stares at Corinne, then looks back at Carole, then back at Corinne. It's a gesture the sisters have put up with many times in their lives, though it has been years since it last happened.

"This is my sister, Corinne," Carole says evenly. "Corrine—Julian."

Julian says nothing and continues to stare at the twins until Carole taps him in the ribs with her elbow.

"Hi," he finally manages.

"Why don't you go on up ahead," she says pointedly. "I'll catch up."

He nods and closes his mouth, then steps away from the two women.

Corinne raises an eyebrow at her sister. "New man?"

"Not even close—he's someone from work. We're actually in the middle of a big project right now."

"Here? On Canada Day?"

"We're meeting a client," says Carole. She looks carefully at this facsimile, or whatever it is, that is impersonating her sister with growing dread.

"What's wrong?" Corinne asks. "You're acting strange."

*Oh, God*, Carole thinks. What if this 'facsimile' person knows she's a facsimile? What if she knows that Carole knows? Her stomach flips.

"Nothing's wrong, I just...I was just thinking about something else. I gotta go!" she adds, abruptly turning away.

"Nice seeing you!" Corinne calls after her, making no attempt to hide her sarcasm.

Clutching her bag, Carole jogs to where Julian is standing, careful to cradle Mr. Biscuits as she does. She has a sudden desire to be as far away from the sister-who-isn't as possible, wanting only to be with the people she knows are real.

"Hi," she says, catching up. The instant she is back in Julian's presence, she begins to feel better.

"You've got a twin," he says, simply.

"Yes. We're identical. Although you've probably figured that out."

"For a minute there, I mean, you two just look *so* much alike, I thought she was actually you. Like, a facsimile version. And I wondered if there were other versions of the rest of us out there somewhere."

"Oh," says Carole, understanding. "Well, that particular facsimile is doing a pretty good impression of Corinne. It makes my skin crawl." She shivers involuntarily. "Let's get back to the others."

"Agreed."

Julian thinks about the past month he's just spent with his facsimile wife and daughters, wondering once again just who, or what, they are. Whatever the case, he never wants to see them again.

\*\*\*

"There's nowhere to bloody-well park!" Marcy's dad exclaims after driving up and down the street behind the ball diamond twice. "I'm gonna have to go around to the other side," he complains.

"But the game has almost started!" Marcy wails. "I'm gonna be late!"

"Well, you should've thought of that before you spent the afternoon moping in your bedroom."

Marcy scowls. Why did her mom have to tell him about that?

Her dad pulls a U-turn, then double-parks behind the diamond. "Jump out," he says. "I'll go find somewhere to park and I'll see you back here in a minute."

\*\*\*

Chet, Dannicka, Ryan, Julian, and Carole stand conferring beside their cars, solidifying their plan. A car pulls up behind Chet's and, as its driver gets out, the five automatically step closer together, lowering their voices. Almost instantly Carole recognizes him. She instinctively drops her head, hoping he won't recognize her, but within seconds she hears his voice.

"Hi," he says. "We meet again."

"Oh!" Carole turns and faces Marcy's dad with what she hopes to be a pleasant expression. Why did they have to run into him now? She wishes, and not for the first time, that this city wasn't so small. "Hello."

At the sound of his voice, the others turn to look his way. Instantly, all faces—Marcy's dad included—register surprise.

"Oh," he says, confused.

"Hello," Julian says, hoping to come off as professional. In a glance he sees that Marcy is not with her dad.

"We all just...sort of kept in touch after that day," Carole explains weakly, knowing he must be wondering why a group of strangers who happened to be in a coffee shop during a strange event are now spending Canada Day together. "How's Marcy?" she adds.

"She's Marcy," he says, guardedly—looking at the group as though something is amiss.

*Something's amiss alright*, thinks Julian.

"Her game's already started." Marcy's dad looks across the park. "I'd better get going."

"Great," Carole smiles wanly. "Enjoy."

All five watch Marcy's dad walk off toward the ball diamond across the park until he disappears from view.

"Holy shit," says Chet. "Do you think he believed us?"

"Who cares?" says Dannicka dismissively. "He's not real—he may as well be a robot."

"But if he tells Marcy about us, she'll freak out."

"He won't get a chance to," says Carole. "The game's already started. We should go now."

They walk alongside the circular perimeter of the park, keeping a wide berth, until they find themselves parallel to the back of the larger community building. Cutting across the park, they walk—hearts beginning to thud loudly—until they reach their destination. Carole experiences a moment of intuition as they arrive. Not one to dismiss any gut feelings, she tells the others.

"This isn't going to cut it," she says, her voice low. "We're going to have to move in behind that little green shed."

For reasons none of them understand, they all turn to Ryan for confirmation. Shifting his weight, unused to being without his cane, he falters for a moment before nodding in affirmation.

Without another word, the five make their way to the shed about thirty paces away.

"I'm so nervous!" Dannicka whispers. "How long until we know it'll work?"

"The closest she'll be to us is when she stands on first base," says Carole. "That could happen in the first couple of innings."

There is a collective intake of breath.

"I guess now we just wait," says Julian.

*** 

Marcy stands on top of the pitcher's mound and tries to stay focused. She's already struck out two batters, but she's let three more get past her—not at all her usual style. So far, there is no sign of the glowing woman and, mixed with Marcy's relief is a surprising sense of disappointment.

She squints at the new batter before her now and takes a deep breath. The batter, a scrawny girl who is at least thirteen but looks more like eleven, avoids meeting her eye. Without warning, Marcy springs into action, delivering one of her perfect signature pitches.

"Strike one!"

After two more easy strikes, Marcy joins the rest of her team trotting back to their bench. Bernadette, who had missed their last game, is here now. She makes a point of trying to catch Marcy's attention, patting the empty space next to her. Marcy looks away and walks past her, choosing instead to sit at the other end of the bench.

As the first batter from her team walks up to the plate, Marcy notices a faint light in her periphery. Turning her head, she sees that the light is shining around the edges and roof of a small building—some kind of shed or something—just up ahead, only a few steps away from the ball diamond. Unable to look away, the light seems to grow stronger the more she stares at it.

A creepy-crawly feeling begins tingling up through her body. She knows this light—it's the same light that was coming from the glowing lady. Is the building itself glowing? No, she decides. The light is definitely coming from behind it.

"Marcy!" the coach calls. "You're up!"

She snaps to attention and gets to her feet, grabbing one of the bats. She's been distracted—she should have been practicing her swing, not sitting down staring into space.

"Come on, Marcy!" her dad calls, clapping encouragingly.

At the sound of her name, five sets of ears perk up from behind the shed.

Marcy steps up to the plate and tries not to think about the light, which is now so bright it seems to take over everything else in her field of vision.

"Strike one!"

"You can do it, Marcy!" Bernadette hollers.

At the next pitch, Marcy manages to hit the ball between the third baseman and the short-stop. She runs to first base and stays there.

Behind the shed, the five collectively hold their breath. Nothing. A smattering of applause from the crowd follows.

"It doesn't sound like a home run," says Chet, "and I don't think she had enough time to make it to third—so she's on first or second right now."

"This could be it," says Carole. Dannicka grabs her hand and gives it a squeeze. They keep their ears peeled, listening to the crack of the bat and the cheering crowd, trying to guess what is happening.

After a few minutes, they are able to tell that Marcy has crossed home plate.

"It didn't work," says Dannicka. "We're going to have to come out."

Marcy jogs across home plate but, instead of joining the rest of her team, she continues jogging. There will be at least one or two more batters before she will be expected back on the pitcher's mound and she needs to figure out what's going on; the light coming off that little shed-thing is definitely getting brighter now, and no one else seems to see it. It's so bright, in fact, that it's nearly blinding her to everything else.

"I'll be right back," she tells her coach, not giving him a chance to reply. She runs around the fence behind the umpire, past the spectators and up the small hill to the little shed. She slows down as she approaches, realizing that she was correct -the light isn't coming from the shed itself, but from behind it. Gingerly, she walks around to the back, nearly blinded by the light now.

She doesn't know what she expected to see, but it definitely wasn't five very familiar faces, all staring back at her with equal surprise.

"Oh no, oh no, oh no..." Marcy mutters. This is *not* happening. She turns away slowly, as if in a trance, aware that five pairs of glowing eyes are all glued to her. The moment her back is turned, she breaks into a run.

"Oh no!" Julian exclaims, "Marcy!!" He turns to the others. "We gotta go after her!"

Ryan doesn't even know if that's possible. He's been feeling better, sure, but he hasn't exactly been pushing his limits. He hasn't run anywhere in years.

Carole, Dannicka, Julian, and Chet, however, spring into action—racing after Marcy, who runs into the centre of the park and in the direction of their cars.

"Marcy!" her coach hollers.

She ignores him, her only thought to run as fast as possible.

"MARCY!" comes the unmistakeable sound of her dad's voice. This, too, goes ignored.

Marcy has gotten a head start and she's a fast runner, but Chet is faster. He catches up to her within seconds, then continues running past her. Suddenly, he spins around, stretches his long arms out wide, and catches her in a bear grip.

"Let go!" she yells, trying to wrench free.

"It's okay, it's okay!" he tries to tell her, but he knows she's not listening.

Dannicka, Julian, and Carole catch up to them but Ryan lags behind. He stops to catch his breath and is soon passed by Marcy's coach and dad.

"Watch out!" he calls breathlessly, trying to warn the others of the approaching reinforcements.

Dannicka looks behind her, panicked by what she sees.

"Ryan can't run!" she screams. She races back toward him and sees he is grimacing with pain. A few feet away, she hears Marcy scream at the top of her lungs.

"Here!" Dannicka says, reaching for Ryan's arm and draping it across her neck. "Put your weight on me, it's okay!"

Marcy screams again, and Carole, trying to get her attention, says "It's okay, Marcy, I promise! Shhh!"

Behind her, Marcy's dad is shouting, "GET YOUR HANDS OFF MY DAUGHTER!"

He lunges for Chet, but Julian jumps in between them.

"I know this looks bad..." he starts, but is instantly cut off by a fist to his jaw.

"Call the police!" Marcy's coach hollers, addressing the crowd that is gathering around.

Julian feels his head being to reel. He has never been hit so hard before.

"Please!" Carole begs. She jumps between Julian and Marcy's dad, banking on the hope that he will not hit a woman. "We're not going to hurt her, we just..."

We just what? But it doesn't matter because Marcy's dad is not listening. Marcy has turned into a wild animal and her dad is not going to stop until he rescues her. Chet still clutches her in a tight bear grip, but his face grows beet red from exertion. Carole tries to block Marcy's dad but he roughly pushes her aside, slamming her into the coach, who is trying to pry Chet's arms apart. Carole and the coach fall to the ground and she shrieks, instinctively gripping her shoulder bag.

About thirty feet away, Dannicka watches the chaos unfold. How did their plan turn to this? And so quickly? Desperately, she tries as hard as she can to drag Ryan, who is doubled over in pain, toward the group.

"Please, Ryan!" she begs. "We're almost there! Please!"

Ryan's sides are so cramped that he can't stand up straight and the muscles in both legs are seizing. He looks in horror at the situation he has created.

*I pulled these people in here with me*, he thinks in despair, *and I'm going to be the reason they won't get back!*

If it wasn't for Dannicka, he would be lying in a heap on the ground right now. She continues to drag him toward the others, despite his nearly dead weight. He doesn't know where she is finding the strength, but he will need to find some, too, even if it kills him.

"Please, just listen..." Julian pleads, trying again to appeal to Marcy's dad. *We're going to get ourselves arrested*, he thinks. "Listen, I—"

Once again, he is interrupted by a punch to the face. This time, he sees stars. His knees buckle and he drops to the ground, slumping against Chet and Marcy, who also lose their balance. Together they topple to the ground, colliding with Carole and Marcy's coach on their way down.

For an instant, Marcy thinks she has found her chance to break free. Through the tangle of arms and legs, she sees her dad's face looming above her. "Help me!" she screams.

Her dad lunges at Chet now, attempting to grab his arm, but the instant he does, Marcy feels the most unnatural rumbling beneath her.

"It's happening!" Dannicka screams at the group, now just 20 feet away. "It's happening!"

Just as it had in the coffee shop, the rumbling quickly turns into a violent jack-hammer-like staccato. Marcy's ear is squashed up against the side of Chet's face and she swears she can hear his teeth chattering inside his head. Suddenly, the jack-hammering is replaced by that same deep thrum passing thickly through their bodies, as if they are being pulled through a deep pool of quicksand. Mr. Biscuits cries out woefully and Carole grips him to her chest, engulfing him with her curled-up body.

After that, all is silent.

***

Slowly, Carole opens her eyes. She sees Mr. Biscuits looking back at her, shaken but unharmed. She lets out a sigh of relief.

Julian, disoriented, manages to prop himself up on his hands and knees. He braces himself for another blow but, when none comes, he tentatively raises his head.

Dannicka realizes that she has thrown the top half of her body over Ryan's in a protective effort. Ryan lays with his eyes squeezed shut, sweat covering his face and torso. Gingerly, she lifts herself off of him and looks into his face.

"Are you okay?!"

"Mm-hm," he grunts.

She looks up and sees a dazed Julian looking past her, into the park. Following his gaze, she immediately understands the expression on his face—Marcy's dad is no longer there. Marcy's coach is no longer there. The crowd that had gathered around them has also, apparently, disappeared.

Everyone but The Six is gone.

# PART II

# CHAPTER SEVEN

"Get OFF of me!" Marcy grunts.

Awkwardly, Chet gets to his feet, feeling disgusted with himself. It's like he has just beaten up a girl—and a much younger girl, too.

"I'm sorry," he says, panting. He wants to explain what has just happened, why he did what he did, but he has no idea where to even start. Instead, he says he's sorry, again.

Marcy stays where she is, lying on her side with half of her face buried in the grass. Chet extends a hand to help her up, but she swats it away and begins to cry.

Carole crawls over to her, reaches out to stroke her hair, then thinks better of it. Instead she says, gently, "we're really sorry, Marcy. But it's going to be okay."

Carole has absolutely no idea if the last part of her statement is true, but she has to say something—the poor girl is traumatized.

Julian, still on his hands and knees, slowly pulls himself into a sitting position. He twists the top half of his body away from the others and spits a mouthful of blood onto the grass.

"Are you okay?" asks Carole.

"Yeah," he says, his voice thick. "I would've done the same thing if it was one of my daughters." He wipes his mouth with the back of his hand, wincing from the touch, and inadvertently smears a trail of blood across his cheek.

Ryan, still flat on his back, manages to prop himself up on his elbows. His head is on fire but the knots in his legs are beginning to loosen. "What's going on?"

Dannicka looks around at the empty park which, only seconds ago, had been teeming with people. Now, the entire area looks as though there has been an emergency evacuation.

"They're all gone," she says in awe. "Everyone's gone."

She looks to the others a few feet away and hollers, "Everyone's gone,"—as if they don't already know— "and we're all still glowing!"

Carole sees the vacant ball diamond and the abandoned booths where, just moments ago, food and crafts were being offered. One second there, the next second, gone. Everybody gone. Despite this drastic, split-second change, there is a palpable stillness to the air—as though many years have passed since anyone had ever been here. She half-expects to see a tumbleweed drift by.

"Maybe it's much later in the evening," she calls back to Dannicka. But that can't be right—the early evening sun is still as bright as it was right before the shift. "Maybe everyone's gone home," she adds lamely.

Without warning, Marcy suddenly jumps to her feet and starts to run again. She doesn't know what's happening, but she needs to get away from these freaky glowing people, like, *now*.

"Oh, come *on*!" Chet wails, still trying to catch his breath. He jumps up to run after her and catches up within seconds. He reaches out and grabs one of her arms, as gently as possible, and forces her to stop. This time, she doesn't fight.

"Where *is* everyone?!" she wails. "What did you guys *do*?!"

Dannicka stands up and walks over to where Chet has stopped Marcy. Gently, she moves Chet aside and throws her arms around the girl. Marcy, now sobbing loudly, lets her.

"We're so sorry!" Dannicka exclaims. "We had to do it! We're trying to help you, honest to God!"

Her words in no way match the events which have just occurred, but for some reason, Marcy believes her. She lets this total stranger hug her, something she would never normally allow, and can't help but notice how comforting the hug is.

"It's a complicated story, but we'll explain it to you, okay?" Dannicka looks straight into Marcy's teary eyes.

"Okay," says Marcy, nodding.

"Your dad may already be at home. I know that sounds crazy, but we'll explain that, too."

She turns to Chet.

"Do you think you can drive right now? I think we need to get Marcy home."

"Yeah," he says. "For sure."

Dannicka sees the look of worry cross Marcy's face and realizes how the suggestion of being alone in a car with some random guy who has just tackled her to the ground would be beyond scary. "Don't worry," she adds quickly, "I'll go with you."

She looks over to Ryan, who has managed to sit up. To her relief, the colour in his face has returned,

"We'll drive you home, too," she offers. She feels manic. The shift wasn't easy—worse than last time—but at least it happened. And now they can all get back to their lives, right?

Julian spits another wad of blood onto the ground. "I don't think we should split up just yet."

Carole looks at him with concern. "Are you sure you're okay?"

He nods. "I'll be fine. I just think we should all stick together for now."

Carole knows what he's worried about, because she has the same concern—that the shift didn't work. They *have* shifted, that much is certain, but she'll be damned if this is the right place. They're no longer in the Facsimile World, but they're not in the real world either. So, where the hell are they? Catching Dannicka's eye then, she sees the same realization come over her.

Dannicka turns to Ryan. "Do you think you can walk back to the car right now? Probably not, right?" Without giving him a chance to respond, she adds, "I agree with Julian—we should all just wait for a few minutes and give everyone a chance to rest." No point in worrying Marcy even more.

"My gym bag is back there," Marcy sniffs, pointing over to the ball diamond.

"Why don't I go with you to get it?" Dannicka offers, doing her best to stay calm and, hopefully, appear reassuring. She can't have the girl bolting again.

As they walk away, Ryan finally gets to his feet—embarrassed by his inability to run, and humiliated by the way Dannicka had to help him. He joins the others and together they watch the two girls walk back to the diamond.

"I don't know about this being later in the day," says Carole. "The light hasn't changed at all."

"And the cars are still here" says Chet. "So, it's not like everyone just decided to bail."

"They *told* me it would work!" Ryan spits through clenched teeth. "They told me that all we had to do was to *be* together to shift back, and now what the fuck *is* this?!"

"What if we got left behind again?" asks Chet, beginning to feel panicked. "And, what if this world isn't going to last long, either? What if—?"

"We didn't get left behind," says Carole abruptly. "This is a different place. I can feel it."

"In that case," says Julian, keeping his gaze fixed on Marcy and Dannicka, "we definitely should stick together."

***

Marcy is totally confused. She's barely had any time to digest the bizarre chain of events that has just occurred, and doesn't know what to think. She has no idea why these glowing people needed to get to her so desperately and yet, she isn't scared. In fact, she's already starting to feel like she wants to be with them too—it seems like the safest choice, somehow, and not only because there aren't any other people around.

After walking a few steps, Dannicka links an arm with hers and it feels like the most natural thing in the world. This is weird, because Marcy would never walk like this with any of her friends. Dannicka, whose name she didn't even know until a moment ago, is her friend, though; she has no doubt about that.

"Something happened to all of us when we went through that earthquake last month," Dannicka begins. She is going to have to be careful with her explanation—Marcy has already been through enough.

"It wasn't really an earthquake," she continues. "We were sort of...pushed into another world, one that seemed almost exactly like ours. You might have noticed some things that didn't seem right."

"Like glowing people?"

"Exactly. And we still don't really know *why* we're glowing. You know, you can't see it, but you're glowing, too."

Marcy does not respond. What is there to say when you've just heard the most mind-blowing thing of your entire life? She holds up the arm not linked with Dannicka's, inspecting it thoroughly. She can't see any glowing skin, but she knows Dannicka is telling her the truth. Just imagine—she's actually *glowing*. Like she's a superhero, or something.

"We might not be back in the right place just yet," says Dannicka carefully. "But the place we just left was not going to last forever. It was sort of...degrading, and we needed to get out."

"But, what about all the people?"

Dannicka braces herself. "I know it's a lot to ask right now to expect you to trust me..."

Marcy cuts her off, "I trust you," she says firmly. She means it.

Dannicka places a hand on Marcy's elbow, which is locked into her own. "When we were 'pushed' into that other world, the one we just left, we were the only people there from the real world. All those people we just left behind were...they were all fake."

She keeps her hand over Marcy's elbow and stops talking, allowing this new information to be absorbed.

"We all just wanted to get back to normal," Dannicka adds after a moment has passed. "And we were told that if we all got back together, it would happen. The very last thing we wanted was to scare you, which is why we were hiding. And when you took off, we didn't know what else to do. We never planned for that, and I'm sorry."

Marcy, grappling with all this information, can only nod.

In silence, they walk beside the deserted ball diamond and over to the benches where Marcy has left her gym bag. The entire area is littered with bats and gloves, baseballs and water bottles.

*None of it was real*, Marcy thinks in awe.

On the other side of the chain-link fence, the same cars are lined up on the street, all of them empty. Her dad's car must still be parked on the other side, but that wasn't really her dad. Who was he?

"This is mine," Marcy says, lifting the heavy bag over her shoulder.

"Do you want me to carry that?"

"No, I got it."

Together they turn and head back to where the others are standing solemnly in the middle of the park, looking like the only other people in the world. Just before they get within earshot, Marcy leans in.

"How do you know all this?"

"Well," Dannicka says, thinking she's already given Marcy enough to think about for now, "I think Ryan can explain that part. I'll introduce you. And, by the way, they're all safe."

"I know."

\*\*\*

It is decided that they will all go to Chet's place first, as he lives the closest. No one suggests they go their separate ways again, or even split up into groups—the idea now seems unthinkable.

"Maybe we could use the phone when we get to your place," says Julian. There's no one to call, and the other adults know it, but Julian's family is in Calgary—he has to at least try.

As they walk back toward the cars, Carole lifts Mr. Biscuits out of her bag, and sets him on the grass.

"Is that...a dog?" asks Marcy, unsure.

Carole laughs a little. "Yes, it is. I know, he's very unusual-looking."

Marcy watches the little ball of wiry fur as he waddles over the grass alongside Carole. She doesn't care that he looks weird—she feels an instant affection for him.

"Well, I think he's cute," she says. Carole smiles, relieved that Marcy seems to be warming to them. It's the only thing to be relieved about. Something feels very...off. It's not just the fact that they 've failed to get back, nor that this place appears devoid of life. Something about it is wrong in a way that wasn't present in that previous facsimile world. Right now, she would actually prefer to be back there, degrading or not.

They walk past an abandoned face-painting station, the paints still displayed as if in mid-use. Marcy stops to look at it.

"Where is everyone? I mean, the real people?"

"We're gonna figure this all out," says Julian. He feels guilty for lying, for brushing off the severity of the situation. He always tries to be as honest as possible with his own kids, because kids can usually tell when you're bullshitting them—but he's never been through anything like this before. What can he say? We're all screwed? He has to give her hope.

Chet wants to ask if any of the others can see that weird colour in the sky. It's subtle, but it's there. It's like a faint shade of pale purple. It reminds him of the lilac trees in his front yard, but for some reason it makes him feel sick. He's never seen a sky this colour before and to say he doesn't like it would be an understatement. He wants to ask, but decides not to. It's not just a group of adults anymore—Marcy is with them now, and he's already scared her enough.

When they arrive at the other end of the park, Julian, whose jaw and face are still throbbing, asks Carole if she will drive his car.

"Sure," she says, "Marcy, do you want to hold Mr. Biscuits in the back seat?"

She does.

Ryan and Dannicka climb into Chet's car.

"We'll follow you," says Carole.

She takes the keys from Julian's outstretched hand and gets in the driver's seat before reaching across to unlock the other doors. After getting herself situated, she reaches for her seatbelt and catches sight of the houses directly across from where they are parked. A ripple of fear flutters somewhere inside her chest.

There is nothing extraordinary about the houses—they are well-maintained, average-looking 1960s bungalows, but one in particular seems clouded over with an awful sense of foreboding.

*Something terrible happened in there.* She doesn't know where this thought has come from, but there is no doubt in her mind. She knows better than to say it out loud, especially with Marcy in the back seat. Instead, she starts the car, eager to get away.

Getting to Chet's house proves more difficult than they anticipated. The side-streets are manageable, but the main roads are strewn with abandoned vehicles. Carole follows Chet as he zig-zags between them, sometimes driving over meridians.

"Good thing it wasn't a weekday," she says. "Or rush hour."

Block after block, they encounter the same scene: empty vehicles, no functioning traffic lights, no signs of any life anywhere. Twice, when their path is completely blocked, Chet and Dannicka jump out to move empty vehicles that still have keys in the ignition.

*I could take any one of them*, thinks Dannicka, who has wanted a car for so long. But, as she stands on the overpass overlooking the Whytemud freeway, the idea doesn't seem right. Not from a moral standpoint, necessarily. Something about getting behind the wheel of a vehicle whose driver has just vanished is creepy, to say the least.

"It looks like some kind of post-apocalyptic movie," says Chet.

"I know," she agrees. Only, seeing it for real is not so entertaining.

Finally, they all arrive at Chet's house. He pulls into his driveway and parks beside his dad's car. He has more than a sneaking suspicion that he will not find his dad here, which is just fine as far as he's concerned. What he believed was his dad for the last month was apparently not. How could he have missed that? No wonder he was so anxious. He shudders at the thought of his facsimile parents—eating meals with them, sleeping under the same roof... so gross.

Everything about Chet's large house looks the same as it always has, but now there is a feeling that if he was to walk through the front door, he would be swallowed. If he was alone right now, he would get back in his car and drive as far away from here as possible. So far, this 'Empty World', for lack of a better name, is giving him an extreme case of the creeps.

"Come on in," he says, not wanting to go in by himself. What if there's something worse than facsimiles in there?"

"Do you have anything to drink?" asks Dannicka, reluctantly following Chet into the house. She shivers despite the heat.

"Yeah, probably," he says distractedly. "Help yourselves to whatever—the kitchen's back that way."

He separates himself from the rest of the group and walks cautiously through the house, glancing briefly into each room.

*There's nothing here*, he tells himself. Nothing hiding in any of the closets, no monsters under any of the beds. He's lived in this house for most of his life and only now realizes just how big it is. The labyrinth-like hallways in the basement, its nooks and crannies especially great for hide-and-seek as a kid, all now seem excessive. Still, it's just his house...nothing about it has changed. So, why is he so freaked out?

*Because you've just been through some real messed-up shit*, he tells himself. *Now, quit being a baby and finish your inspection.*

"The power's out," he says, rejoining the others who are somewhat huddled together in the kitchen. This comes as no surprise to anyone.

"The phone's dead, too," says Julian reluctantly.

For a moment, no one says a word. *If it weren't for Marcy*, thinks Dannicka, *I'd be screaming right now*.

Carole looks at Chet.

"Well, you can't stay here alone," she says. "Why don't we all go to my place? We can stay there until...until we get back."

Carole would really like to get the hell out of this house. In fact, she would really like to get the hell away from the entire south-side. She has always loved this part of the city—she nearly bought a house here. But something is wrong now. She can feel it the same way that she feels it will be better at her own house in the west-end.

"It's already nine o'clock, though," says Julian, looking at his watch. "Don't you live quite a ways from here?"

"It's about a fifteen, maybe twenty, minute drive."

"That could take hours. It'll be dark before we get there. Maybe we should just camp out here for the night. You okay with that, Chet?"

"Yeah, for sure."

He tries to hide his relief. There is no way he could spend the night in this place alone. He doesn't want to be separated from the others, either, and he's pretty sure that feeling is mutual.

"Would it be alright if we sit outside?" asks Carole. "I see you have a nice patio out there." *God, get me out of this house.*

"Yeah, for sure," says Chet.

They seat themselves around a large patio table and, for the first time that evening, there is a calm—though it is far from comforting. The silence surrounding them is almost unbearable. There is no din of traffic, no planes flying overhead, no sound of other voices or any other people. Like Dannicka earlier, the other adults in the group feel that, if it wasn't for Marcy's presence, there would be full-on panic—but the desire to protect her is stronger than their fear.

Carole looks over to Marcy, who is clutching Mr. Biscuits like her life depends on it.

"Are you hungry, Marcy? When's the last time you ate?"

"I'm okay."

"We should all eat something," says Dannicka, feeling like this might instill some kind of normalcy. "Is there anything we could eat?"

"Yeah," Chet replies. "Probably."

He leads her into the kitchen where they put together a make-shift meal.

"I thought yesterday was the weirdest day of my life," he tells her. "But, apparently, I was wrong."

Dannicka arranges cold cuts and cheese on a large plate. *Better eat them now before they spoil*, she thinks. Who knows when, or if, the power will come back on. There's running water, though, albeit cold, which is a welcome surprise.

"Tell me about it," she says.

"Hey, did you notice anything weird about the sky back there?"

"Yeah—I didn't want to mention it earlier. That gross pale purple."

"What do you think that is?"

Dannicka sighs. "It's this place, I guess. I don't know, but for some reason, I think it'll be better over at Carole's."

Chet does, too.

When the food is set out, Marcy is the first to eat which puts the others at ease. There will be time to discuss things among the adults later tonight, but for now, Carole wants to keep this gathering as pleasant as possible.

"This is a beautiful house, Chet. Do you have any brothers or sisters?"

"I've got an older brother—he lives in Winnipeg."

"Oh. What do your parents do?"

"My dad's a dentist, and my mom works for the city."

He has to remind himself to continue using the present tense. They're not dead, they're just...somewhere else.

"What about you?" Dannicka asks Ryan, who has not spoken a word since his outburst in the park. "Do you have any brothers or sisters?

"I have an older sister, but I don't see her much. She doesn't live here. And I had a brother, but he died."

"Oh!" she says. "I'm sorry."

"It's okay. I mean, it's not okay, but I never knew him. He died before I was born."

"That's too bad," she says, not knowing what else to say. So far, both of her attempts at conversation with Ryan have managed to bring up something painful. *Way to go*, she tells herself, embarrassed.

"When are we getting out of this place?" Marcy asks, suddenly.

The group falls silent.

"I mean, how do we know we're gonna get out of here?"

Julian clears his throat and tries to explain. "There are...people who have been trying to help us. They want us to get back as much as we do." He looks over at Ryan, adding, "I'm sure they'll want to get in touch with us very soon. Maybe even tonight."

"Where are they?"

"Well, we can't see them. They communicate only with Ryan—through his dreams."

As fantastical as this sounds, Marcy—for reasons she can't explain—knows that these people are telling the truth.

"Where do they live?" she asks, taking a bite of her peanut butter sandwich.

"I don't know," says Ryan. He starts to say something, then stops himself. Instead, he says, "this entire thing is so messed up, Marcy, but I get the feeling that you're a smart girl and I think you can handle it."

She likes the sound of that.

"I don't know where they're from, but I know it's not here. I get the impression that they live...between the worlds. Do you know what I mean?"

She isn't sure, but she nods gravely.

"What do they look like?"

"I've never seen them."

"So, you just hear their voices?"

"Sort of. In the dreams it's my cat speaking to me. But, obviously, I know it's not really the cat."

Marcy looks stunned. After a beat, she bursts out laughing. "That's really funny!"

Her reaction takes Ryan by surprise. "I guess it is," he agrees.

\*\*\*

By eleven o'clock, with no change to their situation, Julian reluctantly suggests they sort out sleeping arrangements. He's spent the last couple of hours hoping against hope for that tell-tale rumble to start up beneath his feet, but is now resigned to dealing with more immediate concerns.

"My bedroom's in the basement," says Chet. "There's another bedroom down there, and then three more upstairs..."

Decisions are made quickly: Marcy and Dannicka will share Chet's parents' room, Ryan will take one of the upstairs rooms, and, to Chet's relief, Carole will take the downstairs room next to his. Julian declines the remaining bedroom, opting to sleep on the couch instead. He doesn't need to say why.

\*\*\*

## SUNDAY, JULY 2

Dannicka is dreaming about a man in a long, dirty coat. He stands on the balcony of her apartment with his back to her, his gloved hands gripping the metal railing. The sky is a sickening shade of lilac stretching out in all directions. Somehow, she knows he is pleased by this.

Completely unnerved, she stands frozen in her living room staring at this unknown man. How did he get in? She didn't let him in, did she? No—she would have remembered that. He must have gotten in without her knowing. Does he know she's here?

The sliding door between them is closed, thank God, but what she doesn't know is whether or not it is locked. Did she lock it? She tries to remember. Should she lock it now? Doing so could alert the man to her presence.

Maybe she should just run.

\*\*\*

Dannicka wakes with a start.

It doesn't take long to orient herself; the scent of unfamiliar laundry detergent on the sheets and a sleeping Marcy next to her are instant reminders of the bizarre situation she is currently in. She sits up and rubs her eyes with one hand, quietly releasing a shaky breath.

*What the hell was that*, she wonders, recalling the dream of the man on her balcony. It's been one of her greatest fears since she started living alone—that someone would break in while she was there and attack her. It's at least half of the reason she lets Todd sleep over so often.

She turns to the nightstand where Chet's mom or dad has placed a clock radio, its giant red digits proclaiming '13:09'. It's weird – it should be 1:09, but the time has obviously been set incorrectly.

Resigned to being awake, Dannicka lies back on the pillow and hopes for sleep to return, grateful for the company of Marcy sleeping beside her.

\*\*\*

5:45 a.m. The last time Chet was awake at this time of day was when he was on the school's swim team last year. That seems like a million years ago, now. Is it too early to get out of bed and go upstairs? He doesn't want to wake the others. He's restless, having barely slept at all during the night, worried about the frickin' boogey man or some other stupid horror-movie shit coming for him. Real or not, he would really like to get a move-on, already, and get the hell out of here.

He isn't alone in the kitchen for long. The others join him, one by one, each appearing to have had as little sleep as he did. Ryan is the last to enter.

"Nothing from Roland," he says before anyone can ask. He's worried about his own Roland, the actual cat, back in the real world. So far, from what he's seen of this place, there doesn't seem to be any animals here, either. Carole's weird dog is here, but only because he was with them during the original shift. That means his real Roland has been alone for an entire month. The thought is unbearable.

"Chet," says Carole, "do you mind if we bring a few supplies over to my place? I don't think I've got enough sheets and towels for everyone."

Together they gather some linens, food, and anything else that might be useful.

"You don't mind if we leave, do you, Chet?" she asks. "Because..."

"No," he cuts her off. "I wanna get out of here."

Carole tries not to look obviously relieved, although she's sure she and Chet aren't alone in wanting to get away from this house.

"I don't think we should bother taking the Whytemud," says Carole. "From what I saw last night, it just looked way too packed. We'll have to take the long way."

Julian shrugs. "What else do we have to do today?" *Besides try to get home*, he thinks, biting back the worry that kept him up all night. He had stupidly assumed they would all just get together and presto, life would be back to normal, never entertaining any real thoughts about failure. *What happens now*, he wants to implore. *What do we do? What the hell do we do?!* Instead, he adopts the no-worries attitude that has gotten him through many of his wife's blow ups and daughters' temper tantrums. He is now responsible for keeping this group together.

As a group, they decide on a route to Carole's house in the west-end.

"We'll be going past my place," says Dannicka. "Does anyone mind if I stop in to get some stuff?"

"Not at all," says Julian.

Dannicka's apartment, which would be a ten-minute drive from Chet's place under normal circumstances, takes nearly an hour to reach. When they arrive, she looks at her building with a sense of dread.

"Would one of you mind coming in with me?" she asks.

Ryan and Chet, both in the car with her, offer their company.

"Maybe we should all go," she suggests. She doesn't say why—she doesn't need to. The three step out of Chet's car and wave to Carole, Marcy and Julian, who have parked behind them.

As expected, the lobby is empty. Dannicka absent-mindedly thinks about checking her mailbox, then shudders—as if she cares about anything sent to her in this place. They climb three flights of stairs, naturally lit through the three-story windows from the lobby, to reach the top floor. The moment she opens the door to the hallway, they are met with total darkness.

"Here," says Ryan, reaching into his jeans pocket for his lighter. He ignites it and holds the flame high above his head.

Together they proceed down the long, eerily silent hallway without speaking. There is nothing behind any of the closed doors they pass, Dannicka knows this for sure, but she wouldn't be willing to test that theory for any amount of money.

"This is it, here," she says, reaching into her purse for her keys.

She unlocks the door and, for the briefest of moments, pauses before stepping inside. The memory of last night's dream flashes through her mind. She can still see that man on her balcony looking out at that sickly sky.

*Maybe it wasn't a dream,* she thinks. *Maybe it was a premonition. He could be here right now.*

She forces herself to step over the threshold, refusing to let her imagination run wild.

Once inside, the three quickly ascertain that Dannicka's place is as empty as Chet's. Strangely, it looks exactly the same as when she was last here, just...yesterday? How can that be? Ryan can't help but notice a few items lying around the apartment that obviously belong to a guy. He is surprised to find himself disappointed. How lame of him—of course she would have a boyfriend.

Something about Chet's house had bothered Dannicka, but as she gathers her things she realizes that her own place gives her the same creepy feeling, and not just because of the dream. The sooner she can get away from it, the better.

"Okay, I think I got everything I need," she says, trying to sound unbothered. "Let's get out of here."

Back outside, the two cars resume their trip, slowly down 109th Street, cautiously down the steep winding road at the end, then on to the Walterdale Bridge. Thankfully, it is nearly empty. As Julian drives across it, Carole—in the passenger seat beside him—experiences a tremendous wave of relief. A huge weight seems to lift from her shoulders, confirming her suspicions that they were right to leave the south-side. There is something dreadfully wrong there—something she doesn't care to investigate. She glances sideways at Julian, who returns her look. *He feels it, too*, she thinks. But neither of them says a word for fear of worrying Marcy, who is in the back with Mr. Biscuits.

The first thing Chet notices as he drives across the bridge, is that the air on the other side is clear, and thankfully normal. There is no sign of that gross lilac-coloured haze.

"Oh my God!" Dannicka exclaims as Chet drives down into the river valley. "What a relief!"

*So, I'm not the only one who noticed*, thinks Ryan.

"Right now," says Chet, "I don't care if I never see the south-side again."

# CHAPTER EIGHT

Ryan wakes up to his new normal—no headache, no pain, and no contact from Roland. He and the others are beginning to think that Roland cannot reach them here; wherever 'here' is. There is also the possibility that Roland has lost them in the second shift and doesn't know where they are now. Ryan is sure he's not the only one who has considered this, although no one has said it out loud.

From across the rec room in Carole's basement, he hears Chet snoring softly. For the past ten nights, they have camped out here—Ryan on a futon at one end of the wide-open room, and Chet in a sleeping bag at the other end. It seems strange that after only a week and a half Chet feels like a brother to him. In fact, the more time they all spend together the stronger the bond between them grows. Because of this, communal living (something Carole actually did for a brief stint in her twenties) has come naturally to them all. This surprises Ryan the most; he's always been something of a loner, and since the accident had become a near-recluse. Now, however, it's been so easy to be around these people. They seem to understand him and accept who he is without any expectations. As crazy as it sounds, he actually feels for them in a way he hasn't felt before—especially Dannicka. Each morning, when he wakes up, she is the one he's most eager to see.

He'd been wary of what shifting for a second time would do to his body, but as each day passes there is a noticeable improvement; he can literally feel himself getting stronger. He ditched the cane a few weeks ago in the facsimile world, but now even his limp is virtually gone.

Ryan gets up easily from the futon and quietly leaves the rec room, closing the door behind him. Making his way past the laundry room and storage area, he walks into the bathroom and braces himself for the ice-cold shower. There is still no hot water to be found in this world, but it's better than no water at all.

After his shower, he gets dressed, then treads quietly upstairs. Wandering into the kitchen, he sees Dannicka sitting alone at the table.

"Good morning!" she sing-songs quietly.

He grins; he can't help himself. "Morning."

He pours himself a cup of coffee, which Dannicka has brewed in the backyard over their make-shift fire pit. She's become the resident fire maker, being far more adept at it than anyone else. No one was more surprised to discover this than Dannicka, who has always hated camping and had never even attempted to build a fire before.

"Everyone else still sleeping?" Ryan asks. He knows that the answer is an obvious yes, but inquires for the sole purpose of talking to her.

"Yeah," she says. "I got up early because Marcy kept kicking me."

He chuckles. "Classic Marcy."

He appreciates the fact that she never asks if he's heard from Roland during the night. None of the others do, either, but Dannicka never gives the impression that she is even thinking about it.

"It's gonna be hot again, today," she says.

"Yeah."

"Do you wanna go on walk about with me? We could go after breakfast, before it gets too hot."

Definitely. "Okay."

"Or—it's so early, we could go now before everyone else gets up, and then we could come back for breakfast."

Even better. He takes a gulp of the hot coffee. "Sounds good."

Every morning for the past week, The Six have split into pairs and explored different areas of the neighbourhood. After a few days, they all realized that there was no knowledge to be gained—no clues as to where they are or what is happening. But they continue with the ritual anyway, still referring to it as 'walk about' even though it's now done on bikes found in Carole's neighbourhood. Ryan, who never imagined he might be able to ride a bike again, loves it. Especially when he's paired with Dannicka.

They get their bikes from the backyard and steer them quietly onto the deserted street.

"Which way do you want to go?" she asks.

He hops onto his bike. "You choose."

\*\*\*

In the first few days after arriving at Carole's, the six made trips to Marcy's house in the west end, and to Ryan's apartment in the downtown neighbourhood of Oliver. Both residences were devoid of any signs of life, as expected. At Marcy's house, she generously helped herself to more CDs from her sister's collection, and quite a few items of clothing from her closet. Ryan entered his own place alone, not wanting any of them to see the state of disarray in which he lived. After checking for Roland and finding nothing, he stuffed some clothes into a gym bag and left without looking back.

Neither Marcy's nor Ryan's homes seemed clouded by that same sense of foreboding they had felt at Chet's and Dannicka's homes on the south-side, but there was no desire to linger in either place.

Unable to get to his own house in Calgary, Julian has had to make do with clothes from Ryan and Chet, neither of whom share his stockier frame. There has been an unspoken agreement not to enter any of the empty homes in the city, where he would likely find more suitable clothes. Somehow, the mere thought is unnerving, like walking on top of somebody's grave. There are plenty of items— like food and toiletries—they could be getting from the houses in Carole's neighbourhood. In fact, Carole's next-door neighbour has become a good friend of hers and would be more than happy to help. However, they prefer the idea of getting what they need from stores and other places in the area that carry no personal attachment. Carole and Julian have discussed it, and if the time comes for more supplies, they will deal with it. In the meantime, Julian has taken to wearing Chet's over-sized rock band t-shirts, which make the others laugh. He doesn't mind, though—anything to make this situation more bearable.

No one talks about whether or not they will actually be able to get back, but the doubt is there, hovering over every conversation and lingering in every silence. Julian tries to shut that thought out, too—the mere suggestions that he may never see his wife and daughters again is devastating.

***

Marcy has lost track of the days. Yesterday, she heard Julian say that it was July 11th and that really blew her mind. It doesn't feel like they've been in this world for eleven days—it feels like they've been here for at least a month, but not in a bad way. Yes, she does miss her parents—although it's not uncommon to go two weeks without seeing her dad—but honestly, she doesn't really miss her sister or brother. Not yet, anyway. She doesn't miss the constant fights with them, that's for sure. And getting to be the youngest in the group, for once, does make her feel a little special. She really likes being around these people, too. She can't explain it; it's like she knows she's safe with them, and none of them treat her like a kid. It sort of feels like they're all on a long camping trip together at the quietest campground in the world.

The absolute quiet did bother her at first; she's never been comfortable when things are too quiet. But, after a couple of days, she realized just how freeing it is—she can scream at the top of her lungs, sing loudly in her off-key voice, and shout at the others whenever they play baseball or soccer together. And no one ever complains—or tells her to be quiet.

She and Dannicka have been sleeping on the futon in Carole's studio, and every night feels like a slumber party. Dannicka is one of the coolest girls Marcy has ever known. And Carole's studio is awesome. There are so many crazy paintings in it, and sculptures, and all kinds of art supplies. It's like being in a little art gallery.

The one thing that Marcy really misses, however, is Bernadette. She's been trying to get it into her head that the whole month of June never happened in the real world—no embarrassing dance recital, and no huge fight with her best friend. Bernadette never really bailed on her, never left Marcy to fend for herself on stage. Marcy was already missing Bernadette after she stopped talking to her in the facsimile world, but now that their fight never happened, she misses her even more.

\*\*\*

Chet finds himself thinking about his parents. Where do they think he is? Have they sent out a search party? Put all of their pictures on posters throughout the province? He thinks about his friends waiting out in the car; how long did it take before they realized something was wrong?

"Carole," he says, changing the subject in his own head, "have you been everywhere in the world?"

He stands in her dining room taking a good look at each of the framed photos in the gallery that covers an entire wall. They depict a wide variety of subjects: landscapes, monuments, ruins, castles, oceans, animals, and a lot of other awesome scenes. Carole is in many of the pictures, often with people who appear to be from all around the world, and in every one she seems completely at home—nothing tourist-y about her. Chet recognizes some of the settings—the pyramids in Egypt, Ayres Rock in Australia—but most of them are unfamiliar.

"I have been to a lot of places," Carole says. "I always tried to spend at least six months somewhere, to really get a feel for the place. I have lived on every continent, except Antarctica."

"Wow. That must've been pretty cool."

"It's not for everyone," she says. "My sister has only ever lived in Edmonton, and she's fine with that."

He notices that she didn't say 'here' ; that her sister has only ever lived 'here'.

*This place looks a lot like Edmonton,* he thinks, *but it isn't.*

"Have you done much travelling?" she asks.

"Not really, no."

Chet's parents have never been big on travelling. Once, when he was a kid, they took him to Disneyland where he'd had a total blast. He was told it was the happiest place on Earth, and that sounded about right. So, what would be the point of going anywhere else? As he listens to Carole talk about her life though, he realizes that he's been pretty clueless about the rest of the world. If he ever gets out of here, he's going to make sure he sees it.

***

It has been too hot in the afternoons to do much of anything, and today is no exception. Not wanting to expend any unnecessary energy, the six lounge in the shade of Carole's backyard. The younger four are reading, having discovered Carole's vast library of books spanning nearly every genre (except romance, which she has no patience for), but Julian, never much of a reader, is helping Carole pick baby carrots from her garden for dinner.

"Should she be reading that?" he asks, gesturing toward Marcy, who is across the yard—immersed in Stephen King's 'The Shining'.

Carole shrugs. "She said she likes to be scared."

"Still..."

"I know, I gave it a second thought, too. But I just hate to discourage young people from reading. And, if she has the comprehension...I read quite a lot of adult books when I was her age," she smiles at Julian, "and I think I turned out okay."

He chuckles.

When Chet and Marcy discovered that they both wanted to read 'The Shining', and that neither wanted to wait until the other was done, they made a deal. Marcy, who grabbed the book off the shelf first, told Chet she would 'share' reading with him on one condition:

that while waiting for his turn, he would read the 'Anne of Green Gables' series.

"Anne of Green Gables?!" he'd wailed. "Why don't I just cut my balls off?"

"You're gross!" she'd laughed. "And they're good books! Take it or leave it."

Now, whenever it's Chet's turn for the Anne books, he makes a loud production of it—groaning, sighing, rolling his eyes...the works. Secretly, he finds them surprisingly good.

In the evening, after the dinner dishes have been cleared and washed, the six once again retreat to Carole's back yard. The four younger members now listening to their Discmans.

"It's too bad we can't all listen to music together," says Carole. She has a portable CD player but batteries don't seem to last in this place—they can't get through one disc without having to replace them.

"We don't all like the same music, though," says Chet, thinking about his contribution to their community CD collection. He's brought some of his favourites including Nirvana, Smashing Pumpkins, and Pearl Jam, all of which have proven too heavy for Carole's taste. She prefers the Jane Siberry CD that Dannicka has brought. She finds the music thoughtful and deep—even the song about dogs, to which she can relate.

"You know, I used to be in a band," says Julian. "Back in the 80s. And we were pretty popular."

"No way!" says Chet. "What was your band's name?"

"New Clear Winter," Julian says, spelling it out for them. "Do you get it?"

Chet snickers, "We get it."

"I have the cassette in my glove box..." he trails off.

"Can I hear it?" asks Marcy.

"Oh, I don't know. It's pretty out there. Really artistic stuff."

Marcy thinks about all the artwork around Carole's house, not just her own creations but other pieces she's picked up from all over the world, and can't see how art would apply to music. "I like artistic stuff," she says.

"Well...are you sure?"

"Yeeess!" she insists.

"Well...okay. Come on out front. I'll use the car stereo so we can all hear it."

"Won't that drain the battery?" Chet asks.

"Yes," Julian laughs. "But it'll be worth it. You can help me jump-start it later."

In the driveway, he opens all of his car's doors and gets inside. He turns the key in the ignition to the accessory mode.

"This was one of our most popular songs," he tells the others. "Check it out!"

He presses play.

*Burning ashes from a cigarette*
*There's just one thing that I still regret*
*It's stepping onto that private jet*
*And leaving you behind...*

"This is so bad," says Marcy.

By the time the song reaches the chorus, Marcy, Dannicka, Chet, and Ryan are all laughing at the crudely recorded, amateur-sounding rock song.

"It's not *that* bad," says Carole. "I mean, for the time period..."

"Check out my drum fills!" Julian exclaims, miming along to each and every one. This sends the group into absolute hysterics. By the time the song is over, there are tears in their eyes. It's the first time any of them have laughed like that since arriving here.

"I didn't think it was *that* funny," says Julian in mock offence.

"Better than 'Kids in the Hall'," Ryan laughs, remembering one of his favourite TV shows. He looks over at Dannicka and sees that she is already looking at him. It's a look he has not received since he last had a girlfriend.

\*\*\*

"Does anyone feel like doing yoga with me?" asks Carole.

It's nearly nine o'clock and the sun is beginning to lower into the horizon. "It's finally cooled off a bit, or at least, it's not so blazing hot—I feel like I've been sitting for most of the day."

"I'll try," says Dannicka. "I've always wanted to do yoga."

"Well, I haven't done it in at least ten years," says Carole. "So, I'm gonna be rusty. What about you, Marcy?"

Marcy is lying on her back on a large blanket with Mr. Biscuits curled up beside her.

"Huh?" she asks, removing her headphones.

"Do you want to try yoga with us?"

"Yeah, okay," she replies, jumping up. She's not even sure what yoga is.

"Gentlemen?" Carole looks to the three men sitting around the patio table engaged in a card game. "Can I tempt you?"

"Not me," says Julian. "I've already been laughed at enough for one day."

"Sounds like it's for girls," Chet adds.

"Ryan?" Dannicka asks, raising an eyebrow.

It's all the encouragement he needs. He jumps to his feet a little too eagerly, stumbles, and the others laugh.

"Oh, knock it off," he mutters, suppressing a smile.

He is suddenly struck by the glaring contrast between his comfortable living situation here and the home he grew up in—where his mom was always tightly-wound and constantly peppering him with questions and concerns (Was he sick? Was he hungry? Where was he going? What did he do when he was out? Was he careful whenever he went out in public? Did he do or eat anything that could make him sick?); where his dad forever buried himself in the newspaper, or the TV, or out in the garage; where his older sister was so frustrated with their parents that she was frequently AWOL until she eventually moved out for good; where the ghost of the brother he never knew hung constantly in the air; where the living room remained closed off, waiting for company that rarely made an appearance.

"I guess I could give it a try," he says, trying to save face by sounding nonchalant.

Chet snickers to himself, and Ryan swats the brim of his backwards ballcap as he walks past.

"It could be really good for you," Carole says. "It could really aid in the healing process."

She spends an hour trying to remember as many of the poses as she can. Dannicka is surprised at how deceptively difficult it is, and Ryan struggles even more than she does. Even though he's been getting stronger, he doesn't have very much flexibility yet. Still, he appreciates the chance to try something new.

Marcy also enjoys the challenge. Unlike the others, she flows almost effortlessly from one pose to the next as though she's been doing this for years. When they are done, Carole tells her how impressed she is.

"Wow—you're a real natural!"

"A lot of it reminded me of stuff we did with The Dancetasticks," Marcy says simply.

At the mention her dance troupe's name, Carole and Dannicka let out a little laugh. They don't want to hurt Marcy's feelings, but they find the name hilarious. Marcy had already told them about her catastrophic performance with The Dancetasticks, and their hearts went out to her.

"You know, Marcy, I used to take dance when I was younger," says Dannicka. "Maybe tomorrow night you could show me some of your moves—we could work on something together."

"What about now?"

"Ugh, I'm too tired." Dannicka stands up and grabs a towel from the back of a patio chair, then mops her face and neck. "But, tomorrow night, for sure."

"I wish it was tomorrow night right now," Marcy says, slumping in her chair.

"Don't ever wish your time away," Carole tells her. "There's only a finite amount of it and we never get it back."

Chet lifts his head from the card game and looks over.

"Okay," Marcy corrects herself. "Then, I'm really looking forward to tomorrow night."

***

At eleven o'clock, Julian stands up and announces that he is going to bed.

"I should go, too," says Carole. "Marcy?"

Marcy is half asleep on a blanket by the fire, once again cuddled up with Mr. Biscuits. Groggy, she gets to her feet, picks up the dog, and walks into the house.

"I'll be there in a minute," Dannicka calls after her.

Dannicka, Ryan, and Chet have routinely stayed up later than the others, but tonight, Chet senses that they want to be alone. He more than senses it, actually—they might as well be wearing neon signs.

"I'm gonna go to bed, too," he says, standing up and stretching. "Night, guys."

He feels a pang of loneliness for Lindsay, which is stupid considering that the dance they shared on grad night, the make out session at the after-grad party, and the subsequent secret phone conversations—all of which he'd felt guilty about—never really happened. For some reason, the idea of Lindsay as a facsimile doesn't bother him like it does with his parents. And anyway, weren't the facsimiles acting in the same way their real counterparts would have? Wouldn't the real Lindsay act the same way in all those situations? It really does seem like he kinda got to know her. And maybe the real Lindsay will want to get to know him, too. If he ever gets back, he's going to break up with Kelley, first rule of business, and ask Lindsay out.

Ryan and Dannicka sit next to each other beside the fire, marvelling at the exquisite array of stars twinkling brightly against the nearly-black sky. The silence of this world, at first unsettling, now feels incredibly peaceful.

"Don't you worry about your parents?" Dannicka asks. "What they're going through with you missing?"

Ryan grunts. "My mom's probably lost her shit completely by now. I know I should feel bad but, honestly, I haven't minded the break. I just hope she isn't turning my dad's life into a living hell over it."

He stirs the embers in the fire pit.

"I guess I'm just feeling guilty," she says.

"What have *you* got to feel guilty for? You didn't do anything wrong—none of this is your fault." *It's mine*, he adds to himself.

"No, not...this," she says. "It's just...my dad and I used to be close, ever since my mom died. But we had this falling out a few months ago. I haven't told any of you guys yet, but my name used to be Maureen. And when I changed it, he got really upset. I don't blame him."

"Why did you change it?"

She sighs. "I'd just gone through this really bad break-up. I just... didn't want to be *me* anymore."

She tells him about her relationship with Eric and how she'd gone to his hotel room that day, painfully recalling how naïve she'd been thinking that they could get back together.

"But you have another boyfriend now," he says. "Is he a good guy?"

"Yeah." She sighs again. "He's fine and everything. I just don't have the same feelings for him that I think he's got for me."

Ryan feels a glimmer of hope.

"If we ever get out of here, I'll have to break up with him."

Her words are music to Ryan's ears.

"What about you?" she asks, trying to sound casual. "You haven't gone out with anyone since that last girlfriend you mentioned?"

"No—I wasn't exactly in the right headspace." He wants to change the topic. "Well, anyways, Eric sounds like a total idiot. If you and I were together," he adds, taking a chance, "I would treat you like a queen."

Dannicka feels a flush rise to her face. She looks down at her hands, folded in her lap.

"We could be," she says quietly. "We could be together."

She lifts her eyes to meet his. She wants to tell him what he means to her, she's been wanting to tell him for some time now, but finds she is unable to speek. Ryan is looking directly at her—his eyes seem to see right through to her very soul. The look is so honest, so profound, it makes her want to cry.

In silence, they simply hold each other's gaze, unable to break away. Dannicka doesn't know if it's the surreal situation, or this surreal place, but she has never experienced anything with this kind of intensity. Through the simple act of looking into each other's eyes, she can actually feel their already—intense connection growing stronger—their energies knitting together, becoming entwined. She had just been talking about Eric—she'd thought he was the love of her life. What a joke. The years she'd spent with him can't even compare with this one electric moment.

As if in slow motion, Ryan raises one hand and gently touches the side of her face. He's imagined many times in the last two weeks what it would be like to touch her, but this has not at all prepared him for the real thing. Her skin is soft and warm, but it is much more than that—his touch has ignited an actual current now running between them. She starts a little, her eyes widening in surprise. Something is happening, something neither of them can explain. The longer he touches her, his hand gently caressing her face, the stronger the current between them grows; resonating, swirling throughout their bodies.

Dannicka sees the light around him, the beautiful glowing light they have become so used to seeing in each other, shine brighter and brighter. Tiny tendrils of light wind their way outwards from his body, swirling up and around the surrounding trees, up into the sky—up into the stars. It is the most incredible sight she has ever witnessed; almost too much to bear.

She wants to speak, to tell him exactly what she's seeing—that he is part of everything here, that it is wonderous and beautiful, but he already knows. He knows, because he is watching the same incredible display taking place around her.

He realizes, in that moment, that Dannicka is him, that he is Dannicka, and they are everything.

# CHAPTER NINE

Thwack.

Thwack.

Chet is standing on Carole's front lawn, playing catch with Marcy who is two houses over. Even at this distance, he can feel the force of her powerhouse throws. The first time they had played together, she had caught him by surprise, nearly snapping his wrist off.

"Holy shit!" he had said. "You can really hurl that thing!"

"I *know*," she had replied. "I *told* you."

If someone had told him a few weeks ago that he would be living at an older woman's home with a bunch of strangers, playing catch with a thirteen-year-old, and actually liking it he would never have believed it. And, as weird as this whole frickin' thing is, he would much rather be here with them than with his fake family and fake friends in that other world. He wouldn't even mind hanging out with these guys in the real world.

Thwack.

If this had never happened, he would be in the real world right now. It's Saturday afternoon, so he would be at the restaurant, toiling away at his shit job. No big loss there. Then he would proba-bly pick up some booze and spend the night partying. That was how he had been planning to spend the summer—working and partying before having to buckle down for university in the Fall. He couldn't wait to do that, and now it all seems so...pointless.

Thwack.

\*\*\*

"We need to do a food run, today," says Carole.

"I figured as much." Says Julian. He knew this time would come, when the non-perishables from Carole's, Chet's, and Marcy's homes would run low, but has put off talking about it. Bringing it up feels like admitting that they might never get out of here. He's been telling himself that it's just a vacation; it's not out of the realm of possibility that he could go away on his own, visit another branch of the family...of course, he would never choose to spend two whole weeks away from his wife and girls—and it's really been a lot longer than that, hasn't it? That whole month of June, he never really saw them at all...

*Stop it*, he tells himself. *There's nothing you can do about it*. He has his other family with him right now, and they need him. *We're just on vacation*, he thinks.

Dannicka is standing at the kitchen sink, rinsing out the coffee grounds.

"We were in that facsimile world for a whole month," she says, as if reading his mind, "and we were okay."

He nods. He's thought the same thing. Maybe these shift things only ever happen once a month. So really, it's only two more weeks.

"Well, I could use some bug spray," says Carole. This place is apparently devoid of all animals. Although there's no shortage of mosquitos.

"And more batteries," adds Marcy, biting into a crab-apple from one of Carole's trees.

"Batteries," Julian mumbles, starting a list. They've been going through batteries like water through a sieve. Maybe that's a sign this world is beginning to degrade, too. What if they don't even have a whole month here?

*I'm just on vacation.*

He takes a few more suggestions for his list, then adds a couple more items.

"There's a grocery store about eight blocks from here," Carole tells him. "You've probably seen it."

"I have. Who feels like going with me?"

They all do. A chance to run around a large empty store seems too thrilling to pass up—as long as they don't focus too much on why it is empty.

Wanting to preserve the gas in their vehicles (for what, exactly? Julian wonders), the six set out on foot. Taking the bikes doesn't seem practical for carrying their groceries home, either.

"This heat!" Carole complains. "I don't remember it ever being this hot day after day for this long! And it's *so* dry."

Of course, she has no reason to recall this particular weather—they're not exactly at home, are they? She wishes she had kept her complaint to herself. She doesn't need to draw any extra attention to their circumstances. She's been so impressed with the other five—they seem to have maintained a sense of calm throughout this ordeal, when she knows for a fact that, unlike her, they don't share her fascination with this adventure.

"Why don't we take one of the cars on the street?" asks Dannicka. "I mean, why not?" It's been long enough now that the idea of borrowing one of these vehicles is no longer upsetting. Going into the houses, however, still seems off-limits, at least to her.

"I guess there's no reason why not," says Julian.

Dannicka points to a 4x4 pickup truck in the middle of the intersection. "What about that one?"

"And I suppose *you* want to be the one who drives it," Ryan chuckles.

"That's right!"

"If she gets to drive that one, then I should get to drive *that*," Chet says, pointing to a Mustang convertible.

"I'm not riding with you," laughs Carole.

"I am!" shouts Marcy, racing toward it.

The road is clear enough that the eight-block drive takes only a few minutes. When they arrive at the store, they park the vehicles and meet outside the front doors.

"We're gonna have to break in," Julian tells the others. "I'll check around back first to see if there's an easier way in."

"I'll go with you," Chet volunteers.

Together, they walk to the end of the strip-mall that surrounds the store, then in behind it. They find a series of metal doors and a large loading dock, none of which seem any easier to get through than smashing the glass in the front.

The idea of breaking and entering, even in a deserted place, is unnerving to Julian. Once, when he was eleven, he had stolen a chocolate bar from a convenience store on a dare. He then spent a few weeks unable to sleep—convinced that God was going to strike him down during the night. The incident ended his life of crime, unless you counted public drunkenness.

Heading back to the front of the store, Chet rushes over to the others. "We get to smash the glass!" he exclaims. "Fuckin-A!'

Carole raises an eyebrow.

"Oops," he says. "Excuse my French."

"What do you think is the best way to—" Carole begins, turning to Julian, but before any discussion can take place, Chet trots into the middle of the parking lot, grabs a shopping cart and runs with it as fast as he can toward the store.

"Watch out!" Carole screams.

Chet rams into the doors and is thrown back as the cart bounces off the glass and slams into his gut.

"You're gonna break your arms!" Carole cries out.

They all rush to where Chet lies on the ground, the wind knocked out of him. He curls into a ball, gasping for breath.

"Are you okay?!" asks Dannicka, leaning over him.

He coughs, clutching his stomach, then starts to laugh.

"Oh my God!" Marcy exclaims. "Boys are crazy!"

"Did I break the glass?" he wheezes, hopeful.

"No, but you chipped it," says Julian, inspecting the door.

"If you give me a minute, I'll give it another go."

Carole raises both eyebrows. "No chance! If you hurt your-self here, it..." she trails off knowing there's no need to finish the sentence.

As the others help Chet to his feet, Ryan wanders through the parking lot, checking out a few of the vehicles.

"Hey, what about this?" he hollers, lifting a sledgehammer from the back of a pickup.

Julian laughs. "That'll do!" He wants to ask Ryan to hand it over, not sure if it'll be too difficult for him to manage, but he also doesn't want to emasculate him—especially not in front of Dannicka.

"Stand back," Ryan warns the group, squaring himself in front of the sliding glass doors. He swings the heavy sledgehammer back over his shoulder, then lunges forward and makes contact with the chipped spot. The glass holds. He repeats the action twice more before small cracks finally begin to appear.

"One more," he says, enjoying his new-found strength. He hauls back and hits the glass again. This time, the small cracks blossom outward to form an intricate web. Panting, he hands the sledgehammer to Julian. "Got it started for ya."

Julian stands back, lifts the hammer over his shoulder, and strikes the doors once, twice, three times. Despite the growing web of fissures, the glass remains stubbornly intact. *God, what are these things made of?* he thinks to himself.

"Just one more," he grunts. He wallops the glass again and something inside him snaps. Instead of passing the sledgehammer off to anyone else, he pommels the doors over and over. Eventually, the glass shatters into a million pieces, littering the ground around his feet.

"Well, that should do—" Carole begins, but she is cut off by an unnatural wail from Julian, who begins beating the second set of doors with the sledgehammer. The others jump back in surprise.

Suddenly, he is out of control—the stress and fear of the last six weeks boils over and erupts out of his body. He continues to scream and holler, attacking the doors with the hammer, sweat pouring off his face. He doesn't stop until there is nothing left but the metal frames. It's only when Carole is sure he has hurt himself that she approaches, placing a cautious hand on his shoulder.

"Julian," she says, her voice quiet and calm. "It's okay." It isn't okay––she knows that.

Carole never wanted to have children of her own, a choice she has not regretted and has only shared with a few. There's a stigma attached; you're either to be pitied for the possibility that something is physically wrong, or (even worse) you've just 'never met the right man'. If the decision is your own, then surely you are selfish or too unenlightened to know what you're missing. But she doesn't have to be a parent to feel compassion and sorrow for what Julian is going through. They have all had to leave loved ones behind, but being torn away from two small children is especially cruel.

Panting, Julian finally lets the sledgehammer fall to the ground with a heavy thud. He bends over, gasping for breath, hands on his waist.

"You guys go on in," he gasps.

No one moves.

Finally, Carole touches Dannicka's arm and nods, silently instructing her and the others to go into the store.

Ryan enters first, using his feet to clear the shattered glass away from the entrance. He takes a deep breath and holds it, aware of the vile stench wafting out through the doorway, then steps cautiously over the threshold.

Behind him, the others—except for Julian—follow silently. Within seconds, the smell is overwhelming; even holding their breath doesn't protect them from it.

"Holy crap!" Chet exclaims.

Dannicka, gagging, rushes past him and out of the store. The others are quick to follow.

"What's wrong?" Julian asks. He's been sitting on the curb and struggles to his feet. "Something in there?"

"Just the most awful smell!" Carole exclaims.

"It's like someone took a giant dump on top of a warehouse full of hot garbage!" Chet blurts.

Despite their discomfort, Ryan, Dannicka, and Marcy laugh.

"Just give me a minute," says Julian, still recovering. "I'll go in."

"No," says Ryan. "Give me the list. If we hold our breath, we can run in and grab one thing at a time. If no one wants to go back in there, I can do all of it—I don't care."

"I can do it, too," says Marcy. "I'm a really fast runner."

"Yeah, we know," says Chet. She punches him in the arm.

"I know the store pretty well," says Carole. "We should divide up the things we need by section and each go to one so we don't all collide with each other. Except you," she adds, turning to Julian. "You should sit this one out."

He doesn't argue.

The others get their flashlights ready, hoping the batteries will at least last the duration of the shopping trip, while Carole quickly assigns the sections.

"You all know where you're going?" Carole asks.

Everyone nods.

"I feel like I'm on some kind of game show," says Chet.

"Let's go!"

Within an hour, they manage to retrieve each item on the list, and a few extras.

"I can keep going," says Marcy. Running through the dark, empty store was a total thrill—stinky or not. She felt like a criminal, swiping armfuls of canned tuna and salmon into her cart, boxes of cereal, cookies, crackers—not caring about money or anything. She's always found grocery shopping about as much fun as sitting in math class, until today.

"We've got what we need for now," says Carole. "But you've done a great job." *And with any luck,* she thinks, *we won't have to come back here.*

***

## SUNDAY, JULY 16

Julian wakes in the morning and checks his watch. 7:45 a.m. He's already decided not to tell the others that today is his forty-first birthday; he has no desire to celebrate or draw attention to it. He thinks about last year when he turned forty. They'd had a barbeque in the back yard and everyone was there—his wife, his girls, his parents and all three of his younger brothers, along with their wives and kids. Many of his friends were also there, with their wives and kids. It was a mad house. There had been a massive cake with sickly-green icing made especially for him by his youngest, who'd been on a Little Mermaid 'Under the Sea' kick. And he'd taken all of it for granted.

He hasn't seen any of them now in...he thinks for a moment... forty-five days. Do they think he has abandoned them? Do they think he's dead? He wonders how they will mark this day without him. Tears fill his eyes and he wipes them away with the back of his hand. The only way to get through this day, as with any day here, is to believe his family is okay and carry on as usual. There is nothing he can do about them here. He's on vacation.

After breakfast, he and Chet take their bikes out for walk-about. At this point, there is nothing to see that hasn't already been seen, but they continue with the ritual anyway. The daily routine that has developed seems to offer some sense of stability: breakfast, walkabout, lunch, reading and/or games, preparing and eating dinner, clean-up and other chores, late evenings around the fire. Sleep, wake-up, repeat, and try not to think. Between the bike rides, the chores, and the make-shift baseball games, Julian at least feels like he's in better shape than he's been in years.

Without a word, he climbs onto his bike and starts to ride. He's sore from yesterday, not to mention embarrassed. He doesn't know what he was thinking, losing it like that in front of the others. Real Uncle Ribbons stuff. Chet senses Julian's mood this morning and rides beside him in quiet companionship, for which Julian is grateful. Their bikes glide silently and smoothly along the sunny, deserted streets.

***

Something up ahead catches Chet's eye. Increasing his speed slightly, he rides over to the spot, then stops and gets off his bike.

Julian, who's been lagging behind, pedals to catch up. "You okay?"

"Look!" Chet whispers, pointing to the top of a tall fence post about thirty feet away. "Is that a bird?"

Julian gets off his bike, letting it fall quietly onto its side. He holds one hand over his eyes to shield the bright sun, squinting toward where Chet is pointing.

"Oh my God," he mutters, stunned by the sight.

It *is* a bird. It's a magpie.

Both men stare silently, astonished by the first sighting of another living creature in this world, beside themselves and Carole's dog. Normally considered a nuisance in the real world, the brilliantly-hued black, blue, and white bird is awe-inspiring here. To Julian's complete shock, he feels his eyes begin to water at the sight.

Leisurely, the magpie grooms itself while perched atop its post seemingly unaware of its own significance. After a moment, it flies off, heading south—its destination unknown. Chet and Julian watch it, still silent, until it disappears completely from view.

Has it been here this whole time? Has it only just arrived as a sign that others are to come? Maybe this is their version of the post-flood dove. Julian dares to hope.

***

"I still can't believe you saw a magpie," says Dannicka during dinner that evening. "I wonder if they've been here this whole time... although, wouldn't we have heard them?"

"If there's one bird that could make it through all of this," says Carole, "it *would* be a magpie. Those things are tough as nails."

"No doubt about that," says Julian. "Once, I saw one flying with a pack of cigarettes in its beak."

Marcy laughs. "No, you didn't!"

"Seriously! No word of a lie."

Carole gets up from the patio table and goes into the house, where she assembles tonight's dessert. It's just a bowl of canned fruit cocktail, but she's precariously perched two small candles in the centre. She lights them carefully, then holds one hand over their flame to keep them lit on her way back outside.

"Happy birthday to you..." she begins, and the others immediately join in. Julian sits at the table, surprised for the second time that day.

"And many mooooorrreee...." Marcy intones at the end.

"Sorry we couldn't get you a cake," says Carole.

Julian is stunned. "How did you guys know?!"

"You seemed funny today," says Marcy. "So, I looked in your wallet."

He fails to see the connection between those two statements. "Well, okay!" he splutters. "Thank you!"

She looks at him wistfully, eyes shining. "Make a wish!"

\*\*\*

Later that evening, Dannicka momentarily disappears into the house, then re-emerges in full hair and makeup.

"Ladies and gentlemen," she announces, "will you please follow me to the front yard and take your seats?"

"What's going on?" Carole asks.

"It's a surprise," says Chet. "All I know is that they asked me to help with the music."

Carole, Chet, Ryan, and Julian all follow Dannicka to the front yard where four deck chairs have been set on the sidewalk facing the lawn. Before taking his seat, Chet opens all of his car doors and gets the CD ready.

"Remember—track four," says Dannicka. She strikes a pose and holds it, nodding briefly at Chet. He presses 'play', then runs over to join the others.

When the music starts, Marcy—who has been hiding in the house until now—bursts out the front door. She, too, is in full hair and makeup. It's the first time she's worn any makeup since they've been here, and it feels great.

She joins Dannicka on the lawn, and together they perform a dance routine that they've been secretly working on for the last few days.

The song they dance to is "Hand in my Pocket" from the same Alanis Morissette CD that Marcy used in her facsimile-world performance. It's become her new favourite album—every song is great. She throws herself completely and unabashedly into the performance.

Ryan has to keep reminding himself to look at Marcy, too. It's hard to tear his eyes away from Dannicka—he has never seen anyone so beautiful, and if he's being honest, so hot. She catches his eye and smiles, as though she knows exactly what he's thinking.

Julian glances from one dancer to the other, tears in his eyes for the third time that day. When the song has ended, Chet runs back to his car and stops the CD. Placing his pinky fingers in his mouth, he whistles loudly over the vigorous applause.

"That was amazing! Just beautiful!" Carole gushes, hugging them both. "I really enjoyed the song, too. Who's the singer?"

"Her name is Alanis," Marcy says, still breathing heavily. "It was my sister's CD."

Past tense.

An hour later, as the group lounges in the yard, there is a low rumble in the sky.

"It's actually going to rain!" says Carole. "Oh, thank God—we could really use it."

No sooner has she said this than large, heavy drops begin to fall. Julian and Carole quickly gather the patio chair cushions while Ryan and Dannicka cover the fire pit and gather the blankets. Chet and Marcy, however, stand outside holding their arms out to feel the rain until they are completely drenched. No one stops them.

***

Marcy lies in bed reliving her dance routine with Dannicka. It was *so* much fun! Even their rehearsals were fun. She thinks about all the rehearsals she'd had with Bernadette and feels a pang of guilt—they'd always seemed so stressful. Marcy realizes now that it was her own fault; she was forever losing her temper with Bernadette. If she ever gets back to the real world, and lately she's not so sure that will happen, she will absolutely apologize. Bernadette is her best friend, no question—and best friends deserve the best treatment. They also deserve honesty, don't they? And, if Marcy's going to be perfectly honest, she'll have to admit her real feelings.

She has always tried to explain her feelings away, ignore them or pretend they were no big deal. But, somehow in this quiet place it's become easier to be honest—to accept what she has known for a long time—and not to be afraid.

She rolls onto her side and opens her eyes, listening to the raindrops tapping lightly against the window. She allows the secret once-scary thought to come to the forefront of her mind, inwardly forming the words as though ready to say them out loud without any excuse or apology.

*I love you, Bernadette.*

She mulls the words over, feeling a fluttery warmth inside her chest.

*I love you.*

And she does. Not just as a friend, or even a best friend. She loves her the same way that Dannicka loves Ryan. And here, in this otherworldly place, that's not so scary anymore.

# CHAPTER TEN

## MONDAY, JULY 17

Carole wakes at five in the morning and cannot fall back asleep. She was awake until after one o'clock thinking about an idea for a painting, but with the girls sleeping in her studio, she was unable to do any work. She wonders how handy Julian is—maybe they can set up some dry wall in part of her basement. There's more than enough space to add an extra bedroom, or maybe even two... She stops her train of thought, knowing she shouldn't entertain these kinds of ideas. They will get back, sooner or later.

After tossing and turning for an hour, she gets out of bed. Maybe she can take some time after breakfast to start on some sketches, then nap later in the day.

"Early morning walk for you," she whispers to Mr. Biscuits.

She dresses quietly and lifts the reluctant dog from out of his bed. In the kitchen, she scribbles a quick note to let the others know where she is, then heads outside. Already she can tell that today is going to be another scorcher. Last night's thunder storm barely cooled things down before burning away with no trace that it had ever happened.

"This place is turning into a desert," she says out loud.

At the end of the street, she decides to turn right. Mr. Biscuits, who is busy smelling something interesting, lags behind.

"I'm going this way," she calls out. He lifts his head and wobbles over to her, tail wagging.

It's been seventeen days since the second shift and Carole is amazed at how well she's adapted to sharing an empty world, and her home, with only five other people. It shouldn't come as much of a surprise—she has adapted quickly to virtually any new environment that she's been in over the years—but sleeping in a Mongolian yurt and navigating the labyrinth of the London Underground required a different kind of adjustment compared to her current living situation. In only a few days, she went from a hectic schedule of deadlines and social engagements to a stillness so absolute that it's made her previous life seem obsolete. Already she has stopped expecting to hear the phone ring, stopped looking around before crossing the streets, and she's taken to letting Mr. Biscuits wander as he pleases without a leash. She has dropped the armour she didn't even know she carried in her day-to-day public life. In this silent world with a population of only six, Carole is experiencing a solace she's never known before.

They cross what was once a busy street and head into another residential neighbourhood, just north of her own. She looks at each familiar house as she passes, thinking about the days ahead. When winter comes, they might have to set aside their reluctance and enter some of these houses. It won't be easy to get to the shopping centres when the temperatures plummet and the snow begins to pile up; when for weeks at a time it can get so cold that unprotected skin freezes within seconds. How are they going to manage?

The pioneers did it, didn't they? Her own grandparents were homesteaders—on the Saskatchewan prairie, no less—and they managed. Winters there were more unforgiving, and they were without all of the comforts that Carole and the others will have: houses full of supplies and non-perishable food, running water, and a well-insulated home. They won't have the luxury of a working furnace, but Dannicka can keep the fire going in the fireplace—she has proven to be a near-expert, and they can all help her. Carole pictures an axe-wielding Marcy ...

"We're not going to *be* here in the winter," she says aloud, overriding her own thoughts. Besides, with the unending heatwave they have been experiencing, winter seems an impossibility——maybe it really is turning into a desert.

She continues walking at a leisurely pace, Mr. Biscuits scurrying from one lawn to another, when up ahead she sees something move. She cranes her head and squints, trying to get a better look. There it is again. She can't make out what the object is, but she can see that it's bright white and on the other side of a hedge. She quickens her pace. The object is moving again. Suddenly it comes into view and Carole is shocked. It appears to be a child, maybe six or seven years old, with its back to her, wearing what looks like the whitest snowsuit she's ever seen.

Carole is dumbstruck. Is it possible that there have been other people here this whole time? And really, why wouldn't there be? If Ryan was kept back from the first shift because of his accident then surely the same could have happened to someone else!

Realizing that she has stopped in her tracks, Carole begins walking again—this time, directly toward the child. As she gets closer, she is able to confirm that it is, in fact, wearing a snow suit with the hood covering its head almost entirely. The poor thing is probably all alone, likely afraid and definitely sweltering in this heat!

"Hello?!" Carole calls out earnestly.

At the sound of her voice, the child turns around. When Carole sees its face, she freezes. What she is looking at may, in fact, be a child, but it is definitely not human—it is missing two features that she believes no human could live without: a nose and a mouth.

It freezes in place, one small arm held up as though it was about to perform some action before being rendered immobile. It stares at her with disproportionately large, whiteish-blue eyes—which seem to somehow look at not only her, but at everything else at once. And its skin...so uncomfortably, unbelievably white; it's practically blinding.

"Mr. Biscuits!" Carole screams hysterically, not realizing that he is right beside her. She looks frantically around before feeling a small lick at her ankle. She jumps and looks down, relieved beyond words. Without a second thought, she grabs the little dog and starts to run.

Only when she's reached the end of the street does she dare to slow down and look back. The creature has remained in the same spot, standing as still as a statue—as if any movement might be impossible. Terrified, Carole turns away and runs the three blocks back to her house as fast as her legs will carry her. Once inside, she locks the front door, something she hasn't done in weeks, then dashes across the house and locks the back door. She locks the patio door, then closes the kitchen window. Desperately, she looks out at the backyard, then out at the front yard. She contemplates waking Julian, then talks herself out of it. What if she was wrong? What if it hadn't been moving and she'd just imagined it? What if it's just some weird statue that—

*It turned around*, she tells herself. *It heard your voice and it turned around. You saw that.*

Maybe she was hallucinating—maybe hallucinations are a by-product of being in this world for too long. She looks out the living room window again, then decides to wake Julian after all. Quietly, she opens the door to his room and tip-toes inside. He is lying face-down on her guest bed, his arms and legs stretched out in every direction like a starfish. She crouches over him and clutches his shoulder.

"Julian?"

"Mrmph?"

"Julian!"

"Huh?" He squints, wondering why Trudy is waking him so early. He's been in a dead sleep—it seems to take forever to orient himself. This isn't his bedroom, he finally realizes, it's...Carole's guest room. And the woman hovering over him is not his wife.

"Carole," he mumbles. His eyes finally come into focus and when they do, he sees the look of sheer panic all over her face. "What is it—what's wrong?"

"We're not the only ones here!" she whispers. "There's...there's someone else here!"

He rolls onto his side and sits up. "What?!"

"There's something here! I took Mr. Biscuits for a walk..." she begins to shake, her teeth chattering despite the warm room. Julian takes both of her wrists in his hands and holds her steady.

"It's okay—what did you see?"

She tells him.

He is wide awake now.

"Okay," he says, trying to think. "Okay. What if... could it have been a kid in a mask or something?"

"Absolutely not."

He takes her word for it.

"What about, like, some kind of robot or something, like some kind of science experiment, or some elaborate toy?"

"It had skin." She shudders involuntarily.

"Was it glowing? Like us?"

She thinks for a moment. "No—it wasn't! That should have been my first warning! Why in God's name did I run *toward* it?!"

"Shh! It's okay!" He places a hand on her shoulder. "Just breathe."

She takes a few shaky breaths.

"It didn't follow you, right?"

"No, it didn't...I don't think so...but it knows we're here! We wouldn't be hard to find!"

He lets go of her shoulder and vigorously rubs his hands over his face. "Okay," he says. "Okay. I'll go get Ryan."

\*\*\*

Chet has not had a panic attack since he has been here, and the anxiety he'd felt in the last world has become a distant memory. He guesses it doesn't hurt that this world is extremely calm. A few days ago, he referred to it as "The Empty World," and was promptly correct by Marcy.

"It's not empty," she'd said. "*We're* in it."

But this morning, as he lies in his sleeping bag on the floor of Carole's rec room, he feels the familiar anxiety creep back in. Although the room is dark, he can see Julian's outline crouched beside the futon, where Ryan sleeps. He can't hear what they're whispering about, but he knows it isn't good.

"What's going on?" he asks, sitting up.

Julian jumps a little.

"Oh! Sorry to wake you. Go back to sleep."

"What's happening?"

Julian has not had time to prepare an excuse. "It's okay, Ryan and I can handle it."

"I can handle it too, you know."

Ryan looks at Julian for a moment, then turns to Chet. "Carole thinks she saw someone outside a few blocks over."

Chet sucks in his breath. "Holy shit. Really?"

"It's fine—" Julian says quickly. "It's probably nothing. Ryan and I are just gonna go check it out."

It doesn't feel like nothing. "I'm going with you."

"You don't need to. Ryan and I—"

"I'm going with you," Chet repeats, scrambling out of his sleeping bag.

Before any further arguing can take place, Ryan makes the call. "He should come with us."

Upstairs, Chet does not like the expression on Carole's face. He realizes that in all that they've been through together, he's never seen her undone. Until now. Within a few seconds, they decide that Carole will take Ryan and Chet back to the spot of her sighting, and Julian will stay behind to guard the house.

"Should we take the bikes?" Chet asks.

"I think you guys should take one of the cars," says Julian. "Carole, did that street seem clear enough to drive on?"

She tries to remember. "I think so."

Before getting in Chet's car, they grab three baseball bats, just in case. As Chet reverses out of the driveway, Julian stands on the lawn watching them go.

\*\*\*

Dannicka is jolted awake by the sound of Chet's car starting. What in the world is going on? She climbs out of the futon, careful not to wake Marcy, and tip toes out of the room.

The doors to both Carole's and Julian's rooms are wide open, but there's no sign of them. Did they all go somewhere? Why would they not tell her?

Just as she's about to worry, she spots Julian on the street in front of the house. He is looking very intently around the area. She opens the front door and he jumps.

"What's going on?" she asks. "Where did Chet go?"

He tells her.

***

"Turn right here," Carole instructs. She can feel her heart pounding in her chest. "It's this street, about halfway up."

Chet turns slowly onto the deserted street, keeping his eyes peeled. Carole has given them a description of what they're looking for, and neither he nor Ryan like the sound of it.

"It's this house up ahead."

Chet stops the car in the middle of the road, gripping the steering wheel. In the back seat, Ryan grips one of the bats.

"It was right here, right beside that hedge. It was doing something to it, reaching into it or something." She cannot seem to get a decent breath.

From their viewpoint in the car, the hedge seems totally normal––no different than it has always looked. In fact, everything about the houses, the yards and the street looks the same as it always has.

After ten minutes with the car still running, Chet begins to worry about gas consumption. At the same time, he's too paranoid to turn the engine off. He checks the gas gauge—one quarter of a tank left. He meant to siphon gas out of another vehicle a few days ago, but never got around to it. Why didn't he? What the hell was he so busy doing?

"I'm going out there," Ryan says suddenly.

Chet's stomach flips, knowing what his response should be. "I'll go with you," he says, swallowing his fear.

"Wait!" says Carole. What should she do? She's not going back out there, that's for damn sure, but she can't very well ask either of the guys to go alone.

"I guess I'll wait here," she relents. "You two be careful. And hurry!"

Ryan grabs his bat and passes another one to Chet. "On the count of three," he says.

Slowly, they open their doors and step outside. For a few seconds they stand silently in the middle of the road. Nothing about their surroundings seems out of the ordinary—the air smells the same, with that faint odor of garbage they've all grown accustomed to, the sun continues to shine, already hot for this early time of the day, and silence hangs over it all.

"We can't stand here forever," Ryan finally says. "If it wanted to get us, it would have by now."

He walks toward the front lawn of the house, eyes darting back and forth. Chet follows, and together they approach the waist-high hedge.

"Hello?" Ryan calls out.

Silence.

"Hello?" he repeats.

Still nothing. He looks to Chet and nods. Chet, feeling as though he's stumbled onto the set of some suspense movie without a rehearsal, nods back and raises his bat as if he's about to hit the home run of the century.

*Please*, he begs inwardly, *please don't let me have to use this.*

Ryan experiences a rush of adrenaline, but he isn't afraid. In one swift move, he thrusts the heavy end of the bat straight into the hedge, ready for whatever might jump out. Nothing does.

Back in the car, Carole watches anxiously, hands covering her mouth.

Feeling more confident, Chet follows Ryan's lead, inspecting the waist-high hedge more carefully now. Just as before, nothing seems out of the ordinary—no unusual sights, sounds or smells.

"We should check around back," says Ryan.

"Sure."

They signal their plans to Carole, who holds up both hands frantically.

"Just wait!" she mouths, hoping they've understood. Twisting her torso, she reaches into the back seat for the remaining bat, then quickly double-checks that all doors are locked.

"Okay!" she signals.

In anguish, she watches as both men disappear behind the house, then waits for an excruciating amount of time. It feels like hours, but when she glances at the clock in the car, she sees it has only been three minutes.

"Breathe," she says out loud.

A terrible thought comes to her regarding the car's hatchback door. Is it locked? Oh, God, what if that...thing...has snuck up behind her? Refusing to turn around, she keeps her eyes glued to the spot where she last saw the guys. To her relief, Ryan and Chet emerge, unscathed, from behind the house. Ryan gestures that they are going inside the house, but Carole rolls down her window in a frenzy.

"No!" she cries. "Come back later if you want! I can't wait out here alone anymore!"

Ryan and Chet share a look, then head back to the car without argument.

"Anything in the back yard?" Carole wants to know.

"Nothing," says Ryan. "I've been in that yard a few times and everything seems exactly the same."

"We need to get back," she says, clearly agitated. "We've been gone long enough and Julian's probably worried."

Back at the house, they are greeted by an anxious Marcy and Dannicka, both standing on the front lawn.

"Julian's keeping watch out back," says Dannicka. "And I've told Marcy everything."

Carole gives her a stricken look.

"There's no point in keeping secrets," Dannicka tells her.

"I'm okay," says Marcy. At least, she thought she was okay until she saw Carole, who looks totally freaked out.

"Where's the dog?!" Carole snaps.

"He's in..." Marcy starts to say, but Carole rushes past her and bursts into the house. After a few seconds, she emerges, clutching Mr. Biscuits in both arms.

Julian hears the three return and leaves his post to join them in the front yard.

"We didn't find anything" Ryan says. "You?"

Julian shakes his head.

"I know what I saw!" Carole exclaims.

"No one is doubting that," says Julian, his voice calm.

"Maybe we should pack up and go somewhere else," says Dannicka. If Carole is this freaked out, it's for good reason, isn't it? What if this alien, or whatever the hell it is, comes after them? "Maybe we should just get out of the city altogether."

Ryan looks at her, not wanting to say the obvious—that packing up and going anywhere would be next to impossible.

"It would take forever to get out of here," he says instead.

"Well, we could go to another part of the city," she argues. "We could try the northside or something..."

"How do we know there aren't more of them there?" Carole exclaims. "There could be tons of them, for all we know!"

"Or downtown, downtown seemed okay..." Dannicka trails off. She doesn't bother to mention the southside. No one wants to go back there.

The more worked up the two women get, the quieter the others become. Julian needs to reign this in.

"Look," he says. "There could be more, or there could be just one. Either way, it, or they, could probably get around the city as easily as we can." *Or maybe even more easily.* "If it wanted to...

contact us, it would have by now." *It still might.* "We've been safe at Carole's this whole time, and I really don't believe it would make sense to go anywhere else. Do you guys?"

"It's tough to say," says Ryan. "If we don't know where it came from, we could wind up heading toward it. It didn't come after you, Carole. It froze, right?"

She nods.

"Not to make light with a cliché," he goes on, "but what if it came here from somewhere else, like we did, and you scared it as much as it scared you?"

"It's a possibility," she reluctantly agrees. *But you guys didn't see it...*

"Well, I don't really want to go back to the southside," says Chet. The mere thought makes him feel sick. "And we don't know what's happening anywhere else..." He tries to imagine the creature that Carole has described—huge eyes, no nose or mouth, shockingly white skin and a blinding-white snowsuit. Part of him now regrets not seeing it himself. Of course, knowing that it's the size of a six-year-old helps.

"Let's just stick close together for now, okay?" says Julian. "We'll see what's what."

Silently, they all agree.

\*\*\*

Hour after hour, the six sit inside the sweltering house, too cautious to open any of the windows. Chet perches in the front doorway, keeping watch over the front yard, while the others take turns pacing from window to window. Finally, Marcy makes a declaration.

"I'm hungry," she announces. "And hot." What she wouldn't give for a popsicle.

"You're right," says Dannicka. "We should all eat something."

Lunch consists of peanut butter on crackers. It's too hot to make a fire and do any real cooking. Besides, they would be too worried that the fire might attract...something.

By late afternoon, Chet moves his post from inside the house to outside on the front porch. He sits under the burning sun and refuses to move. If something is coming to get them, he'll know about it first. And then...what?

Carole's panic finally subsides later that evening—downgrading to just a worry. Maybe Ryan was right, maybe it is more afraid of her than she is of it.

*Or, maybe it's just waiting until it gets dark.*

She shudders.

"We should keep a round-the-clock watch," Julian says, to Carole's relief, "in groups of two. Ryan, your sleep shouldn't be interrupted," he doesn't need to say why, "so you should take the first watch, then sleep through the rest of the night."

"I'll go with him," says Dannicka. "The rest of us will have to sleep in shifts, which I know isn't ideal, but I think it's the only way to go for now."

Carole couldn't care less about sleeping in shifts. Remembering the face of that creature, she doesn't think she'll ever be able to sleep again.

***

# CHAPTER ELEVEN

"We're running out of a few key things," Dannicka tells Carole. "I mean, we can make do for a couple more days, but we're cutting it pretty close."

"I know," Carole agrees. "I've been worried about that, too. I meant to go back to the store that day..." she doesn't need to finish the sentence.

"Well, we should go today," says Dannicka. "It's been three days now...if something were to happen, it would've by now, don't you think?"

Carole is still reluctant. "I suppose."

"I don't mind going—you don't have to. I'm getting a little stir-crazy being inside all the time, anyway. I just need to get out and walk—I don't care who I run into!"

She looks at Carole. "Sorry—that was insensitive."

"No, it's fine. We all need to get out." She tries to smile. "We can't hide in here forever."

Ryan joins them in the kitchen, opening a cupboard. "I think Chet's sick," he says.

"What's wrong? Carole asks, instantly concerned. They can't afford to get sick here.

"He said he's burning up, and he feels exhausted. He asked me to get him a drink of water."

Dannicka, standing near the sink, takes the glass from Ryan's hand and fills it with cold water from the tap. "He sat out in the

180

front yard for most of the day yesterday, too," she says. "Maybe he's got heat stroke."

"That sounds about right," says Carole, relieved it isn't anything worse.

Ryan takes the glass from Dannicka's outstretched hand. "Could be. I'll go find out."

"Well, I guess we won't all be able to go to the store together, anyway," says Carole. "I'll stay here with him."

Julian, who has just completed his new morning ritual of carefully inspecting the front and back yards, joins the two women in the kitchen.

"We have to do a food run today," Carole tells him. "But Chet has heat stroke, or something to that effect, so we can't all go."

"Is he okay?" Julian isn't crazy about the idea of splitting up.

"I'm not sure."

Ryan makes another appearance into the kitchen. "He's definitely got a fever. I can stay here with him if you guys wanna go."

"I'll be here," says Carole. She's about to add, 'so you don't have to stay,' but changes her mind. What if that thing comes back while they're gone? If Chet's not feeling well, he may not be able to help her fend it off.

As though reading her mind, Ryan nods at her. "We'll stay here, then."

"Marcy should stay here too," says Julian. She must be safer here than she is venturing out. He really doesn't want her around if they encounter that 'being' while en route.

"Well, I agree with you," says Carole, "but I doubt Marcy will."

"What won't I agree with?" At the mention of her name, Marcy wanders into the kitchen.

"Julian and I are going out to the store," says Dannicka. "The others are gonna stay here."

"I'm going with you guys," Marcy insists, leaving no room for argument.

At the last minute, Carole waffles. "I really should go with you—you'll need help bringing things back, and I know where everything is in the store."

Dannicka interrupts with a gentle hand on her arm. "Don't worry about it—we'll take the truck and we'll be fine. You just stay here with the guys."

Marcy admires Dannicka's ability to always say and do the right thing at times like this. She sees the effect that her touch has on Carole––how it immediately calms Carole––and wishes she could be more like that. The only physical reassurance she's ever offered her friends is a punch to the arm.

"Well..." Carole trails off, grateful for the response, but disappointed in herself. Why is she being so weak?

*You're not weak,* she tells herself. *You've just seen something no one else has.*

She places a hand over Dannicka's reassuring one. "Thank you."

***

Dannicka, Julian, and Marcy pile into the same 4x4 pickup that they'd taken on their last excursion to the store. The ride is silent. Dannicka drives slower than she needs to, keeping her eyes peeled for any possible creature sightings. Beside her in the front seat, Julian also keeps a vigilant look-out, though neither of them admits to it. They don't want to upset Marcy.

"Well, no sign of them yet," Marcy announces from the back seat, seemingly unbothered.

The adults exchange a side-long glance. Dannicka turns into the parking lot and drives up to the front of the store. As she and Julian reach to undo their seatbelts, Marcy freezes.

"The doors," she says.

"What?" asks Julian.

"Look at the doors."

Julian and Dannicka turn to look at the sliding doors that Julian had laid waste to five days earlier. Now both doors appear perfectly intact.

For several seconds, no one moves or speaks. While Julian replays the door-smashing incident in his mind, second-guessing his memory, Dannicka's eyes dart quickly from one end of the parking lot to the other. Is that creature somewhere around here?

Marcy breaks the silence. "What if it's a good thing? What if that person-thing that Carole saw fixed it?"

"Then it doesn't want us to get any food," says Dannicka, suddenly feeling very cold.

"If we have to, we'll break in again," says Julian. "There's no other option." They *need* food, and breaking in is still better than venturing into any of the other houses. "I'll come back later with the guys."

Dannicka turns over the ignition without argument.

"Hang on a second," says Julian, unable to help himself. "I just want a closer look." He opens the door and jumps out of the truck.

"Wait!" Dannicka calls, making sure the gearshift is in park. "I'll come with you! Marcy, stay here."

"No way!" Marcy exclaims. In one quick motion, she tears off her seatbelt and hops out of the truck.

Together they join Julian, who is now standing at the store entrance.

"These doors haven't exactly been repaired," he says. "These are new doors entirely, I'm sure of it. The design is totally different."

The rest of the building looks the same, as does the parking lot, right down to the sledgehammer that is still propped up where Julian left it. He takes a few cautious steps forward to get a better look and inadvertently steps on the large rubber mat in front. Suddenly, the doors slide apart with an audible hiss.

Marcy and Dannicka, who have been huddled together clutching each other's hands, scream. Julian jumps back and reflexively makes a grab for the sledgehammer. Marcy doesn't know what she expects to come through those doors, but she doesn't want miss it. Dannicka, however, is tugging at her hands, dragging her away.

"Get in the truck!" she screams. "Julian! Get in the truck!"

"It's okay," he calls back. The only thing coming out of the store is that god-forsaken stench. He's never going to forget that smell.

"I *have* to go in," he says. "We're here, and…"

"What if it's a trap?!" Dannicka hisses. Why did they let Marcy come with them? They should have made her stay home and brought Ryan instead! What were they thinking?! She is never going to forgive herself for this.

"I don't think it's a trap," says Julian. "That 'thing' had days to find us if it wanted to." He looks at the new doors, then peers into the darkness beyond.

Dannicka, standing behind the truck with Marcy, is unconvinced.

"It *fixed* the doors!" Julian continues, gesturing with both hands, just in case Dannicka doesn't know what he's referring to. "What if it also needs to get food? What if it's just more technologically advanced than we are, and figured out the whole door thing? It's done us a favour!"

"You could have a point…" Dannicka is forced to admits.

"Look," he says. "You're right—I don't think we should all go in, but I can go. And I can keep a shouting commentary going while I'm in there so you'll know I'm okay. If I stop talking, wait for two minutes, then leave without me."

"Are you *crazy*?!" Marcy wails.

"If you stop talking, we're coming in for you!" says Dannicka. "So, you'd better keep talking."

Without further ado, Julian takes a deep breath, nods at the girls, then runs inside. Marcy and Dannicka go back to clasping each other's hands and, within seconds, they begin to hear Julian's commentary.

"I just passed the deli! It really, *really,* stinks! I'm grabbing some canned tuna!"

In an instant, he is back outside, handing tins of fish to Marcy.

"It's all clear," he says. "The only thing that's different from the last time is those doors. Too bad that 'being' didn't clean up a bit in there, eh? Maybe we should put in a request."

Dannicka looks at him stonily.

"Okay. Too soon. Got it."

"I wanna go in," says Marcy, feeling decidedly more confident.

"You can't!" Dannicka exclaims.

"Why not?"

"Because——"

"What if I just stay at the front of the store? I won't go down any of the aisles. You'll be able to see me the whole time."

"You guys work it out," says Julian. "I'm going back in." He grabs a basket from the stack by the door.

"Well..." Dannicka sputters. "Fine. But stay where I can see you. I mean it!"

Without a moment's pause, Marcy takes a deep breath and dashes inside. Dannicka takes position at the entrance with one foot inside the store and the other on the mat to keep the doors open. Nervously, she glances back and forth between the inside of the store and the truck which is still running out in the parking lot.

Julian and Marcy make a half-dozen more trips into the store, each time emerging with a basket of goods.

"Okay!" says Julian, once satisfied. "I think we're good to go."

"Thank God" Dannicka replies. "Let's get out of here."

***

Chet is still sick.

He has gotten out of bed, but sits listless on the couch wrapped in a large comforter, despite the heat.

"You're burning up," says Dannicka, placing the back of her hand against his cheek. "You really overdid it out there the last few days—no sun for you for a while."

Carole gives him some aspirin and asks if he's eaten anything.

"I don't feel like eating," he says.

"Then, at least keep drinking," she replies. "You need to keep your fluids up."

"Well, you might feel better when you hear what's happened," Julian says, proceeding to tell them about the repaired doors at the grocery store. "I mean, it was totally fine. It couldn't have been easier. If that thing fixed the doors, then I think we can assume it's trying to help."

Carole doesn't believe this for a second.

"Those door sensors are electric," says Ryan. "At least some of the power must be on, then. Were there any lights on or anything?"

"No," says Julian. "But, it's a start." It's a good sign; if this world was degrading like the last one, why would any power be on? There has to be at least a chance that this place doesn't have a shelf-life.

*That doesn't mean we're getting out of here,* Julian thinks. Maybe it's a sign that they won't. He now feels worse than before— the thought of living out his days without his kids is beyond terrible, and staying here with God-knows what other inhabitants is unnerving. He chooses not to share these thoughts with the others. For the first time since Carole's sighting, the collective worry has finally subsided.

As the day goes on, the mood in the house cautiously improves. Ryan and Dannicka take the bikes out for a ride, disappearing together for nearly two hours. Marcy sings loudly while helping Carole to hang the laundry, and Julian beats a feverish Chet at Scrabble. For the first time in three days, the fire is lit and a proper dinner is made. Conversation returns to almost-normal, and the six roast marshmallows over the fire pit as dusk falls. Even Chet manages to eat too.

"So, it didn't have any hair or anything?" Marcy asks, sliding an incinerated marshmallow off her stick and into her mouth. Now that things feel somewhat normal again, it seems okay to ask; she's been dying to for days.

Carole shifts uncomfortably. "No, not on its face, anyway. I don't know what was under its hood."

"And it was small? Like a little kid?"

"Yes."

"And you said it was wearing a snowsuit...that is so *weird.* I wonder if it was cold or something."

"Could be."

"What about its hands? Did you get a look at them? Or was it wearing mittens?"

"Maybe Carole doesn't feel like talking about that," says Dannicka.

"Oh," says Marcy, disappointed. If she'd been the one to see it, that's *all* she would want to talk about. "Okay."

"It's fine," says Carole. She's got to deal with this anxiety and not allow it to envelope her. "I was wondering about that myself." *While trying to sleep last night.*

"Where do you guys think it came from?" Marcy asks.

"If we knew that," says Julian, loading his stick with marshmallows like a giant shish kabob, "we'd be in charge of the whole world. It was probably, as Ryan said, more afraid of us than we were of it. How about no more questions on that topic tonight?" He balances his stick over the fire. "But, on a related topic, I don't think we need to keep up with the all-night watch, anymore. Do you guys?"

"We could take a vote," says Marcy, raising her hand in the air. Cautiously, the others follow suit. Carole, seeing the consensus, joins in reluctantly—although it doesn't matter because she hasn't been sleeping much anyway. She can keep watch without the others even having to know. All she needs is three hours' sleep, really, and she can nap during the day.

Later, those few hours she allows herself would come back to haunt her.

# CHAPTER TWELVE

Chet wakes up early to discover that his sleeping bag is completely drenched. He had no idea that one person could produce this much sweat. Shivering and disgusted, he peels the top of the sleeping bag away from his clammy body and climbs out of it. He carries the sopping-wet bag into Carole's laundry room, where he shoves it into the large sink. He'll wash it later.

Upstairs, he's not surprised to find that he's the only one awake; the sun is just coming up. He pours himself a large glass of water and downs the entire thing in one go, then looks out the kitchen window into the back yard. He wonders if the creature Carole saw could be around here somewhere—or if it repaired something else during the night. Curious, he flips the light switch over the sink, just in case, but it doesn't come on. He tries the hot water tap, letting the water run for several seconds but it stays ice cold. It was worth a try.

Wandering into the living room and over to the front window, he becomes vaguely aware that his face is growing hot again, a flush of heat rising up from his torso. This, however, takes a back seat to the fact that his car, usually parked in Carole's driveway, is not there. Did one of the others take it? Has there been another sighting of the creature? Quietly, he heads to the front door and lets himself out.

His car is nowhere to be seen, but that's not all—Julian's car is also missing. With a quick glance around, he realizes that all the vehicles that were once abandoned on the street are gone.

Still barefoot, and clad only in a pair of shorts, he begins to run. At the end of the street, he turns left and runs down the next street, crosses over and runs down another. Each one is completely devoid of vehicles. Even the two Harleys that he has passed many times...gone.

He runs until he can't run anymore. He stops, now eight blocks from Carole's house, and tries to catch his breath. His face feels like it's on fire, like his head might explode from the heat it's generating. Slowly, he walks back to Carole's with one hand clutching the cramp in his side. As he reaches Carole's street, he sees Julian standing frozen in the driveway.

"They're all gone," Chet shouts hoarsely.

One by one, the others join Julian on the front porch, each making the discovery for themselves. Not a word is uttered—the desire to speculate disappears, replaced by numb apathy.

A heavy silence falls over the group, and remains throughout the day.

***

Marcy has gotten used to the quiet in this world, but what she cannot stand is the silence that now hangs over the entire house. *No one* is talking. It makes her more uneasy than the missing cars. She would like to say something, or to ask some question that might start a conversation, but she can't think of anything that might change the mood.

She looks at Julian, who is sitting at the kitchen table staring off into space. Whenever she sees this look on a grown-up, she knows they want to be left alone. She picks up her Discman from the living room couch, then looks back at Julian. He doesn't seem to notice her. She doesn't know if it's appropriate to listen to music right now, but she has to do something. She carries the Discman past Julian and walks out into the back yard. Dannicka is sitting on a lawn chair with a book, but Marcy can tell she's not really reading. Ryan sits beside her with his head back, eyes closed. Marcy walks past them to the back of the yard, sitting down on a blanket she had left out earlier.

She puts the headphones on, then looks at Ryan and Dannicka to see if either of them tells her not to, but Ryan's eyes are still closed and Dannicka is still starting at her book. Marcy presses 'play', then jumps a little at the volume. It seems so loud even though it's set where she always leaves it. Self-consciously, she turns it down, but somehow it still seems wrong. After only a few seconds, she turns the music off.

***

In the late afternoon, Carole walks into the kitchen where Marcy and Ryan are silently chopping vegetables for dinner.

"Would you two join us outside?" she asks. "I'd like to have a family meeting."

Although they've all considered themselves family since the second shift, no one has said it out loud before. Marcy and Ryan follow her out to the backyard where Dannicka and Julian are waiting. Chet, now listless, lies beside them on a patio chaise with his feet dangling over the edge.

"I think it's safe to say," Carole begins, "that we have absolutely no control over what happens to us in this world. And, I don't mean to scare anybody, but I think we need to be realistic."

"You think we're going to be here forever," says Marcy. It's not a question.

"I don't know what to think anymore. But I want to tell each and every one of you," *while I still can, while we're still here,* "that I'm not sorry this has happened." Carole's lip begins to tremble. "I think knowing you is one of the greatest gifts in my life. So, yes, Marcy, if we have to be here forever," *even if forever is only days from now,* "I will be honoured to spend it with all of you."

"My real name is Maureen!" Dannicka suddenly blurts. "I mean, I changed it a few months ago—I just wanted you all to know."

The others nod, except for Chet, who appears to have drifted off. Carole looks at him as he lies across from her, noticing that the light around him has changed. It's brighter than it used to be—she's sure of it. She glances around their circle, confirming that his light is definitely brighter than anyone else's. She glances back at Julian who is already looking directly at her. She knows he sees it, too.

Suddenly, Chet raises his head and opens his eyes at half-mast.

"Hey," he mumbles, his eyes bloodshot and unfocused. "So, how can we repopulate the new world with just us?"

They all look at him, then at each other, worried.

"We need to get him into bed," says Carole. "Now."

"Let him sleep in my bed," says Julian. "I don't think he can make it downstairs."

Together, he and Ryan each drape an arm around Chet, struggling to get the tall teenager to his feet. With some effort, they eventually manage to get him into the guest room and onto the bed.

"Blanket?" Julian whispers to Ryan. He can't tell whether or not to cover Chet—he's so hot.

"Just do the sheet," says Ryan, removing Chet's sandals. Even his feet are burning up. "And maybe a cold cloth for his head. I'll get one."

Across the hall, Ryan rinses a face cloth in the thankfully-frigid tap water, then wrings it out. As he returns to the guest room, Julian takes the cloth from him and arranges it on Chet's forehead, reminded of the times he's done the same for his daughters. Already, Chet is fast asleep.

"Whatever he's got," Julian whispers as they leave the room, "I hope it's not contagious."

The instant the words leave his mouth, he wishes he could take it back. He should have kept that to himself; the thought of them all getting sick will only add to their already-heightened anxiety.

"Shit," he mutters. "Sorry, I shouldn't have said that."

"It's fine," says Ryan. "We're probably all thinking it."

\*\*\*

"Have you ever had sunstroke?" Dannicka asks.

She lies on her side on Ryan's futon, her head propped up on one hand. Ryan, lying beside her in a mirrored image, shakes his head.

"No," he says. "You?"

"Once," she replies. "When I was in high school. But it didn't go on for days."

She doesn't need to say anything more.

He reaches out, placing his free hand over her hip, giving her an instant sense of security. She loves how he doesn't offer platitudes such as 'everything is going to be okay', or 'I'm sure Chet's fine.' Throughout this entire ordeal, she has noticed how Ryan has continued to face whatever has come their way without so much as a hint of fear––he just braces himself and deals with it. She thinks about Eric and how he was too chicken to even break up with her properly.

She leans in and Ryan meets her half-way, their mouths finding each other with growing familiarity. For a few moments, she allows herself to sink into the kiss, savouring the taste of him and the weight of his hand now grasping her hip, then reluctantly pulls away.

"I should go back upstairs," she says.

His voice is husky. "I wish you didn't have to."

"I know––me too." Especially tonight, with Chet sleeping upstairs and the rec room all to themselves. If it weren't for Marcy...

She sits up, straightening out her clothes. Before she can get to her feet, he reaches out and pulls her back in for one more kiss.

"Tomorrow," he says. "We'll get away again together."

***

"Hello, Ryan."

Ryan is sitting up in the futon in Carole's basement, propped up as if held by invisible hands. At the foot of the futon sits Chet. A small spotlight—the same as the one that illuminated Roland's entire body—highlights only Chet's head.

"Chet? Are you okay?"

"You may call us that," But this isn't Chet's voice—Ryan knows this voice.

"Where have you been?" he starts.

"It has been difficult to contact you," Chet says. He sits on the futon's edge, in a very unnatural pose--his back is stiff and straight, his knees are folded up to his chest, and both hands hang straight down, fingers grazing the floor. While his body faces the wall, his head is turned at ninety degrees to face Ryan straight on. "The laws here," he continues, "are very different."

It is so strange to hear Roland's voice coming out of Chet's mouth. It's even more strange to look into his eyes and not recognize the person behind them.

"We may not have long," Chet says, "as connection is taxing."

Ryan has so many questions, but he nods in understanding.

"We have attempted to shift you," Chet continues, "but have been unsuccessful. It is recommended that you return to the location of the previous shift."

Chet blinks, for what Ryan realizes is the first time during this communication.

"Do you understand?"

"Yes," says Ryan. "Is this world degrading, too?"

"Not degrading. It is being restructured for other uses. You will need to shift before this restructure is complete or risk a permanent stay."

Permanent? Ryan doesn't like the sound of that. He starts to ask another question but is cut off.

"One of you has encountered an Adjuster—you may encounter others from time to time. It is important you not interfere. Allow them to do their work."

An Adjuster?

"How long before this restructure—" Ryan blurts.

Ryan wakes up.

\*\*\*

"Julian?... Julian!"

Julian is sleeping on the couch in the living room, forcing himself awake at the sound of his name. He squints open one eye.

"Chet?"

"No—it's me."

"Oh. Ryan. What's wrong?"

"Roland came."

Julian sits up. "What?"

"Roland."

"No way." He rubs his eyes with one hand. "Lay it on me."

As Ryan begins to recount his dream, they hear the door to Carole's bedroom open. A moment later, she pops her head into the living room and gives them a drowsy wave, then pads over to the guest room where Chet has spent the night.

With a light tap on the door, she quietly lets herself in. She's been in twice during the night and now, for the first time, she sees that the light surrounding him has dimmed back to normal. Relieved, she tip-toes into the room and places her hand on his forehead, then his cheek. The fever is gone.

As she turns to leave, she hears a mumbled "Hello?"

"Sorry to wake you," she whispers. "I just wanted to see how you're feeling."

"Thirsty," he croaks.

"I'll get you some water."

On her way to the kitchen, she sees that Marcy and Dannicka have joined the other two in the living room. Marcy sees her and smiles brightly.

"Roland came!"

***

"So, what I saw was an 'Adjuster'?" Carole asks.

"I believe so."

"And we might see more of them?"

"Possibly. But, like they said, we're to leave them alone."

"Don't worry," she mutters under her breath.

"I doubt they're dangerous," he adds. "They would have told me."

"Maybe I'll get to see one!" say Marcy, hopefully. She wouldn't bother it—she'd let them do their work, just like Roland said to.

She wonders what their 'work' actually is. Do they have jobs, like people? Who's their boss? Where did they come from? She knows Ryan never seems to have enough time with Roland for that many questions...maybe she can suggest to him that, next time he gets a visit, he should talk super-fast.

"Well, be warned, Marcy," says Carole, only slightly reassured by this new information—they might not be dangerous, but knowing there's more than one out there doesn't exactly fill her with comfort. "It might sound exciting," she adds, "but it's very unnerving."

She turns back to Ryan. "So, what about shifting us back? How exactly are they going to do that?"

"Well, I was just telling Julian that they want us all to go back to where we were for the last shift. Back to that park." Ryan says this calmly, hoping not to make a big deal out of what he knows is unsettling information.

Dannicka feels her stomach drop. Yes, she wants to get back, obviously, she just wishes there was another way.

"And we'll need to get there before that 'restructure'," says Julian. "Right?"

"Yeah," says Ryan. "And I'd say sooner than later. Although it's hard to tell what their concept of time is."

"We could go as soon as tomorrow," says Julian, feeling optimistic. "I mean, provided you're up to it, Chet."

Chet sits up in the armchair. "I'm feeling better—we could go today." He says this because he knows he should, but honestly, the thought of going back there is as unappealing as ever.

*Quit being a frickin' baby*, he tells himself, *and suck it up.*

"No chance," says Carole. "You haven't eaten in two days—you're too weak. If we had a vehicle to get there, that would be one thing. But we don't."

He tries not to look relieved.

Carole feels guilty for using Chet's illness as an excuse to not have to rush back to the southside. At the mere mention of the park, she suddenly sees that house flash in her memory; the one they had parked in front of that gave her such a terrible feeling.

She'd put it out of her mind after they'd left, thinking she would never have to go back there again. It's true that Chet would be too weak to travel today without a vehicle, but if she had one more day to get used to the idea of going back there, she might at least feel more mentally prepared.

"By the way," says Ryan. "I think I might have some insight into Chet's fever."

Julian looks at Ryan sharply. *Please don't say you've got one, too. Please don't let this be contagious.*

"I'm so used to calling them, or it, Roland, but it wasn't my cat Roland who paid the visit last night." He turns to Chet. "It was you."

All eyes turn Chet's way.

"Me? What?" He wracks his brain, trying to remember if he'd had any dreams last night, let alone *that* dream, but he doesn't. In fact, he doesn't even remember going to bed. He'd been more than a bit surprised to wake up in Carole's guest room this morning.

"It was definitely you, man. With a full-on Australian accent."

Marcy looks at Chet as if seeing him for the first time. "Did you feel anything?" she asks. "Do you remember doing that?".

"No." The more he hears, the less he likes. He feels a sudden case of the creeps coming on.

"God, you guys are so lucky!" Marcy exclaims.

Dannicka raises an eyebrow.

"I mean, Carole gets to see an Adjuster, Ryan gets to talk to Roland, and Chet gets to *be* Roland! When is something so awesome gonna happen to me?!"

"Isn't this whole thing awesome enough?" Dannicka asks. "I mean, you are literally in another world right now."

"I guess..." Marcy rolls her eyes and sighs loudly as if to say it'll have to do.

Dannicka laughs. She looks over to Ryan, deciding that Marcy is partly right—Ryan is special. He's not like anyone she's ever known. He is somehow set apart and she has the distinct impression that the accident he suffered (the details of which he shared with all but Marcy that first day) is only a part of the reason Roland can reach him.

"Are you going to be 'Roland' from now on?" Marcy asks Chet.

"I don't think they can do that again," says Ryan. "They said that the connection was taxing."

"Thank God for that," says Carole. Chet still looks incredibly drained.

"Well, we could take the bikes when we go," says Julian. He turns to Carole. "And we can take as many breaks as we need. How long would it take to bike there from here?"

"Maybe about an hour, give or take," she answers.

"We'll plan for tomorrow, then," he says, releasing a huge sigh. "Urgh! I can't believe it!" He laughs a little, allowing himself for a moment to imagine going back home tomorrow and actually seeing his wife and girls. It's almost too much.

The day is spent making plans, packing supplies, and getting organized. Chet can feel the excitement buzzing throughout the house, mostly from Julian and Marcy, but his own excitement is non-existent. In addition to his dread about heading south, he can't get past the thought that Roland used him to reach Ryan. He must have sleep-walked downstairs into the rec room. How could they have gotten him to do that, and to use their voice without him knowing in any way? He knows how important their information is, he knows it's what is going to get them home, but he can't help it—his skin is crawling.

***

After the evening meal, the six sit quietly around the backyard fire.

"This might be our last night together," says Dannicka reflectively. "I mean, like this."

"Maybe in *this* world," says Carole. "But I can't imagine not having all of you in my life after this. We are bound together now, wherever we are."

"Yeah." Marcy nods solemnly. After the initial excitement about getting back, she's now starting to feel apprehensive. Naturally she doesn't want to live in an empty world forever, but the thought of being back in her own house, away from her people, is making her feel sad. How can she just go back to her old life?

"Look at that!" Chet suddenly says, pointing over into the distance.

"Look at what?" asks Marcy. She follows his gaze, unsure as to what he's talking about. Then she sees it. "Holy crow!"

The others all turn their heads. North of Carole's house, a few kilometers away, are the tops of what appear to be a cluster of buildings. They are unlike any structures any of them have ever seen, at least in real life.

"Those weren't there before," Marcy says.

"No, they sure as hell weren't." Carole, unnerved, squints into the distance.

"How could they have been built that fast without us noticing?" asks Dannicka. But, before letting anyone reply, she answers her own question. "Never mind. Apparently, anything is possible here."

"I guess that's part of the 'restructure'," Julian says, wondering just how long they have before it's complete. If buildings of that size can pop up in a few hours...

"Carole, do you have any binoculars?"

"I actually do," she says. "For travelling, not for spying on the neighbours," she adds, reading Marcy's mind.

She retrieves them and hands them to Julian. He holds them up to his eyes, adjusting the lenses. The instant the view becomes clear, he pulls the binoculars away.

"What's wrong?" asks Dannicka.

"Nothing, I just..." *don't want to look at them.* "Nothing, they're just really bizarre."

He tries to describe what he saw in that split second. "The shapes of the buildings themselves are...inconsistent. I don't know how they're staying upright. And they're all glass. Except, I don't think there are any windows."

"They make me feel funny," says Marcy. He turns quickly to find her looking through the binoculars.

"Stop it!" he snaps, more harshly than intended. He swipes the binoculars swiftly away.

Her eyes widen in surprise. "Sorry!"

"No, it's okay—I'm sorry. I just don't think we're supposed to look at them. I don't think they're meant for us."

"Okay."

The group is quiet for a moment.

"I wonder what they're turning this place into," Chet says.

No one answers, but they are all thinking the same thing: if they don't get out of here in time, they just might find out.

\*\*\*

Dannicka is dreaming about the man on her balcony again.

He's still there, standing with his back to her, his gloved hands gripping the metal railing. The tails of his long, dirty coat ruffle gently with the breeze. The pale lilac sky frames his silhouette.

Standing nervously in her living room, Dannicka (who has never been a nail biter) has crammed all ten of her fingertips into her mouth trying to stifle a scream or a whimper, or any other sound she feels compelled to make.

*Shut up!* she commands herself. *He'll hear you!*

The sliding glass door between them is still closed, but she doesn't know whether or not it is locked. Should she risk it? Or should she just run?

*No,* she thinks anxiously. *I have to know if it's locked. I need to make sure it's locked.*

She takes one small cautious step toward the door, toward the man in the long, dirty coat. Then, despite her racing fear, she stands perfectly still, waiting to see if he reacts. The man on her balcony doesn't move. She dares to take one more tiny step forward, then another.

There's still time to run.

*No! I have to lock the door, now! Do it, now!*

The instant she reaches for the handle the man on her balcony turns his head and smiles!

Alison Golosky

Dannicka screams. His smile is horrible. There are two rows of lilac-coloured teeth, and that's not all--his entire face is lilac, too.

# CHAPTER THIRTEEN

<u>SUNDAY, JULY 23</u>

Julian has spent another night on the couch after insisting Chet sleep in the guest room, but he has barely slept in anticipation of the day ahead. By 5:00 a.m. he can no longer lie still. He gets up and walks quietly across the house, letting himself out through the sliding doors in the kitchen.

He makes his way over to Carole's garage, unlocks the door and uses a flashlight to check on their bikes within the dark interior. He had chained them together the night before as an added security measure, despite knowing that chains would not deter whatever force might want them gone. With immense relief, he finds the bikes exactly where he'd left them. Thank God.

Locking the door on his way out, he proceeds with his morning perimeter check of the front and back yards, looking carefully for anything that may have changed since yesterday. Everything appears to be in order and he feels himself relax a little. The others should be up soon, and then they can all get going.

*This time tomorrow,* he thinks, *I could be back at home.* In bed with his real wife, his real daughters sleeping in their rooms across the hall. He's going to miss this house, though. No doubt about that. A sudden pang of sadness takes him by surprise. He gazes once more across the yard, standing perfectly still and taking a moment to fully appreciate the silence of this world. It may be his last chance to experience this kind of calm; one way or another, it is going to change.

After a few moments, he starts walking toward the house and something catches his eye. Quickly, he turns back and discovers he is only six feet away from what must be an Adjuster. Julian freezes. It's just as Carole described—the size of a small child, no bigger than his eight-year-old, with skin so glaringly white that its massive whitish-blue eyes stand out like headlights. But, of course, the most striking thing about it is not the features it has, but the ones it doesn't have—a nose or a mouth.

The head-to-toe snowsuit it is wearing is so unbelievably white that Julian feels the need to shield his eyes. He resists the urge to make any sudden movement and stands completely still, heart thudding, staring at this being with incredulity.

What is it? Where did it come from? It dawns on him then that perhaps it is from right here, in this world. It may be wondering just what the hell Julian is, and where *he* came from.

Remembering his manners, Julian forces some semblance of a smile. The Adjuster remains completely still, not reacting in any way. It's impossible to tell if this creature is actually looking at Julian, even at this distance. Its eyes, though large, do not appear to be focused on anything in particular.

Julian can practically hear his heart thudding inside his chest. It's so loud that he wouldn't be surprised if even the Adjuster could hear it. Do they have ears? Oh God, he really should just get out of here!

Slowly, cautiously, he begins walking backwards in the direction of the house. He's been told not to interfere and to let it do its... work, but somehow turning his back seems risky. It's only when his heel scrapes the edge of the deck that he dares to turn away, scrambling quickly up the steps and back inside the house. Slowly, he closes the sliding glass door, carefully eyeing the Adjuster, who may or may not be eyeing him.

Before the door closes completely, Julian is struck by a worrisome thought. Unable to help himself, he pops his head back out the door, smiles as if trying to placate a difficult customer and says, "we need those bikes, okay? Thanks!"

The Adjuster, still motionless, does not react in any way. Julian slides the door closed, then locks it. He wonders if he should have thanked the Adjuster for repairing the doors at the store. For a fleeting moment, he contemplates opening the door again and doing just that, before realizing how crazy that would be. Instead, he backs away slowly, creeping over to the kitchen sink where he cautiously peers out the window. There is no sign of the Adjuster anywhere.

He releases a huge gust of breath, not realizing he'd been holding it in.

*The bikes!* he thinks suddenly. *Shit! What if it took the bikes?*

He has to go back out there. He feels for the garage keys in his pocket, and takes a deep breath. He wants to make a mad dash back out there, check inside the garage and then race back to the house, but his better judgement tells him to go slow.

He sticks his head out first, looks from side to side, then ever so slowly extricates himself from the safety of the dining room. He stands still for a full twenty seconds before beginning an excruciating slow thirty-pace trek to the garage. Nervously, he begins to whistle softly, then stops the moment he realizes what he's doing.

When he reaches the garage, he pauses again before putting the key in the lock. With another glance from side to side, he finally opens the door and shines the flashlight inside.

The bikes are still there.

"Yes!" he whispers.

*This time tomorrow,* he thinks, *I could be away from all this weird shit.*

\*\*\*

Ryan wakes up alone in the rec room. He rolls over on to his back, opens his eyes, and sits up with an ease he'd never dreamed possible.

*Better enjoy it now,* he tells himself, *because it's never going to be like this again.* If they get back to the real world, he'll go back to his real-world body. He knows this to be true. He wonders what it would have been like to wake up next to Dannicka, to hear her breathing beside him, to have spent the whole night with her.

That's never going to happen either—it couldn't have happened here because Marcy depended on her during the nights, and in the real world, he will never be able to let Dannicka into his life. How could he do that to her? It wouldn't be much of a life for her, at all. It would be a sentence. He can't stand the thought of her being trapped with a miserable invalid, missing out on all the things she deserves to have, to experience. As messed-up as this world has been, it's been amazing, too. He's had a life here—a chance to feel whole; something most people in his situation never get. He is grateful for that. And now, he needs to let it go.

***

Marcy wakes up.

Beside her, Dannicka is curled up in a ball, her hands clenched into fists, covering her face. Marcy wants to hug her. She has never shared a room with her 'real' sister. She couldn't imagine ever having to, and now she can't imagine not sharing a room with Dannicka. She sits up and leans over, concerned by the expression on Dannicka's face.

"Are you crying?"

Dannicka, eyes open, has woken up with a start, expecting to see the man with the lilac face. Instead, she sees only Marcy and is immediately relieved.

"No," she says, catching her breath. "I'm not."

She blinks her eyes firmly to clear her vision, then focuses back on Marcy. "Are you?"

Marcy nods.

"Come here." Dannicka reaches out for the younger girl, who gives in readily to the embrace. If Marcy had seen what Dannicka just dreamed, she'd be crying even harder.

"We're going to see each other when we get back," Dannicka says, wanting it to be true and wanting to reassure herself as much as Marcy. "All the time. It's gonna be great. We'll have our other families, and our other friends, and we'll have each other, too."

She kisses the top of Marcy's head, trying to comfort her, trying to erase the image of those flashing lilac teeth. A terrible thought comes to her mind and she can't shut it out.

*He's over there. And he knows we're coming.*

\*\*\*

Carole wakes up, thinking about the five people now sleeping in various rooms throughout her house. She has always preferred to be alone here, her home has always been her sanctuary, but now she can hardly bear the thought of waking up tomorrow alone. She wipes the tears from her eyes, telling herself that they will still see each other; and it won't have to be in a world shared with Adjusters.

\*\*\*

Chet lies on Carole's guest bed. He does not wake up.

\*\*\*

Marcy sits up suddenly in bed, clutching her chest.

"Whoa!" she exclaims. "That was weird! It just felt like all the air in my lungs got, like, sucked out or something!"

She looks over to Dannicka, who is standing at the end of their shared futon, one hand holding her own chest.

"You felt that, too?" Dannicka asks, catching her breath.

"Yeah...but I think I'm okay..."

A terrible feeling descends upon Dannicka, so sudden and shocking, like being doused with a bucket of ice water.

"Something's wrong!" she cries. Instinctively, she bolts out of Carole's studio and races over to the guest room.

"Chet!" she screams, banging on the door. "Chet!"

Without waiting for an answer, she flings the door open and bursts into the room. Chet is lying face down on the bed, the light that had emanated from him so brilliantly is gone.

"No!" she screams in panic. "No!" She rushes over to him and tries desperately to turn him over, but he's too heavy!

"Marcy!" she screams. "Help me!"

Carole, Ryan, and Julian, all of whom had experienced the same sensation in their own lungs, rush into the guest room on instinct.

"Let me through!" Ryan demands, pushing his way past the others. He desperately hopes that he will remember the CPR training he had done two years ago. With one swift move, he turns Chet's body over as Marcy and Dannicka jump out of the way. Ryan climbs on top of him and starts a series of chest compressions, followed by mouth-to-mouth resuscitation. Chet doesn't respond.

"Come on!" Ryan grunts. "Come *on!*"

Maybe he's not doing it right. Maybe the compressions aren't hard enough—Chet's a big guy. Is he counting right? Is he going too fast?

*Come on,* he tells himself. *Concentrate!*

He does another set of compressions followed by more mouth-to-mouth. He tries not to see that Chet's lips are blue, that his skin is an ashy grey.

*Concentrate.*

He becomes so focused on his task that he doesn't hear Marcy sobbing uncontrollably. He doesn't see Dannicka, helpless and horrified, trying her best to offer comfort. He doesn't notice Carole and Julian standing at the foot of the bed, holding on to one another in disbelief. One more set of chest compressions, one more attempt at mouth-to-mouth.

*This isn't happening,* he tells himself. *This is not happening!* They're supposed to be getting out of here.

For nearly ten minutes, the others stand by as Ryan does everything he can to resuscitate Chet's lifeless body.

"The bed's got too much give!" he shouts. "Help me get him onto the floor!" Goddammit, why hadn't he thought of that the minute he got here!?

Carole breaks away from Julian then, and speaks in a low voice.

"Ryan."

He doesn't hear her. He continues on with another set of chest compressions.

"Ryan," she says, a little louder. "Stop."

Ryan, pale and exhausted, ignores her and continues on.

"Ryan. Stop."

"I can't!" he says through gritted teeth.

Dannicka unpeels Marcy's arms from around her waist and goes over to him, placing both hands gently on his back.

"Stop," she whispers. "He was already gone when we came in."

Ryan covers his face with his hands, forces back the sobs that are welling up from deep inside. Dannicka keeps both hands gently but firmly on his back, feeling the sorrow radiating out of him in waves, flowing into her hands and up her arms, swirling through her body and mixing with her own.

Finally, he climbs off Chet, off the bed, and slumps onto the floor. For several seconds, no one moves.

"Come on," Julian tells Marcy. He shouldn't have let her see this. Placing a hand on her shoulder, he tries to guide her away but she shakes him off.

"No!" she says, her voice thick with tears. "I want to stay."

He doesn't argue.

Marcy had always thought that seeing a dead body would be the worst thing in the entire world. But this isn't a dead body. This is her brother. Wiping the tears from her face, she walks over to the bed and kneels beside it. She slides one hand under Chet's and holds it gently. His large hand is so cold. She places her other hand on top of his, clasping it firmly. No matter how long she sits there, it does not warm up.

\*\*\*

Four hours after they have found Chet dead, Julian says what no one else had wanted to say.

"We still need to leave."

"We're not leaving him here," Carole snaps, with more than a hint of hysteria in her voice.

"No, we're not. We're bringing him with us."

"Will he still be able to shift with us?" asks Marcy.

"I hope so," says Julian. "His parents will want to see him."

While sitting around the kitchen table, they begin the difficult discussion about how to transport Chet's body. Ryan, who has not spoken in hours, suddenly gets to his feet, roughly pulling his chair out of the way. He stomps out of the kitchen and slams the front door on his way out of the house.

"Where's he going?" asks Marcy.

"I don't know," says Dannicka, "but we'll let him be."

Ryan rushes down the front sidewalk, down Carole's street, then breaks into a run. He runs for several blocks, each step landing heavily on the pavement, until he can hardly breathe. Unable to keep up his frenzied pace, he stops in the middle of the street and screams—a pained, guttural sound.

"It's MY fucking fault!" he hollers desperately into the silence. "I should have fucking *DIED* in that accident!"

There is no response to his outburst—just the incessant brilliance of the sun beating down on him.

"I should have FUCKING DIED!" he screams again.

He is only a block away from the grocery store, he can see it from here, and he begins striding toward it. He tells himself that if the doors won't open, he will smash them in with his bare hands. He is almost disappointed when he steps on the mat to find they slide open easily.

Holding his breath, he runs into the store without realizing that it no longer smells. In the back storeroom, he quickly finds what he's looking for thanks to one large halogen light glowing dimly from the ceiling. The fact that the light is on goes unnoticed—he only cares about what he's come here for.

He walks over to a flat metal cart that looks about five feet long. It won't be long enough for Chet's 6-foot-4-inch frame, but it will have to do. Ryan manoeuvres it out of the back room and into the store. Clumsily, he rolls it down one of the long aisles, the front corner colliding once or twice into food items on the lower shelves, sending them sprawling.

When he reaches the end of the aisle, he sees what he knows must be an Adjuster standing behind one of the tills as if waiting to ring up Ryan's groceries. Even through his grief and anger, the sight of the Adjuster is jarring. Ryan jumps a little, stopping in his tracks.

The Adjuster stares blankly at him. At least, Ryan thinks it's staring at him—it's almost as though its eyes are looking everywhere at once while at the same time showing no sign of movement. For a few moments, they both stand frozen in place.

"I'm taking the fucking cart!" Ryan shouts, breaking the silence. "Just try and fucking stop me!"

He stares at the Adjuster, daring it to retaliate, but it does nothing.

"Fuck you," he mutters. He shoves the flatbed cart roughly past the Adjuster and out the doors, into the glaring sunshine.

***

While Ryan is gone, Carole heats a pot of water over the fire, pouring it into a large bowl and adding dish soap. She carries it carefully into the guest room, setting it down on the nightstand. She sets up a folding chair beside the bed and begins to wash Chet's body with a soft cloth. When Dannicka sees what Carole is doing, she fills another large bowl and joins her. In silence, the two women carefully wash and dry each part of Chet, struggling against the rigor mortis that is beginning to set in. When they are done, they dress him in his favourite shorts and t-shirt. Carole finds a fresh sheet and together they wrap his body.

By one thirty that afternoon, the six are ready to go. Carole, Julian, Ryan, Dannicka, and Marcy carry heavy backpacks full of supplies. There is no way to predict how long they will be on the dreaded southside, nor exactly what they will find when they get there.

Chet's shrouded body lies on the cart before them. Julian has attached a sturdy piece of plywood under his legs to extend the length of the cart. Under Chet's head is a small pillow, that Marcy had suggested and lovingly placed. She refused to turn away as Julian and Ryan secured his body with ropes. Dannicka, on the other hand, could not bear to look until the process was complete.

Chet's backpack, which he had packed for himself the night before, was momentarily placed on the cart next to his legs, but it seemed somehow disrespectful—like his body was also luggage. Instead, Julian volunteered to carry the extra pack along with his own.

Carole and Ryan take their positions at the cart's handle. The excursion, meant to be a one-hour bike ride, will now take hours on foot.

"Let's go," says Carole grimly.

The house—which the six had been sad to leave only hours before—now stands empty and ominous behind them.

No one looks back.

# CHAPTER FOURTEEN

By two o'clock, the blazing sun feels like absolute punishment. Carole, already sore from pushing the heavy cart this far, wipes her forehead with the back of her hand.

"Okay," she says. "Time to rest."

"I can keep going," says Marcy, who has been carrying Mr. Biscuits for most of the trip so far.

"It's too hot," Julian tells her. "We need to stop every half-hour."

They sit on the front lawn of a 1950s home in the shade of a large pine tree. The cart, too difficult to manoeuvre over the tree's protruding roots, stays where it is on the sidewalk, under the fiery sun. No one wants to mention the fact that Chet's body is beginning to smell.

"We've done about 14 blocks," says Carole.

Julian nods, then takes a large swig of water. "So, from here," he thinks for a moment, "it's about twenty-five blocks to the bridge, right?"

"Give or take."

The group falls back into silence. Marcy carefully pours some water into her hand, then watches as Mr. Biscuits eagerly laps it up. Dannicka sits next to Ryan, linking an arm through his for comfort, despite the heat. Ryan feels no comfort from the gesture, overcome with guilt. Her pain, and the pain of the others, is his fault. And he will never forgive himself.

After only a few minutes' rest, he gets back to his feet.

"You wanna get going?" asks Julian.

He nods.

"I'll take your place at the cart, then."

Ryan adjusts the straps on his backpack. "No, I got it."

Julian knows better than to argue. "I'll take your place then, Carole."

Marcy adjusts her over-sized sun hat, something she never would have worn around her friends in the real world, and picks up Mr. Biscuits.

"Ready," she says.

After another fifteen minutes, they find themselves standing outside of the Grabbajabba parking lot. Without a word, they stop to look.

"Do you guys think it would be worth it to go inside?" asks Dannicka. "What if we can shift from here?" *What if we don't have to go back to the southside*, she wonders, thinking about the freakish man in her apartment. She hasn't told anyone about the dreams. She would have this morning, if...well, she would have told Ryan, at least. Now, it seems unimportant in the grander scheme of things––she doesn't need to add to the already-terrible situation. But if she could just get that lilac face out of her mind...

*...They were just some fucked up dreams about a monster in my apartment,* she tells herself. *And we're not even going back there.*

"They," Ryan catches himself before saying 'Chet', "specifically said 'the previous location.' I dunno. What do you guys think?"

"Sure, let's stop," says Carole.

Dannicka relaxes ever so slightly. The thought crosses her mind that even if they did shift from here, it might not get them to the right place.

"Why don't I go have a look," says Julian. He leaves his place at the cart and ventures forward, remembering how anxious he had been about coming back here the first time. Though still wary, his criteria for what scares him has changed now—and stepping into the Grabbajabba is pretty low on the list.

Carole stands in the parking lot, watching as he cautiously opens the front door of the coffeeshop.

"It's a hair salon!" he calls to the others.

Marcy sets Mr. Biscuits down and follows him then, curious to see for herself. After poking her head in for a moment, she, too, addresses the others. "It's true!" She looks back at Julian. "But the outside still says Grabbajabba."

"I guess it's in transition."

"It's cool in here," she says, venturing inside.

At first, he thinks she's referring the design of the salon, then realizes she was speaking literally.

"You're right," he says. "There's air-conditioning in here."

The power is coming on in bits and pieces. How long do they have before the restructure is complete?

"There's air-conditioning!" he calls to the others. "We might as well take advantage of it."

"Maybe we shouldn't all go in at once," Carole calls back. "What if we end up shifting to the wrong place again?"

Dannicka looks over to her. "I had the same thought," she confesses.

Julian wipes his forehead. "Right. Well, I'll wait outside—"

"I'll stay here," says Ryan, both hands still gripping the cart handle.

Behind him, Dannicka places a hand on his back. "I'll wait with you."

"No—you should go in and cool off."

"At least wait in the shade, then, okay?"

Ryan complies, rolling the cart over a few feet.

Julian holds the door open for the rest, turning back to Ryan before going in. "Ten minutes, okay?"

Inside, the cool air feels like a blessed relief after weeks of soaring temperatures. While the others sink into chairs, Julian wanders into the back room, which appears to serve the same function as it did when the place was a Grabbajabba. He flicks the light switches on and off, but none of them work. Neither does the computer sitting silently on a small desk.

In the main area of the salon, Marcy scans the rows of mirrored stalls where tables used to sit. She remembers sitting in the middle of this room with her gigantic hot chocolate. And Chet was stand-ing right...there. She shuts her eyes and tries to remember what he looked like back then. She tries to remember him talking, moving, laughing, desperately wishing she could erase the thought of what he looks like right now.

The door to the salon opens and everyone jumps. It's Ryan, but he only peers in for a moment. "We should get going," he says.

"Don't you want to come in?" Julian asks. "I was just going to step out..."

"No."

Carole walks over to the entrance.

"Ryan, you really should cool off, it's only going to get hotter out there."

"I'm okay."

She nods, knowing she can't change his mind. She just wishes they could rest for a few more minutes; the heat is really getting to her.

Dannicka follows Ryan back to the cart, re-adjusting her backpack.

"Let me trade places with you," she says.

Stubbornly, he shakes his head.

"Then I'll push with you."

Together, they manoeuvre the heavy cart out of the parking lot and into the street.

Once past the Grabbajabba, they enter the neighbourhood of Oliver. Ryan's apartment is just a few blocks away, but he has no desire to go there. It occurs to him that since Chet is dead, his Roland—back in the real world—must be dead, too. They've both been used up. And, for what? So that some mysterious beings could get a message through? Beings who have that much power in the universe but don't know how to use a goddamned telephone?

There is another half-hour of walking in silence, after which Julian announces that it's time for another break. Ten minutes of sitting quietly, replenishing fluids, contemplating the next leg of the journey. Restless, Ryan announces once more that they need to move on. This time, Carole takes Dannicka's place at the cart.

Minutes later, they reach the crest of 109th Street, which leads down onto the High Level bridge. From here, they can see the river, and across it, the southside. Dannicka feels her pulse quicken, along with a renewed sense of dread—that unnerving lilac hue she had noticed the last time they were here seems to have intensified. She's not the only one who thinks so, either. Even though no one has said anything, there's a palpable increase in their collective apprehension; Carole's fear alone is practically wafting over Dannicka in waves.

"Let's stop for a second," says Julian, assessing the grade of the slope leading down to the bridge. It doesn't seem like much when you're in a car; but on foot, and with such a substantial burden, it is completely daunting. Chet's body has been well-secured to the cart, Julian made sure of that, but he still worries that it won't hold.

"Carole, why don't you hold the cart with Ryan and I—we're gonna need all the strength we can get."

"Okay."

"Here," says Dannicka. "You guys give your packs to me and Marcy; we'll carry them to the bottom."

They accomplish this in two trips, dropping each heavy knapsack with a thud onto the walkway beside the bridge.

"I can't watch this," says Dannicka. It's too awful. She turns her back, expecting Marcy to do the same, but Marcy faces the others stoically.

"I'll tell you when to look," she says, reaching out and placing a hand on Dannicka's shoulder.

At the top of the slope, Carole, Ryan, and Julian brace themselves.

"Ready?" asks Julian.

"Ready."

Almost instantly, Carole feels her grip slipping.

"You can let go," Ryan tells her, grimacing from the effort. "We've got it!"

"No!" she exclaims. She wraps her right arm around the handle so that she is pulling from her inner elbow, then does the same with her left. Adrenaline she didn't know she had kicks in. She hunches over and uses her thigh muscles to keep her feet from slipping. Her knees bump repeatedly into the top of Chet's head, upsetting her terribly.

"Sorry!" she gasps, as though he can hear her. "Sorry!"

Muscles aching and dripping with sweat, the three make it safely to the bottom with Chet's body still secure.

"It's okay," Marcy tells Dannicka. "You can look now."

Dannicka opens her eyes and turns back just as Carole, overwhelmed, bursts into tears. Without a word, Julian puts both arms around her, holding her while she cries. The others stand silently beside them. In the distance, Dannicka can see that awful lilac-coloured haze sitting heavily over what is visible of the southside. It has definitely gotten worse. A wave of revulsion passes over her.

*Suck it up,* she tells herself angrily. *No one wants to go there, but we* have *to. So, suck it up.*

\*\*\*

After another short break, they begin the dreaded trek across the High Level bridge. Dannicka takes another turn at the cart beside Ryan, who remains steadfast at the handle. Marcy, Carole, and Julian lag behind.

"I've never walked across here before," says Marcy, breaking the silence. She pauses briefly to look down at the water one hundred and fifty feet below her. She would never have been allowed to walk along here in her old life. She wishes she could have done this under much different circumstances. It could have been fun.

Dannicka thinks of all the times she has walked across this bridge, and how much she always loved doing so. But now, it will never be the same again. She cannot reconcile the beauty of the sun reflecting brilliantly upon the water—giving the appearance that the entire river is sparkling—with the dead body of someone she has loved like a brother tied before her to a storeroom cart.

Part way across the bridge, Ryan spots a small figure standing at the other end of the walkway. Dannicka, who has been looking out at the river in an attempt to avoid the lilac air looming ahead, does not notice.

"I don't want you to worry," he says, keeping quiet, "but there's an Adjuster up ahead."

She turns to look and catches her breath. It is too far away for her to make out any features, but the mere sight of another being, after weeks of being alone, is shocking—human or not.

They bring the cart to a slow stop.

"We've got company," says Ryan tersely.

The others come to a stop behind them, spotting the Adjuster in the distance.

"It'll be okay," says Julian. "I didn't get a chance to tell you... earlier, but there was one in Carole's back yard this morning. I was out there, too, and it didn't do anything. I just went back in the house," *where I didn't know Chet was dying, or dead,* "and, by the time I looked out the window it was gone."

He doesn't tell the others that he spoke to it, tried to interact. He should have kept his mouth shut. Maybe that's why...

"I saw one today, too," Ryan admits. "At the store." He doesn't tell the others about his verbal assault, though he's not sorry for it.

"I think we should stop here for a minute and not look at it," Julian suggests. "If we continue forward, it might take that as a threat."

"It's small," says Marcy, surprised. "It's smaller than me."

Carole stares at it for a moment, in defiance. *I'm not scared of you*, she thinks. But she is.

Together, the group turn away, facing the river as though this was the point of their trip.

After a few moments, Marcy, who just cannot help herself, turns her head ever so slightly. She slides her eyes as far to the right as she can, just in time to see the weird little creature move. It springs suddenly to life as though shocked by electricity, then waddles in a mad dash to its immediate left. The way it moves reminds Marcy of her brother when he was little; trying to play tag in the winter and running awkwardly, constricted by a stiff, unyielding snowsuit.

What happens next is even more bizarre—the Adjuster pulls open what looks like a small sliding glass door perched right in the middle of the air, and hops inside, completely disappearing from view! Marcy's eyes widen in surprise.

Glancing down at his watch, Julian sees that two full minutes have passed. He waits for another minute to go by before slowly looking over to the end of the walkway. There is no Adjuster in sight.

"I think it's okay now."

"I peeked!" Marcy confesses. "I couldn't help it!"

"Marcy!" Carole admonishes.

"Did you see anything?" asks Dannicka.

"I saw it leave. It moved sort of, sideways. And it pulled open this little glass door in the air, or something. And it went inside."

"What do you mean, a glass door?" Julian asks.

"Well, I could see right through it, like it looked like clear glass, but it was warbly. And, after the Adjuster walked through it, it totally disappeared!"

"Like a door that you open, or like a panel, like sliding patio doors?"

"Like sliding patio doors. It guess it was a panel then."

*More like a portal,* Ryan thinks.

"Can you see the panel now?" Julian asks.

Marcy squints into the distance. "No."

"They probably appear, then disappear," says Ryan, sounding like he couldn't care less either way.

"Well, we should keep going," says Julian.

At the end of the bridge, Marcy points out the area where she saw the glass panel.

"It was right here."

Upon closer inspection, they find nothing around the area to suggest anything unusual; plants, bushes, and the end of the walkway all appear as they always have. Dannicka has walked past here more times than she can count—she should know.

"These panel things are probably all over the place," says Carole, unnerved.

Julian, however, is now more concerned with the incline on this side of the bridge—it's much steeper than the north side. Even with three people at the cart, it will be too difficult to push it that far at that angle.

"Ryan," he says, pulling him aside, "I think you and I better carry Chet up the hill."

"I was thinking the same thing."

They begin loosening the knots they had so carefully tied back at Carole's house. The odour coming off of Chet's body is now impossible to ignore, and at this proximity, Julian has to fight his gag reflex. He holds his breath, but all he can think is that he's now ingesting the gasses being emitted into the air. He hates himself for thinking this.

Ryan sets about untying the knots and pulling away the ropes in a perfunctory way, seemingly unaffected by the stench. Behind them, someone is crying softly. He's not sure who, but it sounds like Dannicka.

When they are done, Julian steps back, stealing a massive gulp of fresh air. "Okay. So, how should we—"

"I'll take his shoulders," says Ryan. "You take his feet. On the count of three."

With great effort, the two men lift Chet off the cart. Ryan, walking backwards, begins carefully making his way up the incline. Julian follows, verbally instructing Ryan to head right and left as the path snakes its way upward.

Without a word, Marcy puts Mr. Biscuits down and begins loading the backpacks onto the now-empty cart. Carole and Dannicka help her and, when they are done, they silently push their cargo up the hill.

After their climb, Julian doesn't need to remind anyone to take a break. Exhausted and sweating, they sit in the only bit of shade they can find. The strangely coloured sky above them stretches out as far south as they can see, reflecting a pale lilac hue on everything around them. Every time Dannicka inhales, she feels as if she is swallowing it. She turns her head in a useless attempt to find unpolluted air.

Across the street is a diner where, in another life, she used to work as a waitress. She eyes it for a moment. "Maybe that's got air conditioning, too," she says. "Why don't I run over and check." *Why don't I go indoors and get away from this disgusting lilac fog?*

She crosses the main road and walks up to the front door of the diner. Gingerly, she pulls it open and is met with a blast of air so cold that she is instantly chilled to her bones. It's dark inside, almost impossibly dark considering the bright—albeit lilac—daylight. It takes a few moments for her eyes to adjust. When they do, she jumps back and slams the door shut, then turns and rushes back to the others.

"What's wrong?" asks Carole.

"It's cold in there, alright," she says, teeth still chattering. "But you don't want to go in there—it's a morgue."

"You mean, as cold as a morgue, or...?" Julian starts to ask.

"An *actual* morgue," she shudders. It's not at all like the funeral home her mother was in, with a depressingly formal reception room at the front, an austere and heavy atmosphere made even more so by attempting to downplay what lay in the next room. This is *only* a morgue; slabs, and tubes, and sinks, and formaldehyde. Since when are there morgues that you can walk right into from the street?

"Are there any bodies?" Carole asks.

"No," she says grimly. "Not yet." But someone is looking forward to filling it up. Someone who she now believes may, in fact, be real.

There are many other stores and restaurants on this stretch of 109th Street, all as innocuous from the outside as the surprise-morgue, prompting the quick and unanimous decision by the five not to enter any of them.

"We've got whatever we need anyway," says Julian. "Let's just keep going." Whatever is going on in this part of town, he doesn't want to know about it.

Together he and Ryan begin the laborious process of securing Chet's body back onto the cart. When completed, the group resumes its journey, plodding slowly down the middle of the deserted street.

Forty blocks to go.

\*\*\*

At seven thirty that evening, they arrive at the Lendrum park where, twenty-two days earlier they had shifted for the second time. Marcy and Ryan let the cart roll to a stop as the group visually survey the area.

The park looks very different than when they left it. Gone are the booths, Canada Day decorations, the baseball equipment, and the vehicles. There are no signs of any activity at all, except that someone, or something, has cleaned up.

"Well," says Julian, "we may as well make our way over to the exact spot."

He and Ryan silently untie Chet's body, freeing him from the cart which will be too difficult to roll through the grass while weighted down. Carole rolls the empty cart behind them, following the men as they carry Chet once again.

Marcy sets Mr. Biscuits down and watches as he wobbles through the neatly-cut grass. She remembers the first time she saw him here—she remembers how she ran from these people. She remembers Chet catching her, twice, in a giant bear hug, and how she fought against him. A massive lump forms at the back of her throat and she cannot seem to choke it down. Without a word, Dannicka puts an arm around her shoulders and silently walks in step.

When they reach the exact spot in the park where their second shift occurred, they all stop walking. Ryan and Julian return Chet's body to the cart, then join the others who have collapsed, exhausted, onto the grass. Dannicka feels ashamed for finding the smell wafting from Chet's body unbearable.

"What do we do now?" asks Marcy.

Julian looks once more around the park. "We wait."

\*\*\*

Hours later, when the sun begins to lower in the sky, Dannicka builds a fire.

\*\*\*

The decision to spend the night outside is unanimous. No one wants to miss their chance to shift—it could happen at any time—and besides, no one wants to sleep inside any of the houses. The house that caught Carole's attention the last time they were here still gives her the same foreboding feeling. She had hoped that it wouldn't be as bad as she anticipated, that it was only her anxiety making the memory of the house seem worse than it is. But here in its vicinity, the terrible energy emanating from it is undeniable. Do the others sense it, too? She doesn't know, but decides to keep her worries to herself. Other than one quick glance when they arrived, she has kept her back to that house whenever possible. This hasn't been much of a comfort, however—she still knows it's there. It seems to have eyes, watching her every move.

As the others begin to unroll their sleeping bags and attempt to get settled, Julian takes Carole aside.

"I'm going to check out that house across the street," he says quietly, pointing to the exact house that she's been avoiding.

Carole looks startled. "Why?! Why would you want to–?"

"I *don't* want to!" he snaps. "But, if it starts raining or something, we're going to need shelter. And I'd rather make the decision as to where that's going to be now, and not when we're in a rush to vacate."

She knows he's right, it's just...no one has wanted to go into any of the houses in this world, not even in Carole's neighbourhood let alone this disquieting part of town. They haven't been thinking straight. They should have brought tents.

"And anyway, we could use a place to go to the bathroom and wash up."

"Okay," she says reluctantly. "But, just don't go into *that* house." She eyes the other homes on the street. "That one," she says, indicating a similar house two doors to the left. "That one's okay."

He doesn't question her. They've all come to trust Carole's instincts.

"And don't go alone. Take Ryan with you."

They turn to look at Ryan, sitting next to Chet's body as if turned to stone.

"On second thought, I'll go with you."

"Then let's go now," he says. "Before it gets completely dark."

Armed with flashlights, Carole and Julian walk to the south end of the park, across the street, then up to the house she has deemed safe, or at least, safer. On the porch, Julian stops and looks at her. "Here goes nothing."

The door is unlocked. Cautiously, he pushes it open and waits. When nothing greets them, they venture slowly inside.

Julian finds a light switch and flicks it on, to no avail.

"Let's just do a quick check through, then get out of here," says Carole. "And, for the record, I'm not going into the basement."

"No argument there."

"Let's split up—we can get through this quicker."

He looks slightly surprised at her suggestion. "We're okay to do that?"

"Yes."

"I'll take the bedrooms, then."

"Fine."

It's an elderly couple, she soon decides, who must have lived here. She bases this on the furniture and décor, as well as the large framed photos in the living room which span at least six decades. In an instant, Carole is able to decipher the story of this family. She thinks about her own mother, hoping that Corinne is taking good care of her.

In the kitchen, she gives a quick once-over, then hears Julian in one of the bedrooms.

"All clear," he calls out.

"Here, too," she says. "Let's go."

Julian closes the door behind them then follows Carole down the walkway and onto the street. He turns to look back and his stomach drops—the door of the house two doors down, the one he had initially suggested, is ajar.

"That door is—"

"I know," she says, "Keep walking."

\*\*\*

"I'm staying up," Ryan announces.

The others can see how exhausted he is, from the traumatic day, and from pushing the cart for their entire journey, but no one argues. They don't want to risk another visit from Roland, either, though it's probably unlikely; one of them would have had a fever by now, if that was the case. Without further discussion, the others get into their sleeping bags and prepare for whatever amount of rest will be possible.

Julian hardly sleeps. He is worried about the partially opened door. He keeps turning toward it to check on...what?

He is worried, too, about the restructure—wondering just how long before there are animals and birds that might be attracted to Chet's body. Insects have settled in already, now that the cart has been parked in one place. Ryan has hung repellent-soaked cloths over Chet, but it doesn't seem to be very effective.

Restless, Julian opens his eyes and looks once again in the direction of the opened door.

Marcy, sleeping fitfully, repeatedly kicks Carole, who is next to her, throughout the night. Carole doesn't mind—it serves as a reminder that Marcy is still there.

As she continues to wake with each jab to her shins, she notices that only Dannicka seems to be sleeping soundly.

\*\*\*

Dannicka is dreaming about the man with the lilac face.

# CHAPTER FIFTEEN

## MONDAY, JULY 24

Dannicka is dreaming about the man with the lilac face. This time she is not in her apartment, but sitting on a cold metal slab in the morgue-that-used-to-be-a-diner. The man with the lilac face sits on the slab across from her, grinning broadly. The sight is terrifying. It's not just the pale purple-greyish hue of his skin that scares her, it's the frantic excitement in his eyes. This morgue is *his* place, she realizes. One of his places. And she walked right into it just yesterday. Why did she do that?

He wants to fill this place up. He wants them all here—he wants this to be their home. She needs to get the hell out of here. Now.

She tries to move, but can't. Her body is stuck to the cold slab like a tongue on a metal railing in the winter. She tries to scream, but no sound will come out. Oh, God. Oh, Jesus. Why did she come in here?! She squeezes her eyes shut, unable to bear the sight of this bizarre, horrible person. It's no use, though—she can still see him with his lilac-coloured skin, and teeth, and eyebrows. Even his greasy brown hair and filthy coat are now seared into her brain.

She dares to open her eyes again, too afraid not to see what will happen. He lifts one hand and points, deliberately, first to himself and then to her as if using a rudimentary form of sign language. And, just in case she's unclear about his meaning, he speaks aloud through his lilac smile. His voice is gravelly, as though he hasn't used it in years.

"You," he says. "And. Me."

*** 

Dawn.

Carole opens her eyes.

*Still here,* she thinks grimly, wishing that by some miracle, they might have shifted in their sleep, or perhaps woken up to find that the last twenty-four hours were just a bad dream. But as she looks over and sees Chet's body, she knows that neither wish has come true. If this next shift doesn't happen soon, she is going to have to leave. She honestly doesn't know how long she can stand being here on the southside—this place is going to drive her insane.

Sore from pushing the cart and from sleeping on the ground, she forces herself up into a seated position. The others are all asleep— even Ryan, she notices with relief.

Mr. Biscuits, still curled up beside Marcy, thumps his small tail at her. She pats his head then quietly gets out of her sleeping bag. Slipping into her shoes, she begins walking over to the house that she'd chosen the night before. They have taken to calling it the Designated House. It has proven itself to be safe, as she'd suspected, and she feels no trepidation about heading there alone now.

As she gets closer, she sees the door to the 'Other House'—the one Julian was first going to enter—and immediately stops walking. Last night, the door was slightly ajar. Now it's open half-way.

Without realizing, she covers her chest protectively with both hands and begins walking almost sideways to the left. She turns her head away, refusing to look at it any further, not wanting so much as a glimpse into the darkness spilling out of that house, its door hanging open like an unhinged jaw. She scurries quickly past it, allowing a wide berth on her way to the Designated House. When she reaches the front walk, she runs to the front door and dashes inside, quickly shutting the door behind her.

After using the bathroom and washing up, she discovers that the power is on in the kitchen. They could make a proper dinner here.

*Oh God, please don't let us have to. Please let us be out of here before dinner.*

She wanders to the living room window to check if the coast is clear before heading back out. She can see the others are still asleep on the grass. Ryan is curled up next to the cart a few feet away, staying near to Chet's body, apparently unbothered by the smell which the rest find increasingly difficult to bear.

The vignette displayed before her is so depressingly awful that Carole begins to cry. She covers her face with both hands and allows herself to weep aloud, but only for a few moments. Then, wiping the tears away, she tells herself to get moving.

Lifting her head, she looks out the window once more. The group is still asleep on the grass, but now, they are no longer alone—four Adjusters, one in a pink snowsuit and the others in white, are standing in a circle around Chet's body.

Carole bursts out of the front door of the Designated House as though she has been shot from a cannon.

"GET AWAY FROM HIM!" she screams with all her might.

The others wake at the sound of her voice, at first disoriented, then immediately at attention. Marcy grabs Mr. Biscuits and scurries out of her sleeping bag. Ryan, who is the closest to the Adjusters, puts his hands in the air but refuses to move away.

"Careful, Ryan," says Julian evenly. He keeps his eyes on the Adjusters while simultaneously signalling Carole, who is racing toward them, to stop. "Don't come any closer," he tells her.

"Please," says Dannicka gently. She addresses the one in the pink suit, guessing that it is the one in charge. "Please don't take him. We're trying to bring him home."

Julian is more than worried now—if this isn't interfering then he doesn't know what is. So far, it appears that the work these Adjusters are doing involves renovation and clean up. What if Chet is something that they intend to clean up? He can't let that happen!

Slowly, the Adjuster in the pink suit begins to move. It raises one of its little hands and places it on top of its head. Marcy is surprised to see that it has four fingers and a thumb—she'd expected something different considering all the other weird things about them.

In watching this strange display, all five are brought to sudden silence. Mesmerized, they stare at the Adjuster, with its tiny hand now resting atop the hood of its parka. Somewhere in the foggy recesses of Julian's mind, he finds himself wanting to make a joke—wanting to ask the Adjuster if his wife left a red sock in the wash—but this thought, along with all others, begins to melt away.

From her viewpoint on the street, Carole thinks the Adjuster is trying to communicate something, but what? She cannot stop staring at it—she is completely spellbound, even from this distance, staring right into its huge blue-white eyes. It's looking right at her, too, isn't it? She can't tell.

Ryan stands frozen in place, both hands held up in surrender. Four seconds ago, he was about to go completely ballistic on a non-human being, and now, for the life of him, he can't remember why.

Several seconds pass before the pink-suited Adjuster moves again. This time, it slowly removes its hand from atop its head. Dannicka thinks she sees a small flicker in the blue-white eyes then, like a projector changing its slide. With its first and second fingers, the Adjuster touches its own eyeballs.

*That's weird, isn't it?* she thinks, dreamily.

After that, everything goes white.

\*\*\*

Marcy finds herself sprawled on the grass and can't for the life of her figure out why. Did she fall asleep? Why would she have gotten out of her sleeping bag? Why is Carole sleeping way over there?

In an instant, it comes back to her. The Adjusters! She scrambles quickly to her feet and looks around the entire park, seeing no sign of them anywhere. Around her, the others are lying on the grass, sleeping or unconscious or something!

*We've been knocked out!* she thinks. *They stunned us!*

Chet is still there, on the cart, which is a relief to see. Her relief is short-lived, however, when she realizes that none of the others are waking up.

"Dannicka?" she asks in a panicked voice. She leans down and shakes her a little, but there is no response. "Dannicka?"

She rushes over the Carole, shaking her, too. "Wake up!"

Mr. Biscuits sits beside Carole's head, whimpering and trembling. Marcy picks him up.

"Ssh," she soothes. "Ssshh. It's okay."

But it isn't. What if they're all dead now? How is she going to manage alone?

"Ryan?" she pleads. "Julian?"

As she leans down to shake the man she has come to think of as her second dad, he drowsily opens one eye. Marcy is flooded with relief.

The other eye opens and for a fleeting moment, he seems not to recognize her. Then, all at once, he sits up.

"Where's Chet?!"

"He's still here," she says. "He's right where we left him."

He glances at the others anxiously. "What just happened?"

"What the hell..." Ryan sits up, confused.

"We're all still here," Julian says, getting to his feet. He walks over to where Dannicka and Carole are, and the two regain consciousness as he approaches. He helps them both to their feet.

"We're all here," he tells them. "Including Chet."

"What happened?" asks Carole.

"They stunned us!" Marcy exclaims.

Together, Ryan and Julian look over Chet's body, swatting away the flies in frustration. It doesn't appear that the Adjusters have altered it in any way, although, how would they really know? Neither of them wants to unwrap Chet—that goes without saying—but the ropes are at least still intact.

"How long were we out?" asks Carole, struggling to shake off the lethargy.

"Not long, I don't think," says Julian. "The light is the same."

Carole looks over to the street, to where she was standing when Julian told her to stop running. "I was over there," she says. "I was on the pavement...how did I get over here on the grass? Did any of you move me?"

The looks on their faces answers her question.

"*They* moved me? They *touched* me?" she wants to leap out of her skin, panic once again starting to take over.

"Hang on," says Julian, trying to gain some control. "*If* they moved you, then it was probably to protect you."

"From what? An on-coming car?!"

"From hitting your head, or hurting yourself," he says. "Think about it—it makes sense."

"Nothing about this makes sense!" she snaps. She looks down at her arms, then the rest of her body searching for any sign that those tiny white hands touched her. She feels a sudden urge to jump into a hot shower.

"What do you think they wanted?" asks Marcy, more scared than she wants to let on. The grown-ups have no control here, and they're scared, too. She can tell.

"I just don't know," says Julian. "But at least they haven't hurt us."

"They haven't helped us, either," says Carole. "I've had just about all I can take of this place."

\*\*\*

By late afternoon, Dannicka is able to convince Ryan to move away from the cart and join the others a few feet away. The flies swarming around Chet's body are now loud enough that it's becoming difficult to hear each other over their drone.

"You can still keep watch from here," she says. "Besides, I'd like to have a family meeting."

She takes him by the hand and leads him over to the make-shift fire pit. Carole and Julian are huddled together in quiet conversation and Marcy is playing in the grass with Mr. Biscuits a few feet away. If it wasn't for the dead body behind her, this could be an idyllic summer afternoon.

"Can I talk to you guys?" she asks. "I need to tell you something." She looks at their faces, sees the strained looks. "I'm sorry—I know we already have more than enough to worry about, but I think this is important."

She pauses, running a hand nervously through her hair.

"I've been having these dreams. Not like Ryan's, or anything, but... I had the first one when we were here the last time, and then, like, two more since then." She pauses. "There's a man with lilac-coloured skin, like a lilac face, and teeth..."

"Oh," Marcy whimpers.

"I know," Dannicka says. "It's that colour we've been seeing here. And this man—" She stops herself from saying that he wants them dead because Marcy is already scared enough. "He knows about us. He knows we're here."

Before losing her nerve, she quickly describes each of the dreams in detail, leaving nothing out. Around the circle of faces she sees the looks of strain morph into fear.

"And it's not Roland?" Ryan asks.

"It is not Roland."

*Of course not,* Ryan thinks. Roland needs a host. This man, whoever he is, came on his own.

"And it's my fault," Dannicka continues. "He knows about us because I walked into that stupid restaurant."

"That's not your fault!" says Carole. "And anyway, you said you dreamed about him back at Chet's."

"I know, but going into that restaurant was like announcing to him that we came back!" She starts to cry, overcome by anxiety, exhaustion, and dread.

"We've got to get out of here," says Carole. "It's been nearly twenty-four hours—we should have shifted by now!"

Julian feels a jolt of panic at the mere thought of leaving. "This could be our only shot to get the hell out of here!" he exclaims. "They said the laws are different here. Just because it didn't happen instantly doesn't mean it *won't* happen!" He can't seem to keep his voice from rising.

"We can't spend another month here!" Carole argues. "We're like sitting ducks right now! Those adjuster things could come back at any time, and I don't know what the hell Dannicka's dreams mean, but I don't think they're a coincidence! Are we just going to sit here and wait to see if that man shows up, too?! We need to get somewhere safe––"

"THERE'S NOWHERE ELSE TO FUCKING GO!" Julian explodes.

All fall silent and Julian's last statement hangs in the air.

He wishes he'd never said it.

Marcy silently watches the exchange between the grown-ups. She needs to do something to make things better, now, before everyone loses it.

"That man with the lilac face was just in your dream, Dannicka," she says. "He's not here with us. He isn't real. I've had scary dreams before, too, and they really do seem real at the time, but..." she trails off.

Dannicka gives Marcy's hand a half-hearted squeeze, but doesn't reply. He is real––she knows this, and he can hurt them.

"One more day," says Julian. "Can we just try to stay one more day? And if there's no shift, we can get out of here." He looks directly at Carole, his voice calm. "Wherever you want to go."

***

At dinner time, Julian and Carole go into the Designated House to try and put together a meal, even though no one is even remotely hungry. On their way, they allow themselves a quick glance at the Other House, noting that its front door is still open halfway, its darkness is seeping out like blood from a wound. There is a noticeable drop in temperature as they walk past and Carole shivers involuntarily.

Inside the Designated House Carole passes the wall of framed photos, noticing that many of the people in them have changed completely from the portraits she had seen yesterday.

"The restructure is going quickly, now," she says.

"I know," says Julian.

"If we don't make it out in time, we're going to have to dispose of Chet's body."

"I know."

"If we end up staying here, do you think we'll meet ourselves? How's *that* going to work?"

She opens a kitchen cupboard, slams it shut, opens another, then slams that one shut, too.

"I really don't know."

"And, if we do shift out of here, if we actually make it back, how exactly do we explain Chet's death?" Hysteria begins to rise in her voice. She opens another cupboard and slams it shut. "Not to mention, where we've been for the last two months?"

"I've been thinking about that, too."

"And what if we shift somewhere else completely?" she questions. "We think it can't get any worse than this, but what if—"

"Carole."

"What?"

He places both hands on her shoulders, looking directly into her eyes. "Wherever we go next," he says, "we'll be together."

\*\*\*

As the sun begins its descent in the lilac sky, a street lamp behind the ball diamond sputters to life. The five, sitting around the fire, look at it in silence. A few other lights have also made an appearance from an apartment building not far off in the distance.

Marcy, leaning back against Carole, stares up at the new light source.

"How much longer do we have before it's done?" she asks.

"I don't know," says Carole.

"It feels like soon."

"Yes, it does."

Julian places a hand on Ryan's shoulder.

"Ryan," he says, lowering his voice. "We have to think about Chet, and what to do with his body if we don't make it out in time."

Ryan stares ahead into the growing darkness. He knows Julian is right, but he just can't talk about that right now. He'd wanted to honour his brother, to treat his body with dignity—or, at the very least, to bring him home in one piece. But the maggots have settled in now, he can hear them. Chet is being taken away from them bit by tiny bit. He can't bring himself to talk about it. Not right now.

"Tomorrow," he says.

Julian nods.

\*\*\*

## TUESDAY, JULY 25

Dannicka looks at her watch. 3:45 a.m. Not that it really matters. She tip-toes over to Ryan's sleeping bag, kneels down, and gently touches his cheek.

"Mmm?"

"It's your turn," she whispers. He nods and sits up, surprised he was able to get any sleep.

"Nothing to report," she tells him.

He watches as she crawls into his sleeping bag, savouring the warmth he's left behind. He kisses her tenderly on the forehead and tells her to get some sleep.

"I don't want to."

She doesn't have to say why. The moment she closes her eyes, she knows she'll see him. It's getting easier for him to get through now.

Ryan sits beside her and strokes her hair. "I'll stay right here beside you."

\*\*\*

Dannicka is sitting on the grass, on the swell of the small hill in front of the little green shed. She is looking out to her right, over to the middle of the park where her friends lie. Four of them are sleeping. One of them is dead.

It is warm out, bright and sunny, but in the space surrounding her friends, it is the darkest of night. She wonders how she became separated from them. She doesn't want to be, but she also doesn't want to go back into the darkness of that foreboding circle.

"Wake up!" she says, knowing they can't hear her. "Wake up!" she calls again, louder. "Over here! It's warmer here!"

"It really is, isn't it?"

She jumps at the sound of the voice, turning sharply to her left. It is the man with the lilac face, now sitting next to her. He is wearing the same long coat he always wears and, at this close proximity, she discovers how terrible it smells.

How did she not realize he was here? She wants to scream, to run, to get away from him as fast as possible, but she's completely immobile.

"You know," he says, conversationally, "I've just been here for so long. For *sooo* long, you just stop taking notice of certain things. But you're right—it is warmer here. You were right to come here."

*But I didn't!* she wants to protest. *I didn't want to come here!*

"Yup. *Sooo* long." He releases a loud, airy sigh, his warm breath washing over her face, making her want to vomit.

He looks wistfully out into the park, at the darkness enveloping her friends. He points to Chet's body.

"Where's he going?"

Dannicka feels her panic rise.

"He's coming with us!" she says, finding her voice.

The lilac-face man grins, displaying his prominent rows of perfect teeth. "With you and *me*, you mean," he says. He's coming with *us*. I like Marcy, too," he adds as an afterthought.

Dannicka was wrong. He doesn't want them dead. He wants so much more.

\*\*\*

"Dannicka."

She opens her eyes in fear, expecting to see that horrible face. Instead, she sees Ryan. She is lying in his sleeping bag where she had dozed off hours ago. She hadn't meant to fall asleep. How could she have let herself? It's already broad daylight!

"He's coming!" she says. "If he isn't here already, he will be! We've got to wake the others up and get out of here!"

She scrambles out of the sleeping bag and begins to holler. "Wake up, everybody! Wake up!"

It doesn't take much coaxing.

"What's happening?" asks a bleary Marcy, rubbing at her eyes.

"He's coming!"

"Who?"

With one look at Dannicka's expression, Marcy suddenly knows the answer. She was wrong to try reassuring Dannicka yesterday— she gets that now. The man with the lilac face must be real, and he's coming for them.

Marcy grabs Mr. Biscuits, looking around frantically. What should she take with her? How much time do they have?

Ryan has run back to Chet's body, single-handedly trying to wrench the heavy cart free from the ruts it has created in the grass. Carole and Julian, still slightly disoriented, gather up the contents from their open packs and begin to tie them closed.

"There's no time!" Dannicka yells. "Let's just—"

Before she can finish her sentence, there is a deep, familiar rumble beneath her.

"It's happening!" she hollers. "Marcy, run!"

Julian and Carole drop their packs and begin to run over to Ryan and Chet. They shouldn't have slept so far from the cart. But the smell, and the sound of bugs...

Marcy clutches Mr. Biscuits, reaches for Dannicka's hand, and together they race toward the cart.

*We're going to make it!* Carole thinks. *We're actually going to make it.*

The five create a tight circle around Chet's body, gripping each other's hands for dear life.

*Here it comes,* thinks Dannicka. *Oh God, here it comes...*

But something is wrong. The rumbling, though unmistakeably familiar, seems weaker, somehow. It should be strong––it should be shaking the ground beneath their feet by now. She glances around the worried faces in their circle, then around the park beyond, searching for that telltale distortion of air. In the process, she sees that the door to the Other House is now wide open.

*Who cares?* she tells herself. *It doesn't matter anymore—we're all going to get out of here, any second now... Stop looking at it!* But she can't look away, because there is a leg protruding from the darkness of that gaping doorway. It's a man's leg. A glowing leg. Then a glowing hand, an arm, a shoulder...

She starts to whimper, "Oh no, oh no..."

"Dannicka?" Carole, looking at her with growing concern turns to follow her gaze, toward the one place she has tried desperately not to look. To her absolute horror, she sees the now-wide-open door, but that's not all—something is crawling out through it, limb by limb. And it's not an Adjuster. It's much, much worse.

The group watch in terror as the man with the lilac face emerges like an actor stepping into a spotlight. He stands on the porch of the Other House, facing them straight on, and grins maniacally from ear to ear, flashing perfect lilac teeth. He turns around and shuts the door behind him, then, unbelievably, performs an over-the-top pantomime of pretending to lock it. When he's finished, he turns back to the group and displays an equally-outrageous mime of straightening an imaginary tie.

"What the fuck?!" Ryan exclaims, watching in disbelief. He can't get past the man's face—his face is fucking purple!

Slicking back his greasy hair, the lilac man brushes off each shoulder, then, still grinning, claps both hands together twice.

"It's time!" he shouts, and with that he begins striding confidently toward their group.

"Oh, God. Oh, Jesus. Oh, my God..." Dannicka begins a frenzied half-prayer, squeezing both Ryan and Marcy's hands for dear life.

"Just hang on!" Julian shouts, trying in complete vain to keep some kind of calm. The shift is finally happening—the rumbling beneath them drums into a loud crescendo now, but he can tell that it's taking too long. That freak of...not nature, that's for goddamn sure...is going to reach them any second. To his complete horror, he watches the lilac man break out of his confident stride and into a run. He is running toward them and there's *nothing* they can do.

"Hurry up!" Carole screams, as if the shift itself can hear her. "For God's sake, HURRY UP!"

Suddenly, Marcy tears free from the circle, turns around and shoves Mr. Biscuits into Carole's arms. She can't just stand here and let this happen—she won't!

"Marcy!" Carole screams in astonishment. "Marcy!!"

But Marcy is running away from the group and back over to the fire pit. She bends down and swiftly picks up a potato-sized rock, then spins around and, incredibly, races straight toward the man with the lilac face.

"MAR-CY!" Dannicka screams.

The lilac man seems surprised, thrilled with this recent turn of events. He begins running even faster toward the girl, his long filthy coat-tails flapping out behind him like wings.

When they are twenty feet apart, Marcy hauls one arm back and fires the rock with all her might. The rock, still warm from its position near the fire, hits the man with the lilac face square in the throat. He staggers back, arms flailing, falling over in an awkward convulsive dance. Marcy hears a horrible gagging sound, an awful choking, but she can't waste another second. She hears the others screaming her name hysterically, but she is already racing back toward them as fast as her legs will go. Julian is running toward her now. She reaches for his outstretched hand and feels his fingertips just as the force of the shift slams into them.

# PART III

# CHAPTER SIXTEEN

"What the hell is taking him so long?!"

Raja cracks his knuckles impatiently. From the front seat of Chet's car it's impossible to see inside the coffeeshop, but nobody has come in or out of the place in ages. What could be going on in there?

"You could've gone in to help him," says Lindsay, still sitting beside Jessica in the backseat.

Raja smirks. "I thought *you'd* wanna help him."

"Why? Because I'm a woman?!"

This time, Raja laughs out loud. "No! Because you wanna be alone with him! It's so obvious!"

"Oh, shut up!"

"It's true!"

"He's got a girlfriend!" Lindsay argues. "I'm not—" she interrupts herself, something odd catching her eye. "Whoa! Look at that!"

Raja and Jessica follow her gaze to the front window of the coffeeshop.

"Look at what?" Jessica asks.

"That, like, ripple of air, or something!" she says. "Can't you guys see that?"

"No," says Jessica.

"It's going right past the window! Like, right inside the store!" Lindsay points to the exact spot. "Right...there!"

"I don't see anything," Raja squints. He turns to Lindsay and grins. "Drink, much?"

Lindsay ignores him, keeping her eyes on the store front. She has never seen anything like this; it's as though the air inside the shop is totally warped. After only a few seconds, it is gone. She sits back in her seat, wondering if she had imagined the whole thing or if her eyes are going funky.

"Huh," she says. "That was totally weird."

Jessica groans loudly. "Oh, my God, this is taking forever! I'd like to get to the mall to-*day*..."

Lindsay opens her car door. "Fine! I'll go in."

Raja and Jessica watch as she walks up to the shop and lets herself in. In a flash, she is sprinting back out the front door and toward the car.

"Something's wrong!" she shouts. "Something's wrong!"

Raja and Jessica get out of the car at the same time. At the sight of Lindsay's ashen face, Raja knows it's serious. He rushes past her to the shop where he pulls the front door open with so much force that he nearly tears it off its hinges. The moment he sees what's inside, the state of the door is the last thing on his mind.

"Oh, my God."

There are four, no, five bodies lying on the floor, and they all appear to be unconscious. Chet is sprawled in front of the counter in a puddle of splattered coffee drinks.

Raja's first thought is that there's been a mass-shooting, but he doesn't see any blood. And there were no gunshots—they would have heard those, wouldn't they? He's never heard a gunshot in real life, but it has to be super loud. He stands frozen in the doorway for a moment. He should go in, shouldn't he? He just can't seem to. He's too chicken.

*Grow some balls!* he tells himself. He takes a deep breath.

"Don't go in there!" Lindsay yells. "It could be a gas leak or something!"

Relieved, he backs out of the store and lets the door close.

"We need to call an ambulance!" says Jessica.

Raja scans the rest of the area, spotting a quiet-looking clothing store. "I'll use their phone," he hollers, running over.

Minutes later, Chet's friends, huddled together in the High Street parking lot, hear the sounds of approaching sirens. Soon the entire square is teeming with police, ambulances, a fire-truck, and even a hazmat team. In shock, the three teenagers watch as officers in SWAT gear swarm the coffeeshop.

Hours seem to pass before they finally spot Chet strapped to a stretcher, lifeless. It all seems surreal. Half an hour ago, he was fine—driving, laughing...

Lindsay sees his slack-jawed face beneath an oxygen mask and feels herself grow faint.

"Are they...is he...dead?!" She doesn't think she can bear to hear the answer.

"He can't be," says Jessica. "They would've covered his face."

Five more stretchers follow; five more bodies, including one that Raja hadn't counted.

*Six people in there,* he thinks. It could easily have been more had any of them gone in, too.

*** 

SATURDAY, JUNE 3

Corinne picks up the morning newspaper from the mailbox and reads the headline on the front page: 'THE MYSTERIOUS GRABBAJABBA SIX'. The subsequent article describes the six coma victims, one of whom is her sister, and how there are still more questions than answers.

She walks into her kitchen and tosses the paper onto the table in disgust. 'The Grabbajabba Six'? What idiot came up with that one? It's bad enough that her sister is in a coma, but having it reported by the media is intrusive, not to mention embarrassing.

She glances back at the newspaper and scans the photos of the victims. The picture of Carole was taken at their mother's birthday a few years ago.

*It might as well be my face,* Corinne thinks before realizing that, upon closer inspection, it actually is. Angrily, she turns the paper over, not wanting to see it anymore. How hard is it, she wonders, to do something right? It was their mother who provided the photo to the newspaper and, after forty-two years, she apparently still can't tell them apart. What a stupid mistake!

*She probably wishes it was me in the coma,* she thinks. It's no secret, at least to Corinne, that their mother has always favoured Carole. It's always been Carole's latest adventures: where she's been, what she's done, and isn't *her* life so exciting? While Corinne had stayed close all those years, it was Prodigal Carole who got all the fuss for finally deciding to come back home. Now she's gone again. And this time, it might be forever.

Her eyes sting with the threat of tears, but she shakes her head, refusing to let them go any further. She's just tired, that's all. Sitting up all night at your sister's hospital bed will do that to you.

\*\*\*

For the past seventy-two hours, Ryan's parents have taken turns keeping watch beside his hospital bed in a terrible state of déjà-vu. Numbly they answered the doctor's questions about possible organ donation——the same questions they had been asked the last time. Their answers are the same as before: no, no, and no. At least this time his body isn't mangled beyond recognition. In fact, he looks the same as he had a few days ago, when they last saw him. He just won't wake up.

A few of Ryan's friends, including his ex-girlfriend Amy, and even his physiotherapist, have stopped by, only to be turned away by hospital staff. Their cards and flowers are forwarded to Ryan's mother, who refuses to bring them into his room. Who knows what germs they might carry? Instead, she keeps them at her home, telling herself that Ryan can see them when he wakes up. He *is* going to wake up. And when he does, he'll move back home with her where she can keep an eye on him every day. Permanently.

When she first heard about this incident, she had been convinced that it was some neurological remnent from his previous accident, and didn't she just know this would happen? She *knew* it! And she *told* those doctors, who don't know anything, that he needed twenty-four-hour care.

When she eventually calmed down enough to listen, and realized that five other people were similarly affected, she was forced to think otherwise. Something must have gotten into that shop, something toxic, and when Ryan wakes up, they are going to sue that awful place for everything they've got.

In contrast to Ryan's stark side of the room, Chet's side is festooned with cards, flowers, and gifts. Ryan's mother hates looking at it; to her, it's like some kind of macabre party and there is *nothing* to celebrate. Some people are incredibly insensitive.

\*\*\*

Chet's mother sits beside her son's bed, keeping a quiet vigil along with her husband. She knows they have been here for three days because that's what they tell her, but there is really nothing to mark the passage of time. It has been one constant state of surreal. She looks at her son's face, she watches his chest move up and down with each breath, she watches his monitors. She looks back at his face, then back at his chest, then back at the monitors. And on it goes.

She and her husband have attempted to interact with Ryan's parents, who sit stonily at the other side of the room, but their efforts have been unwelcome. Chet's mother doesn't blame them. She has, nonetheless, begun to feel a bond with the other patients' families: Marcy's parents, Julian's wife Trudy, Maureen's dad and step-mom, and to a lesser extent, Carole's twin sister, Corinne.

At 3:00 p.m., Chet's mother stands up and stretches her arms above her head, sore from sitting in the same uncomfortable chair for so long. She looks at her son's face, at his chest, at the monitors.

"I need to move my legs," she whispers to her husband.

"Go ahead," he whispers back. He stands up and moves over to where she's been sitting.

As she passes Ryan's mother, she pauses briefly. "I'm going to get a coffee," she says quietly. "Can I get you anything?"

Without making eye contact, Ryan's mother shakes her head no, wondering just how stupid this woman must be. Does she honestly think she would want a coffee, of all things, while her son is clinging to life? Before Chet's mom has even stepped away, Ryan's mother gets to her feet and briskly closes the curtain around the bed, sealing herself and her son inside.

Chet's mom looks over at her husband, and they exchange a brief look of annoyance. She steps out of the room then, and out into the hall.

Outside Julian's room she sees his wife, Trudy, in her usual chair beside his bed. She is holding Julian's hand.

Chet's mother pokes her head in the doorway. "Hi," she whispers. "How are you doing?"

Trudy looks up and they share a knowing look. She shrugs. "You?"

"Same. I was going to get a coffee. Can I get you one? Or something to eat?"

"A coffee would be great." Trudy reaches for her purse.

"Please, it's my turn."

"Thanks." Trudy smiles weakly and Chet's mother nods.

She continues down the hall, stopping at the room shared by Marcy, Maureen, and Carole. The area around Marcy's bed resembles Chet's—surrounded by gifts, cards, and flowers. A home-made origami mobile hangs suspended in one corner. The out-pouring of support they have all received has been both overwhelming and incredibly moving. Chet's mom hadn't really realized how many people care about her family, although she knows she would be just as supportive to anyone else in a similar situation.

*Why does it always take a crisis?* she wonders.

"Hi," she says, addressing Marcy's parents and Maureen's father, who are talking quietly together. There is no one at Carole's bedside, although her mother and twin sister have made frequent appearances. "Does anyone want to come with me on a coffee run?"

Before there is any chance to respond, a voice over the intercom announces a 'code blue'. They have all been in this hospital long enough to know what that means.

Chet's mother looks at the others in alarm, then instinctively rushes out of the room. At the end of the hall, she sees several hospital staff heading toward her son's room.

*No! No! No!*

She breaks into a run.

"You can't come in here!" a nurse exclaims. She holds one arm out toward her, but Chet's mother is not going to let anyone stop her from entering. She pushes her way past the nurse and forces herself into the room and over to the bed.

"He's my son!"

"You have to let the doctor do his work!" the nurse orders. She grabs at one of her arms and holds her in place, but, having recognized who she is, does not ask her to leave.

Chet's mom looks over to her shocked husband. "What happened?"

"His heart stopped!" he exclaims. "It just stopped!"

She hears the monitor wailing in a long, even tone and screams. She watches in absolute anguish as her son's gown is torn open and paddles are applied to his chest.

"Clear!"

Chet's body jerks upward violently, but his face remains lifeless.

"Clear!"

Chet's mother clings to the nurse in desperation. *This can't be happening! Please, oh please, God, oh please...*

"Clear!"

And then, as if her prayers have been answered, the monitor returns to a consistent steady beat. As the staff in the room attend to Chet, the nurse holding his mom's arms adjusts her grip into an embrace.

"It's okay, he's okay," she soothes, letting Chet's mom cry onto her shoulder.

When the horrible episode is over, the room returns to its uneasy state of normal. Chet's mother resumes her post at her son's bedside, then sees that Marcy's mother, Maureen's father, and Trudy are waiting anxiously in the hall. Chet's mother looks at her son's face, his chest, and once more at the monitors before walking over to the doorway.

"He's okay," she says, beginning to sob.

The three concerned family members hold their arms out to her and she gratefully falls into their embrace.

Behind them, the curtain surrounding Ryan and his mother remains closed. Not once, the others notice, did Ryan's mother check to see if everything was okay, or to offer any support.

Within the curtain, Ryan's mother holds both hands over her ears, eyes squeezed shut. Her mouth hangs open in a silent scream.

# CHAPTER SEVENTEEN

Marcy wakes up.

At least, she thinks she's awake—she can't, for the life of her, open her eyes. Her lids seem to be weighted down; her lashes knitted together as though sewn shut. She tries raising an arm, wanting to rub at her eyes, but she is unable to do that, either.

There is a low hum in this place, whatever this place is, mixed in with the hushed murmur of voices. Where is she? They did shift—they must have, because she remembers how hard the force was against her body. The question is, to where?

As she slowly regains consciousness, she becomes aware of something covering her nose and mouth. Again, she tries to raise each of her hands, wanting to get rid of whatever it is, but her arms remain completely immobile.

Each new realization causes her more worry, more fear. She needs to look around. She needs to sit up. She might need to run.

All at once, her last memory comes flooding back; the man with the lilac face, racing toward her, laughing maniacally, and she toward him—hurling the rock straight for his face...

Oh, God, is he here?! Did he shift with them? She needs to move!

She tries squeezing her eyes shut even harder and discovers that it's something she can actually do. She squeezes them tightly, then relaxes them, repeating this over and over again until finally, a sliver of dim light appears.

*Come on!* she commands herself, willing her eyes to open, giving herself a headache from the exertion. With each attempt, her lids pull a little further apart, eventually allowing a hazy glimpse of her surroundings to finally become visible.

Through a fog, she sees what appears to be two figures standing a few feet away. Their heads are bowed together in conversation, but she can't make out what they're saying. Squeezing her eyes shut once more, she forces them back open, trying to focus with everything she's got. Now she can see that she's lying in a bed—her feet look like two bumps under a cotton blanket. The lilac man must have captured her, drugged her, and tied her to this bed!

"Marcy? Marcy! Oh, my God!"

What follows is a cacophony of voices, some yelling, some crying, faces peering over her own. She blinks repeatedly, trying so hard to clear her blurred vision. In a few seconds, the shadowy shapes around her head morph into clarity—two faces. Two sets of eyes. No noses, no mouths.

Marcy discovers that she can scream.

***

Someone is being tortured.

Dannicka is forcing herself into consciousness, fighting the overwhelming desire to stay asleep, because someone is screaming.

It's not her...it's not one of the men...it doesn't sound like Carole. It has to be Marcy.

*Wake up!* she tells herself.

Her eyelids feel like they have been glued together and there's something blocking her mouth. She can't seem to move any part of her body. What is happening?!

*Wake up!*

With all the effort she can muster, Dannicka forces her eyelids apart. Her vision is so hazy—she squeezes her eyes shut, then opens them again, but all she can see are the dark outlines of other bodies. Oh, God, where have they shifted to this time?

"Maureen? Maureen?!"

They know her other name. They know her. The man with the lilac face knows who she is, and he's told them.

She feels hands on her and wants to recoil from their touch. *Oh, God, get me out of here!*

Marcy is screaming, her voice scratchy and hoarse. In a panic, Dannicka tries to move, but can't. At least her vision is finally starting to clear; the blurry figures around her are moving swiftly, barking out fragments of sentences she doesn't understand. One of the figures bends down, its face looming above hers. No nose, no mouth.

Dannicka starts screaming, too.

***

Across the room, Carole drowsily opens her eyes just enough to form two narrow slits. She can't really see, but she can hear panic, screaming, voices shouting. Someone, or something, is torturing them. She knew this would happen. She knew that the next place they shifted would be worse!

If only she could move. They've paralyzed her——she's forced to listen to the agony the others are suffering.

A face appears in her view. No nose, no mouth. She was right! But she's not going to go down easily.

***

Chet's mother feels her anxiety rise.

"Maybe you should see what's going on," she tells her husband. She won't leave Chet's side, not now; but the shrieking and hollering coming from the women's room is extremely upsetting.

On the other side of the room, the curtain surrounding Ryan, his mother, and now his father, remains closed. It has not opened since Chet's scare three hours ago.

Chet's father walks past the enclosure and out into the hall. Seeing Trudy standing a few feet ahead, he rushes over.

"What's going on?"

She turns toward him. "The women and Marcy have just woken up! They're all hysterical!"

"What? They *all* woke up? At the same time?"

"Yeah, I think so!"

Together, they look down the hall, unable to see into the room, unable to get any closer.

"What if..." Trudy starts to say. She looks at Chet's father, and without another word, they both rush off toward their respective rooms.

"What is it?" Chet's mom asks.

"The women have regained consciousness," says Chet's dad. "All at the same time."

He looks hopefully at his son. "Is he...?"

Chet's mom looks at her son's face, at his chest, at the monitors. She bites her lip and shakes her head. Both parents watch anxiously for the least little change in their son, anything at all, but nothing comes.

After a few moments, the sound of a chair scraping wildly across the floor comes from behind the curtain, followed by a frenzied shout.

"He's waking up!"

Chet's parents, startled, watch as the curtain separating them suddenly tears open and Ryan's mother bursts through and out of the room.

Looking back at her son, Chet's mom silently prays. *It's going to happen to us, too,* she thinks.

It has to.

At the nursing station, Ryan's mother can't find a doctor, or anyone, for that matter. What kind of two-bit hospital is this?! Is the entire staff in that one room? She turns and runs toward it, only to collide with Trudy, who is heading in the same direction.

"Julian's waking up, too!" Trudy says. "Is Ryan—?"

Ryan's mother does not have time for conversation. She needs a doctor. Now.

The women's room is in an absolutely frenzy. Marcy is screaming and clawing at everyone within reach, Maureen and Carole are hollering, and the others in their room seem unable to get control.

Ryan's mother has spent a lot of time in hospitals and has never seen anything so chaotic. She panics and grabs the arm of the closest doctor.

"My son is awake! And he needs someone NOW!"

The doctor quickly assesses the situation and barks out an order. Two staff members immediately turn to follow Ryan's mother back to her room but Trudy stops them in the doorway as they pass.

"My husband's waking up!" she says.

The staff members stop in their tracks, conferring with the doctor in charge.

"Come ON!" Ryan's mother screams. She shoots daggers at Trudy with her eyes. If something happens to Ryan now, she'll know who to blame. How long before he starts lashing out, too? How long before he hurts himself and causes permanent damage? He's not as strong as the others!

Within seconds, a number of hospital staff gather around Julian's bed, and Ryan's, preparing for a similar reaction to those of the women. Chet's parents keep their eyes glued to their son, searching desperately for any signs of revival, but still there are none. His mom holds one of his large hands in both of hers, remembering the first time she had held his tiny little fist. When did he get so big? He's nearly a man.

*Please, Chet. Please, my only boy. Please, wake up.*

She doesn't know she is crying until two giant tears fall onto their entwined hands.

***

"He may be disoriented."

Julian, eyes open, has not said a word. He looks at the doctor, at his wife, at the nurses, then back at the doctor. Fear and confusion are written all over his face.

"It's okay," Trudy soothes, relieved beyond measure to see her husband awake after more than three days; three excruciating days fearing that she would never see him awake again. She reaches out to touch his face, but he flinches, recoiling from her hand.

Her relief vanishes. He must have brain damage; he doesn't even know who she is.

"The girls?" This comes out as a whisper.

Trudy feels a glimmer of hope. "They're here! They're in the cafeteria with your parents—they're going to want to see you!"

"Where are the others?" he croaks.

"What others?"

"The ones I came in with."

Trudy pauses momentarily. "They're here. They're in the hospital, too. Don't worry about that now. Everything's gonna be—"

"Where's Chet?"

How does Julian know Chet's name? Did they get to talking before they all collapsed? Even if they had, what are the chances Julian would actually remember his name? Trudy has so many questions but she knows they'll have to wait. Her husband is obviously disoriented.

"He's here," she says. "Don't talk right now, just get some rest."

"We tried so hard," Julian tells her. And to Trudy's astonishment, he starts to cry.

*** 

Ryan is lying in wait, ready for an opportunity to present itself. He hears his mother's voice—she's having a melt-down about something, as usual—soon joined by his father's voice, and there are other voices he doesn't recognize. He doesn't know if they are real or not, and he doesn't really care. He needs to find the other five.

"I *saw* him open his eyes!" his mother exclaims.

The paralysis that Ryan experienced upon waking is lifting away. He's sure he could move now, but doesn't want to risk it. Carefully, he opens his eyes ever so slightly—anyone who glanced at him would think they were still closed, and when he sees another face come into his limited view, a face whose only feature is a pair of eyes, he takes his chance.

In an instant, both of Ryan's hands are locked around the doctor's throat. Immediately, the doctor pushes him away with his forearms, forcing Ryan's much weaker arms to buckle. More hands start grabbing at Ryan's arms, shoving them to his sides and locking them down. Something, or someone, pins down his kicking legs. There are too many of them to fight off—he's just not strong enough. He hollers in frustration.

"You're hurting him!" his mother wails. "For God's sake!"

It is only once Ryan has been completely immobilized that he begins to realize where he is. This is a hospital. And that thing with only its eyes showing is a doctor in a mask.

"Where are the others?" he demands. "Where are the other five?"

No one is answering, they are all too busy shouting at each other and trying to contain his mother. And then, cautiously, an unknown face comes slowly into his view.

"They're all here, son," says this man, kindly.

"He's *not* your son!" Ryan hears his mother snap from somewhere across the room.

He looks at the man who has answered his question. He has never seen him before, but he looks so familiar it's what Chet would have looked like years from now. Ryan starts to cry.

"I'm so sorry," he tells Chet's father. "Chet died because of me."

\*\*\*

"I'm sorry for losing control," says Carole. "I thought you were... someone else," she adds, weakly.

The doctor, with his face mask now hanging loosely around his neck, turns off the light to his scope.

"Don't worry about it. How many fingers am I holding up?"

"One."

"Follow it, please."

She keeps her eyes on his finger as it moves up and down, then side to side, giving her a chance to see Marcy and Dannicka across the room. Their beautiful light, which she had never stopped marvelling at, is now completely gone. Her surprise registers.

"Everything okay?" the doctor asks.

"Yes. Fine."

"Any blurred vision, now?"

"None."

"We've given you a mild sedative." He says, addressing all three patients. "Get some rest—we'll keep you monitored and I'll see you all for further testing in the morning."

After he leaves, Marcy looks at her parents warily. "Are you guys real?"

Her dad, aware of the confusion she and the others are apparently experiencing, treats his daughter's question seriously. "Yes. We're real."

"We're real, sweetheart," her mom adds, holding Marcy's hand.

Marcy is having serious doubts. First of all, to the best of her knowledge, no one has ever called her 'sweetheart'—she's just not that kind of person—and, secondly, she can't honestly remember the last time her parents were together in the same room. This can't be the right place. Even with that needle they gave her––the one that's making her feel kind of floaty––she can't relax.

"Where's my family?" she asks. Her parents exchange a look.

"We're right here," says her mom. "Your brother and sister..."

"No, my *other* family," she demands.

From across the room, Carole hears their conversation and interrupts. "Everyone's here, Marcy." She doesn't actually know if this is true, but she needs Marcy to stay calm until they can figure things out.

"Everyone's real?"

Carole wonders what Marcy's parents must think about this odd exchange. They must, at the very least, want to know how she knows their daughter, let alone why Marcy is looking to her as the voice of reason.

"Yes, everyone's...really here."

Dannicka's dad and stepmom, witnessing this strange conversation, share a concerned look.

"I need to sit up," says Marcy.

"You can't do that." Her mom places a hand on her arm. "It's too soon."

"I need to sit up, NOW!" She can hear Carole and Dannicka, but she needs to see them with her own eyes—and if her parents won't help, she'll sit up on her own.

"Oh, for God's sake," her mom mutters. She looks at her ex-husband. "Just raise her bed, okay?"

Marcy feels her bed shift to an upright position. She sees Dannicka lying in a bed next to her, and Carole across the room. Her relief is instant but short-lived: neither of them is glowing.

"Excuse me," says Carole, to anyone who will listen. "I can't seem to really move that well—can someone please raise my bed, too?"

Dannicka's dad is closest, and he obliges. He turns back to his daughter. "Do you want me to move yours, too, Maur—Dannicka?" At the last second, he stops himself from using her former name.

She has never heard him call her Dannicka before—he swore he never would. She's not entirely sure she's in the real world, but this gesture on his part fills her with hope.

"Yes, please."

All three patients are now able to see each other. Marcy scrutinizes Carole and Dannicka silently for a moment, realizing that it might be true: they might actually be home.

*If we were in the right place,* she realizes, *then we wouldn't be glowing, would we?*

"So, *they're* real?" she asks Carole, pointing to her parents while looking past them dismissively. Carole returns her gaze and nods assuredly. Finally, Marcy begins to relax.

"Where are the guys?" she wants to know. She sees looks of confusion pass between her parents, but she doesn't care. "*Where* are the guys?!"

"Um, one of the men that you were with is next door, and the others are down the hall," says her dad.

"Where's Chet?"

Marcy's parents are confused, wondering how these people all know each other. The doctors have already cautioned against questioning them this early, or causing any undue stress, not yet knowing the full extent of any possible damage done. Questions will have to wait.

"Yes, Chet's here, too."

*In the morgue, no doubt,* thinks Carole. Aloud, she asks, "Does anyone know about my dog?"

"I think your sister said she had him," says Dannicka's dad. "She was just here with your mom earlier today, but they left to get some dinner."

"Is he okay?"

"The dog? Oh—I don't know. I think she said she had him at her place. They found him with the rest of you."

She is afraid to ask, but she needs to know. "Where did you find us?"

Another puzzled look is exchanged between each of the other family members in the room.

"At the Grabbajabba on the High Street."

Carefully, Dannicka asks, "What day is it?"

"It's the fifth," her stepmother replies.

"Of August?"

The looks that pass around the room are more than concerned.

"Of June. It's Monday, June 5th. We found you on Friday."

All three patients fall silent.

*I need to talk to the guys,* Carole thinks. *Now.*

"Dad?" Dannicka asks, breaking the silence.

"Can you go see the guys and tell them we're okay? Their names are Ryan and Julian."

It doesn't cross the mind of Dannicka's father to wonder how she knows the other patients—his daughter has her own life, her own friends. But what does bother him is how troubled she's acting, as though she's afraid of something.

"Sure. I'll tell them."

\*\*\*

"The girls are here to see you," says Trudy. "And your parents, too." To her daughters she adds, "be gentle with your dad."

When Julian sees his daughters, Pandora and Lexie, his eyes fill with tears. He holds out both arms and the girls, wary from seeing their dad in such a state, walk cautiously into his embrace. He feels their little faces against his, smells the familiar scent of their hair, and instantly knows they're real.

He didn't realize, until this moment, just how much he had missed them. He never acknowledged how hard he had worked to keep himself from thinking about it. The giggling, the tears, the tantrums, the questions, the joy––the love they have given him, the love they have made him feel. He has missed all of it, and now, he gets to have it back. He actually gets to have it all back.

"Are you crying cause you're sick?" Lexie asks.

He laughs a little. "No! I'm fine. I'm just so happy to see you."

Over their heads, he sees his parents. It's only been two months since he last saw them, but they appear to have aged years. He knows they have been worried. They really don't know just how worried they should have been.

"So, how long have we been here?" Julian asks, hoping the question doesn't sound too odd.

"You got here Friday," says Trudy. "I came out that night, and your parents brought the girls the next day."

That wasn't what he meant.

"What's the date?"

Trudy shares a look with Julian's parents.

"It's the fifth."

It was the twenty-fifth when they shifted. He's been here since...

"We've been here for nearly two weeks?"

"No, it's been three and a half days." Trudy can see her husband becoming upset. "We can talk about it later."

"Sorry to interrupt..." A voice in the doorway prompts everyone to look over.

"I'm Maur—Dannicka's dad. She just wanted me to let you know that she, Marcy, and Carole are okay."

Trudy turns to Julian and sees the worry on his face replaced by noticeable relief.

"Oh, thank God," he says.

"They're right next door. So, I'm just gonna go pass the message on to Ryan, now. I guess Chet still hasn't woken up yet, eh?"

"What?" Julian asks.

"He's still in the coma," Trudy explains. "He had a scare earlier this afternoon."

She has no idea about the scares they've had recently, but it's the first part of her statement which has his attention.

"A coma?"

"Yes."

"You mean...he's still alive?"

"Well...yeah."

To everyone's surprise, Julian bursts into tears. Not the tears of joy he had shed to see his daughters; this is all-out sobbing. It's hard for Trudy to see him like this, not that she ever has before. Julian is usually the sarcastic one; he never gets ruffled, is more likely to crack a joke during a serious moment and, for as long as she has known him, has never been prone to crying. He needs rest. He's clearly not himself, yet.

"It's just a bit too much for him," she explains. "Would you mind leaving us?"

"Not at all."

***

"What do you mean, Chet *died* because of you?!"

Chet's mom looks over at her son, hears the respirator, and sees the monitors blinking rhythmically. "What does he mean?!" she asks her husband. "He's not dead!"

"Stop yelling at him!" Ryan's mother shouts. "He doesn't know what he's saying!"

Why couldn't they have been put in a private room? What kind of hospital is this where severely injured people are penned in together like cattle? It's worse than being in a third-world country. She might just consider suing this place, too, when all is said and done.

"He's not dead!" Chet's mom announces again, as much to convince herself as anyone else.

Ryan hadn't considered that Chet's parents wouldn't believe him, that he'd have to convince them he's dead. Unless they've shifted somewhere else, and there's another Chet...which means there's another Ryan.

Ignoring his mother, he waves his hand in the direction of the other adults in the room. "Where is he?"

Chet's dad comes back into view. "He's right here. Beside you."

So, he did shift with them, after all. Thank God for that, at least.

"He hasn't woken up yet," Chet's dad adds.

Hasn't woken up? Are these people in total denial, or what?

"I need to sit up!" Ryan says. His mom protests, but he ignores her. He would be sitting up already if it wasn't for whatever-the-hell they injected him with. At least the restraints are gone.

He struggles into an upright position and sees, sure enough, that Chet is lying in a bed next to his. It's not a different Chet, he knows that for sure, but somehow, he's still alive. Ryan can hear the hiss from an oxygen tank; and the horrible smell of decaying flesh that had permeated everything around him is gone.

Ryan hears himself moan. Can this really be happening?

"Excuse me, sorry to bother you guys..."

Ryan turns at the sound of the voice in the doorway.

"Dannicka wanted me to let you know, Ryan, that she, and Marcy, and Carole are all okay."

Ryan, now a total roller coaster of emotions, bursts into tears. He realizes that the stranger in the doorway must be Dannicka's dad and curses himself. What a lame first impression he must be making! He's crying like a loser and can't seem to stop.

"Would you leave us alone?!" Ryan's mother barks.

Dannicka's dad steps back, surprised. "Sure. Sorry!"

Chet's dad steps toward him. "Thank you for letting us know."

"Tell Dannicka I love her!" Ryan blurts out, barely recognizing the slobbering baby he has apparently become.

Dannicka's dad raises an eyebrow. It's a gesture he has seen Dannicka make many times.

"Oh-kay," he says. "Will do."

\*\*\*

Corinne arrives home from her afternoon hospital visit only to receive a phone call informing her that her sister has woken up. Immediately, she heads back out to pick up their mother and within minutes, they have returned to Carole's bedside. They are shocked at the transformation she has undergone in so little time— only an hour ago, Corinne wondered if she would ever see her sister awake again.

"Where's Mr. Biscuits?" is Carole's first question, something she instantly regrets. Why wouldn't she first have thanked them for coming to see her every day?

"He's at my house," says Corinne. "He's fine—I wanted to bring him, but they wouldn't let me."

Carole is overcome with relief. "Thank you. Thank you for taking care of him. And for coming here, too. They said you've been here every day."

"Why wouldn't we?"

Normally, Carole's instinct would be to snap back, but she doesn't have it in her. It's not just that she's exhausted from the last two months—she's tired of the constant not-so-underlying tension between herself and the person who was once literally a part of her. She has missed her sister. She has been missing her for years.

As though reading her mind (and they used to do that, didn't they?), Corinne reaches for Carole's hand and gives it a warm squeeze. It's a simple gesture, but to Carole, it speaks volumes. In that moment, Carole knows without a doubt that this is the real Corinne and not just a facsimile. Despite the anger and resentment they have felt—and may continue to feel—and despite their differences, both imagined and intentional, she and her sister are one and the same. They are as stubborn as each other, but underneath it all and their love is fierce.

\*\*\*

The pain starts in his lower back. From what Ryan has been told, he's been lying in this bed for nearly four days, something he won't even bother to question, so he tries to tell himself that the pain is merely a result of being in one position for so long. As the day progresses, however, so does the agony. It creeps down into his legs, and up into his neck and arms. He knows this pain all too well, and he knows what it means—he is settling back into this world, back into this world's body.

*I don't belong here.*

He does not mention it to the hospital staff, but his mother can see the agony written all over his face. Despite his protests, he is administered a heavy pain killer through his IV drip and soon falls into a thick, fitful sleep.

\*\*\*

At 9:00 p.m., a nurse walks into the room shared by Carole, Dannicka, and Marcy, and informs the visiting family members that they will have to leave.

"It's okay," Dannicka tells her dad. "I feel fine, honest to God."

She looks into his eyes and sees a wave of emotion and exhaustion. He must have gone through hell over these past few days, wondering if he was going to lose her, too. He leans down to kiss her cheek.

"I love you," she whispers. It is the first time she has said this to him since her mother died. She is going to tell him more often from now on.

"Do we both have to go?" Marcy's mom asks, indicating both herself and her husband. "Can't one of us stay?"

"I'm sorry, but since the patients are stable, we have to follow regular restrictions. If you'd like to spend the night, there's a family room, but you can't stay in here—these guys are going to need their rest."

*And time together to talk*, thinks Dannicka.

After their families have gone, the three hear a voice that they have come to recognize as Ryan's mother. She is shouting something at the nurses now, probably after being told to leave.

"Can't wait to meet her," says Carole, dryly.

When the commotion settles, Marcy looks at her roommates. "Is it really true that Chet's still alive?"

Carole wants to believe it. "That's what they're telling us."

"They're also telling us we've only been here since Friday," says Dannicka skeptically.

"It might have only been three days, here," Carole says, "but we were definitely gone for those two months. No one can convince me otherwise."

"But *how* is that possible?!" Marcy wants to know. "Did we just, like, dream it up?"

"There's no way we all dreamed that," Dannicka says, thinking about the lilac man—what would that make him? A dream within a dream? If only that were the case.

"But how could we be there and here at the same time?!"

Carole sighs. "Marcy, there are an infinite number of mysteries in the universe—things we will never understand. And we only caught a glimpse."

"But how are we going to explain it to everyone?"

She looks gravely at the younger girl. "I don't think we are—I don't think anyone would believe us."

"That's an understatement," Dannicka says. "We can't even explain it to ourselves."

Marcy looks at the two women in disbelief "So, we just pretend it never happened?!"

"We can always talk about it with each other," says Dannicka gently, hoping that this will be enough.

Marcy cannot imagine keeping something like this from Bernadette. But, when she thinks about it, she knows they're right––she has no idea where she would even start. No one would believe her. Not even her best friend.

***

Julian lies in his hospital bed in the dark, alone for the first time since he regained consciousness. He has pieced together the unbelievable sequence of recent events, and has come to the following conclusions: either they were somehow in two different places at the same time, or their bodies remained here while their consciousness shifted. He doesn't know which is true, and he doesn't know what either one means for Chet. Chet's alive now, but he's the only one who hasn't woken up yet. Maybe his death in the other world was foreshadowing for what is about to happen here. He wishes he could see for himself. He contemplates sneaking out of his room, but knows it would be impossible—he's hooked up to too many machines. Trudy swore that she saw Chet just today—he will have to take her word for it. Tomorrow, though, he will insist on seeing him first thing.

He closes his eyes, then opens them again. Who is he kidding? There's no way he'll be getting any sleep tonight.

# CHAPTER EIGHTEEN

## TUESDAY, JUNE 6

He has never slept this heavily in his entire life. This is beyond sleep, beyond dreams. It's way stronger than the anesthetic he was given last year when he had his wisdom teeth taken out. It is an all-encompassing state of heaviness, separating him from this world. He wants to stay like this forever, but something is telling him it's time to wake up.

He struggles against this desire for oblivion, knowing somehow that he should wake up—that he needs to—but he can't seem to... connect. He drifts off again, sinking down into welcomed nothingness. Time passes, impossible to measure. And, there it is again, swimming back up to the surface.

*Right. I'm supposed to wake up.*

Something, or someone, touches his arm, followed by the sound of a woman's voice.

"His vitals are normal."

"Oh," another voice responds quietly. "I thought I saw something on the monitor. Sorry to bother you."

This second voice sounds like his mom. How is that possible?

From somewhere beside him, a faint, incessant beeping keeps a steady beat. A pungent, sterile odour fills his sinuses, and it takes a moment to place it. He's starting to think he may be in a hospital.

Did they shift? How could they have shifted without him realizing? Maybe they didn't shift at all—maybe the Restructure is complete. Maybe this is the new world. Still, why would he be in a hospital?

It's too exhausting to think about. Without another thought, he fades back into unconsciousness.

\*\*\*

Chet resurfaces for the third time, this time with a clarity he didn't have earlier, wondering about the strange dream he'd had—he was certain he had heard his mother's voice. There had been a rhythmic beeping sound, and the smell of disinfectant...

He breathes in deeply, the earthy scent of grass and dirt filling his lungs. Unable to open his eyes, he strains to hear that beeping sound from before, but there is only silence.

He must have fallen asleep outside. Maybe he was sleepwalking again. He needs to get up and back into Carole's house before an Adjuster finds him. When he tries to move, though, he finds he is completely paralyzed. He can't even open his eyes. What did they do to him?!

For several seconds, he struggles to pull his eyelids apart, and finally succeeds, but barely. It is pitch-dark out—if it wasn't for the array of stars above him, there would be nothing to see.

He blinks several times, willing the blurriness to clear, each time succeeding in forcing his eyelids further and further apart. He has a better view of the stars now, recognizing that something about them is wrong—they aren't as bright as they should be. There's a haze, or a film; something obscuring their light. Something the colour of lilacs.

His heart begins to pound. Oh, Jesus, no—he's on the southside.

Still unable to move the rest of his body, his eyes dart desperately around, then down, landing on the sight of three figures encircling him. They are clad in blazingly-white snow suits which, in glaring contrast to the darkness around them, is nearly blinding.

At first, he tries to figure out who they are—maybe Marcy, or... but as his eyes adjust, he soon sees that none of them are from his group. In fact, they're not people at all—at least, they're not human.

One of the Adjusters (that must be who these creatures are) reaches a very small hand toward Chet's face. Instinctively, he wants to recoil, but can't. He's still completely paralyzed. He watches helplessly as the little white hand draws closer, wondering what it will do to him.

In one quick motion, the Adjuster reaches toward Chet's mouth, deftly removing something Chet didn't realize was there. Before he has a chance to freak out about it, another thought hits him—he can breathe better now.

The little hand moves upward until it is resting on Chet's forehead. It is surprisingly warm. Within seconds, his vision begins to clear and he is able to fully see the strange face hovering over his.

It's just like Carole said—the large, incredibly white-blue eyes, the lack of a nose or mouth. He wonders if they have ears; he can't tell because of the fur-lined hoods covering their heads.

He is so mesmerized by these creatures that several seconds pass before he realizes he is in the middle of a wide-open park—the same park where they shifted for the second time. He has some kind of enhanced vision now and can see everything around him without even turning to look: the schools, the ball diamond, the little green shed, the houses surrounding the park. Even the hospital bed he is in, the machines and IVs he is hooked up to, the curtains, and the two slumped figures sleeping in chairs beside him. He sees all of this at once, and is suddenly aware that he is in both places at the same time.

He turns his attention to the other two Adjusters beside him. One of them places one hand on Chet's chest and the other on the beeping monitor. Its hand is also very warm, sending a tingling heat radiating throughout his torso. He understands, now, what these creatures are doing. He understands that he, and they, are in both the park *and* the hospital.

He needs to let them do their work. *I'm supposed to leave them alone,* he thinks, dully. But he can't help it—he needs to know.

"Is my mom here?"

There is no response to his mumbled question. Instead, the third Adjuster, standing completely still at the foot of the bed, raises its arms and places its small hands on the soles of Chet's feet. A rush of warmth surges up through his legs and swirls rapidly throughout his entire body. He is wide awake now.

From somewhere else in the room, a fourth Adjuster appears. Unlike its counterparts, this one is wearing a soft pink snowsuit. Instantly, Chet understands that it is something special, something different from the others, and not only because of its clothing. With an air of solemnity, the pink Adjuster approaches the bedside, holding two tiny fingers on one hand out in front of its face. It places its fingers directly onto its own unblinking white-blue eyes, then places the fingers of its other hand over Chet's eyes. Everything goes white.

"His oxygen mask came off!" Chet's mother cries. She rushes over to her son to ensure he is still breathing. Simultaneously, the on-duty nurse rushes in and attempts to reapply the breathing apparatus.

The Adjuster in pink takes its fingers off of Chet's eyes and Chet gradually regains his sight.

"His eyes are open!"

He is aware of his mother's voice, but he can't think about that right now. His eyes are locked on the Adjuster in pink.

"Who *are* you?" he tries to say.

The Adjuster does not answer.

Because he can't, Chet realizes. There's no way for it to speak.

"Because you can't," he says, feeling a depth of emotion he doesn't really understand.

He wants to thank this creature, to somehow express his gratitude for all that is happening here, but there's no way to communicate—it can't hear, it can't speak his language...does it know what he's thinking?

The Adjuster, keeping its mesmerizing gaze fixed solidly on Chet, begins to fade into translucence. Chet doesn't want it to go. He stares fixedly back into those incredible eyes, never breaking his own gaze, until all the Adjusters, the park and everything around them evaporates, leaving only the hospital room.

He hears his mother crying. He hears the voice of his father, along with other voices he does not recognize. He is surrounded by people, by real humans. And, in the cacophony, he hears Ryan's voice.

"Ryan," he mumbles.

\*\*\*

Ryan has woken up in a morphine-induced fog, but the commotion going on in the room sobers him quickly. Something is happening to Chet.

"Hey!" he croaks, his voice raspy and thick. "Hey! Open the curtain!"

His request goes ignored. He tries to reach over himself, but can't, and for once his mother isn't around, either. He clears his throat and tries to call louder.

"Hey!"

No response.

"Open the frickin' frackin' curtain!"

He doesn't want to swear out of respect for Chet's parents, but he's losing patience. If someone doesn't open that curtain pretty damn quick...

In a flash, the curtain tears away and Ryan sees Chet—his head turned to the left, eyes opened, looking directly at him, mumbling his name.

"I'm right here, buddy!" Ryan never imagined he would see this—see Chet's eyes, awake and alive—ever again. "I'm right here!"

"Are we home?" Chet half-whispers.

"Yeah. We made it."

"The Adjusters..."

"They're gone, man. Don't worry."

Chet squeezes his eyes shut. They *were* here.

Even through their overwhelming joy and relief, Chet's parents find this conversation odd. They know similarly-strange things were said by the others upon waking––it must be some kind of side-effect. It won't last long, though––the others are all back to normal and Chet will be, too. Oh, thank God, thank God...

***

"Carole, are you awake?"

Dannicka is sitting up in bed, trying to figure out what in the world is going on down the hall. Across the room, she sees a clock, sees that it's 6:00 a.m., and knows it's too early for any doctors to be stopping by. The ward still has a middle-of-the-night feel to it, making whatever is happening feel especially jarring. It isn't coming from Julian's room—he's right next door and it's not close enough for that—which means it could be from Chet and Ryan's room.

"Carole!" Dannicka stage-whispers, not wanting to wake Marcy.

Carole stirs in her bed. "Hmmm?"

"Something's going on! Listen!"

It doesn't take much to alert her. Remembering that she's in a hospital––that they all are––Carole sits up. It's difficult to tell who exactly is yelling, but there are at least three, maybe four, different voices.

"I'm calling for the nurse," Carole says, reaching for the buzzer beside her bed. After several seconds without a response, she tries again.

"I wish I could just rip these damn tubes out and go out there myself!" she exclaims.

"What's going on?" asks a waking Marcy.

"We don't know," Dannicka says, worried. "It's either Ryan, or Chet, or..." She doesn't know which would be worse.

Marcy sits up, noticing right away that she already feels way better than she had the day before. The grogginess is gone and she feels back to herself. But there's something else she notices, and she doesn't like it.

"I can't tell what's happening to you guys, here. I can't feel you anymore."

"I know," says Dannicka. "I miss that, too."

"Where the hell is the nurse?!" Carole exclaims, pressing her buzzer again.

As though on cue, one appears in the doorway.

"We're fine," says Carole, "but what's going on over there?"

"It's the last member of your party," the nurse says. "He's awake."

*\*\*\**

After morning rounds, Julian, Carole, Marcy, Dannicka, and Ryan are declared fit to be discharged the next day, pending observation. There is nothing, apparently, wrong with any of them.

"Of course, we'll be following up with you through your own G.P.s," says the doctor.

Julian reads his name tag. Dr. Myers.

"That's it?" asks Trudy. "We don't even know what happened!"

"That's for the police to investigate," Dr. Myers says. "I've been informed that they're already looking into it." He turns to Julian. "They'll want to talk to you and the others once you're able to. I've told them you should be ready by tomorrow."

*That's good,* thinks Julian. He'll need some time to get his story straight.

As soon as Dr. Myers has left the room, Julian throws off his blanket and swings his legs over to one side of the bed.

"I'd like to see the others, now," he says, trying not to show Trudy just how anxious he is to do so.

"Are you sure?" she asks. "You haven't even stood up yet."

"I'm fine," he says. And he is, which is bizarre considering all he has just been through. He rises from the bed, steady on his feet.

"Hang on," she says, grabbing her purse. "I'll go with you. And put your robe on, for the love of God."

He slips into his robe, not bothering with the sash. His heart starts pounding as he turns right, toward Chet's and Ryan's room. He needs to see for himself if what he has heard is true: that Chet is alive, awake and okay. He can't allow any relief, or even hope, to come creeping in until he is certain.

At Chet and Ryan's room, they are turned away.

"The doctor is still with them," says the nurse.

Julian and Trudy turn and head over to Carole, Dannicka, and Marcy's room, instead. Julian knows he will have to maintain a poker face when he sees them, not wanting to give away the true depth of their relationship. How could he possibly explain to Trudy what they mean to him?

He taps lightly on their open door. "Can we come in?"

"Julian!" Marcy exclaims. She rushes over and hugs him exuberantly.

*So much for the poker face*, Julian thinks, avoiding his wife's gaze. Carole and Dannicka see the look of surprise on Trudy's face and refrain from hugging Julian themselves, though they both want to. Trudy decides to dismiss Marcy's reaction as that of a teenage girl, but she cannot explain the looks she saw on the faces of the other two women upon seeing her husband. This entire situation, as strange as it already is, keeps getting more bizarre. And Trudy doesn't like it.

"Hi, I'm Carole."

Trudy turns and shakes the outstretched hand being offered to her.

"And I'm Dannicka."

"Trudy. Nice to meet you. I'm Julian's wife." Which she senses that they already know. "I've met some of your family," she continues. "It's great to see all of you awake."

"You must be exhausted," Carole says, wanting to deflect the scrutiny from Julian's wife, "having to sit here for days on end."

"Here's my Dad!" Marcy announces as he enters the room.

*Saved by the bell,* thinks Carole.

Julian flinches involuntarily at the sight of Marcy's father, remembering the powerful blows he'd suffered at the hands of the facsimile version. His face, when last Julian saw it, had been contorted with anger, but now displays the most grateful of expressions. He holds out a hand and shakes Julian's vigorously.

"Marcy tells me you took good care of her at your coffee shop!"

Julian pauses, wondering what exactly Marcy has told him, and how he should respond.

"I told him how you let me use the bathroom, even though I wasn't a customer," Marcy volunteers.

"Well," says Julian, "I have daughters of my own."

"I've met them," says Marcy's dad. "Very nice girls."

"Even the youngest one?"

"Julian!" Trudy admonishes.

Marcy's dad laughs for a moment, then sobers. "So...what *did* happen in there?"

All eyes turn to Julian and he repeats what he has already told his family.

"Well, I haven't really figured that out. All I remember is that there was a kind of rumbling. I thought it was an earthquake. And it was followed by a deep, like *deep* in your eardrums, sound." He figures that it would be best to tell the truth about that much. This way they won't have to worry about keeping their stories straight. "And, the next thing I knew, I was waking up here."

"Geez, Louise," Marcy's dad mutters under his breath.

Julian turns it back on him. "What have you guys heard?"

"Nothing. The police just said that you were found unconscious and they didn't know why. I think they're gonna want your statements once you guys get out of here."

A look passes between Carole, Dannicka, and Julian that is nearly imperceptible, but Trudy notices.

"Well, what there is of it." Julian tries to laugh.

"Do you think we can see the guys, yet?" asks Dannicka, not only to change the subject, but because she and the others have waited long enough.

Carole answers. "Let's go find out."

The group is stopped by a nurse outside Chet and Ryan's room. "You can't all go in at once," she says. "It'll have to be two at a time."

Carole looks at the others, then nods at Dannicka and Julian. "Why don't you two go first? Marcy and I can wait."

Without a word, Julian and Dannicka nod back before heading into the room.

Trudy watches this display of efficient decision making and is struck by the realization that these people know each other. And not just from a chance incident four days ago.

*How?* She wonders. They make an unlikely group of friends. Could it be AA? Julian had mentioned going to a few meetings in Edmonton some years ago, but why wouldn't he tell her he still goes? Maybe he's not really doing as well as he's been leading her to believe. Lying is always the first sign. She looks at Marcy. Does this mean she's in AA, too? Do they let kids join? Marcy strikes Trudy as a bit...tough. She wouldn't be surprised to learn that she had been in her fair share of trouble.

From the hallway, she watches Julian enter the room and approach Chet's bedside. She sees him lean down to hug the boy, shoulders shrugging up and down. At first, she thinks he is laughing, then realizes that he is sobbing. She feels a pang of...not jealousy, but...betrayal. He did not give his own daughters this reception.

All Dannicka can do when she sees Chet and Ryan is cry. She doesn't know who to go to first, but Julian rushes over to Chet making the decision for her. She throws herself into Ryan's arms, and he holds her while she cries.

"You're in pain," she says, breaking away and looking into his eyes. "I can tell."

"I'm fine," he tells her. "Go say hi to Chet."

\*\*\*

That night, when the families have gone, the nurse on duty allows the six to gather together in Chet and Ryan's room. Chet, still very weak, sits propped up in his bed.

"But I don't even remember how the shift started," he says. "Do you guys?"

He sees the looks on their faces and it doesn't take a genius to figure out that they know something he doesn't.

"Okay." He braces himself. "What's wrong?"

With great difficulty, Julian describes Chet's death in the Empty World, and how it had occurred two days before they all shifted. Chet listens, incredulous, feeling as though all the blood is draining from his face. He doesn't bother asking how this could possibly be true—he knows it is, and he knows that the five people in front of him do not have the answers. He had thought his experience with the Adjusters, all of which he described to them in detail, was about them helping him shift back home. He didn't know that he was dead. Actually dead. Not just flat-lining on the table with a beautiful 'I-saw-myself-floating-above-my-body-with-an-incredible-light-calling-out-to-me' story. Just...gone.

He should feel incredible. He should consider it a miracle, like Jesus.

He doesn't.

"What happened when..." Marcy begins. "Do you remember, like..." she pauses again. "Where did you go?"

He tries to recall what happened to him before he woke up today in the park. They were at Carole's place. He'd had a fever and Ryan told them that Roland had used him to send a message. And then they'd spent the day getting ready to leave for the southside. That night, he saw those weird buildings—the ones that had not been there before.

*After that,* he thinks, *nothing.* Two entire days of absolutely nothing.

"I don't know,' he says, finally. But the real answer is that he didn't go anywhere, did he?

*Because,* he thinks numbly, *there's nowhere else to go.* There's nothing out there, at least, nothing beyond this life.

A strange, unsettling feeling comes over him: what if he isn't human at all? What if he's some kind of computer, or something, that just got shut down, then booted back up?

*I'm somebody's program.*

Suddenly, he feels very cold.

Carole sees the ashen look of concern cloud over his face. She places a hand over his. "Maybe," she says gently, "we're not meant to remember."

"Yeah," he says. "Maybe." Another thought strikes him—what if he's dead right now? Would he even know? Maybe this is where the Adjusters brought him—a world that seems familiar, but isn't real, where he'll be trapped, like in some kind of...what do they call that? Purgatory.

Aloud, he asks, "but, all the cars were gone...how did you get me all the way to the southside?"

Ryan clears his throat. "On a flatbed cart."

"On foot? But that must have taken—"

"Don't make us talk about that."

"Okay."

A silence falls over the group as each member, aside from Chet, relives that terrible journey.

"Anyway," Dannicka continues, "we got out just in time. There was someone else in that world."

She tells him about the lilac-faced man, feeling her fear come crawling back from reliving her encounters. Somehow, she doesn't feel safe, even here. There are too many possibilities, now.

When she is finished recounting the details, Marcy speaks up quietly.

"I killed him, didn't I?"

"You didn't kill him, Marcy," Julian looks her straight in the eye. "You just knocked the wind out of him. And that's all."

But he saw how hard she threw that rock—it's entirely possible that she shattered his wind pipe. In fact, it's entirely probable. He will never admit this, though—at least, not to her.

"Why did he have a lilac face?" she asks. "And teeth?"

*Shit,* thinks Chet, in awe of what he missed.

Julian sighs. "God only knows. Something could've happened to him, or maybe he was from somewhere else."

"But he was glowing—that means he wasn't supposed to be there, either, and I stopped him from getting out! Maybe he just wanted..."

"He wanted to hurt us," Julian interrupts. "You did what you had to do to protect us."

*What I should have done,* he thinks. He should have been the one to face the monster, to shield his family. How could he have left that up to her? He will regret that for the rest of his life.

He places both hands firmly on her shoulders. "You protected us, Marcy. You saved us. And that's all you need to remember."

But she will remember it all. You can't just kill someone and never think about it again.

Dannicka doesn't share Marcy's remorse—she is beyond relieved that the lilac-faced man did not shift through. He's still out there, somewhere though—and in the years that follow, as Dannicka continues to see him in her nightmares, she will feel as though he did shift with them after all.

"Time for bed," announces a nurse, peering into the room.

"Just five more minutes!" pleads Marcy.

"Five minutes, and that's all."

Carole looks at the others. "About tomorrow—I agree with Julian. When we give our statements to the police, I think we should say exactly what happened to each of us up to, and including, the shift. Or, earthquake, I guess we should get used to saying. And then we say that the next memory we have is of waking up here. What do you all think?"

"I can do that," says Marcy. She means it. She will never tell another soul.

"Well," says Carole, "goodnight, all."

She reaches for Julian's and Marcy's hands on either side of her. Marcy reaches for Ryan, who reaches for Dannicka, who reaches for Chet. Chet holds his other hand out to Julian, who clasps it warmly.

In their circle of six, they remain silent for a few solemn moments. What is not spoken among them is felt, resonating deep within each of them, long after the circle is broken.

# CHAPTER NINETEEN

THURSDAY, JUNE 8

Dannicka wakes up alone in her own apartment for the first time in twenty-three days. The feeling is strange, and lonely. It's weird not to have Marcy beside her—she had actually gotten used to the periodic kicking—and it's still more unsettling to know that the others are not here under the same roof. She knows she would have been welcome to stay at her dad and stepmom's last night, and even more welcome at Ryan's, but she had needed to face her apartment alone.

Falling asleep, however, was nearly impossible. She had been acutely aware of everything around her: the traffic, the sirens, her neighbours in the apartment below...she can't believe how easily she'd tuned all of this out before. She's going to have to find a place for herself amidst the cacophony of this world.

Throwing off the covers, she pads over to her bathroom, momentarily surprised, then instantly grateful for the hot water coming from the taps. After a luxuriously long shower, she wanders into her small kitchen to make an entire pot of coffee just for her. She marvels at the simplicity of it—pouring water from the tap into the machine, adding the grounds, pressing the 'on' button. She thinks about what it took to make coffee while she was at Carole's, beginning with having to start a fire. She will never take something like this for granted again.

She opens the fridge and finds a carton of cream, purchased the day before the first shift. According to her memories, that was more than two months ago, but here in the real world, it was only last week. She opens it and cautiously sniffs the contents. Satisfied, she pours some into a mug, then tops up the rest with coffee. Coffee with real cream is something else she's gone without for the past month. She won't take that for granted again, either.

Cradling the hot mug, she carries it over to the living room. She's missed her apartment. She eyes the stack of records on the floor where she'd left them last night. Her first order of business when she'd gotten home was to check her 'Big Country' album. It wasn't until she saw the word 'country' that she fully accepted she was actually in the right place.

Over in the corner, her phone sits on a side table, its message light blinking incessantly. She couldn't bring herself to check the messages last night—being back here has brought on a kaleidoscope of emotions, not the least of which is feeling overwhelmed. She doesn't want to hide, though. She spent so much time wanting to get back here—at least, in the beginning, anyway...

She looks back to her phone. Time to face the music.

The most recent message, sent an hour ago, is from Marcy.

"Hi Dannicka..."

A short pause follows. Marcy, it seems, is at an atypical loss for words.

"Um..."

In the background, another voice can be heard: "You said you wanted to go to school, today! You're gonna be late!"

"Okaaaay!" Marcy shouts. Then, more quietly into the phone, "I miss you! Have a good day!"

Dannicka, having heard her voice, now has the strength to hear from the rest of the world. There are tons of messages from various friends, two from her boss, two from Eric—which she immediately deletes—and five from Todd. She will have to call him.

A thumping knock on the door startles her, and she actually jumps.

"Dani?"

She opens it to find an incredibly relieved Todd, who throws his arms around her.

"You didn't call! I phoned the hospital and they said you'd been discharged yesterday!"

"I'm sorry, I was with my family. I got in late."

He looks at her, scrutinizing. "Are you okay? What the hell happened?!"

She feels an incredible wave of guilt.

*Well, let's see—first, I cheated on you, then I was sent to a different world, and then into another one, where I actually met someone else...*

Instead, she answers his question with the perfunctory story that she and the others are becoming used to telling.

"Holy *shit*!" He is holding both her hands in his, looking at her with so much concern that her guilt begins to feel unbearable.

"Where are the flowers I sent?" he asks, glancing into the apartment. "Didn't you get them?"

"I did. They were really pretty." She tells him that before leaving the hospital, she dropped them off at the palliative-care ward. Todd looks puzzled. She doesn't tell him that her donation also included an ostentatious bouquet sent by Eric.

"You've been so good to me," she starts, "and I hate to say this—"

"Then don't."

"I have to break up with you," she blurts, ripping off the band-aid.

"Why?"

"It's not right, I just, I don't have the same feelings for you that I think you have for me."

"Dannicka," he says patiently, "you just got out of a frickin' coma! Don't you think you should give it a few days? You might not even realize what you're saying."

"I'd been thinking about this even before the coma," she says gently. "I'm really, *really* sorry!"

In her old life, she would have found this situation with Todd to be the height of emotional drama. She would have fixated on it for weeks, discussed it over and over with her friends. Now, in the very grand scheme of things, she sees how very small it is. It's not small to Todd, though—she can empathize with that—but he will be better off.

"I'm gonna call you in a few days," he says, soberly. "Then you can tell me if you still feel the same way."

"Okay," she relents. She doesn't need a few days to know that she will never feel for Todd the same way she feels for Ryan.

*****

Julian drops his daughters off at school, something he doesn't usually get to do.

"Have a great day!" he sing-songs out the window. Pandora looks around nervously to see if any of her friends have witnessed this embarrassing display from her uncool dad. Lexie, on the other hand, runs back to the minivan, steps up on the runner-board, and kisses him squarely on the cheek. Julian practically floats out of the parking lot.

He drives back toward home, resisting the urge to pull onto the Deerfoot and confirm that the missing foothills are back where they're supposed to be. On the drive home to Calgary yesterday, he'd been afraid to look, but the relief he had felt upon seeing them nearly brought him to tears. The icing on the cake, however, was hearing about Tawnee's beaver play—not only was it nowhere near a Broadway stage, it wasn't being performed on any stage at all. It had closed early due to poor ticket sales.

*Home at last,* Julian thought.

He parks the minivan in his driveway and trots up to the front door.

"Hello?" he calls, stepping through the doorway.

"In here," Trudy calls back from the kitchen. Julian walks up behind her, catching her in a tight embrace.

"Guess what?" he asks. "We're actually alone!"

He turns her around and kisses her deeply, feeling a surge of desire.

She breaks away. "Do you think this is a good idea? Do you think you're well enough?"

He presses himself against her. "You tell me."

Later, they are lying together on the floor of the living room basking in the freedom of having the house to themselves; of not having to be quiet in their bed, behind a locked door.

"Man, did I need that," he gasps, catching his breath.

Trudy rolls onto her side, one leg curled up over his, her hand flat against his chest. He's been trying to figure out how to tell her what really happened to him––to all of them––but he doesn't know what to say. It's not like talking to a friend or parent; she's his wife. He should be able to tell her anything. How would he even start?

*Okay, so what we thought was an earthquake is actually something called a 'shift'. Our world shifts regularly, and apparently, it's something no one ever notices, except the six of us were accidentally shifted into a Facsimile World, and then into an Empty World, because Ryan isn't vibrating fully on this world's frequency. And there are these creatures called Adjusters...*

He can picture the look he'll see on her face. She will likely start thinking about Julian's uncle. She will think about schizophrenia, and mental illness, and worry about its heredity. She will force him into a series of doctor's offices and psychiatry appointments. She will want to keep his daughters away from him.

"Have you been going to AA in Edmonton?"

Her question catches him off-guard. Why is she asking? She knows he goes to meetings here in Calgary every Wednesday.

"No. I went a few times there, but that was a couple of years ago."

He feels her body stiffen. She sits up and begins to get dressed.

"So, now you're going to tell me that those other people are just your customers," she says, pulling her shirt on over her head. "And you've gotten so close just from pouring them cups of coffee."

He bristles. She has managed to belittle his career in one sentence, a career that supports their family, but it's more than that—he wants to tell her about new worlds, and she wants to accuse him of secret AA friendships. He realizes she is never going to believe him.

He should be grateful—she has just handed him the perfect excuse. "It's supposed to be anonymous," he says flatly. He sits up and starts putting on his clothes.

"Well, you didn't have to lie to me about it," she says. "What am I supposed to think, when you keep that kind of thing from me? Have you been drinking when you go up there?" She looks at him pointedly as if searching for some telltale sign.

"No." He zips up his pants and reaches for a sock. He wants to remind her about the eight-year sobriety chip he received a few months ago, but doesn't bother. "If I was drinking again, you'd know."

"So, you've just been going to meetings out there, then."

"Occasionally," he lies. "I guess I should have mentioned it." He puts on his other sock with a muttered, "Sorry."

She fluffs a hand through her hair. "Yeah, you should have. And what's with that Marcy girl? They're letting kids into AA now?"

He gets to his feet. "She's a teenager. They allow teenagers."

"Well, she's got a great start in life," Trudy says sarcastically.

Her words sting. It's as though someone has just insulted his own daughter. He says nothing, but his suspicions are confirmed—he is never going to be able to make his wife understand. It would be futile to even try. He also realizes is that he no longer cares to.

\*\*\*

Ryan wakes up, alone in his apartment. The pain he had just gotten used to living without reminds him that he is at home—in his real world. He lies curled up in bed, bracing himself for the unravelling of his limbs, and the subsequent agony this will bring. This time, he will not have the comfort of Roland, his Roland, to help him through.

While in the hospital, Ryan's parents had led him to believe that Roland was in their care. It wasn't until he was discharged yesterday that his parents told him the truth. Roland had been found dead, which Ryan had already suspected.

"This wouldn't have happened if we had a key to your apartment," his mother had said, missing the point, as usual. "Your landlord didn't let us in until Saturday afternoon—that cat had been alone for twenty-four hours!"

"That wasn't why he died," Ryan said, dully. "Cats don't die from being alone for a day."

He didn't bother to ask his parents why they pretended Roland was still alive up until the moment they dropped him off at his apartment and were forced to tell him the truth. Ryan sat numbly in the back seat, wishing he had never agreed to let them drive him home. With Dannicka already gone, he had simply followed his parents out to their car like an automaton, going into shut-down mode the way he always does in their company.

"You shouldn't be staying by yourself!" his mother had exclaimed, changing the topic. "I don't even know why we came here! I mean, look at you, you can't take care of yourself." She went on with that intense and frenzied tone she had whenever he was the topic of conversation. She turned to her husband, who was sitting obediently behind the wheel of her car. "Let's just take him back home with us," she said, as though talking about some wounded animal they had found by the side of the road.

Ryan opened the car door and got out without a word, slamming it shut. He didn't argue, and didn't ask them why they had lied. He knew why: he knows his mother has some kind of mental problem, he's known it his whole life and his dad has tried his best to accommodate her. Ryan had simply decided that he'd had enough.

His mother quickly opened her door and scrambled out to block his path.

"Stop," he said, his voice low. He put one hand out like a traffic cop, but close to his body like there was an invisible force field around him. Keeping his eyes locked on hers, he shook his head slowly.

"Stop," he repeated, even more quietly. And by some miracle she did. She froze in her tracks, staring at him, seeming unsure about what to do next.

He kept his eyes locked on to hers, shaking his head slowly, knowing for certain that this time she actually understood: he did not mean 'stop-in-this-moment', he meant permanently.

It is no small thing to sever yourself from your parents. For Ryan, it was something he had never wanted to do, but now it seems his only option. He isn't even angry with them anymore. What does piss him off though, is that they were the ones to find Roland—it should have been him. He would have held him one last time, thanked him for being such a true, beloved companion, and for sacrificing himself to save Ryan and the others. He would have buried him somewhere meaningful, or had him cremated and spread the ashes. His parents, however, just left him at the vet with no instruction. There is nothing left of him, now.

Still in bed, Ryan lies flat on his back, arms at his sides. He takes a deep breath and slowly opens his eyes. Within seconds, dozens of tiny stars start to twinkle in front of his vision.

"Oh, shit!" he says out loud. Struggling against the all-encompassing pain, he forces himself to get up and look desperately for his migraine medication on the night stand. It's still where he left it, thank God. He takes two wafers out of the package and places them under his tongue.

The thought of spending the day in bed, no matter how shitty he feels, is too depressing. Instead, he grabs his blanket and takes it into the living room, tossing it onto the couch. After a brief stop in the bathroom, he absentmindedly reaches for the cupboard where he used to keep Roland's food. Realizing what he is doing, he closes it gently.

As the pain in his head continues to blossom, he makes his way over to the couch and turns off the ringer on his phone. After an hour of throbbing pain, someone begins knocking on his door. Each rap sends a wave of agony piercing straight through to his skull, as though he is being struck by a hammer. He lies still on the couch, clutching his head, wishing desperately for the knocking to end.

"Ryan!" a voice calls out. "It's Dannicka! Are you okay?"

Dannicka.

"I'm sick!" he yells. "I'll call ya later!" He can't handle the thought of her seeing him like this.

"I'm not going anywhere!" she calls back. "I'll just wait until you feel like you can open the door."

Every move he makes is excruciating, but he cannot bear the thought of leaving Dannicka in the grungy hallway. He forces himself to stand.

"Coming," he says, wincing. He takes small, shuffling steps, each one sending bolts of pain through his head, until he reaches the door. When he opens it, he is overwhelmed by the sight of her.

"Oh, Ryan."

He can't respond.

She helps him back to the couch where she covers him up with his blanket. This is one of his nightmares come true—having a girl-friend who is forced to become his nurse.

"I'm taking care of you," she says, as though reading his mind, "just like I know you'll take care of me if I need it."

He can't argue with that.

"I need you," she says. "And I'm not going anywhere."

He relents.

She stays for the rest of the day; quietly tidying his messy apartment, somehow making meals from his meager pantry supply, curling up to read with his feet in her lap. Despite his initial reservations, he eventually allows himself to accept her comfort.

At the end of the day, she helps him make his way back to his bed. "I'll sleep on the couch," she says. "If you need me in the night, just call."

"I'm gonna give you a house key," he mumbles.

She kisses him on the mouth. "Go to sleep."

\*\*\*

Carole scoops up Mr. Biscuits in both arms and, for the first time in nearly a month, carries him into her real studio. Being back in her house is not as difficult as she thought it would be. For one thing, the house looks very different from the one they had left in the last world. In fact, there was no trace of the others here at all. The studio is still a studio, not a guest room, and the basement is not set up as a place to sleep, either. There is no fire pit in the backyard (although Carole thinks she will put one in), and the guest room looks completely untouched. She may never erase the memory of Chet's death, of preparing his body, but at least she knows that he did not die in *this* house.

Also making the return home easier, was the small gathering of close friends who had welcomed her when she arrived from the hospital. But now, tonight, she is content to be here alone.

Setting Mr. Biscuits down on his bed, she glances around her art studio as though reacquainting herself. Brushes, paints, canvases, drop cloths and cleaning solutions, her smock hanging from its hook are all as she had left them. Propped up in one corner sits the 'No-Think' painting she had done the night before the first shift— before it was altered. She lifts the canvas off the ground and places it back on the easel. She mixes her colours until she is sure she has achieved the right shade. Then, with a steady hand, she begins to paint three small circles in the top left-hand corner.

As she works, she thinks about the Adjusters, and how her perspective has changed—when Chet described his encounter with them, and what they had done, she finally understood. They saved his life, or, brought it back, or...something to that effect, anyway. She now believes that's what they had been trying to do the entire time. It is probably what the one in the backyard had come to do, and the one they spotted on the bridge...If only she'd left them alone, like she'd been told.

She squeezes her eyes shut for a moment, recalling those moments on the bridge, seeing everything that happened like watching a movie—only this time, knowing the ending. She had spent so much of that time being afraid of the Adjusters, and she didn't have to be. What were they?

*Incredible beings,* she answers herself. *And, you got to see them.*

She steps away from the easel and surveys her work. She will hang it in her living room. Eyeing the three cobalt-blue circles approvingly, she gives the painting a title: "How I Spent My Summer Holidays".

***

## FRIDAY, JUNE 9

"Hello, Ryan."

Ryan is sitting up in his bed, head still throbbing with pain. At the foot of the bed sits Roland, but it's not his Roland. It is a two-dimensional projection of the cat who once was, before he was used and discarded. The sight of him sends a stab of grief straight through Ryan's heart.

"Your animal served us very well," this Roland says, as though this makes up for anything. How is it they still have a hold on him here?

"We've been authorized," the cat continues, "to give your animal a gift."

Are they fucking serious? Don't they know what they did to him?

"He's dead," says Ryan, grimacing with pain.

"We've been authorized to give him the gift which he has wanted," this Roland says genially, as though Ryan has not spoken.

Before he can argue, this Roland tips his head back and opens his mouth wide, showing two long rows of very small teeth. Tiny two-dimensional stars begin to drift out of his mouth, floating lazily up and into the air around both their heads. Ryan's anger dissolves into understanding. Mesmerized, he follows the bright little stars with his eyes, observing their two-dimensions morph into three. They hover around his head, dancing slowly, dreamily, over his face and throat.

Moments later, when he wakes, the migraine is completely gone.

***

## FRIDAY, JUNE 16

"I am so proud of you!" Chet's mother says. "I don't know where the time has gone."

Her eyes well up with tears.

"Okay, let's keep it together," says Chet's dad. "We haven't even left the house yet."

"I just want one more picture. Why don't the two of you stand beside the car?"

"Mom, I'm gonna be late," Chet complains, but he smiles warmly beside his dad.

"Why don't you take one of me and Mom?"

His mom rushes over and hands the camera to her husband. Chet puts an arm around her shoulders and smiles.

"Do you have your speech?" she asks.

"Right here." He pats the pocket of his suit jacket. This time, he will not leave it behind.

"See you guys there," he calls. He jumps into his car and reverses out of the driveway.

Four days ago, when he showed up for his social studies exam, the entire gymnasium had cheered. He'd felt completely overwhelmed. He learned later that Raja, Lindsay, and Jessica were also heralded as heroes for acting quickly and calling the police.

"I saved your life, dude," Raja told him. "And, don't worry—I won't let you forget it!"

"No doubt," Chet laughed.

His teacher had offered to make a special accommodation for him to opt out of the exam, but he nobly refused. Naturally, the fact that he already knew what was on the exam went unsaid. Still, the first thing he did when the papers were handed out, was to look for the word 'company' in place of 'country'. When he saw that the exam was as it should be, he breathed a sigh of relief.

He approaches the turn-off for Kelley's street, but does not slow down. He continues driving for a few more blocks, and within minutes, arrives at Lindsay's house. He pulls into the driveway, and before he can even turn the car off, she appears at the front door, smiling.

"Hi!" she waves.

She is wearing the same sleek dress that he saw her wear in the Facsimile World. He was hoping that she would.

"Nice dress," he says.

She smiles. "Thanks. I feel kinda...I dunno, like I can't move properly in it."

"Well, you look great."

She smiles again. "You do, too."

When they arrive at the school's parking lot, she begins to laugh. "Who brought the limo? What is this, the Oscars?"

Chet rolls his eyes, knowing exactly who it is. "Don't look at them," he says. "They want you to."

Last week, when he broke up with Kelley, she did not take it well. Now, she tells people that Chet's 'not himself' since the coma, and what can she expect. He couldn't possibly care any less.

He takes Lindsay's hand as she gets out of his car, and together they walk to the cafeteria. Once there, they put on their caps and gowns along with the other students.

"Good luck with the speech," she says, giving his arm a squeeze.

"Okay, grads!" the Vice-Principal hollers. "Everyone, line up the way we rehearsed! Two-by-two, alphabetical order!"

Chet turns to Lindsay. "See you on the other side." He leans down slightly, kissing her on the cheek.

Finding his place in line, he is soon joined by the same nerd-girl that he stood beside at his facsimile grad. The nickname he had given her seems harsh to him now.

"Hi," he says, offering a smile.

She looks away quickly.

With an intense feeling of déjà-vu, he turns around to look at the back of the long line. Sure enough, Raja is there, just as before. Chet gives him the finger. Raja, faking offence, reciprocates. Chet laughs.

"Ladies, and Gentlemen!" a voice announces through the loud-speakers. "Please rise for your Graduating Class of 1995!"

He hears the opening notes of the grad theme song, 'We May Never Pass This Way Again,' also familiar. The march begins. When he enters the gym, there is a noticeable increase in applause. He passes his parents and nods, seeing that they both have tears in their eyes. He hears the lyrics of the grad theme song and begins to laugh; quietly at first, then out loud. He can't help himself––it all seems so incredibly bizarre. The nerd-girl gives him a quizzical look, as do the girls in front of him.

"Sorry!" he laughs. "Sorry!"

Settling himself, he wipes the tears from his eyes.

When his name is announced later in the ceremonies, Chet once again makes his way to the podium. This time, the speech he is about to deliver will be real. There won't be anymore do-overs—at least, he doesn't think so.

He clears his throat into the microphone. "Good afternoon, parents, teachers, friends and family, fellow grads. Thank you for electing me as your Class Historian."

The applause is thunderous. It's getting to be embarrassing. He continues with the rest of his speech, this time with confidence. He reads from his notes, word for word, until he comes to the last paragraph, where he has scribbled in a new ending.

"I didn't think I would be here, today," he says.

Silence falls over the entire gymnasium.

"In fact, I'm not even sure how it's possible that I *am* here. But right now, in this moment, apparently, I am. I am here with all of you. And, in order for us to be here, each one of us, whether we realize it or not, has done or has gone through something important. Something difficult. Something amazing. We are not the people we were when we started here. We know so much more now, and sometimes, the more you learn, the more questions you have."

He pauses for a moment, looking sagely over the crowd.

"But, like the song says, we may never pass this way again. This could even be true. So, while it's great to look back and remember the good times, or to wonder what your future holds, don't forget to appreciate where you are right now."

The applause is deafening.

\*\*\*


## WEDNESDAY, JUNE 21

"I guess I still don't know why you had to re-arrange your work schedule to attend a teenage dance recital."

Julian sighs. "It's important for her that we're all there—I've told you."

"Well, you can't make a habit of it," says Trudy. "I can't have you leaving town every time one of those people wants something."

"This is the first time," Julian says, putting his toothbrush into his travel bag. He stops himself from saying that he already missed Chet's grad, thanks to her, which he deeply regrets. He should have been there.

"It better be the *only* time," she complains. "Because you've got a family here, in case you've forgotten."

He quashes his rising anger, closes his travel bag, then forces himself to kiss her on the cheek. "I haven't forgotten."

Not one bit.

\*\*\*


Chet pulls his car up to the front of Ryan's apartment building and honks the horn. Upstairs, Dannicka peers out the window of Ryan's suite and waves.

"Chet's here."

"Do I look okay?" Ryan stands before her, not used to wearing dress clothes.

"You look great." She smiles and kisses him. "Let's go."

At the front door, she puts on her shoes and grabs her purse. Ryan reaches for his cane, and locks the door behind them.

\*\*\*

When Carole sees Chet's car pull into her driveway, she feels like her heart may burst. She could have driven herself, but didn't want to miss out on a few more minutes to visit with the others. She doesn't imagine that it will happen too often. It's been two weeks since they've last seen each other, but it feels like months.

"Carole!" Dannicka calls, jumping out of the car to greet her. The two women embrace. Back in the car, Carole pats Chet on the shoulder.

"Here," she says, handing him a small box. "Grad present and birthday present, all in one."

"Thanks! Do I open it now, or—"

"Open it later," she tells him. "When you turn eighteen again."

***

Marcy sits at the same make-shift dressing table in one of her school's classrooms. What she is feeling, she knows, is more than mere déjà-vu.

"Trust me," she tells the other girls in the dance troupe. "You're gonna have to wear *way* more make-up than usual."

She looks at Cody, the only male dancer in their group. "You, too. Seriously."

"No way!" Cody sputters, face turning pink. Marcy smiles.

"Marcy!" Mrs. J hollers. "There's someone here to see you! Be quick!"

Marcy rushes over to the classroom door, thrilled to see Dannicka standing there.

"Just wanted to let you know that we made it," Dannicka says. "All of us."

Marcy hugs her.

"Mrs. J! This is Dannicka, the one who choreographed my routine!"

The teacher, obviously distracted, glances over only briefly. "Nice to meet you."

"Okay!" she hollers to the rest of the troupe. "Everyone get into line! We're on in five minutes!"

"Break a leg!" Dannicka says, then heads back toward the gym.

As the Dancetasticks take their place on stage, Marcy catches Bernadette's eye and pulls a face. Bernadette laughs.

Marcy is beyond happy to have her friend back. When she'd gotten home from the hospital, she'd raced over to Bernadette's place right away. Bernadette threw her arms around her, making Marcy feel like her heart would burst.

She wanted to tell her—she had promised herself back in the Empty World that she *would* tell Bernadette about her true feelings. But somehow, she just couldn't—she completely chickened out. Seeing her best friend again, and looking into her eyes, told Marcy all she needed to know. As much as Bernadette loves her, she will never love Marcy in the same way. Maybe one day, Marcy will tell her who she really is, but it doesn't seem to matter just now. And anyways, it isn't her biggest secret anymore. Not by a long shot.

What Marcy did say, though, was that she'd decided to call off their duet.

"You're not ready," Marcy said, "and that's okay. I'm gonna do a solo."

Bernadette looked unmistakeably relieved.

As the opening notes of the first song ring out, Marcy spins around and strikes her defiant pose.

Later in the program, she waits backstage, jumping up and down in the wings. She watches as Mrs. J walks over to the microphone, just as she had before.

"Ladies, and gentlemen!" she announces. "Our next performer gave us quite a scare a few weeks ago, and now, we are so very grateful to have her back. Let's give a big hand for Marcy!"

The applause is super loud. Marcy walks on to the stage to take her place, and to her surprise, receives a standing ovation.

*But I haven't even danced yet,* she thinks. Tears spring to her eyes, but she shakes them away. *Focus.*

Finally, the applause dies down. 'Ironic', the song Marcy has now intentionally selected, begins to play, and this time she is ready. She moves deftly, even gracefully, through the choreography that she and Dannicka had come up with together. She feels the eyes of everyone in the audience upon her.

As she performs her routine, Marcy feels something she can't describe. She feels like she becomes more than just herself, more than the limits of her body; transcending beyond conscious thought. It's as though a part of her that she hadn't been aware of is awakening. For the first time in her life, she experiences complete freedom. She gives herself over to it, no longer counting each beat, no longer aware of the audience. Like a conduit, she allows the artistry and the energy of the performance to flow through her.

As the song ends, Marcy stands at centre stage, facing the audience head-on. In each hand, she holds a lit sparkler, unaware of how beautiful, vulnerable, and wise she looks. In the audience sit five people who, for just one moment notice that the sparklers are not the only things that glow.

# EPILOGUE

*One year later*

<u>FRIDAY, JUNE 21, 1996</u>

"The Shivasina pose is possibly the most important pose of your yoga practice," says Dannicka, addressing her class in a soothing tone. "It allows the body to rest fully, and to integrate the work you have done."

Barefoot, she walks silently between the rows of yoga mats scattered throughout the studio floor. She looks very different than she did a year ago, although her friends and family can't explain how, exactly. There is a serenity about her, a grounded-ness, that was not there before. She is no longer addressed by anybody as 'Maureen'.

This is only the third class that she has taught, but she already knows that this is exactly where she belongs. In a few months, she will receive her full Yogi certification—and, in two years or so, once she has saved up enough money, she will be able to continue her study, in India. The thought is very exciting.

She sees Ryan at the back of the room, lying on his mat with his eyes closed, a peaceful expression on his face. Some of the things that have been said about love are true—the sky seems bluer, the world more beautiful...but real love, she is discovering, is not a shout-it-from-the-rooftops thing. It is deep, it is elevating. It is powerful.

She still dreams about the man with the lilac face, though not as often. She is working on letting go of her fear, handing it back to the Universe, which both she and the lilac man are a part of.

***

Ryan lies on his yoga mat, eyes closed, listening to the beautiful sound of Dannicka's voice. He wouldn't have blamed her if she had broken up with him—in fact, he'd tried to convince her that she should. He is miles away from the strong, energetic Ryan of the Empty World, and he had worried that he would only bring her down. But Dannicka has slipped into his difficult life with absolute ease, as if she had always been there. She doesn't see him as an invalid—she doesn't see him as a crumpled body with a cane used so often that it's practically an appendage. She sees him as a person, as a soul. She has helped him to realize that the guilt he has held onto about the shift, about his condition, about the accident, was never his to carry.

While the pain in his body remains, the migraines have become a thing of the past, thanks to Roland. He thinks about his little pet, and how his one wish was to put an end to Ryan's suffering. The thought can bring tears to his eyes.

He senses Dannicka as she glides silently past him. He resists the urge to reach out and grab her ankle.

***

Across the room, Carole lies on her mat, eyes closed, allowing her thoughts to wander. She thinks about the painting she is currently working on. She thinks about Mr. Biscuits and his hilarious face. She thinks about her newly-installed fire pit and how she will sit beside it with Ryan and Dannicka after tonight's class is over. She thinks about her sister—that it's time to schedule the monthly dinner-and-a-movie date that they've been doing over the past year. She thinks about the many blessings in her life. She has experienced something incredible—something most people could never even imagine. And for all of it she is truly grateful.

\*\*\*

Across the city, a fourteen-year-old Marcy prepares for her first baseball game of the season. Over the last few weeks, she has struggled during team practices—she cannot seem to throw the ball without seeing the man with the lilac face in front of her. Every time the ball slams into the catcher's glove, she hears the sound of the rock hitting the lilac man's throat. She hears him gurgling and it makes her feel sick. She thought it would be better by now because that was a whole year ago—last year, when she got out of the hospital, she couldn't even play baseball at all. Maybe it's never going to go away. If that's the case, she knows she only has two options: keep trying, or quit. And right now, she honestly doesn't know which it will ultimately be.

"Focus," she mutters to herself. She stands nervously on the pitcher's mound, arms at her sides. Without warning she springs into action, trying to deliver one of her signature pitches. But she falters, and the next sound she hears is the crack of the bat. Only, to her it is the choking strangle of a dying man. She watches in dismay as her once-perfect pitch soars past her and into the outfield.

\*\*\*

Across the province, Julian sits at his desk finishing his work for the day. It's late, after seven o'clock, but he's come to accept the long work days. He knew he would be putting in more hours when he accepted the promotion. It also means no more trips to Edmonton, which brings a heavy sadness, but he knows how much it satisfies his wife. And keeping Trudy happy, however possible, is his main priority right now. It's a small sacrifice to ensure he can raise his kids in the way he feels best; where he can live under the same roof and not have his wife turn them against him. And she would.

His youngest is nine now; that leaves nine more years until she turns eighteen and becomes an adult. Nine more years of keeping the peace, of giving Trudy whatever she wants. Then he will be free to see the others, his other family, after having spent a decade apart. Hopefully, his daughters will want to get to know them, too.

In the meantime, he has been taking advantage of a new technology called 'email' to keep in touch with the other five. It is a weak substitute for a real relationship, but it's better than nothing. Shutting down his computer, he stands and stretches. He taps his pockets, checking for his wallet and keys, then heads out of his office.

He had a memory surface from his thirteenth birthday recently. Uncle Ribbons had given him $50, which was a lot of money in those days. Julian had used it to buy his first drum kit. Whatever happened to his crazy uncle? He can't ask his mom about her brother—that subject has been off limits for years. Maybe his dad will know.

\*\*\*

Across the world, Chet unpacks his things in the tiny room where he'll be spending a few nights while he's in Portugal. He spent the last year working to save up for this trip, and this is the first stop. His parents didn't want him to go travelling at all—they'd wanted him to start university right away and become a dentist that much sooner. Chet had never given a second thought to becoming a dentist—he'd always just assumed he'd follow in his dad's footsteps. And why not? His marks were high enough, and dentists make a lot of money. It seemed like a no-brainer. But, to say that he will never see his life, or this world, in the same way again is the understatement of the century.

Through his own research, he has been looking into an exciting branch of science called Quantum Physics, and now he knows what he'll commit himself to. He wants to study the mysteries of the universe. He wants to study the human brain. He wants answers. But, for now, and for the next two months, he is going to see as much of Western Europe as he possibly can.

Reaching inside his backpack, he retrieves the gift that Carole had given him one year ago. It is a miniature painting—only seven centimetres by eight centimetres. "So you can take it with you wherever you go," she had said.

Against the white background, in the top left-hand corner, sit three tiny dots in cobalt blue. Scrawled in small letters in the middle of the painting are three words: You *Are* Here.

He'll have to take her word for it.

# ACKNOWLEDGEMENTS:

Having a visual disability has made writing a novel an interesting and challenging experience. It has created a lot of extra work, mostly for other people. I'd like to express my gratitude for the following:

Charmaine Wallace – typist

Yvon Loiselle – typist

Julie Golosky Olmsted – creative consultant

Ariana Villars – editor and typist

Rosemary Bell – administrator

I would also like to thank the friends and family members who read earlier drafts and offered valuable feedback.

And an extra-special thank you to my husband Darren.

CPSIA information can be obtained
at www.ICGtesting.com
Printed in the USA
BVHW031352110422
633959BV00006B/239